Juliette Mead was born in 1960. After graduating from Oxford University, she pursued a career in finance, working in Dallas, New York and London for various investment banks. She left the City after a brief stint as a headhunter, and now lives in Wiltshire with her husband and four young children, where she writes full-time. She is the author of *The Headhunter*, *Intimate Strangers* and *Sentimental Journey*, shortlisted for the 1998 Romantic Novel of the Year Award.

# Jack Shall Have Jill

### Juliette Mead

POCKET
B O O K S

LONDON · SYDNEY · NEW YORK · TOKYO · SINGAPORE · TORONTO

For Julia, Jo and John,
with happy memories of Kingston Road

And for Archie

First published in Great Britain by Simon & Schuster UK Ltd, 1998
This edition first published by Pocket Books, 1999
An imprint of Simon & Schuster UK Ltd
A Viacom Company

Simon & Schuster UK Ltd
Africa House
64-78 Kingsway
London
WC2B 6AH

SIMON & SCHUSTER AUSTRALIA
SYDNEY

A CIP catalogue record for this book is available from the British Library.

1 3 5 7 9 10 8 6 4 2

ISBN 0-671-85579-4

Extract from *A Subaltern's Love-song* by John Betjeman reproduced by permission of
John Murray (Publishers) Ltd
Extract from *Penguin Small* by Mick Inkpen reproduced by permission of Hodder &
Stoughton Ltd
*Once In A Lifetime* words and music by David Byrne/Chris Frantz/Tina
Weymouth/Jerry Harrison/Brian Eno © 1982 Index Muzic Inc./Bleu Disque Co
Inc./WB Music Corp/EG Music Ltd. Warner Chappell Music Ltd, London W6 8BS.
Reproduced by permission of IMP Ltd.

Typeset in Berkeley by SX Composing DTP, Rayleigh, Essex
Printed and bound in Great Britain by
Caledonian International Book Manufacturing, Glasgow

# Acknowledgements

So often when it comes to gratitude, it's a question of rounding up the usual suspects:

My dear friends Tina, Janos and James, and my husband Guy for reading early drafts and giving me confidence and necessary corrections with an equally gentle touch, and my equally dear friends Georgie, Marilyn and Jenny for giving me confidence without correction. Ginny and Toby for developing the original idea with me. My two sisters and parents, for taking late night phonecalls, listening to my whingeing and offering advice. My children, who can't understand quite why it takes me so long to write a book; Becky, Nora and Lynnette for distracting the children when the going got tough. My friends Jocelyn and Sophie for their input on Rome and all things Italian. Marie Beresford, for generously teaching me the mysteries of the Tarot at short notice and with remarkable intuition. My mother-in-law Jillian and sister-in-law Lucinda for their input on Oxford. Hazel Orme, a wonderful and tactful copy editor. And Jo Frank and Marian McCarthy, formerly of Simon and Schuster, for being in on the early stages, and always eager to see the book through.

Most of all I am indebted to my friend and agent Carole Blake and my friend and editor Clare Ledingham; how tough things would be without their talented and enthusiastic support.

# The Rules of the Game 1

## Oxford, December 1985

At the end of the Michaelmas term of their third year, the residents of the house decided to have a traditional Christmas dinner party. The term 'residents' has to be used loosely, as it encompassed the three who paid rent (Olivia, Pip and George); Olivia's non-paying, semi-resident boyfriend, Jerry; Pip's occasional tutorial partner and occasional boyfriend Michael; and any one of a string of girls on whom George had designs, the current lucky lady being a Somerville second-year linguist called Sarah. The plan did not originally involve outsiders; the five regulars were élitist by nature, and Sarah was as yet provisional, so did not qualify for a vote. Besides, in common with many students, they felt that the social lives they had established by their third year needed no expansion.

A week before the scheduled date of the dinner, Olivia announced that they needed to invite two more guests: six did not a dinner party make. George rattled off a string of suggestions, mainly Old Marlburian cronies, only to be snapped at for being insular. Pip, knowing Olivia all too well, suggested Justus O'Keefe, and Olivia, feigning nonchalance, agreed. He was, after all, a stranger in a strange land, and would be alone at Christmas, a feeling that Olivia claimed to know only too well. It was easy coming up with a fourth female to even up the numbers – they settled on Wilhemina, better known as Billy, a German art student at the Ruskin, who would further contribute to the foreign flavour.

Purporting to be a traditional British Christmas, the dinner had more in common with a French *réveillon* – oysters, platters of cold meat, and various puddings purchased from the nearby Maison Blanc. They moved from the dining room to the sitting room at about two in the morning, hazy with the potent cocktail of youth and sexual tension, liberally laced with alcohol. Pip and Jerry were apparently deep in a political argument that was going nowhere; neither could be bothered to concede, and Jerry was too busy eavesdropping on Olivia's conversation to follow his own. Billy was idly decorating a wall of the room with a life-size sketch of a male nude while holding forth on the dimensions of Leigh Bowery's genitals to no one in particular. Landlord George, who would normally have protected the décor, was too drunk to care, and too busy trying to persuade Sarah to dance with him. Sarah was enjoying his attention, but reluctant to take centre stage before a group of third-year students. Michael was opening a seventh bottle of fizz from the case that George had contributed. Olivia was listening intently to Justus expound on themes in twentieth century American fiction.

'You could say American writers made some traditional ideologies peculiarly their own – Freudianism; the New Frontier, the flight of the hero from social conditioning and so forth,' Justus drawled, his eyes locked on Olivia's, and thinking that, good-looking as she undeniably was, what attracted him most was the intensity with which she listened. Most good-looking women didn't bother to learn how to listen. 'The alienated individual, either trying to escape social convention, or belong to it.'

'Gatsby?'

'Gatsby for sure. You've read Emerson?'

'Should I?' Olivia gently nudged Jerry's hand off her thigh, and Justus watched her doing it before he replied.

'Darn right you should. I'll lend you some. Tell you what, I'll *give* you some. For Christmas.' He flashed a sudden smile, his perfectly even and whiter-than-white teeth glinting in his permanently tanned face. 'Emerson started it all. Henry James took up the mantle. I can kind of see you as a Jamesian heroine. Isabel Archer – all that searching for a deep interior life.'

'Implying I haven't got one already?' Olivia raised her eyebrows.

'This is meant to be a party, not a sodding tutorial.' Michael undid the top two buttons of his shirt. The room felt hot, despite George's refusal to have the thermostat above 60 degrees.

'Let's play a game.'

'And I thought that's just what we were doing . . .' Justus said softly to Olivia. She was dimly aware that Pip and Jerry had stopped talking, and that George and Sarah were snogging on the sofa against the far wall.

'Who's up for Sardines?'

'Oh, grow up, Michael. Billy, are you *quite* certain that's in proportion?' Pip squinted at Billy's nude as she emptied the dregs of the wine into Olivia's glass, and waggled the bottle. 'What about Spin the Bottle?' She placed it on the table and gave it a preliminary twirl.

'What's Spin the Bottle?'

Jerry leaned forward to answer Justus's question. 'The truth game. A version of it. Maybe not an idea that travels across the Atlantic. I doubt there's much call for truth there, judging from the ethics of your politicians.'

'I don't know about that. Folks back home just say what's on their mind. They don't tend to need artificial aids.'

3

Jerry shrugged and spun the bottle a few times on the low oak table. 'It's simple. Someone spins, and asks a question, any question, of whoever it points to. When they've answered truthfully, they take a turn at spinning the bottle, and so on.'

'Sounds riveting,' Justus said, with casual sarcasm.

'It can be. It depends how far people are prepared to go.'

Sarah led George back to the table, checking her face in the mirror as she passed.

'Bags I start.' Michael Marsden sat heavily on the floor and spun the bottle. It selected the American. 'Piss.' He grunted. 'I wanted one of the girls. So, Justus, what do you make of Oxford, then? What do you make of us lot?'

'I think you are very . . . interesting. I'm not sure –'

Michael cut him off. 'OK. Boring question. Let's get on to something juicier.'

They watched the green bottle twirl on the table until it slowed to Olivia.

'If you had to be a literary heroine – no – if you had to choose between being Isabel Archer or Cleopatra, which would you be?'

'Shakespeare's or Shaw's?'

'Oh, for fuck's sake.' George put his head in his hands. 'Could you two *stop* wanking off about bloody literature? I'm going to need some whisky if I have to listen to this sort of drivel.'

'Shakespeare's.' Justus ignored George.

'Isabel Archer, then.'

'Why?'

'One question, chum. You get one sodding question, that's the rule. Get on with it, Liv.'

Olivia let her gaze linger on Justus as her hand closed around the base of the bottle. Jerry's chest tightened in apprehension. He dreaded watching her manipulate a gentle half-circle so that she could ask the American a follow-up. He dreaded any further evidence of her interest in Justus: she'd already spent most of the night talking to him. Olivia gave a forceful spin and it pointed to Jerry himself. She smiled seductively at him, batting her lashes in flirtatious parody. 'Darling Jerry; do you think we'll always be together, you and me?'

Jerry rubbed his chin. 'I used to be certain of it. It'll be up to you.'

'We don't want to hear about your romantic angst, Jerry! Give us some sex, gossip – something we don't know, for God's sake.'

'Shut up, George,' Olivia commanded, and turned to Justus apologetically. 'You'll have to excuse George; he tries ever so hard to be a member of the human race, but he hasn't even passed his Common Entrance.'

It was George's turn in the spotlight.

'Uh . . .' There was not much more that Jerry wanted to know about George Upton. 'Right. Sex. Do you believe that romantic love is a by-product of physical lust, or that lust is a manifestation of romantic love?'

George groaned. 'Bloody hell . . .'

'Stop being a dickhead and answer, if you can even understand the question,' Olivia admonished.

'Righty-o. As I see it, love and lust are quite separate. Sometimes they act in conjunction – like us two,' he patted Olivia's thigh to Sarah's confusion, 'and sometimes they don't.'

George was bored by the others; if things didn't hot up, he'd rather take Sarah to bed. He spun carefully. 'Livvy, my darling, have you slept with anybody in this room? Apart from Jerry?' He wanted to tease her in front of her friends; most, he wanted to set the cat free.

'Yes,' she answered quickly. All of a sudden, George panicked. The cat was prowling on the window-ledge, ready to leap.

'Who?'

'It's my turn to spin.'

None of the following questions were of any significance or interest: some were too drunk, some too inhibited to get to the bone, until the bottle was once again spun by George and pointing at Olivia. George was quite oblivious to discretion.

'How many people in this room have you slept with?' George wore a smug smile, which did not flatter him. Pip leaned forward as Justus leaned back with a broad grin. Jerry did not move.

Olivia gave George a long, steady stare, with only a hint of irritation in her eyes, then gripped the bottle as she replied, 'Two.'

That single word had enormous effect. You could almost hear the pigeons' wings flapping as they looked at each other.

'Livvy, you're plastered.'

Olivia laughed at George's disapproving expression, and glanced at Jerry from under her lashes. He was staring at her intently. 'Isn't this something we might have discussed in private? Or am I taking too much for granted?' he asked, but Olivia only shrugged. It was just as she'd predicted; they had all jumped to the wrong conclusion – that she would observe the rules.

'Well . . .' Pip drawled. 'That's the whole point of the game, isn't it, public confession I mean?'

Sarah looked around the floor for her bag. 'I really ought to be going . . .'

Billy, standing on the back of the sofa, still daubing the wall in great swirls of sepia, extending the abstract yet unmistakable shaft of the penis with every stroke, paused to gaze at the ceiling and said reflectively, 'I will tell you how many men *I* have slept with. The first was my uncle. After him, fifteen.'

Michael eyed the developing mural dubiously. 'Who were they? The bloody All Blacks?'

Justus sat as still as a cat and noted each reaction.

Olivia twirled the bottle distractedly, without enthusiasm. She knew, as well as any of them, that the game was nearly over.

Not one of them felt able to voice his true thoughts. What a remarkably cool liar she is, Pip thought at once, and then wasn't so sure later that night when the party had finally broken up. Olivia and Jerry were a steady item, but why hadn't Olivia ever confided about George? Surely it couldn't be Justus, Pip thought as she pulled up the sheet: they barely know each other. I'm meant to be her best friend; I'm meant to know everything. She couldn't have bonked Michael – she *couldn't*. Sod it. I wish I was more like her. I wish I had her boobs at least.

Michael lay on his stomach next to Pip. Apart from registering that he was the only bloke in the room Olivia *definitely* hadn't shagged, and pondering whether there might be a chance to rectify that the following term, he gave her little thought. He was more concerned whether size really mattered to women; it apparently did to Billy. He toyed with asking Pip directly how he measured up, but she hadn't complained so far, and there was no point in handing her an invitation to start now. He plummeted into sleep with the abruptness of a child.

George, on the floor above, also in bed but alone, found himself more preoccupied with Olivia's response than Sarah's sudden departure. *Two*? Which two? he thought. She's baiting me. She hasn't slept with Michael or Justus – she can't have. I'm drunk. Why should I even care about Livvy's games? Cow.

Sarah sat drinking coffee in her own house four doors away. It was quite obvious to her that George and Olivia had been and possibly still were involved: there was an unmistakable intimacy between them. Jerry and Olivia were known to be lovers; Justus and Olivia might be as well, from the looks they were giving each other. What it must be to have men throwing themselves at you all the time. They all frightened her, and though she decided to stay on her guard, she recognised it was a rather delicious fear.

Justus walked all the way back to Magdalen without a second thought as to how many people Olivia had slept with. He was certain she had lied, but whether it was more or less than two was irrelevant. He wanted to know why she hung out with that crowd in the first place. She seemed smarter than the rest of them. I wonder what she'd do in bed, he mused. I wonder what she wouldn't do. It wouldn't matter if she did nothing, just lay there. She's no Isabel Archer – she was lying then, too. She's Cleopatra; maybe worse.

Billy did not go to bed. She returned to her studio and continued to work. As she painted, she mentally dismissed the game and most of the players. Very stupid; very British. They are always silly about sex. Did they even know I was here? I would like to paint Jerry. Not Olivia, she is too obvious, and the American man is too strong – only good for photographs. I like Pip – she has acidity in her. I can imagine how she looks without her clothes.

Jerry looked at Olivia sleeping soundly next to him and resisted the urge to kick her hard in the shin. What more does she want? he thought. What's she playing at? Shit, how I hate these games . . . Next time I won't even pretend to play. Why do I love her so? Why don't I even want to stop? He breathed out softly, whispering her answer in the darkness of her bedroom, 'Two . . .'

Olivia was not asleep: she sheltered behind her eyelids, heard him, and lay still, wondering exactly why she had been moved to lie, and whether she'd made a mistake doing so. In the main, she blamed her companions for believing her.

# I am fond of them all . . . .

What do you think of these people? Do you hate them already? You'd have grounds to. They are, after all, students – and don't we all love to hate students? Privileged, not paying their dues, not even thinking that they ought to pay their dues, not even realising that there are dues to be paid – let alone tuition fees, back in those days. Unappreciative of how lucky they are. Completely irresponsible, and convinced they are entitled to be. Worse, this lot are all relatively attractive, relatively well-off, relatively secure, academically successful, yet treat each other, in a word, shabbily. If young people with all those advantages can get away with acting so callously, what hope is there for the rest of us? Not the most endearing cast of characters, I admit.

Perhaps you are more generous. Perhaps you don't feel that you know them well enough to know if you like them or not, although I think we are all inclined to make face judgements, however much we tell ourselves not to. In exchange for your patience, I am prepared to do something very dangerous: to enter into a Faustian bargain. If you will do me the service of letting me tell you more about each of them before they landed in Oxford, and what happened some ten years after they left, I'll make a bet with you. I bet you'll end up liking them – yes, all of them. I did. There are no heroes, no villains, in my opinion. I know them all still, and even if I do have my favourites, I am fond of them all.

Let's start with George Upton, the 'landlord' of 12 Kingston Road. Much of what I will tell you I heard from his own lips, but I believe it to be true; George is an honest man. George was the sort of boy whom everybody liked. At school, he was greatly admired for his sporting prowess. The heavily partisan supporters on the Marlborough College side of the rugby pitch would always, at climactic points in the game, take up the cheer of 'Up-*ton*, Up-*ton*, Up-*ton*! Come on, Maaall (this first syllable growled) braaaaa!' (the second bellowed). His teachers were fond of him; how could they not be? He was bright, far brighter than he was prepared to let on; he was confident, socially and academically, and if they wished that he applied himself a little more rigorously to the curriculum, they had to acknowledge that George Upton was that model modern Marlborough Man, an all-rounder: captain of rugby; a decent spin-bowler; head of house and thus a white tie (school jargon for a prefect); a senior figure in the CCF; a mainstay of the town's many pubs; and a stud in the eyes of the sixth-form girls. By the age of seventeen, George had discovered not only that the world was his oyster but that he held it comfortably in the palm of his hand. There were a few jolly years to spend – he had yet to sit A levels, but viewed them as a trifle; he had to hurdle the Oxbridge entrance exams, but had little doubt of securing a place at Merton College. Three jolly years there, then who knows? He'd take his pick from the City, the Army, Westminster, perhaps; a gorgeous wife, definitely; inheriting the old house near Blandford when his father's toes pushed up the daisies, saving any unforeseen disasters . . . He was big and blond and in every way golden.

You may find yourself itching to dislike George at this early stage, but my first comment was a true one. For all his blessings,

George had no arrogance; he had recognised at an early age that his advantages were unearned. For all his rowdy confidence, he was a gentle soul at heart, and despite his head start in life, George had as many fears and doubts about the future as the next teenager. At seventeen, his preoccupying concern was women. In common with most schoolboys of the era, he thought of – and addressed – members of the female sex as 'women' as soon as they turned fifteen. The only thing that kept young George Upton awake at night was the vexing problem of how to lose his virginity. He'd had a couple of opportunities with some of the local girls around Blandford, but they were too close to home and altogether too scary. With the help of a few magazines, he fantasised his perfect partner. A girl who was willing yet not experienced enough to know that it was his first time. One with a touch of exoticism that would make the event memorable and provoke the envy of the lads at school, who should be able to admire her from a distance. His day-dream expanded and matured to star an older woman, who would positively welcome his inexperience and consider him a stallion . . . Might he even, perhaps, be doing *her* a favour? George liked this twist very much: a beak's wife, perhaps, a pretty, outwardly composed blonde wife of a language master, walking her dog along the rugby pitch, letting her eyes linger that touch too long on the muscled thighs of the prop forward (George's own position, by happy coincidence), then one afternoon letting her hand trail lingeringly down his chest as she congratulated him on his third try in front of her husband, all the time her passion simmering beneath the surface. . . And then one night, one warm, sultry evening at dusk, he'd be alone in the changing rooms, and he'd hear a woman's voice – not even the voice, perhaps she'd just clear her throat, a little husky, a little nervous, very needy, and he'd step out in his towel to see if she needed any help, and my God, would she ever

11

need help, *his* help . . . Sleep usually came more easily after this.

George was waiting for a suitably pretty, suitably old (say mid-twenties) and understandably frustrated schoolmaster's wife to appear. In the meantime, he casually informed his cronies that he'd had two 'women' at home that summer, and it had been an easy business, not really possible to describe until they'd been there themselves, but a wink and a laugh and an elbow in the ribs served to make his point. The September after he had supposedly shed his virginity as effortlessly as puppy-fat, George nonetheless joined his mates on the benches that lined Court to watch the annual parade of the new sixth-form girls. It wasn't that he, George, was interested in the babies joining the school, he took pains to point out: it was simply a school tradition, to score the new women, let them know what was ahead and toughen them up for College life. It was part of being a lad; it was playing the game, and George was good at games. The lads did their best to welcome the female intake on their way to the first Chapel of the new school year by calling scores out of ten and the odd encouraging remark from the safety and superiority of the spectator benches.

Some of the bolder girls pretended not to see the boys sitting there. They clustered together, shoulder to shoulder, tossing their heads like spirited fillies and swinging their hips with the disdain that only a pack of sixteen-year-old females can muster. Those were the ones with good bodies and tight skirts. There were a couple of solid types with toothy smiles and sensible hair who marched along, pumping their arms like soldiers on parade; then a few stragglers, shuffling along with their eyes glued on the path, baggy old skirts down to their ankles.

'Ginger Nut, seven and a half.'

'Hey, Curly, decent boobs, six for effort!'

'Nice face – shame about the legs!'

As the final bell for Chapel rang, George spotted a girl walking apart from the rest, reading a book. She didn't toss her head, or blush, or in any way acknowledge the reception party. At first sight he thought she looked pretty enough, tall and long-waisted, lovely luminous skin, her pallor alluring rather than sickly, but she wasn't what he would have called knockout: she simply looked different. The funny thing was that all the lads, even the notoriously crude, shut up as she walked past. It just didn't seem right to score her. She didn't seem to be part of the game at all.

That was George Upton's first meeting with Olivia Fletcher-Smith, if it can be called a meeting, seeing as they did not exchange a single glance. He was to meet her many times, but that first encounter, the very first, cast something of a spell over George.

Now I must turn to Pip, or Ginger Nut as the lads christened her that first day. Even at her birth, Philippa Renfrew must have been a shocking sight. Her hair was of such intense red, such wild flame and so plentiful that she seemed to be on fire. Her father reputedly held her in his arms and glanced quickly at his dark-headed wife, while rubbing his own black one. He did not have a red-headed relative; nor did Mrs Renfrew. Nor did she, mercifully, have a red-headed friend or a red-headed milkman. The babe was theirs, her hair a whimsical tease. They'd comforted each other that it might all fall out in a few months, and be replaced with the familial black shaggy tresses.

It didn't; it wasn't. At sixteen, Pip, as she was known, was crowned with a tangled mass of hair so vibrant it looked artificial. It wasn't only the arresting colour, it was the shocking contrast it made with the bone-white forehead above her small but piercing green eyes.

She hated her hair, and blamed it for her essential shyness, a trait she combated with ferocious pugnacity. This resulted in people saying that her feistiness was in keeping with her hair colour. Kind friends complimented her startling looks, but Pip never wanted to startle, she wanted to glow and float, and drift and swoon like a latter-day Guinevere. How could you be a dark-haired, doe-eyed Guinevere floating and swooning in long-waisted green velvet, she ranted, when you were five foot one and looked as if you'd plugged your finger into a live socket?

Before going to Marlborough College, Pip had endured the nickname Carrot Top. She smacked a few girls for using it, was vicious on the hockey field and became accustomed to fighting her own corner. When she was eleven, a new girl came to St Mary's with the right hair, and eyes more grey than green. Pip cemented herself to Olivia Fletcher-Smith's side and swore eternal love. And as young girls do, they shared their intimate moments: at twelve they bought a box of tampons from Boots and examined them in mutual horror in a lavatory cubicle. They whispered their crushes into each other's ear, initially pop stars, then more lasting romantic figures, Lancelot for Pip, Heathcliffe for Olivia – the consequence of a school outing to the film of *Wuthering Heights*.

Three years later they faced and hurdled their O levels. When the Renfrews decided to move Pip to Marlborough College for the sixth form, it was inconceivable that the girls should be parted, and as Olivia was blessed with a biddable if absent father it was quickly agreed that the two girls should move on together. Over those years, their behaviour changed along with their bedroom walls – from ponies to pop stars to Escher prints and finally, at Marlborough, to Italian Renaissance annunciations. Their musical taste changed accordingly, climaxing, at eighteen, in 'Sad-eyed Lady of the Lowlands', set on continuous replay. And, needless to say, their taste in men changed too, if less dramatically; they never forgot their first romantic fantasies, and sought them in future men for many a year to come.

14

Now we'll turn to Jerry, a tricky customer to describe, if only because he played with different personae as if he were dressing up for a costume ball. The first time that Jerry Milton came to Kingston Road, at Olivia's express invitation, she and Pip grilled him about his life while George noisily vacuumed the carpet around their feet. Other than admitting to membership of the New College Junior Common Room, Jerry was strangely evasive. When Olivia asked what he was reading, he shook his shaggy head, pulled his oversized greatcoat tightly around him, sank his chin on his chest and muttered, 'No, no; far too personal.' Harmless questions such as 'Where do your people live?' and 'Where did you go to school?' were met with wild but silent gesticulations of his overly long arms and legs. George's rhythmic vacuuming slowed to a small fixed patch under Jerry's feet, as if the machine itself was magnetically impelled towards the stranger. Finally he stopped altogether and wandered over to the stereo.

'Anything you'd particularly like to hear, Jerry? Your name is Jerry, isn't it?'

'That's what some people call me.'

'What d'you fancy? Dylan? Springsteen? Bob Marley? Jazz?'

'I couldn't possibly tell you that.'

'Livvy, are you sure you didn't damage his brain when you knocked him over?'

There had been only one major drawback for Olivia in accepting George's invitation to move into Kingston Road. Three weeks into the Michaelmas term of their second year, Olivia was put on notice by her tutor at Brasenose that she could not persistently turn up fifteen minutes late for tutorials and maintain his goodwill. There was no alternative but to join Oxford's ten thousand cyclists. It is said that once you learn to ride a bike you never forget it, but Olivia had never learned, and at nineteen considered herself far too old to start. Pip and George took her in hand, selected a second-hand bike and spent a day taking turns holding on to the seat and pushing her around the back streets of Jericho. The next morning Olivia was on her own, and wobbled precariously down the road while Pip and George fell about laughing on the doorstep of Number 12. One morning, running five minutes late for a tutorial on the 'Faerie Queen', she wobbled across the cobbles of Radcliffe Square and ran into a very tall young man with light chestnut hair and deep-set blue eyes. Ran over, to be accurate, as he was sitting on the pavement outside BNC with his legs bang in the middle of her path. Apologising profusely over her shoulder as she raced into college, she shouted her address and invited him to come to tea that afternoon. And there he was, drinking coffee.

'He seemed perfectly normal this morning.'

'Well, he doesn't now.'

The three housemates observed their guest as if he were a zoo exhibit, or a piece of instalment art – too bizarre to reject out of hand, definitely incomprehensible, and vaguely funny.

Jerry looked back at them dolefully, and sighed with resignation. 'All right. If you insist on probing into highly personal and private matters, I might as well tell you the truth. I call myself Jerry because it is easier for Anglo-Saxons to get their lips round it. My real name is Jérzy. I'm illegitimate – the only son of a minor Scottish laird and a Hungarian opera singer turned prostitute.'

Pip was leaning so far forward in her chair that her knees were almost on the floor. George stood frozen at the tape deck. Olivia, who knew exactly what it was to be partly British and dramatically unBritish, and so was on her guard, smiled slowly and refilled Jerry's coffee cup. 'Do go on, Jérzy . . .' she breathed with perfect pronunciation, and heavy emphasis.

'I grew up partly in Budapest and partly near Fort William. I had intended to pursue a blossoming career with the Hungarian National Junior Football team, but my dear mother begged me to attend Heidelberg University, where I began a thesis on Hegel, before switching to Wittgenstein, or 'Aulde Witts', as we call him back home. After I was arrested for certain . . . political activities, my father decided that I should transfer to New College to take a degree in physics. Here I am. Is there anything else you need to know?'

'That's just amazing,' George began. 'Oxford certainly attracts all sorts, hmm? Livvy's never brought a physicist home before. Fancy that. So you speak Hungarian, do you, um, Jérzy?'

'Sadly no longer.' Jerry paused as he decided quite how far to push their gullibility. When he saw Olivia struggling to keep a straight face he decided to let rip. 'During my short but unpleasant period of incarceration under the German philosophical thought police, I received several severe blows to the head, which induced a partial but permanent amnesia in the area of the brain that controls linguistic memory. I have only one remaining word of Hungarian: *gulacz*. And in German, I only remember *Götter-dämmerung*. My English is also rusty.'

George snorted, but at Jerry's baleful expression disguised it into a cough. 'Bloody hell. You poor sod.'

'Excuse me? I don't understand your English idiom.' Jerry turned up the collar of his greatcoat.

'Then you won't understand if I call you a complete wanker, will you?' Olivia smiled prettily, and unwound her corkscrew-curled legs.

'Don't be so hard on the bloke, Liv. For all you know he might be bonkers.'

'He's obviously suffering from all sorts of disorders, though none as permanent as your idiocy, George. D'you want more coffee, *Jérzy*, or d'you want a glass of wine?'

'D'you mean to say he's taking the piss?' The light dawned slowly on George. Jerry inclined his head graciously.

Olivia felt she knew everything about Jerry, and it took only another hour or so for her to know just about as much as he did, and only a few weeks for the pair to become inseparable. A month later he told her he would adore her till the day he died. Everything about him intrigued Olivia, even his choices from the menu at Brown's. He came from Cambridge, where his father was a professor. He took up student causes and attended demonstrations, only to find himself protesting as often against the protestors as alongside them. Despite a profound distaste for football, rowing and cricket, he admired those sportsmen who competed as individuals, and regularly watched the racing at either Brands Hatch or Epsom on the sets of those friends who owned televisions. He was not a member of any university society, despising the Bullingdon and ignoring the Piers Gaveston. He did not attend a single JCR meeting throughout his Oxford sojourn. He looked for the mystical in everything. From the start of his second year he spent most of his evenings, many nights as well as some mornings and afternoons, at 12 Kingston Road. He was the last of the household to realise that far beyond adoring Olivia, he was falling ever more deeply in love with her.

Now I must talk of Justus, who was always the most foreign to me, literally and in spirit. In his second year at the university, shortly before I first met him, Justus O'Keefe stood for election to the prestigious presidency of the Oxford University Dramatic Society, OUDS. He was well regarded by most of the dramatic cliques; he must have known he could count on the votes of an overwhelming percentage of the female members of the society who, while earnestly assessing his thespian talent, secretly rated him Oxford's biggest heart-throb. Surprisingly, men were drawn to him too, and Justus received admiration with no more awareness than a beautiful woman has crossing the street, ignorant of the broken hearts she leaves at the traffic lights. Once the election was over and the presidency his, he resigned immediately, pleading the pressure of completing his thesis. From then on he was known as 'the *Acting* President of OUDS', a pun that amused him and seriously pissed off his successor. Most of the members of the society were too in thrall to judge Justus's quixotic behaviour critically, but some resented the way he had manipulated them and disobeyed the rules of the game for the sake of his image. This was, if you'll excuse the pun, an injustice to a man who simply set out to have it all while deciding which bits of it all he particularly wanted to keep.

Justus was the only child of a pair of Boston-bred Wall Street lawyers, who, like most Americans, had given their son the best education their wallets allowed (which was substantial) and asked only that he lived up to their expectations of his future (which were enormous). He had not yet blotted their checklist, ticking off scholarship as well as sporting prowess at Hotchkiss, reinforcing both at Princeton, and then proceeding rapidly on to a Rhodes scholarship at Oxford. The O'Keefes had felt momentary disappointment that their golden boy had not chosen to follow in their footsteps in the busy courtrooms of America, but it was early days yet, and if an Oxford M. Litt didn't immediately qualify him for one of the more lucrative professions, their resources were more than adequate to provide for further graduate education of his choice.

By the time he arrived at Oxford, Justus had progressed well beyond the adolescent sexual issues that preoccupied Jerry and George. He had not experienced George's seventeen-year-old virginity trauma because he had lost his own at fifteen before it had become an issue. He did not go to university with Jerry's contradictory urges of rampant lust and the proper subjugation of the flesh because he saw no rational reason to subdue any of his impulses. At Princeton he became a serial seducer. By the time he got to Oxford – and he was, after all, a couple of years older than most of the undergraduates – he had long stopped counting the notches on his bedpost. He had found women generally irresistible, and few of those he encountered showed signs of wanting to resist him, but by twenty-three he had become a little bored by all too easy conquest and had tired of playing a game he knew too well. As his dad said, 'If you know you can have it, son, you'd be a mug to want it.' This had proved true with the OUDS appointment; now he was looking for something a little further out of his grasp.

At the time he became a fringe member of the 12 Kingston Road clique, Justus had two passions, a genuine one for literature and another for drama, but he distrusted the pretensions and affectations of those who formed the nucleus of the drama world at Oxford. Perhaps this drew him towards Kingston Road; I have often wondered. Back in the winter of 1985 he found there a contained, incestuous collection of people who didn't appear to have any goals at all and apparently had abandoned acceptable extra-curricular activities completely, occupying their time dealing with each other and talking with no apparent focus or intent. He studied them as he might study a play, making preliminary stage directions in his mental margins. They baffled him by their lack of purpose; they also intrigued him – at least, the two women did; he may have regarded the men as nothing but a stage set against which the female drama would be played. He suspected them all of reckless idleness, and himself of envy; Justus was incapable of being idle.

Oh, yes: there was one other rather strange thing about Justus:

at that time he had many friends but very few close friends – very few indeed. When I first knew him this puzzled me. When I eventually recognised his great gift, his star quality, if you will, it ceased to puzzle me. Justus O'Keefe had the innate ability to make people pay attention to him. This is an extraordinary asset, but in my experience, although it may easily inspire love, it does not facilitate friendship.

How can I begin to tell you about Olivia? I have decided that the obvious access to her – and let me warn you, all paths to Olivia have a tendency to wind up the garden – is through her parents and their marriage. Even as a young girl Olivia must have thought a lot about marriage. Barring marriages of necessity, whether for financial motivation or paternal shotgun, she once told me she believed there to be three general 'types' of marriage. There were youthful, whimsical marriages when two people believe themselves to be wildly in love, and can't tolerate the idea of life outside each other's pocket. There were calmer, more reasoned marriages, when a man and a woman take a long, cool look at each other and know that, all considered, they are embarking on a partnership, founded on friendship, physical attraction and mutual respect and bolstered by shared aspirations for future life. Then there were marriages that just happened, out of the blue, as if predestined: one day you turned around and saw the man you were going to marry. Her own parents had broken the rules, doing the passionate-love-at-first-sight tango when they were both in their late twenties and inconveniently married to other people, and somehow remaining passionately in love ever since. As a child, Olivia thought that grown-ups had a duty to think about how their type of marriage would affect their kids because, as far as she could see, it was her parents' marriage that had messed up everything in her life.

The marriage of Peter and Domenica Fletcher-Smith was the talk of their social set for thirty-odd years. Olivia's parents had met at an art gallery function in Venice. They had fallen in love on sight, begun an affair that night and legal proceedings shortly after, and had been able to tie the knot some three years, one divorce and one tricky annulment later. Family friends would take Olivia aside and tell her how lucky she was to be the end product of such naked devotion. It was often said of Peter that he appeared to desire his wife even more, after ten, fifteen, twenty years of marriage, than he had when they first met. Those in their social circuit looked on this reciprocal obsession with wonder and envy. To their daughter Olivia it meant simply that neither parent had room in their lives for her.

Peter Fletcher-Smith had been born in England but was one hundred per cent an expatriate. His ailing career, as well as his ailing heart (handcuffed to an amiable but stolid English girl from a village near Wolverhampton) had been rescued when he met Domenica Makridakis. The daughter of a Greek shipping boss who, while not quite a magnate in the Onassis sense, was more than a businessman, Domenica had cajoled her father into finding her second husband a place in the Makridakis empire and had enough private income to allow Peter to pursue his shambolic but hugely enjoyable calling as a professional dilettante. Peter and Domenica began their married life with a well-situated and gracious apartment in the Via del Corso in Rome, a compact but charming new villa in the hills outside Athens, and open access to the family's several properties on the island of Chios. Peter felt that God had blessed him, and when Domenica became pregnant two short years after their marriage he felt he had fulfilled all that could be asked of him.

Olivia would admit that she was not an easy child. As a baby, she regarded her parents with a serious, studied frown. As a toddler, she had been wilful and difficult to please, and had been increasingly left in the care of the retainer Domenica's father had sent to Rome to enable his daughter and son-in-law to travel. On her first day at nursery school she had disdained the sandpit and climbing frames, and had sat inside on the floor with a pile of books. Her mother described her as a problem child – resentful, obstreperous and resolutely unfeminine; an ugly duckling, no less. The little girl was expelled from ballet class as irredeemably uncoordinated. She resisted every attempt to comb her hair, let alone plait it. Once a month or so, Domenica would steel herself to groom her daughter herself. The child would kneel between her mother's knees with her head bent, her eyes screwed tight and her neck rigid as Domenica tried to drag the comb through her thick dark hair. Time and again she threw the comb aside in frustration, and only then would the little girl raise her head and stare at her mother with eyes the colour of the sun seen through green glass, the opposite of Domenica's, which had the glossy sheen of black olives. Domenica would turn in frustration to her Tarot cards. Long after, Olivia retained a mental image of her mother, devoutly unfolding her husband's red silk cravat in which she wrapped the deck, pressing the cards between her hands and laying them out, quite oblivious to the child who lingered in the doorway. By the time her daughter was eight, Domenica had abandoned any attempt to influence her.

Peter, on the other hand, adapted easily to the child's moods. Olivia never felt the absence of his love so much as the absence of any genuine interest in her. The easy, affectionate manner that had made him the darling of the expat cocktail circuit charmed her, too, despite her efforts to resist it. She thought he would have been perfect, if only he had been an uncle. Peter found solace in the notion that Olivia was not so much a problem child as a gifted child, and convinced himself that his daughter's aptitude for

23

reading and her natural reclusiveness – as well as her green eyes – proved that she took after his (English) side of the family, and thus would be happier in England. His paternal duty was to return her to a society where she would feel at home, and where his wife would be spared the stress of raising a cuckoo in her tidy nest. Peter took the eight-year-old Olivia to England, appointed his childless sister Melanie and her husband Tom Barkham *in loco parentis*, and found her a place at a small, all-girls school. When he had opened a bank account in his sister's name and deposited adequate if not extravagant funds, he flew back to Italy and Domenica's slim, strong arms with a light heart. Olivia made dutiful family visits throughout her childhood and adolescence, but she did not come back 'home' to Rome until she was nearly twenty-two.

Need I tell you about Sarah? I would prefer to let her speak for herself, something she rarely did at Oxford, and to be frank, I barely knew her in those days. I could tell you a great deal about Billy, the German artist, but I cannot, hand on heart, state that any of it is true: Billy is quite insane, and I mean that as a sincere compliment. As for Michael Marsden, you will hear all you need to know of him anon.

Who am I to judge these people? you're probably asking. Well, I was there at the time, not that I ever chose to be a protagonist in their individual stories; I was rather taken up with the notion of being a passive observer. But I *was* there, and I did know them, as much as they would let me, and felt angry with and sorry for each of them in turn, then and in what followed. I wouldn't have written it down at all, if it wasn't for the fact that I bumped into Pip Renfrew on the street yesterday. 'Good God!' she said. 'Isn't it funny how the least likely people keep cropping up in your life, for no apparent reason, decade after decade, just when you're wondering if they're dead, and quite certain you've seen the back of them?'

Not a terribly pleasant thing to say, but she didn't mean any harm by it. Honestly. I always thought she was the nicest of the bunch of them – but what did I know back then? Anyway, what she said haunted me.

Before I describe what happened some ten years after they left Oxford – and I'll try not to wander off the point – let's play a game. Write down now on a piece of paper how you think each person is going to end up. I'll give you a clue: four of them got married between 1986 and the summer of 1997. Two of them nearly did. One of them, I regret to say, was badly treated but thankfully rose above it. One of them is an irrelevance. Take a guess. Do it now – write it down now, and we will review it all at the end, after I have told you their story. It is not a test; there is no one correct answer. Let's just call it a game, between you and me.

# ten years just thinking about stuff . . .

**Rome, May 1997**

Olivia Fletcher-Smith, thirty-two-year-old spinster of the parish of Santa Maria in Trastevere, dodged the traffic in the Piazza del Popolo on her way to meet her fiancé and wondered which of the three categories of marriage she was about to enter. It certainly wasn't love-at-first-sight, romantic bliss; it wasn't a sensible, considered, strategic marriage at all – far from it! She barely knew him, not really. It had to be fate; and being a woman who had grown, if anything, more superstitious with age, she thought fate was probably the soundest of the three alternatives. As she swung her long legs past the crowded tables outside Rosati's several male voices called out to her, 'Miss, Miss! Here! Over here!'

She turned to see a table with five of her students – four boys and one girl – and strolled over to them. 'What are you lot doing in one of the most rip-off bars in Rome? Even if your poor parents are paying, haven't you got any pride?' Her hands rested lightly on her hips as she shook her head in mock indignation. 'Anyway, you all ought to be working. I take it you've finished your assignment for me?' As a specialist coach, she had no responsibility for the extra-curricular lives of her students.

Black-eyed and catwalk-handsome Luca rose and offered her his seat. 'Please join us. If we have a lesson in the sunshine, perhaps we'll write better essays.'

Olivia sat down after glancing at her watch, noting the immediate disappointment on the face of Lizzie, a luscious sixteen-year-old who had clearly engineered to be the only female present at the gathering. 'I can only stay a moment. How are you getting on with *A Midsummer Night's Dream*?'

'Ghastly. It makes me want to puke.' Lizzie rolled her eyes, her gaze coming to rest on Luca, who had pulled his chair so close to Olivia's that their knees rubbed. 'It's all about fairies, and magic crap. I wish we could have done one of the real plays, Miss.'

Olivia didn't disagree: it was a tossy play to study even if you loved Shakespeare, and most of these kids didn't. Few of them ever would.

'Just think about the opening premise as if it were real life – as if it were you. Egeus goes to Theseus, the top dog in Athens, and asks him to agree that if his daughter Hermia refuses to marry the man he has chosen as her husband – Demetrius – then she should be condemned to death. Hermia, meanwhile, is madly in love with Lysander.' Olivia rolled her long dark hair around her hand, and knotted it into a loose bun that held and coiled against the nape of her neck. 'The Duke gives her three options, and only four days to decide: she can either marry the man she doesn't love, spend the rest of her life in a convent, or die. Pretty rough, no? How would you feel, Lizzie, if you had to face that?'

'I'd tell my dad to get stuffed.' Lizzie Roberts darted a knowing look at her companions and slouched, her too-large biker jacket, probably Luca's, swallowing her hands in opposite sleeves.

'I'm sure you would; but the law of Athens wouldn't let you do that. Imagine that you couldn't tell your dad to get stuffed. Death or lifelong celibacy?'

'I'd still tell him to screw himself.' The group sniggered, and Lizzie's confidence grew. 'Wouldn't *you*, Miss? You wouldn't marry someone just because your dad told you to.'

'I hope I would be able to convey my feelings in a slightly more cogent style, Lizzie, but you're right, I wouldn't have liked it. Nor does Hermia for that matter.' Olivia inwardly cursed the examiners who had selected the play. What she wouldn't have given for a third year of *King Lear*.

Lizzie was now in her element, and not prepared to let any opportunities slip by. 'Besides, I don't want to get married at all – to anyone, ever. I don't see the point. I mean, there's nothing to gain, is there? Even Shakespeare knew that.'

'How so, Lizzie?'

'Well, he never wrote about happy marriages, did he? The only people he ever describes being properly in love aren't married – Romeo and Juliet, Antony and Cleopatra, Henry Whatsit and that French skirt, Kenneth Branagh and Emma Thompson in Italy . . .'

'*Much Ado About Nothing*, please; it isn't just a movie.'

'Whatever. None of the married ones are happy, are they? Lady Macbeth. Desdemona. That woman who turns into a statue. All his love stories end at the wedding. I bet if he'd done a sequel they'd all end up divorced, or killing each other or something.' Having made her contribution, Lizzie was blatantly adjusting a stocking top for the benefit of the boys from the back row, but Luca's intense eyes were fixed on his teacher.

Olivia sighed. 'So what would you do if you were Hermia, and you couldn't get away from the law of Athens?'

Pretty Lizzie flung her blonde hair back from her face in a gesture of such disdain that Olivia was torn between wincing and inwardly punching the air. 'I'd run away. I'd elope.'

'But that's *exactly* what she does!' Olivia unbuttoned the top of her shirt. It was barely summer but already sultry in the city. 'I first read this play when I was about your age. I'd seen it several times before – in England every am-dram company plus some supposedly professional ones puts it on in the summer – but I never remembered that opening scene. All I remembered was the fairies, and Bottom, and tedious stuff about people changing their minds about whom it was they loved. When I was your age I was forced to read it a couple of times, and I still didn't get it.' She leaned closer to them, aware of their growing disaffection. 'OK, guys, let's call a spade a spade. I thought it was the direst crap.' Their attention returned at once. 'Then I went to a lecture given by a teacher at my school. He said that there were only twenty good lines in the play, and that a key Shakespearean instruction occurs in the first scene. That first, forgettable, yet shocking scene. Theseus says to Hermia, "Take time to pause." Take time to pause. Think about it – we can apply that to many of Shakespeare's plays – Lear's heath, the forest of Arden, *The Tempest* . . . It's something I want to talk about next term. So remember that: "Take time to pause".'

'I don't know what it means.'

'Work it out.' Olivia gave them a slow wink.

'But, Miss, I thought the play was all about magic and stupid games and kids' stuff.'

'It is. All about magic, and games, and love. *And* betrayal, and identity, and insecurity. Call it kids' stuff at your peril.'

'You don't believe in magic, do you, Miss? And fairies? You can't. Not at *your* age.'

Olivia smiled. 'I'm not ancient – not yet. But believe in magic? I certainly do. I believe in it more every day.'

'Maybe we can't understand this play,' Luca drawled, pouring her a glass of wine from the carafe. 'Maybe you need to have been in love to understand what it is to change your mind about who you love.'

'Whom. *Whom* you love,' Olivia corrected mechanically.

'Take me, I wouldn't be interested in a foolish girl who did what her father said – I wouldn't be interested in a girl at all. But an older woman, a woman who knew what love meant, who knew what she wanted . . . That would be interesting . . . Have you been . . . Are you . . .' The boys grinned and chirped in anticipation. ' . . . in love, Miss?'

'As a matter of fact, Luca, I have been and I am. I'm getting married in London this summer. When I come back, I'll be very interested in the group's assessment of the play – especially yours. No doubt you'll have read it several times, and I look forward to marking your first essay on it. Remember? "In what sense does the Athenian wood represent a time to pause for all the characters in the play, and what do they learn during that pause?" '

They groaned. Antonio, the most studious, asked, with a grave face, 'Miss, please, Miss, explain what "time to pause" means.'

'It's easy. Tell you what, I'll give you a big clue.' Olivia smiled at him. 'Don't rush into the essay, or into anything else.'

'Miss? Miss? Please, Miss?' Lizzie smirked as she mimicked Antonio. 'Who are you going to marry?'

'*Whom*. I'll tell you next term, after I've done it.'

'Does your dad approve?'

'As a matter of fact, yes, he does.'

'Che peccato! é bono come me?'

Olivia shook her head and tried to look severe. 'English, please, Luca. You must always speak English to me, in class or out of it.'

'I don't know how to say *bono* in English.'

Olivia smiled. 'You'd say, is he a stud – like me? And you'd probably flex your arm to show your pecs. I give up on you lot, I really do. Have a happy summer. Work hard!' She did not need to turn back to know whose lips had formed the wolf-whistle as she re-engaged battle with the traffic.

31

Olivia had been coaching the children of wealthy Italians and more or less wealthy English and American expats for six years. She had no idea what she would be doing in the future, whether, indeed, she would return at all after her wedding. The proposal and her acceptance had come so fast, so furiously, they had made barely any plans. She walked down the Via del Corso, the spine of Rome, past the house where her parents had lived when she was a little girl. As she passed by the front door she touched the spot where the brass plaque used to hang: 'Signor e Signora Fletcher-Smith'. The same plaque now hung outside a luxury apartment in the Teatro Marcello.

Olivia continued down the Corso to the Piazza Venezia, the city's pelvic bone. At the grandiose monument to Victor Emmanuel II she cut along the Tiber to the Piazza della Bocca della Verità. It was dusk, and although the noise of traffic raged around them, the Bocca itself was surprisingly free of tourists. No one really knew the origins of the carving; it looked like a vast marble disc secured to the wall, perhaps some three feet in diameter, and sculpted with a face that seemed to some ferocious and to others benevolent. Both its name, the Mouth of Truth, and its legend derived from the gaping mouth that dominated the carving. Justus was waiting for her there, in the portico of the church of Santa Maria in Cosmedin, facing the marble plaque with his back to her and the hood of a grey sweatshirt pulled up over his head. From the rear, he might have been a twenty-year-old tourist. She walked up behind him and slipped her arms around his waist. 'Hello, sexy.'

'Hey.' His face lit up in a boyish grin. 'I was just thinking about you.'

'Fibber. Go on. Put your hand in and say that.'

'What? In the lion's mouth?'

'It isn't a lion, you berk. It's said to be the god Oceanus.'

'Looks like a lion to me.'

'I thought so too, when I was little. The truth is nothing so romantic. It's a Roman drain cover, or so they say. Go ahead. Put your hand in.'

He didn't obey her instruction immediately. First, he placed both his hands on either side of her face and nuzzled her neck. 'You smell amazing. But, then, you always did. It's one of the things I always remembered about you.' He inhaled the heady fragrance of lavender and roses, honeysuckle and jasmine. It might have evoked old ladies and stale drawer liners, but her scent was honeyed and resinous. 'I could smell that for the rest of my life.'

'Why you want to sniff chalk and smelly adolescents I don't know.' She nudged him. 'Go on. Put your hand in, if you're an honest man.'

'Just my *hand* right?' He winked at her and obliged, putting his large right hand up to the wrist into the maw of the marble face. 'Guess I can risk one. What do I do now?'

'You tell me stuff. Make promises, whatever you want. No – I'll ask you questions, and you answer, but be warned: if you lie, the water god –'

' – the lion.'

'All right, the lion will bite your hand off.'

'I'm not scared.'

'I've never seen you scared. I don't believe you're capable of it.'

'Bullshit. I was scared last month when I asked you to marry me.'

'I don't believe you.'

He withdrew his hand and waggled his fingers before her. 'See? I was telling the truth.'

'Put it back. Question number one: am I the most beautiful woman you have ever clapped eyes on?'

He cocked his head as he studied her. 'Objectively? Nope. Not even in the top twenty.'

'I said be honest, but you don't have to take it to extremes! A simple "No" would have done me fine. Number two: are you marrying me for my money?'

This time he laughed. 'Oh, sure. What kind of idiot marries a teacher for her money?'

'Your kind of idiot. Do you love me?'

'Yes. Madly.'

'Will you love me forever and ever?'

'Yes, yes, yes. . .'

'Are you a good actor, or a ham?'

'I am a *great* actor . . . Aarchh!' He snatched his hand out, pulled it up his sleeve and tucked it under his armpit in a fair impression of Gregory Peck in *Roman Holiday*. 'Bastard bit me!'

Unlike Audrey Hepburn, Olivia didn't scream. She shook her head slowly. 'You're not a proper actor, you're a phoney. Vaudeville. A clown. Anyway, I bet your hands are insured.'

'Sure they are, but at least I've named you as the beneficiary. Now let me say my own stuff. I love you, Olivia Fletcher-Smith, in spite of your truly ridiculous name –' she kicked him in the shin '– I love you. I want to marry you. I want to live with you all my life, and have babies . . .'

'Careful.'

He waved his fingers again, and put them back. 'I adore you. I thank God – any and all of 'em – for letting me meet you again. I love the fact that you're so much the same. I love your back, and your shoulder blades, and your butt –'

'For God's sake, we're on the threshold of a church.'

'And your eyes and your hair and your quite amazing mouth. I even like your mother.'

'Liar.'

34

'As a matter of fact, I *do* like your mother.'

'I know. That's the problem. She likes you too, which is a bloody good reason not to marry you.'

'You need to learn respect.' When he saw her frown, he grinned again, and held her left hand in the Bocca, pulling her down so that they perched buttock-to-buttock on the edge of the pedestal before the carving. 'It's your turn, babe. I wish I had a camera.'

Olivia stared at their hands, his gripping hers at the wrist. 'I've been trying to teach *Midsummer Night's Dream* this afternoon.' It was one of a series of fateful connections that had brought them back together after ten years, having seen him play Oberon at Oxford so long ago, finding herself teaching it, then bumping into him so suddenly when he was shooting a film in Rome. The random timing of it all.

'No kidding. What did you say?'

'I told them I'd once seen a production with an unforgettable Oberon.'

He relaxed his grip and she moved her fingers gently. 'See? I wasn't lying. What I failed to say was that the performance was unforgettably awful. For starters, the costume left something to be desired . . .'

'Nice phrasing. It left a *lot* to be desired, as the Cherwell reviewer said. An *enormous* amount.'

'You vain git . . .' She leaned her head against his chest. If she were honest – and what better place to be honest – it was that first sight of him in a green body paint and very little else that had inspired her obsession back at Oxford.

'C'mon, Olivia. Tell me you love me like I love you.'

'There's no way I can know how you love me. I can say I love you in my own way . . . which I do.' She dipped her head in an odd twisting movement, like a swan stretching. 'I do,' she repeated, in her soft, deep voice.

'And you know I love you?'

'I think you do.' Olivia withdrew her hand and buried it in her pocket. She shivered. 'I hate this place.'

'So why did you want to meet here?'

'I thought it would amuse you.'

'I like to think of you coming here when you were a little girl, putting your hand in and saying, "No, I didn't steal the sweeties!" and running away screaming with horror. I wish I'd known you then.'

'You've known me long enough.' She slipped her arm through his and tried to edge him away from the Bocca. 'Besides, I never came here as a little girl. I didn't spend much time in Rome, and when I did my parents weren't interested in visiting churches. The first time I came here properly was with George and Jerry, in fact, when we were about nineteen. I don't think I've been back here since.'

'That's typical of you, Olivia, to arrange a romantic tryst with your fiancé at the site you met your old boyfriends.'

'George was never a boyfriend. Not like that.'

'We're not done yet, lady. Put your hand back in and promise me we're getting married this summer.'

Olivia rolled her eyes in mock frustration, her hand resting in the jaws of truth, the mouth worn so smooth and cold by the millions of hands that had stroked it, pilgrims making promises they intended to keep as often as those they knew they wouldn't. 'I am going to marry you this summer. Providing you take that stupid hood off.'

He dropped the hood, and Olivia was struck by the strength in his face. 'Say that you *want* to marry me this summer.'

As Olivia obediently began to repeat, 'I *want* to marry you,' there was a loud bang, like the retort of a gun. 'Jesus!' she cried, instinctively snatching her hand back from the marble jaws, and could not prevent herself from examining it for damage, her eyes wide. Her fingers were intact, the skin unbroken. She twisted the large diamond ring on her fourth finger round and round, but it was unmarked.

Justus laughed. 'Gotcha.' She stood, shaking her head and looking around, still nervously wringing her left hand in her right. 'Wow. That really scared you, didn't it? For a second, I thought you were actually hurt. It was a car back-firing, OK? A car.'

The hand returned safely to her pocket, but Olivia had been reduced to a state of whispery shock. 'I do want to marry you, I thought, for a moment . . . I can't stand this game-playing. I hate games. I *hate* them.'

He feigned amazement. 'You, the Spin-the-Bottle queen? The mistress of ceremonies? Miss I-can-handle-anything-you-throw-at-me? The creator of – what the hell did you call it, the if-he-or-she-were-a-car crap? *You* hate games?'

'I loathe them. I'm useless at them, I always have been. There was a time when I tried to be good, but when I realised I couldn't do it, I decided to stop trying. Forget it. Come on – let's see the church as you're leaving tomorrow. You've been a crap tourist so far.'

'I've been working.'

'No excuse.'

After a perfunctory poke around the interior of Santa Maria they headed back across the river towards Olivia's flat in Trastevere. As they walked, Justus read aloud from the brochure on the Bocca della Verità.

'You got it all wrong, Livvy. You're an incompetent guide, even in your home town. It says here that it wasn't a drain cover, or Oceanus. Listen.' He began to read aloud, adopting a heavy cod Italian accent. ' "The work in question is a symbolic representation of the divine form of the god Faunus, an Italian divinity often confused with the Greek god Pan".'

37

'Pan, Shman, one god's as good as another. Hey, did you know that "panic" comes from Pan?' Perhaps that explained her momentary seizure at the Bocca.

'Of course I did. Shut up and learn something. "God of fields and herds, he was also venerated because of his connections with untamed nature." I like that. Untamed nature. "Among his attributes were the gifts of fertility and prophecy." Better and better . . . "Perhaps due to its centuries of continuous veneration, today the Mouth of Truth instills in its visitors an overpowering sensation of the pagan spirit, often heating the blood to such a temperature that visitors have been known to rip their clothes off, fall to the ground and fornicate".'

Olivia snatched the pamphlet. 'Where the hell does it say that?'

'Only kidding. I knew I should have prayed for babies.'

'Let's go see Cecilia.'

'Is she beautiful? Will she be home? Is she a friend I should meet?'

'She's utterly stunning and definitely at home, but she's been dead a while. It's a statue, you philistine, an effigy of Santa Cecilia by Canova. You're going to learn something if it kills me.'

'Please, Miss, please, Miss, couldn't we quit the cultural lecture for a drink at some point? Or head for your place? I might not see you for a month. If Cecilia's waited this long for me she can hang on another few months.'

'I want to go say hello to her on the way home. She *is* sort of a friend, my favourite Roman. I want to light a candle.' They had only been together for a month; she wanted to be sure he knew all the things that mattered to her.

They eventually settled at a table outside the Hostaria La Canonica, just off the main Trastevere piazza and in literal spitting distance of her flat in Vicolo del Piede. Justus was leaving for France the next morning, and Olivia herself would go to London and wait for his arrival there.

'Did you invite your parents to the wedding?'

'I didn't have to. They'd already accepted.'

'Are they pissed we're not getting married in church?'

'How can they be? They're not entitled to be holier-than-thou. Mother was born Orthodox, I assume, but now claims she's Catholic. My dad was a Prot ripe for conversion. They're both divorced – even if my mother had to screw three cardinals to get her annulment.'

'You're kidding me?'

'Yes, I'm kidding you. But she would have, if that's what it took. Strings were pulled, that's all. They're just relieved I'm getting married – and to a celebrity, no less.'

'Actor, please. What about witnesses? You said you wanted Pip?'

'If that's OK by you. And by her. God knows how she'll react when I turn up in London. I don't even know if I'll be able to find her.'

'I can't work out how you lost touch. You were best friends all your life, then you up and leave London, come back to Rome, and never hear from her again?'

'It was complicated, Justus. You upped and left London, too; *you* didn't stay in touch. You know what it's like. At Oxford – school, even – we lived in each other's pockets. I suddenly had this road-to-Damascus revelation that I didn't want to go down from Oxford, share a flat in London with the gang, buy three power suits and save for a down payment. I just felt like coming back to Rome and thinking about stuff for a while. It's the best place in the world to spend ten years just thinking about stuff, and not doing much in particular. Maybe Pip was pissed off with me.'

'Didn't she contact you?'

'Maybe she thought I "abandoned" them, or was criticising their choices by not following suit. I don't know. I can't remember that far back. We lost touch, OK?'

'Not really, but I get the distinct feeling you're not going to tell me any more. What about Jerry? Did you stay in touch with your shadow?'

'Why do you call him that?'

'He was like a puppy, trailing round after you and whining if you went out of sight.'

'Don't let's talk about Jerry.' Olivia did not want to discuss quite how isolated she had felt for the past ten years in Rome. Oh, she had friends here, many; she'd had boyfriends too. But severing herself from the friends of her youth had cost more than she was willing to admit.

'You couldn't have understood.'

'I understood the first time I met him. He was hopelessly in love with you.'

'Everyone was hopelessly in love with someone all of the time – just like *Midsummer Night's Dream*. We just couldn't always keep track of which person we were meant to be in love with at each precise moment,' Olivia said cynically. 'That was the point of going to Oxford, wasn't it?'

'So are you going to look up Jerry when you're in London?'

'Just Pip. If I can track her down, and providing you're happy for her to be our witness.'

'Sure I am. She's a great girl.'

'She's thirty-one or -two by now.'

'So are you, but you're still my girl. Don't we need two witnesses?'

'How about your female lead?'

'Ophélie? I doubt she's capable of witnessing anything in English, given she can't speak a word of it. Not that that's prevented the casting director making her a quasi American.' The actress's incapability of maintaining an English accent – *any* accent – for more than three consecutive lines did not do much for either the cast's or the director's equilibrium. 'It's thanks to Ophélie Arcier and her incompetent pig of a dialogue coach that we're now twelve days behind schedule in the shoot. Not that I'm complaining, as she's given me two more weeks with you.'

Olivia wondered if he would have proposed quite so impetuously if his schedule hadn't been so frantic. Not that she regretted it. 'She's terribly lovely. Gorgeous. And young. Don't tell me you don't fancy her?'

'Fancying, as you put it so quaintly, is the last thing on my mind. I could happily strangle her. I just want you to know that if you want to ask George – Jerry, even – that's fine by me.'

'I told you, I'm not going to see them. I haven't spoken to any of them in ten years.'

'You are a strange and mysterious woman, Olivia Fletcher-Smith.'

'I wish you'd stop calling me that.'

'It's your name, isn't it?'

'Fine, but most people don't use the full handle when they address their loved one.'

'George always used to call you by your full name, didn't he?'

'Most of the time he called me Fletcher-Dunn. Remember the Betjeman poem – "Miss Joan Hunter Dunn"?'

'Can't say I had much time for Betjeman.'

'I bet you didn't. It was a favourite of George's.'

Justus held her hands and looked at her. He was quite certain that he wanted her, and he knew perfectly well that he wanted her because he felt it was time to marry, and she had known him before he had become a celebrity, before any success, and equally because he felt that he had not known her, and he had always been

41

intrigued by the challenge of discovery. Overruling all, her presence made him immediately happy, and that was a sure sign of love.

'I'll be back in London sometime in late July, definitely by the end of the month. We can fix a date at the registry office any time in August – the sooner the better. I want to give you the number of my hotel in France, and the keys to my flat in Kensington.'

'Your flat in Kensington? First I've heard of a flat in Kensington.'

'There's a lot we don't know about each other, but hell, that makes it more fun. Don't get excited, the flat's not much. I bought it when they commissioned the third series of *The 87th Precinct* just to keep a toe in England. Maybe I had some sixth sense we'd meet again.'

'I still haven't seen you as Carella. People talked about it – people who had satellite. That was the first time I'd heard your name since we left Oxford. Suddenly everybody started talking about this American TV series, and this unbelievably sexy detective.'

'Why didn't you call me?'

'Oh, sure; I was going to call up – God knows where – and say, hey, Justus, remember me? Now you're a big famous star? I used to know you at Oxford.'

'We could go a tad further than saying we "knew" each other.'

'You think I should have written and said, "You may not remember me, but we had sex during our last term at Oxford"?'

'I would have written back. I always thought about you.'

'Easy to say now. As I saw it, if we were meant to meet, we'd meet. And we did.'

They had, indeed, met quite by chance six weeks earlier. In less than a month Justus had proposed and she had accepted. Since then they had spent nearly every night alone together, although Justus had to be on set every day.

'Use my flat while you're in London. I'd like to be able to

imagine where you are. It's not much,' he repeated. 'We'll get something better when there's time to look.'

'Kensington will do fine.'

'And I want to give you this.' He pushed an Amex card across the table. Olivia noted it was in her name and pushed it back.

'I have my own money.'

'I know you do, sweetheart. I also know you're brighter than me, and more independent, and more beautiful, and freer and wiser and nobler and one hell of a lot touchier, but couldn't you bite down hard, sign it and pop it in your wallet just to put my mind at ease? In case you saw something we needed?'

'Like a flat in Belgravia, perhaps?' Olivia suggested sarcastically.

'Shit, girl, you don't let up! God knows why I want to marry you. Like a first edition of Keats, or diamond ear studs, or a painting, or a present for your aunt Mel. Don't you understand it gives me pleasure to indulge you? Don't you understand that I can't think of any greater happiness than making my new-about-to-be-wife happy?'

'I don't know. The whole thing scares me. I haven't seen you in ten years, haven't heard from you, and then I walk smack into you in Rome, and suddenly it's love and marriage and diamond ear studs and presents for all Rabbit's friends and relations. It scares me.'

'Because you think love should be all blood, sweat and tears? I've thought about you, had you locked up somewhere deep in my mind. All the time. When I saw you on the set, that afternoon, I knew at once. I felt so in love, so suddenly. I knew what I'd lost, what was missing in my life, and I saw a chance of taking it back. I'm not going to blow it. I love you, Olivia, I want you more than I've ever wanted anything. And I don't give up easy. My feelings haven't changed for a minute since I saw you again. If you've got cold feet just say so – but that doesn't mean I'll give up.'

'Of course I want to marry you. I'm just frightened of the stuff that goes with it.'

'Like Amex cards? Rip it up.'

She rescued the card before he could reach it and slipped it in her bag. 'Not Amex cards. That. All *that*.' Olivia inclined her head towards a table inside the restaurant where two couples were pointing and staring at them. 'That's what scares me.'

As if Olivia's nod had been a prearranged signal, the two women rose from their table and approached shyly, blushing and holding out a postcard and a guidebook. Justus stood and chatted with ease for a couple of minutes, introduced Olivia as his fiancée and signed his name.

When he sat down, Olivia took his hand and said, 'When I fell in love with you you were nothing.'

'Hang on a second – '

'OK, so you were a Rhodes scholar and a good-looking son-of-a-bitch. I lusted after you, that's all. It was nothing but sex.'

'Liar. You've already confessed you fell in love with me.'

'Did I? Maybe I did. I don't know what I felt except that I couldn't stop thinking about you. Is that love?' She smiled at him tenderly. 'It wasn't anything like what I feel now. I remember the second time you came to Kingston Road for dinner –'

'We played that stupid game. You said you'd slept with two people in the room. You lied to get them worrying what was going on between us.'

'No, that was the first time. The second time we played a *different* stupid game. When you left you asked me to dinner and I refused. I remember leaving a note in your pigeon hole the next day saying, very casually, I could, after all, do dinner. You didn't even reply. You didn't call or anything. I couldn't sodding think about anything except you.'

'I thought you were playing. I thought that's the way you liked it.'

'Not with you. Justus, darling, we had a brief affair, but the briefest. Ten years later I meet you and, God help me, I still feel the same way. Only now, half the world agrees with me and votes you the sexiest man on earth. You're in the Italian *tabloids*, for heaven's sake. They describe every woman you ever had.'

'You're exaggerating. I was voted America's fifth sexiest bachelor by the readers of the *National Enquirer*. And they missed some of the women and got the rest wrong. I haven't had time to work and have sex with that many people.'

'You're still a household name,' Olivia insisted. 'Like Andrex. Like Tampax.'

'How you flatter me. For the record, most people who see me do *not* recognise me. After this current piece of garbage, my career will be in the toilet –'

'Like I said. Like Andrex. Like Tampax,' Olivia interrupted mischievously.

Justus ignored her. He had enough stage experience to know how to deal with hecklers in the audience. 'And we'll have to sell the London flat in order to eat. Fine by me. I'll get a teaching job. Maybe we could open a school together. I don't care. I only want to be with you.'

'What makes you so sure you could teach, even if you wanted to, which I do not believe for a moment? You know, when I was young –'

'Wow! The old days.'

'Stop teasing and be serious, you berk. It's not that I don't want to marry you – I do. Very much. It's fate. But I haven't changed, I come completely unencumbered. You? You're a sodding Hollywood A-list star. It's the baggage you see – it's like marrying a man and taking on twenty stepchildren.' She grinned at his offended expression.

'If you are referring to my fans, I hope I have more than twenty.'

'Seriously, can you blame me for being frightened?'

'I couldn't blame you for a single thing.'

'You have no idea what you are talking about. You have no idea what I can and can't be blamed for.'

Justus leaned back in his chair and observed her; he wondered if she would move him so powerfully if she was less opaque, if he knew all of her, every second of her past, every inch of her present. 'How can I, baby, if you won't tell me?

'Are you sure you even want to know?'

'Is the Pope Catholic? Does Clinton play away from home?' he affirmed.

'One day I'll tell you anything, but not on our last night. Let's go home.'

They stepped across the street to the large wooden door of the house where Olivia occupied the top floor. The two American couples and the Italian waiters watched them leave. The American women were excited – it had put the froth on their cappuccinos to see Justus O'Keefe in an intimate liaison with an unknown woman he described as his fiancée. The Italian waiters were equally curious: Olivia had been living in the neighbourhood for a long time; they had seen her in the company of several Italian boyfriends, but the American seemed different. Waiters have a gift for summing up relationships in a matter of minutes. They are highly experienced, after all, and those in the Hostaria La Canonica deduced that Justus and Olivia had made a fair exchange.

When you fall in love there is far more involved than character and appearance. It is often the other person's range of experience that carries the strongest magnetic force. Each party buys into the whole package of what the other represents – there is an exchange, a reciprocal borrowing of status and image, which may explain why young women fall so easily in love – or homage – with older men (and older men with young women), why the attraction of a war hero, a statesman, an elderly artist, can be so compelling: their past experience itself carries a certain suggestion of the future. As Victor Hugo said, the young man is handsome, but the old man is great. Now the waiters cannot have missed the fact that Justus was still young, and very handsome, but it was his casually worn yet incontestable status that they believed significant. Their interpretation of the essence of attraction may have been old-fashioned, but it is still commonly held. It did not allow for appearances being deceiving.

# The Rules of the Game 2

## Oxford, January 1986

George looked sideways at Olivia and thought he could quite happily murder her, if only he didn't adore her so much. Even if Pip was the official instigator of this game, Olivia was equally culpable. The two girls loved games. Even though they had only two terms to go before finals, there was always time for games. It was a rare night that the evening's entertainment at 12 Kingston Road didn't end in a bout of Spin the Bottle, Adjectivally or some such nonsense. With all the regular suspects gathered in the sitting room, George had let himself be bullied. He really wanted to be left in peace to have another bash at seducing Sarah; the last time he'd tried – after another bloody stupid game – she'd scuttled off home like a frightened rabbit and he hadn't seen her since. She'd make a suitable finale to his Oxford conquests if Olivia and Pip would ever grant him an hour's privacy. Bloody Olivia had spent most of the Christmas vac tucked up all cosy with Jerry, leaving him like a sodding gooseberry, and his women didn't even have the grace to give up the sitting room now that he'd enticed Sarah back . . .

Pip was standing in the middle of the room, arms akimbo,

rallying her lethargic troops like a miniature, red-headed Henry V. 'Come *on*. We're going to play If He or She Were a Car, What Car Would They Be? D'you know how to play, Sarah? Justus? One of us goes out of the room, and the others choose a person in the room to describe.'

Olivia was lying on the sofa, eyes closed, her head on Jerry's lap, her legs flung across George's, bare feet hanging over the arm. 'You forgot to say it can also be the person who's *left* the room.'

'That's right. It can be any of us here now.' There were eight of them that night: the three girls and matching three boys, Justus, who had tipped up on the doorstep, and a chum of Michael's called Mark. Billy had not been invited back, although her presence lingered on through her painting on the wall.

'So the person comes back in and they get to ask three questions. If he or she were a movie, which movie would they be? Stuff like that. Everyone in the room gives their answer to each question, but the rule is, it has to be a genuine answer – what you really think. Only the person who's the subject is allowed to give red herrings. Then you have to guess who is being described.'

Sarah cleared her throat nervously. 'Maybe I'll just watch. I don't really know any of you that well.'

'You must know by now that in this house knowing the rules is not a requisite for playing the games,' Jerry drawled. 'And knowing the people is irrelevant. The object of the game is to flatter or piss off as many people as you can, as fast as you can, with a cast-iron alibi. Don't you *like* games?'

Sarah shook her neat brown head. 'Not much.'

'Nor me,' Jerry agreed, stroking Olivia's hair. 'Even when I know how to play them.' Olivia kept her eyes closed, but a smile flirted around the corners of her mouth.

'I'd still rather play Sardines . . .Why don't I ever get to choose the game?' Michael ogled Pip lasciviously to no effect.

'Tell you what, I'll go out first, so Sarah and Justus get a chance to see how it works.' Pip picked up her glass of wine and left the room.

Olivia rose slowly from the sofa. 'Who's it going to be? You, Jerry?'

'No, thanks. The last time you said that if I was a food, I'd be a vegetable. Let's make it you, Livvy.'

She shrugged, and George shouted in game-host fashion, 'Come on down, Philippa Renfrew!'

'If he or she were a flower, what flower would they be? Livvy?'

'A wallflower.'

'George?' George dragged deeply on his cigarette, and stared at the ceiling for inspiration.

'Come on, Upton! Don't drag it out!'

'I've got it, I just don't know what it's called . . . Something exotic, hothouse. Vivid colour, papery petals, very tender.'

'Justus?' Pip turned to the American, who hadn't spoken for some time.

'I don't see him – excuse me, or her – as a flower at all. A tree, maybe. A tall tree on a distant horizon.' There were appreciative murmurs around the room, and another slow smile from Olivia.

'Sarah?'

She dipped her head, and answered uneasily, 'A rose.'

'Michael?'

'Yeah. A rose without a thorn.' He put his palms together in prayer and pulled a worshipful face.

'Mark?'

Mark Jacobs grinned, and twisted the end of the joint he was rolling. 'A lily.'

'Jerry, your turn.'

Jerry stared straight at Justus O'Keefe. 'Venus Fly Trap.'

Pip folded her arms across her narrow chest and scolded them. 'Well, thanks, guys. That was crap. Round again, and speed it up; it's meant to be your first impression. If he or she were a country, which country would they be?'

They answered in the same order.

'Finland.'

'Greece.'

'The Land of the Free.'

Silence.

'Sarah? If he or she were a country?'

'Oh, God, I don't know.'

'Just answer. Anything that comes into your head.'

'Italy – no – France?' She waited for George's nod. 'Yes, France. Definitely.'

'Cyprus . . . but I say it for a reason,' Michael contributed, with heavy portent.

'Occupied Poland.' Mark followed his friend's lead.

'No man's land.' Jerry emptied the bottle into his glass, shaking out the last few drops.

'So we've got a heavy Mediterranean bent, plus the usual wackos. Last question. If he or she were a car, what car would they be?'

'Four-wheel drive, off the road vehicle,' Olivia replied immediately.

George: 'Something stylish, sporty but upmarket. An Aston Martin.'

Justus: 'I'll second that.'

Sarah: 'A Mercedes? Maybe a convertible? I don't know very much about cars.'

Michael: 'Nah, something sexier, yet classic. Big and smooth. Timeless. The Citroën DS.'

Mark: 'My dad's old Bentley. Distinctly unreliable.'

Pip waited for Jerry to answer. He had picked up a book from the arm of the sofa, propped it on top of Olivia's head and appeared to be engrossed.

'Jerry?'

'Oh, am I up? What was the question again?'

'If he or she were a car, what sort of car would they be?'

Jerry's eyes returned to the page. 'A hire car.'

Pip: 'You berks. It's obviously Livvy.'

Two hours later Sarah Matthews had found her courage and was trying to persuade them to play yet another round of If He Or She Were A Car, longing, secretly, to be the subject . . . Michael and Mark were staggering back to Balliol. George was wondering if he was too pissed to take Sarah to bed and if she was pissed enough. Jerry and Pip were being polite to Sarah, while hinting that you could have too much of a good thing. Olivia escorted Justus to the front door. She leaned against it

'I bet you think we're really childish.'

'Hell, no. I had a real good time.'

'So you'll come back?'

'Just ask me. Wouldn't miss entertainment like that for anything. It's best as a spectator sport, like watching ice hockey – you wince every couple of minutes. Maybe we could have dinner together sometime?'

'I'm sort of busy the next few weeks . . .' She wanted to sound aloof, but feared she sounded stupid.

'I can wait.' He placed his palms against the door, an inch to either side of her head, trapping her.

'I just mean I've got a lot of work, and I may be doing a play.'

'Oh, yeah? Me too.'

'Which one?'

'Worcester Buskins' *Dream*. What about you?'

'Oh, I probably won't get a part.'

'If I was the director, I'd give you any part you wanted.'

'You haven't seen me act.'

'Oh, yes, I have.' The second she saw his head move down, she knew at once that he was going to kiss her, and closed her eyes. Justus did not kiss her: he reached behind her bottom for the doorknob. 'But you haven't seen *me* direct. Yet.'

Olivia followed him on to the top step; he walked down Walton Street without a wave or a backward glance, his hands thrust deep in his jeans pockets. If he hadn't given her that intimate smile as he pulled open the door and she opened her eyes she would have felt an utter fool. In the space of sixty seconds he'd made her feel both a boring blue-stocking and an empty-headed bimbo. She went back inside, wondering why Jerry had called her a hire car. He could have meant that she was a slag, but that was probably her guilty conscience talking – if she hadn't been waiting like a fool for Justus to kiss her that would never have crossed her mind. He might have meant that she was her own boss, could be borrowed, but never owned; a far more attractive interpretation. Knowing Jerry, he probably meant nothing at all. The sitting room was dark apart from the glow of the dying fire. She switched on the lights and two shapes moved on the sofa. Olivia apologised and retreated to the kitchen where Pip was doing the washing-up while Jerry sounded off.

'What kind of a name is Justus anyway, for Christ's sake? *Justus*. It sounds like a nineteenth-century slave: "Yassuh, mastuh, Justus'll pick cotton, now the cotton is high . . .Yassuh . . ." I'll bet his family owned a couple of hundred slaves. What a smug dick.'

'You've barely met him, Jerry. Don't be so prejudiced. I think he's . . . interesting. Don't you, Pip?'

'He's incredibly sexy, if that's interesting. But I don't trust him an inch.'

'That's because you're a clever girl, unlike some I could mention. *Justus*. I've never heard of anything so pretentious.'

Olivia tossed him a dishcloth. 'Don't be so anti-American.'

'It's nothing to do with his being American. I wouldn't give a toss if he was called Brad, or Bud or Butch, even . . . But *Justus*. I bet he made it up.'

'He didn't. I've seen his passport. Pip, do you think we could make it a house rule not to have full-on sex on the sofa? George is such a fusspot about keeping things tidy, and then bonks –'

Jerry's hand froze in the act of drying a plate. 'What do you mean you saw his passport?'

'Passport. You know, the funny little books that grown-ups use to go to foreign countries?'

'When did you see it? I thought you hardly knew him?'

'It was lying on his desk when I went round yesterday to borrow his notes on Donne.'

'Why did you need *his* notes on Donne? There are plenty of other people. I could have given you some notes –'

'Oh, I see. Rather than read Justus's notes on Donne, who happens to be the subject of his thesis, I should have improvised with *your* notes on Hume. That makes a lot of sense,' Olivia teased.

'Why can't you see he's a phoney? Why do you waste so much time with jerks like Yankee Doodle?'

'You're just –'

'Don't say it, Olivia. Don't say it.'

'You're just –'

Jerry cut in crisply, 'I am not.'

'Just –'

'Don't. If you say it, you'll make it come true, Livvy. Don't say a word.'

'Jealous.' She flicked on the kettle and took three chipped mugs out of the cupboard. 'For Christ's sake, Jerry, don't get so worked

55

up. It was only a game. Look at you, you're a medical miracle: two legs, one prick, not much belly to speak of,' she poked him in each body part until she reached his head, 'and absolutely no trace of a brain.'

## the tender skin below his right eye . . .

Olivia left Rome nearly as abruptly as she had once left England. This time, however, she did phone her friends to tell them she would probably be back at the end of the summer, when they would celebrate her marriage and meet her husband properly. Her friends, male and female, were not surprised; not even her parents were surprised. This was, after all, typical behaviour. Olivia shut up her flat, packed a suitcase and got on a plane three days after Justus had flown to France with full entourage of minder, cast and production team. On the flight to London she was given a complimentary copy of *The Times* and skimmed it absent-mindedly until she hit the obituaries page. She didn't bother with the obits themselves: her eyes dropped immediately to the gazette entries of births, marriages and deaths at the bottom of the page. She read two entries carefully:

**Carruthers**, Wing Commander Robert St. Clair, DFC, DSO. On 31 May 1997, suddenly but peacefully, during a performance of his favourite concerto. Beloved husband of Constance, much loved brother of Lydia, adored father of Celia, Mary and William, devoted grandfather of Holly, Henry, Lucy and Gabriel, godfather and member of the congregation. Funeral at

St Mary's, East Hendred, Oxon., at 11a.m. Saturday 6 June. Family flowers only, but if desired, donations may be sent to the RAF Widows and Orphans Fund.

**Fletcher,** on 30 May, peacefully at his parents' home, Hovingham, Joseph Leo, aged 30 years. Beloved youngest son of Richard and Anne, affectionate brother of Neil and Sophie and brother-in-law of Steve. Received into St Aidan's Church' North Burbage, for Requiem Mass Friday 5 June at 12 noon. Funeral Mass at the Holy Cross Church, Pewsey, Saturday 6 June at 11a.m. followed by interment. R.I.P. Donations in his memory if desired to the Spina Bifida Association.

They would both have appealed to Jerry; he would have agonised over the schedule clash. She wondered if he still went to strangers' funerals; ten years ago, she was certain he would have set off for East Hendred – probably borrowed her car to do so and coaxed her into going with him. He never looked forward to anything with such keen anticipation as the funeral of a complete stranger, not because he was morbid, but because Jerry was so emotively in tune with the mourners that each and every funeral moved him greatly. She tore out the item and put it in her wallet.

Arriving at Heathrow Olivia bought a packet of cigarettes, having not smoked for nearly eleven years. Justus would kill her long before smoking could, but Justus need never know. She settled into his flat looking for traces of him but there were few to be found. Olivia sat inside for a day doing absolutely nothing. It was close to eleven years since she had been in London, or contacted any of her old friends. She would sit in the dark with a packet of fags and a bottle of wine, looking down on the street and gathering her thoughts. It took several days to work up the courage to call

Pip, during which she made deals with herself. She knew that in September 1986 Pip had gone to work for the BBC. She would call Broadcasting House to ask if they had a Philippa Renfrew in the directory; if not, so be it. If Pip had changed jobs, which was highly likely, knowing Pip (if she *did* still know Pip), then Olivia wasn't intended to find her; it would be the mirror image of the way that Justus had found her, which clearly meant they *had* been intended to meet again. And the way she and Jerry had not.

'Excuse me, do you have a Philippa Renfrew on your list?'

'Putting you through.'

Olivia clenched the telephone, heard Pip's voice and hung up. She waited until lunch-time to call back in the hope that Pip would be out of the office and she would be able to speak to a machine.

'Philippa Renfrew.'

'Hello, Pip.'

'Hello? This is Pip Renfrew. Who's that?'

'Pip. It's me.'

'I'm sorry?'

'Pip, it's me,' she repeated. There was no reply. For a moment Olivia thought Pip had hung up. 'It's Olivia. Do you . . . remember me?'

'Jesus Christ. Is it really you, Livvy? I don't believe it. Where the hell are you?'

'In Kensington.'

'In *Kensington*? For fuck's sake, Livvy. How long have you been there? Don't tell me you've been living in London all this time, please God don't say that –'

'No, I only arrived a couple of days ago. I wanted to get in touch. Catch up.'

'Catch up. I don't know what to say. So . . . can we meet? Tonight? No, I've got some sodding conference tonight. Can we meet tomorrow? What are you doing here? How long are you here for? What the hell happened to you?'

'I don't really know . . . I just wanted to talk to you. How are you?'

'Where do we start, Livvy?' Olivia heard her old friend draw in her breath. 'How are *you*? Where *have* you been? What is it – ten years? Eleven?'

'Nearly eleven. I've been in Rome mainly. I travelled a bit.'

'I wrote, you know. I phoned. For *years*. I spoke to your parents several times – did you know that? They didn't know where you were. We all tried.' Pip's voice dropped. 'We thought you might even be dead. Your parents were so odd. Then their number changed, ex-directory shit. What the hell happened to you?'

'Pip, I don't want to talk about this over the phone.'

'Did you get my letters?' Pip demanded fiercely. 'Did you get Jerry's? Or George's? Christ, Livvy, we went *mad*. Do you have any idea what you did?'

'Not really, I couldn't think straight.'

'But what *happened*? We thought you'd had some sort of a breakdown. Did you?'

'No, not the way you mean.'

'I don't believe I'm talking to you. I assumed you'd run off and married some Greek tycoon. I read sodding *Hello!* magazine for *two years* in case I'd see a glimpse of you. *Are* you married?'

'No. Are you?'

'No.'

'What about everyone else?'

'Who do you mean everyone else?' Pip's voice shifted. 'You mean Jerry?'

'Jerry, George, Michael . . . The gang.'

'How can I put this?' Olivia listened to the ominous silence

60

before Pip resumed. 'When you left, we were all about to start real life. The four of us were meant to be renting a house together in Shepherd's Bush, remember that? I don't suppose you're calling to get your share of the deposit back?'

'No.'

'Good. We lost it, now I think about it. I think George paid your share. After you vanished, Jerry pulled out. George and I couldn't afford the rent without you two. Anyway, water under the bridge, as they say. So . . . I went to the Beeb. George went off to his bank – he's still there, some big-shot director, making shit loads of money – and Jerry . . .' Pip's voice died away.

'What? What happened to Jerry?'

'You don't know?'

'No.'

'It's funny. I've always had the weirdest feeling that you and Jerry had been in touch somewhere along the line, even though he claims he never managed to find you. You never spoke to him?'

'Not since I last spoke to you.'

'How odd. Maybe my sixth sense isn't all it's cracked up to be. Well, Jerry disappeared too, for a while. He jacked in his place at King's – you remember he'd been offered a post-grad place? – and fucked off; India, Tibet, Africa, God knows where, looking for you and the Grail and God knows what else. Then he came back, bone thin, two years later, to see if you'd been in touch. You know he went to Rome to look for you?'

Olivia gripped the phone so that it pressed hard against her ear, cheekbone and chin. 'I don't know anything, Pip.'

'You should call him. Seeing as you're in the mood for catching up. He lives in Notting Hill and runs a gallery off Cork Street. He has the most fantastic stuff. George is still in town, too. *He's* married.' At last Pip's tone became conspiratorial, the voice she had adopted when sitting on the edge of Olivia's bath at

Marlborough and gossiping about who had been seen snogging whom. 'D'you remember Sarah?'

'Sarah Matthews? That Somerville girl?'

'The very same. He married Sarah ages ago. Not that long after you vanished. He was desperate for you to come to the wedding. Shall I give you their numbers?'

'Pip, are you angry with me?'

'Angry? I'm fucking *furious* with you. It makes me so angry to hear your voice, I'm finding it hard to speak. Why *have* you come back, Livvy?'

'I honestly don't know. Maybe I shouldn't have.'

There was a long sigh and a longer pause. 'OK. Look, I can't deal with seeing you for a two-hour lunch, wondering if you'll piss off for another ten years. It's Friday tomorrow. I'm booked to have lunch with – oh, never mind who – I could cancel, but I'd still have to be back here by three. How about we meet on Saturday for lunch, and take it from there?'

'You could come to me.' Olivia gave her address.

'Well, wow. Sheffield Terrace. Moving up in the world.'

'It's not my flat.'

'I can't wait to hear whose it is. Shall I give you those numbers?'

'No. I can't call the boys. Not yet at least.'

'Jerry's place is called Samsara. You can look it up. George works for Bartle Greenberg.'

'Don't be angry with me, Pip.'

'I probably won't be by Saturday – but you owe me, Liv. By the way, George has two boys. Real sweeties. I'm the older one's godmother.'

'What a thought. And Jerry?'

'What do you think? See you Saturday.'

Olivia had absolutely no intention of contacting Jerry, but on

Friday morning she caught the bus from Kensington High Street, got off on Piccadilly, and began to wander around the Cork Street neighbourhood wondering what it would feel like just to 'see' him. She traced and retraced her steps down every side and cross-street around the Royal Academy, and at eleven a.m., in the cul-de-sac of Boyle Street, she found him. The street was half a demolition site. The gallery was small, only one building-width wide, modern, with some Persian miniatures in the window and African masks and spears on the walls. Twice she walked quickly past, then stopped on the far side of the road sheltering behind some scaffolding. Inside, she could see Jerry talking with a man she took to be a client. It was like watching a silent movie through the glass of the gallery front. Jerry was not much changed: he had the stoop he'd already acquired when she'd first met him, the same way of inclining his head when he listened and the same gestures. An elbow cupped in one hand, his cheek cradled by the other, long fingers tugging gently at the tender skin below his right eye. She thought how many times she'd watched those hands caress a gearstick, or stroke a book in turning the pages, and waited for him to glance up and spot her. She tried to establish the forfeits of the game: if he sees me now, we're destined to be together. No: if he catches sight of me, I'll run, and never come back. She was furious with herself for being a fool at thirty-two, and an indecisive fool at that. She stood in the rain and watched him talk. He looked lovely: confident, urbane, worldly. The client was waving his hands in the air, Jerry was laughing, then he touched his long fingers together in five steeples, flexing them in and out, before putting his index fingers to his lips. The familiarity of this gesture made Olivia's head swim. She turned away.

She did not go home. She walked up and down, wondering whether she knew Jerry's tastes well enough, still, to be able to predict where he would go for lunch. There had been a time when she could have selected not only the restaurant of his choice, but also what he would order, what he would drink, even what he would feel about his meal once he had eaten it. They had once gone to Blackwell's together, formally handed each other twenty pounds and made a bet that they couldn't each choose the books the other would buy. She had been spot on – at least, he *said* she had been. He'd been close to spot on, though she told him he'd missed by a mile. Now, as she walked the rain-washed streets, she played the game: on days when he'd arrived late into the gallery, he'd grab a sandwich at one of three Italian sandwich shops in the immediate neighbourhood; but which of the three? She settled on the one with the old man in charge, wiping and wiping away at his spotless counter. The *padrone* would greet him – 'Buongiorno, Signor *Meel*-ton, *va bene?*' and Jerry would take pains to ask after the proprietor's three daughters, remember their names, praise their brains and beauty, and duplicate a father's shrug of frustrated resignation when the old man complained that none of them wanted to marry. But he wouldn't always go there – he looked smartly dressed today, and Jerry wouldn't want to burst the atmospheric bubble of the café with his Italian suit. He might favour the Japanese noodle bar, where he could be in and out without so much as a nod from a waitress. The smart restaurant with its cappuccino soups, pumpkin ravioli and mussels *en papillote* with lemon grass would only be patronised if he were dining with a client. Olivia wallowed in idle speculation. As the time neared lunch, she moved further away from the gallery itself, and found herself outside an Irish pub, its outside blackboard menu boasting wild smoked salmon and native oysters. This is where Jerry would come if he was with a male friend, a mate. He was older now: he'd value his pleasures and his food more than he had when she knew him. He'd unfold into a wooden chair, loosen his collar, clasp his hands behind his neck and lean back, tipping the front legs off the floor and laugh . . . And he'd eat oysters like a man from the nineteenth century – two dozen at a time, with nothing. Not even lemon. Just washed down with a pint of Guinness. It was a quarter to one and Olivia was hungry. The only risk was the disappointment, once inside, of proving to herself how little she now knew him. She went in, ordered a glass of white wine and lit a cigarette. It was her second packet since she'd returned to England – but only her second packet in ten years, and the only bad habit she had returned to. She was wary of recidivism, but perhaps not wary enough.

The bicycle accident in Radcliffe Square had had two immediate results: first, Olivia took driving lessons before buying an old 2CV; second, Jerry became so frequent a visitor at Number 12 that at Christmas George presented him with a bill for one quarter of the term's utilities bills. One of the shabby armchairs in the sitting room became Jerry's, and it was a rare evening that the household ate together without Jerry joining them. If Pip and George were not wildly impressed by Jerry's culinary creations of brown rice, steamed vegetables and harissa, they enjoyed his outspokenness and used him as a testing ground for their opinions. Jerry introduced them to a host of Oxford characters they might not otherwise have met: defrocked priests, Ruskin art students (Billy among them) and a sprinkling of young dons whose eyes burned with fervour into the small hours. Number 12 developed into an Oxford-style salon, soaking people up like a sponge, and if it was Jerry who introduced the more unusual guests, Olivia was the undisputed hostess. Jerry's arrival in their lives suited them all very well; George liked having male support in disputes with his 'women'; Pip and Olivia loved him. As for Jerry himself, he found George amiable, Pip endearing, and Olivia entrancing. It was half-way through the following Hilary term that Jerry and Olivia became lovers. They remained pretty much inseparable until the end of the summer after finals, the end of their Oxford sojourn, when Olivia had left England and vanished off the face of the earth.

Olivia ordered a second glass of wine and a round of smoked-salmon sandwiches. As she bit into the first brown quarter the door swung open and Jerry Milton walked in. He glanced around the room as if he had arranged to meet someone there. When he saw her he stood quite still for a moment then turned on his heel and stepped back outside. Olivia put her head in her hands, heard the soft thwup, thwup of the door again, and the scrape of the chair opposite her. It happened so fast that she still had a mouthful of unchewed sandwich and had to swallow hard. He spoke quietly, in a controlled voice, but she could see a muscle working in his cheek. He looked pale and suddenly exhausted, quite unlike his relaxed appearance in the gallery.

'What are you doing here?' His voice was the same, perhaps a touch deeper, perhaps a touch tighter in enunciation.

'I came to see where you worked – just to *see*, you understand? Pip told me you had a gallery near Cork Street. I only wanted to *see* you. I don't want to bother you.'

'Why should it bother me? You should have called. You should have come into the gallery and made yourself . . . uncomfortable.'

'I ought to go – you're obviously expecting someone else –'

He grabbed her wrist and held it far more tightly than Justus had at the Bocca della Verità.

'I could hardly have been expecting you. My God, Olivia. What on earth brought you back?'

'I didn't mean to come back. I'm not staying, just passing through.'

'I couldn't give a frog's fart why you're back. I *would* rather like to know why you left.'

'I had to.'

She lowered her eyes to the sawdust-strewn floor to avoid his. 'I had to, Jerry,' she repeated quietly. 'I'm sorry. It must have seemed odd, but I had to.'

Jerry gazed at her and rubbed his lips hard. 'Yes, I have to admit it *did* seem odd. I could have accepted your swanning off, telling me to get stuffed, saying you'd changed your mind about everything. Actually, I could almost have predicted one of those, but not your vanishing without a trace and without a word. Not your failure to reply to my letters. That seemed more than "odd".' He stood up and she winced as the chair scraped angrily. 'Would you mind if I get myself a drink? Can I get you another one?'

She was so relieved he wasn't leaving that she smiled. 'I'd love one. Whatever you're having.'

Jerry walked to the bar stiffly. If she had said, no, thanks, I must be off; if she had asked for something utterly preposterous, as she so often had when he had been unable to supply it – the Campari and sodas she demanded in his room at New College, Old Fashioneds, all to tease him, only on the next visit, when he had stocked up with the requisites, to ask for a Negroni – but to say 'whatever you're having' took away his thunder.

The twelve-month flood of near daily letters with different postmarks from Jerry to Olivia became an eighteen-month trickle of postcards. Perhaps, if he had carried on writing eight and ten-page letters, year after year, she might eventually have replied. The final card, sent to her parents' address in Rome three years after she had left England, said only, 'Olivia – where in hell are you?'

He came back to the table with three whisky and sodas. He seemed composed again; his eyes now looked sleepy. She saw that he had aged, that his chestnut hair was both shorter and darker than it had been, his face more lined and rather thinner. She looked at the three glasses he placed on the table.

'You *are* expecting someone?'

'A friend.'

'I'll go when they come.'

'Let me try to get this straight. You left because you had to, have I got that right?'

It was impossible to talk to him as her old . . . whatever it was he had been. Lover. Friend. He was a different man; a stranger. She nodded.

'And you've come back because . . ?'

'I wanted to.'

He leaned back in his chair, but not in the insouciant posture she had envisaged. 'Olivia, Olivia . . . You haven't changed at all, have you? "I had to"; "I wanted to". Here you are, what – thirty-one?'

'Thirty-two in August.'

'Fine, thirty-two, and still talking like a teenager.'

'I know you're angry about what happened. I haven't come here to apologise, nor do I expect you to understand. I certainly didn't expect it still to matter much to you. I wanted to catch up. I suppose I just wanted to settle things, once and for all.'

He could have told her that nothing is ever settled once and for all. You couldn't even brush your teeth in the morning and say it was settled 'once and for all'. The best you could hope for was 'done for the time being'. A week after Olivia had vanished, he remembered spending an evening in a bar in Crawford Street with Pip and George, and George saying, 'That's that, then. Done and dusted. That's what she really thinks of us.' Jerry had thought George a fool – not callous, he knew that he'd loved Livvy, Jerry could recognise love in others if not always in himself, but he had dismissed him for a fool to believe that life could let you go so easily. Jerry knew that once life got its claws into you, it did not let go. You could rip it out like a tick off a dog, but only at the risk of the teeth staying festering somewhere in the flesh. It had been late summer; there had been a series of departures. Justus O'Keefe had hightailed it back home to the States; Olivia had disappeared some weeks later; Jerry himself had gone mid-September. It had taken him years to come back, make a life, and give up on Olivia.

'May I ask you something?' Olivia had pulled her hair over one shoulder and was wrapping it around her fist, as he had watched her do many times before. 'Do you remember one night, when we were all at Kingston Road, and we played that game about describing people?'

'There were a lot of nights you played games at Kingston Road.'

'It was early on in Hilary term of our final year. You and I were . . .'

'Lovers.'

'Yes.'

'The second night Justus O'Keefe came to the house?'

'I don't know, it was nothing to do with him. Anyway. Whichever night it was. We were playing the game, Pip was guessing, and you had to describe me as a car, and you said if I were a car, I'd be a hire car. Do you remember that?'

'Yes.'

'What did you mean?'

'That's harder to recall, but I can remember what I thought about you then, so I can guess at it.'

'I thought you were calling me a tart.'

'You were always so literal. How could I have thought that? Even if I had, would I have been so crass as to say it? You never understood what I thought about you.' Jerry waved his hand as if shooing a fly. 'And it *did* have something to do with O'Keefe. I was annoyed that you were my girlfriend, had your head on my lap, yet kept looking at him. I probably said it to annoy you.'

'I remember you were nasty to me afterwards.'

Jerry half laughed. 'I was never "nasty" to you, Olivia. I wasn't capable of it. I would have jumped off a bridge if you'd asked me to, just to amuse you. You were quite right to despise me.'

Olivia was on the point of saying he bloody well hadn't jumped off Magdalen Bridge when she'd begged him to, but bit her tongue. Jokes were hardly appropriate. She had never despised him. Jerry knew perfectly well she had never despised him; that hadn't been the problem. Neither of them noticed Pip come into O'Neill's until she stood behind Jerry's chair facing Olivia.

'This is just like the old days. *Plus ça change . . .*'

'Sit down, darling. You remember Olivia Fletcher-Smith? – I'm sorry, *is* it still Fletcher-Smith? Funnily enough, Livvy and I were just chatting about the old days.'

Olivia stood up. Pip shook her head slowly.

'You look amazing. More beautiful than I imagined, and I was already giving you the benefit of the doubt.'

'You look wonderful too,' Olivia said sincerely.

'Sit down, I'm not staying. If I did, Jerry and I would only talk about you. I'll leave you guys to talk.' She squeezed Jerry's shoulder. 'I'll call you, hon, OK? See you tomorrow, right, Livvy?' Olivia, uncertain and still poised to leave, nodded. 'You *do* look great. Bitch.' Pip grinned broadly, and kissed Olivia's cheek, then hugged her. 'It's good to have you back.' She was gone.

'You and Pip have stayed in touch?'

Jerry rubbed his eyes. 'Yes. In touch. What are we going to do now? Play Twenty Questions? You get one, then I get one? What are you? Animal, vegetable or mineral? Go back to where we left off, but do not pass Go, do not collect two hundred?'

'If that's the way you want to do it.'

'When has what I wanted ever entered into your master plan, Livvy? You come; you go; you come back. You hold the cards, you choose the game, you make the rules. The best I can do is ask why.'

'I think I should go.'

'Oh, no.' Jerry gripped her wrist again. 'Not just yet. When you've answered my questions you can go. I don't have many, to be honest. Only three.'

Olivia lit a cigarette. She'd forgotten how usefully time-filling an occupation it could be.

'Why did you seek me out? Why have you come back?'

'I'm getting married. I felt I had unfinished business that . . . I wanted to finish.'

'Before you get married?'

'Yes.'

'Neat. I can understand that, that you'd want to tidy up. Fine.'

'Aren't you interested who I'm marrying?' Away from her students, Olivia's grammar was slipping.

'Not in the slightest. Why did you leave?'

'Don't you know why I left?'

'I haven't got a clue. Surely that was obvious from my letters?'

'Are you saying that in all these years, Pip never told you?'

'Pip? She didn't know any better than I did. Nor George. The three of us sat around speculating for weeks. I wrote, I phoned, I telexed. I went to find you. I saw your parents. They didn't know where you were, but mentioned you had explicitly told them that I was the last person on earth you wanted to see. I pursued you relentlessly. I went to see your grandfather. Interesting old man, isn't he?'

'He was. He's dead.'

'I'm sorry; I liked him. He also said he had no idea where you were and that you were a stupid girl. I believed him, though not your parents.'

Olivia drained her glass and smoked nervously. 'I didn't know that you came to Rome.'

'Then you didn't get my letters. Or you didn't read them.'

She shrugged. 'Some.'

'Some. I must have written to you three or four hundred times. Is four hundred "some"?'

'I got some of your letters,' she repeated. 'I can't have got all of them. I was moving around. I never knew you came to Rome.'

'You must have known I would come after you. How could I not? I was in love with you. I thought you were in love with me. We were planning to live together – do you remember *that*? We decided to get married. . .'

'We talked about it, Jerry. We only *talked* about it.'

'That's strange. I remember you agreeing. You still haven't said why you went.'

'I'm sorry. I can't.'

'It's such a long time ago, there can't be any reason to keep secrets. You were bored of me, England, everything. Just admit it.'

'I can't.'

'Where have you been?'

'Mainly in Rome, for the past six or seven years anyway. I went back to Rome and I've been teaching English Lit there. A-level coaching.'

'I've got one more question, right?'

'As many as you want.'

'Easy to say when you don't choose to answer them. Lord. I'd like to know how long you're going to be around, how you feel about getting married, what you think of me, if you ever think of me, why you toyed with me for so long, what happened that morning in St Sepulchre's, but if I have to put it all in one question . . .' Olivia, upset, didn't trust herself to speak and shook her head slightly. She didn't want to play games.

'Would you let me show you my gallery? Spend the rest of the day with me?'

Olivia could easily have said no and it would have been a grown-up, sensible decision to avoid conflict. But the fact that she was nearly thirty-two did not mean that Olivia was grown-up and certainly not that she was sensible. Easy as it was to come up with reasons for flight, it was far easier to find excuses for staying. She had not, after all, planned to meet Jerry; it had been an accident. Her intention to sort things out once and for all before she and Justus married was a sensible and proper one. She owed Jerry the truth, even if they were now strangers. She was genuinely surprised that Pip had never explained her departure to the others. She was intrigued – and perversely irritated – by the tangible intimacy between Pip and Jerry. Most of all, she had nowhere to go, and nothing to do, and she wanted to look at him for a little bit longer.

'Yes, I'd like that very much.'

that was all she said. It's raining . . .

George Upton was in a rage, which meant very little – George's rages were the equivalent of most people's tetchy moods. He sat in the boardroom with his feet on the table and his hands behind his head, addressing the speaker-phone.

'No, Hal, it isn't going to happen. I've had it with that tosser. If he's going to piss around like an incontinent old fart about the commission rates at this stage in the game, he can take a running jump. We've got far too many people tied up on this as it is, and I am not going to be messed around at the eleventh hour by some incompetent who can't tie his own shoelaces. If he wants to take his business elsewhere, tell him he's welcome, not that anyone else –' a temp came into the room – 'hang on, Hal. Yep? What is it, Lucy?'

'There's a lady holding on the other line – Pip? – She says it's personal, but urgent.'

'If she can hold I'll be with her in five ticks. No, take a message and I'll call her back. Hal, are you there? Bottom line, we're doing this for two and a quarter, or we're not doing it at all, and I wouldn't crap myself about which way it goes, right? I am not going back to the syndicate desk with revisions, and that's final, OK? No – that's it. You go back to your people and tell them to crap or get off the pot. Now about the Finns. I'll be in Helsinki next week, and it's our last chance to show them that Merrill sucks donkey dick.' He took his feet off the mahogany table and raised his voice a decibel or two. '*What* does Merrill do, Hal?'

'Sucks donkey dick, George,' came the obedient reply

'That's my boy! So, what progress on co-lead indications?'

As Hal ran through the numbers, the temp came back in and scudded a slip of paper across the table to him. George craned his neck and read: 'Hey, Georgie-Porgy: Three guesses who's in town? Wrong, wrong and wrong again. PTO.' He turned the paper over, and read the single word, 'Olivia'. George smiled slowly. 'Sounds good, Hal. You're doing a great job. I'll call you from Helsinki. Fax me all the stuff tonight – home and office – and we'll get on it and ram it down their throats.'

He clicked off the phone, stretched out his legs and picked up the note from Pip. 'Bugger me,' he said aloud, 'little Livvy.'

In Olivia's first year at Marlborough College, George had had very little to do with her. There had been only one 'encounter' and it was not a pleasant memory for him.

Though a recognised front-runner in the field of liberal education since the 1960s, Marlborough College clung to certain traditions, one of them being that every member of the school had to serve at least one year in the CCF. This was just about endurable for the boys, but the sixth-form girls bitterly resented the requirement, not least because it obliged them to exchange mufti for distinctly unflattering uniforms. George had risen rapidly through the ranks of the CCF because Major Wainwright (who ran it) and his father had served together in the army, and this had been enough to convince Wainwright that George Upton was cut out for a dazzling military career. George couldn't quit the Corps without offending the Major and he was far too well-mannered to do that.

One wet Wednesday afternoon, the seventeen-year-old George was drilling the pack of miserable fourteen-year-old boys and the handful of girls that Barmy Wainwright had entrusted to his charge. George had no intention of an Army career, but he found it provided an effective method of venting surging adolescent hormones – bawling, '*Drraapp* and give me twenty!' like a crazed drill sergeant in an American movie. Blasting the wretched twerps in the Remove had done wonders for his young ego, and set him on the path that was sure to lead him all the way to a safe seat on the board.

He'd started his drill: 'A tenn . . . shun! By the left – quick march!'

Out of the corner of his eye, George had spotted Olivia Fletcher-Smith break ranks and lean against the wall. She appeared to be absorbed in her own fingernail. He'd toyed with the idea of turning a blind eye, but the lads were watching him, snivelling and sniggering like the little oiks they were. George had started to march over to the girl, thought better of it, and summoned her to him.

'Why aren't you doing drill?' He intended to sound severe, but his voice betrayed him by squeaking.

'It's raining.' That was all she'd said. It's raining.

'What did you say?' he'd roared, feebly.

'I *said*, it's raining. Sir.'

George sat in the boardroom thinking about the seductive talents of the sixteen-year-old Olivia. She had given no overt demonstration of impudence, or provocation, or petulance; she had said those simple words plainly and directly. But when he had looked into her clear green eyes, he felt some part of him, some essential dignity, the conviction of authority that had always come so easily to him, expire with a sad gasp. What he had read in her eyes was a speech, something along the lines of 'Do you take me for a complete idiot? Do you honestly think that I'm standing on God's green earth purely for the pleasure of marching up and down some stupid cement track? Do you genuinely believe my sole purpose in life is to make you feel like a grown man?' ('Yes! Yes!' he'd wanted to shout.) 'I am not about to strut up and down like a clockwork *rabbit* merely because you have nothing better to do with your time than shout "shun!" twenty times a day. If you could shake your thick stupid head until you get some sense into it, if you could attempt to see beyond the bridge of your ugly nose – overlooking the putrid zit perched on the tip of it – if you could think of anything other than your petty rank in this ridiculously antiquated hierarchical game, you might notice that it is, indeed, raining, and agree to call it a day.' That was one thing that couldn't have changed about Livvy; she'd always had the most expressive eyes. One little glance could tell you everything and more. Talk about windows to the soul: in Olivia's George had seen several different souls all at once.

Recounting the tale at Oxford, Olivia had always claimed George made her drop and give him twenty. This was untrue. He had sent her back to her study, and told the little turds it was her time of the month – female trouble, which made him feel rather worldly and sophisticated at the time, and shut them up. He had given her a wide berth for the rest of that year, pretending not to see her in pubs when he was on vice squad, and turning a blind eye if he spotted wreaths of smoke wafting above the Master's summer-house, just in case Olivia was among the offenders; they did not speak again until the summer holidays before his Oxbridge term.

After his A levels George had decamped from his parents' house in Dorset to his grandparents in the village of Compton Abdale with the avowed intention of putting in eight hours a day of study.

In the week that had passed he had gone so far as to purchase the books on his huge pre-Oxbridge entrance summer reading list and thoughtfully peruse their jackets, but had not as yet opened one. Other daily tasks presented themselves as more pressing. One Friday evening, George was in the kitchen, cleaning his grandfather's gun in a desultory fashion. His grandmother sat opposite him at the kitchen table, sketching a plan for her new herbaceous border.

'Any plans this weekend, darling?'

'Just work, Granny. I'm going to get myself in gear tomorrow and get cracking. Doc Peters will slaughter me if I get back without having read the stuff. It's a bloody shame, but if I'm to have any chance of getting into Merton, it's nose to the grindstone.'

His grandmother misguidedly feared the effect of 'all-work-and-no-play' syndrome on her eldest grandson, and had decided that George's summer study programme should be balanced with stimulation of a different and more pleasurable kind.

'You don't want to become a brain on legs, darling. I've asked the Barkhams over for a game of tennis tomorrow.'

'They're too old to see the ball, surely? Won't be much sport, zimmer frames getting tangled up in the net.'

'You wicked boy! They're in their prime compared to your grandfather and me. Melanie Barkham can't be more than fifty.'

'Don't worry, Gran, you'll thrash 'em. A slip of a girl like you.' His grandmother patted his arm dotingly. 'So you need a ball boy?'

'No. We thought we'd separate the generations. We old folks can play a set, and then you can play with their niece.'

'Oh, Lord, you don't want me to baby-sit, do you?'

'She's not a child, Georgie. She's at school with you.'

'Barkham?'

'Olivia Fletcher-Smith. Do you know her?'

'*Ker-rist*, yes, and a royal pain in the arse she is too. I nearly had to bust her a couple of weeks ago, stupid girl. If I hadn't taken pity on her she'd have been gated for the rest of the term, if not for the rest of her life.'

'Now you'll have the chance to make friends. You can partner her at tennis.'

'I'd rather partner R. W. Southern in *The Making of the Middle Ages*.'

'Georgie . . .'

'All right, Gran. Whatever you say.' George stepped into the boot room to find some more gun oil. The shelves were lined with prescription medicines for long-dead dogs.

On Saturday afternoon, Melanie and Tom Barkham arrived in tennis whites, eye shields and elasticated wrist-bands. Olivia was wearing what looked like a pair of prep-school boy's blue shorts with a bare-midriff cheesecloth shirt, and didn't even have socks on. She had a bit of yellow wool tied around her hair in a scrubby pony-tail and when she saw George her face set in an I'd-rather-be-dead-than-be-here-with-you look. It was a pity that George had no guardian angel, no benevolent seer who could have said, 'Head up, old boy, here comes someone who is going to play a big part in your life,' but he didn't; few of us do. George put down his book with an exaggerated sigh, and stood up to greet the guests.

'Why don't we "wrinklies" play first, and you young things can amuse yourselves until the court is free?' George loved his grandmother, but he cringed when she tried to prove how hip she was by using shorthand she shouldn't have known existed. He also cringed when she addressed him as 'Georgie' in public. 'Georgie, why don't you take Olivia off and show her the garden?'

The two teenagers spoke at once.

Olivia: 'I'd really much rather watch you play tennis, Mrs Upton.'

George: 'I ought to be catching up on some work.'

Veronica Upton dismissed them both with an imperious wave. 'Nonsense. You two must have millions of things to talk about. School, for instance.'

The two older couples strolled down to the tennis court, leaving George and Olivia standing uneasily on the lawn. They had barely spoken to each other since the unpleasantness on the drill court. They moved in different sets, George with the prefects of the Upper Sixth and the rugby fifteen, and Olivia in two cliques that George would have described as the low-life lads who spent their afternoons droning along with Lou Reed, and the arty pseuds who wailed along with Van Morrison. George now looked at her with curiosity. Though conscious of the occasional stiffening when he regarded one of the sixth-form girls, he was not prepared at school to chance his arm and run the risk of a first refusal. His explorations in the realm of sex to date had been limited to snogging the local girls who hung around the pubs in Blandford Forum, and whose interest in him was heightened by the knowledge that he was the eldest son and scion of the largest private brewery owner in the West Country. With his fairer schoolmates he restricted himself to the casual insult or studied indifference. However tempting the promise of sexual gratification, the risk of injured pride and loss of face was far more daunting to his eighteen-year-old ego than the chance of a quick grope was satisfying. He might have behaved quite differently with Philippa Renfrew or a handful of the other girls with whom he had a decent chance of inspiring a response other than disdain, but with Olivia he found himself quite tongue-tied.

'D'you spend much time in Compton Abdale?' he opened.

'All my time. Outside school. I grew up here.'

'Funny we haven't met before. I mean, here.'

'I suppose.'

'Would you like to see the garden then?'

'I don't much care.'

They walked down the path to the first of Veronica Upton's series of connecting walled rose gardens. George began to find his stride. 'My grandmother has one of the most prized collections of old-fashioned roses in the country. She doesn't open the garden to the public much – three or four times a year. Can't really be dealing with the *hoi-polloi* scattering ice-cream wrappers and taking cuttings and the like. People say this garden is as fine as Mottisfont.'

'Do they?'

'Absolutely. Don't you like roses?'

'I couldn't give a sod about them.'

'Oh. So how are you finding College? You're in C2, aren't you?'

'Yes.'

'With Bugger Bailey. He's not a bad sort – took me for history in the hundreds.'

'He's a creep.'

'Not a bad historian, though.'

'I prefer Doc Peters.'

'Well, yeah. No contest.'

At this point, George pushed open the gate to enter the second of the three rose gardens, and the one he considered his inner sanctum. He had set up a table there that very morning, and piled his textbooks prominently, with R. W. Southern's *Western Society and the Church in the Middle Ages* displayed on top. He had not as yet sat down at the wicker chair and done any work, but that morning he had laid out an old essay, and a couple of pens (tops off) to make it look as if Olivia had interrupted an intense study period.

'I can't really spare the time for tennis at all. I've been trying to make a head start on my reading list – out here every morning, cold flannel on head, you know – what with Oxbridge next term and everything. I'm going for a place at Merton to read history. I suppose you've got nothing on this summer? God, the joy of the upper sixth – just another idle year dossing before you sit As.'

'Actually, I'm doing Oxbridge next term too. Fourth-term entrance.'

'What crap.'

'I am. RBW suggested it.'

'Crap.'

She shrugged. 'You'll see for yourself. I'll be joining some of your history classes next term, for my general paper. Doc Peters agreed.' Her hand trailed over the pages of his essay, and then her index finger jabbed at a sentence. 'That's wrong, by the way.'

'What's wrong?'

'Well, the date's wrong. Athelstan succeeded in 924, not 926. But really the whole thesis is wrong. Athelstan established the peace that let Edgar incorporate the Danes.'

George hurriedly turned over the essay. 'I suppose there's no harm in having a trial run at it in some plonker's subject like English,' he said, swinging his racket in what he hoped was a nonchalant manner. 'Then you can resit the following year. So. What do you fancy? A gentle knock-up? I promise I won't make you run around too much.'

'Actually,' Olivia replied, fixing him with a gladiatorial stare, 'I'm fucking good at tennis.'

Olivia had not lied. She was very good at tennis, with a strong forehand, a vicious backhand and a deeply unsettling serve. The tennis court was one of the few arenas in which she did not feel clumsy. She had spent hours and hours of her childhood playing by herself against a wall, with a ball on a piece of elastic, and with anyone who would play with her during her lonely holidays. She thrashed George Upton effortlessly, and he loved it. During that game, George fell hopelessly in love with her and his life was never the same again. He was more frightened of her than ever, but now he adored her. For all his buffoonish ways, George was not stupid. That summer, he and Olivia studied together two or three times a week, and their conversations about Thomas Hardy and the Avignon papacy were not interrupted by misguided attempts to snog her, or misplaced hands on her nubile body. George was biding his time. When they returned to school, he championed her on her weekly visits to his Oxbridge history class, making sure that the elder candidates did not take advantage of her relative youth, and seconding her opinions when she voiced them in discussions. Doc Peters, fountain pen stuck permanently in the corner of his mouth and sucked thoughtfully like an everlasting lozenge, noticed the shift in the dynamics of his class but did not comment. He merely brushed the chalk dust off his pale linen jacket, his eyebrows twitching in barely suppressed amusement. When George saw her arm in arm in a pub with one of the rugby fifteen – or even worse, as he did once, snogging a disreputable sixth form 'poet' in the art block – he turned his back and felt a searing pain run through his chest and stomach. He never once touched her, made a pass, or gave a hint of how fiercely his heart and loins ached for her. He bided his time. When he secured a place at Merton, his joy was bridled until Olivia came bursting into his bedsit to say that she had just heard she had a place to read English at Worcester. His secret fear had been not that he would fail to make the grade, but that she would end up in the Other Place. As a prefect, he was entitled to visit the town pubs, and as a prefect, he was entitled to take sixth-form guests, and he took Olivia to the Sun and ordered a bottle of champagne to celebrate. Olivia told him how happy she was that they would be at Oxford together. George privately regretted that he had applied to Merton rather than Worcester.

Their friendship during George's final term was founded on

deep mutual support, subtly inlaid with flippancy. When Olivia was intellectually cocky, George brought her down to earth with a bang. When she was insecure, he soothed her as a mother would a fretful child. After intensive tutorials, they would retire to George's bedsit for coffee and cramming.

'You can't ever trust an official biographer. Einhard was a sycophant. If you want to know the truth about Charlemagne's court, you're better off with Notker.'

'*All* biographers are sycophants, Livvy, official or not. It's just a question of comparing all the primary texts.' George kept his head deep in his book, but drew deeply on the scent of Olivia's perfume that would linger on in his room for hours after she herself had left it.

'Yeah? Well, I wish they'd all bloody written in English. George?' He didn't look up from his book. '*George*? Do you think I'm getting obscenely fat?' Olivia pinched the inch of flesh at her waist.

'No.' George wouldn't even raise his eyes from the text. 'I think you *are* fat. Always have been. A complete porker. A blubberous whale. You knock the spots off Moby Dick.'

Some evenings they strolled together over Granham Hill, and talked not only about work but about how much they would miss their schooldays. Contrary to most teenagers, this pair found it easy to accept that these had been the happiest days in their lives.

'This place – the past eighteen months here – have been the closest to a home I've ever had,' Olivia remarked one night, as the sun sank over the brow of the hill. 'It's pathetic, isn't it? I care more about the people here – you, Pip, Doc Peters, RBW, even Bugger Bailey – than my own family. They never loved me, Georgie, not even when I was born. Never at all. What makes me so unlovable?'

And because George knew that she spoke the truth, and knew how much it hurt her, it made his own heart ache. 'You're full of crap, Olivia. You sound like a bad B movie. Of course they love you. Everyone does – I have my doubts about Bugger Bailey, his tastes lean in a different direction – but everyone else can't help themselves. Your parents probably spend their lives talking and worrying about you, stupid old farts.' At the age of eighteen, he was quite wise enough to know instinctively that friendship requires the absolute denial of truths that hurt and the casual confirmation of untruths that comfort.

In the years that followed, George Upton found it difficult to understand why he had been so reluctant to take the initiative as far as Olivia was concerned. He was not introspective by nature, but at times, with hindsight, it occurred to him that he might have had Olivia then, sexually and romantically, and kept her his for ever. She was, after all, as she never tired of saying, very fond of him, and had, after all, been ripe, curious and unattached. George himself was deemed eminently eligible within the Marlborough mating pool: as captain of rugby, an Oxbridge candidate and a prefect, he straddled three of the major peaks of public-school achievement. Olivia often dropped the names of girls who wouldn't have refused a rendezvous in the squash court with him. But George declined. The late adolescent years between fifteen and nineteen are known to be formative – and Lord, which years aren't? – but for George, they were the moulding, firing and the polished glaze of his future. As easily conditioned as Pavlov's dog, he came to associate real desire with ultimate disappointment, and could not for the life of him consider himself Olivia's equal. Something about her made him choose to protect her and not threaten her; he feared that if he came on too strong, she would run away and be lost to him forever. George determined to cut his sexual teeth elsewhere, and then lay claim to her when he was confident of his abilities and self-control. In the meantime, he was resigned to watch others playing for, and winning, her attentions. When he quite literally bumped into her in the Magger's Garden one night, deep in the embrace of a notorious sixth-form shit, he had found his cheeks mysteriously moist as he walked away. He restricted himself to asking sporadically why she wasted her time with such prats, to which she replied quite simply that she liked them.

George left school that December with his place at Merton confirmed, intent on nine months' travel before he went up to Oxford. He spent six months swanning round South America with a fellow Marlburian, funded by a generous allowance from his father. He missed Olivia terribly, and in Rio, cut his sexual teeth painfully and in a foreign language.

Olivia spent her last summer before university in Greece. She had asked her grandfather if she could borrow one of the smaller villas in the Makridakis property portfolio, and he, of course, denied her nothing. She invited five of her schoolfriends to Chios for a final fling pre-university. George came for a week, and was sickened to find Olivia sharing a bedroom with his successor as captain of the cricket First XI, a strapping blond with the emotional depth of a handkerchief and matching absorbency for insults. He left the island by boat, the image of Olivia waving from the shore, her chin raised and her lips pouting as she blew a kiss, imprinted forever on his mind. The following September George and Olivia were reunited, as arranged, at the King's Arms in Broad Street one rainy Monday night.

George left the office early that Friday in an attempt to beat the traffic on the way to the farmhouse in Suffolk where his wife and children were waiting. He tried to reach Pip on the car phone, but got only her answer-machine. He made good time to Woodbridge, and could have been home in time to read his boys a story, but instead he chose to stop off at the Rose and Crown for a swift pint and a little peace and quiet for his memories.

trouble enough for any man . . .

Olivia picked up a five-inch by two-inch Persian miniature of a battle scene, admiring the intricacy of the work, the near microscopic flashes of gold on the costumes of the warriors and the trappings of their horses.

'What would this cost?'

'That one?' Jerry looked over her shoulder. 'Tricky to price. It's worked on ivory, which shows quality. The artist is rated; El Fharmi was the court painter, as it were, to the last but two Shah. It's a very good example of his work. On the other hand, it's relatively modern, being Pahlavi period, and he was prolific, so it has little rarity value. If you want to see something more unusual, if less charming –'

'No. I really like this one. How much is it?'

'Two and a half grand.'

'I'd like to buy it. Do you take Amex?'

'I'm sorry, but it's not for sale. The miniatures in the window –'

'You would have sold it to the man who was here this morning.'

'Which man?'

'The client who was here at about eleven o'clock. The one you were laughing with. I bet you would have sold it to him.'

'I assure you I wouldn't. That was my accountant.'

Olivia replaced the miniature on a shelf, and sighed. 'Lord, Jerry, how you've grown up. I would never have expected you to have an accountant.'

'I would never have expected you . . .'

'To what?' Olivia met his eyes.

'Never have expected to see you again.'

'What's the most beautiful thing, the best piece in the gallery?'

Jerry opened his mouth and shut it; he smiled. 'I nearly paid you a nauseatingly obsequious compliment. The *best* piece? Hard to say. My taste is eclectic – I have some interesting tribal art and do very good business with some of the American collectors. If by best you mean most valuable, it's probably one in the strong room.' He led her through a door, down some steps and tapped in numbers on a security door.

'Aren't you worried I might come back and rob you?'

'No.' He swung the door open.

'It's like Aladdin's cave!' Olivia exclaimed.

Jerry had no need to point out an enormous carved ivory tusk, supported by a cast brass head, its height several inches greater than his own; it dominated the room. 'This is the most important piece I have. It's a memorial head of an Oba and Benin Tusk, recently sold by the Pace Gallery in New York. It sold for a hundred and sixty-two thousand dollars.'

'Jesus wept! You paid that?'

'On behalf of a client. Would you like to hear the story behind it? It is believed to be one of six ancestral altar tusks from a Benin shrine, early nineteenth-century, commissioned by Oba Obanosa to commemorate either his father Akengbuda or his mother Ose. From the motifs along the tusk,' Jerry's long index finger trailed over the carvings of warriors and animals that ended in the head of a woman, 'scholars have concluded that it commemorates the mother, which makes it more interesting. Obanosa, you see, ascended the throne at an advanced age, in eighteen-o-four. After his coronation, he gave his elderly mother Ose all the lands and privileges that accompany the title of Iye Oba, or Queen Mother, and in return, expected her full support and allegiance. The Benin tradition is that any mother so honoured must emulate Idia, the mother of the great sixteenth-century ruler, Oba Esigie. Idia was no mean mother – rather like my own, I've often thought. She ran the military on behalf of her son, and was a dab hand at sorcery; by all accounts, a force to be reckoned with.' Olivia leaned with her back against the wall. Throughout Jerry's tale she studied him rather than the tusk, watching his fingers stroke the detailed work, listening to the rise and fall of his voice. 'Oba Obanosa was less fortunate in his maternal parent – Iye Oba Ose's primary allegiance was to a rather dashing rebel called Osopakharha, who attempted to overthrow her son. Unsuccessfully. The rebel was executed for treason, and general havoc ensued. The Queen Mum, or the Empress, to give her her proper title, continued to support the rebel forces against her son, and was accused of employing witchcraft when Oba Obanosa fell prey to a mysterious and debilitating disease. The treacherous Iye Oba was also put to death, at the order of her son, but according to Benin custom, the king was nonetheless obliged to erect a suitably grand memorial altar to her memory. In the final throes of illness, he commissioned the altar from which this tusk was taken, and then died in agony.'

He turned to face her.

'Tricky spot to put a son in, isn't it?'

'Other mothers have done it. Volumnia played pretty close to the bone . . . Do you believe the story?'

'Certainly. You read a tusk like a book, starting at the bottom and moving upward along the convex curve. This one is unusual: most have predominantly male figures, with the Idia image used once, possibly twice, to indicate that the Oba's kingship is supported by powerful female energies. This tusk uses the Idia motif four times – and the final one is unique, as far as we know. It emphasises female ritual and magic, rather than military power. Come closer, let me show you.'

Olivia shook her head. 'No, thanks, I can see it well enough from here.'

'You should touch it. It represents five hundred years of female strength – for good and bad. Maternal loyalty and treachery. And it's likely to be your last chance, anyone's last chance. My client will have it locked up in Germany. I doubt he'll ever display it.'

'So that's your favourite piece?'

'Only the most valuable. My personal favourites are over here, the Lobi pair.' Jerry indicated two rough nudes, a male and a female, with ledge-like bottoms and heart-shaped faces. 'I find them a very well-matched couple. I admire his worried expression, and her knowing one. They could be yours for a fraction of the price of the tusk.'

She followed him upstairs. 'I never knew you had such an interest in African art.'

'I didn't either. And, to be honest, I specialise more in Islamic and Turkish than Tribal. I prefer the household accoutrements – ceramics, cutlery, textiles, jewellery – things that individuals kept about them in their lives. You don't want to know about this.'

'How did you get into it all?'

'Through you, of course.' He began to lock up the cabinets and set alarms while Olivia watched him. 'I suppose I'd always had an interest in what we can learn about people from their possessions – that grew out of going to funerals. I used to go to the estate sales after a funeral to learn more about what the person had been like – it let me feel closer to them. But the Eastern and African interest was certainly thanks to you. When you left, it seemed logical to follow you, and luckily for me my great-aunt had died and left me some money, enough to bum around for years, so long as I stayed in the cheapest places. Rome was the appropriate starting point, although it was hard to find anywhere cheap. Then Greece. From Greece, I think I was looking for the end of the earth . . . I continued east, gradually as far as Burma, without success. So I went back to Rome, in case you had returned, which you hadn't. I then found myself in North Africa with nothing to do, and time on my hands. I spent about eighteen months wandering around and about, up and down the continent.'

'Collecting?'

'Oh, I picked up the odd tourist bauble, but I returned empty-handed. I hadn't gone to learn a trade, or shop, I had gone with one sole mission. To find you. I'm sorry, am I embarrassing you? You look uncomfortable.'

'Not at all. I'm just curious.'

'That's right: you said you wanted to "catch up". Somewhere between the Ivory Coast and Burkina Faso I developed a secondary ambition – to find out why men fall in love, and how to fall out of it. Shall we move on? It's nearly dusk.'

'You said why men fall in love – did you mean the human race, or just men?'

'I meant just men. That was my preoccupation at the time. And no, before you ask, I didn't find an answer, although I think witchcraft may have something to do with it. Don't look so glum! We should celebrate.' He offered her his arm. 'Where shall we go? What would amuse you?'

'A funeral?' She looked up at him through the corners of her eyes.

Jerry took it in his stride. 'You're forgetting. Not much we can go to on a Friday evening. Tomorrow morning, on the other hand, there might be something of interest. . .'

'Carruthers and Fletcher,' Olivia said quickly. It sounded like a song-writing partnership.

'What?'

'Nothing. Why don't we have a drink? Several. I feel like getting completely smashed.'

'Wouldn't that be dangerous?'

'Why should it be?'

'Mightn't you say something you'd regret?'

'Why do you think I have things to regret?'

'Doesn't everybody?'

'Am I the same as everybody?'

'Isn't regret the essence of the human condition?'

'Did you discover that on your epic journey?'

'Wouldn't you just like to know?'

'Uh, uh . . .' Olivia laughed. It had been another game, and Jerry had always been better at it than she had been; he still was. 'Yes! I *would* like to know.'

'Tough. The trouble with you is you always want to know everything.'

They walked in silence for several blocks, and Olivia found herself thinking of a May morning that had stretched into a long afternoon. She and Jerry had gone down to Magdalen together at dawn to hear the choir, and she had dared Jerry to jump off the bridge, a suggestion he had firmly rejected. After dropping in on several parties, and a late breakfast in the covered market, they had returned to Olivia's bedroom in Kingston Road still arguing, as they undressed, about whether or not he lacked courage. Olivia had not used the word courage; she stated – not once, but several times – that he didn't have the balls.

'The trouble with you, Jerry, is that you want to believe you're this incredibly unconventional, free-spirited, impulsive *life force*, and actually you haven't even got the guts to get your feet wet. You probably don't go out in the rain without an anorak. At least thirty men had the balls to jump in the river –'

'And about twenty women, not that you were among them.'

'Stop changing the subject.' Olivia unbuttoned her shirt and threw it on the floor. Jerry immediately picked it up and put it on the chair. 'There. I rest my case. You're so conventional that you can't even stand mess. Some Bohemian, huh? The kind of maverick who eats just enough fibre for breakfast to keep his bowels regular.' She took off her jeans and waved them tantalisingly in the air. 'Shall I drop them? How much would it upset you? Would you rush to fetch the iron?'

'That you are spoilt, slovenly and sluttish, my darling, does not justify your criticism of my consideration for others. I prefer not to sleep in a pigsty, that's all.'

Olivia threw her jeans across the room so that they strangled the bust of Socrates that Jerry had given her for one birthday. 'So you're intending to sleep all day? No need to dwell on your virility, then, is there? They don't call you Jerry No-Balls for nothing, do they?'

'Come here, you . . .' He growled as Olivia danced away.

'The trouble with you is that you're all show and no performance. All bark and no bite. All meat and no potatoes . . . No – don't you dare touch me – I haven't finished yet.'

'God, how many dreadful clichés do I have to listen to?' Jerry climbed naked into the bed and pulled the duvet over his head.

'The trouble with you –'

'Shut up and come here. Sit down. Let me tell you, for a change, what the trouble with *you* is. The trouble with *you* is that you are the sort of person who likes summing people up by saying, "The trouble with X . . ." and then sitting back smugly while everyone else marvels at your perspicacity.' He removed her bra while Olivia sat meekly listening, folded it and laid it carefully on the chair.

'You can't resist pigeon-holing people, it's the only way you can deal with them. And I can tell you where you slot people before it even comes out of your mouth. Take Pip for example.' He proceeded to imitate her likely pose, expression, even her voice. ' "The trouble with Pip is that no matter how many people tell her she's wonderful, and loveable and gorgeous, she doesn't believe in herself enough to make other people believe in her, and if you ask me, she never will".'

'What a horrible thing to say.'

'You might not have said it, but I know you've thought it. Haven't you?'

'I wouldn't have put it like that, but . . .'

'Precisely.' He eased her pants off as she wriggled up the bed beside him. 'Now, let's take good old George. "The trouble with George is that he can't be bothered to use what brain he has because he's never needed to – he's always going to just chug along like some sort of steady, reliable car. The most unpredictable thing he's ever going to do is overheat slightly".'

'That's foul.' Olivia laughed.

'It is, but you said pretty much the same thing to me less than two weeks ago when George was in a strop about the phone bill. Or let's take your buddy Justus.' He paused, chin in hand, fingers pulling at the corner of his eye, thinking hard. 'Casting aside the dreadful thought that you might not think Justus *has* a problem, let's try this: "The trouble with Justus is that he's never had to struggle, he doesn't know what sacrifice is about – everything in life comes too easily for him." How's that? Hmm?'

Olivia looked at him bleakly. 'Not bad, for off-the-cuff stuff. And what would I say about you?'

'You'd say, "The trouble with Jerry is that he's hung up on dreams and ideas, and won't ever pull his finger out and *do* anything." You'd say, "The trouble with Jerry is he's just not a fighter, he hasn't got what it takes. He hasn't got the balls." But, of course, you'd be wrong.'

'If you're so smart that you not only know what I think, and what I'd say, but you also know the truth, you tell me: What *is* your trouble?'

'The trouble with me, my darling, is simply that I've had the misfortune to fall in love with *you*. That's trouble enough for any man.'

It was strange what she remembered, and what she could not. She could remember many times at Oxford, but they were not the obvious times, not the big, red-letter days, but fragments of perfectly ordinary ones. Certain conversations she thought she could recall verbatim – from others, faces, names had vanished without leaving a discernible trace. For example, right now, as she walked through Berkeley Square with her arm held stiffly through Jerry's crooked elbow, she could not remember the time she had first slept with him. Oh, she knew *when* all right – she knew it had been the second or third week of the Hilary term of her second year, and she knew where, and she could visualise her Kingston Road bedroom with perfect recall, but she could not recapture what had happened, or what had been said, or how she had felt. She could see Jerry preening the following morning, her short white dressing gown revealing his scarred knees and lean thighs, but even then she could not remember if they had earnestly discussed their relationship, or joked about sex, or what. Now Justus – she could remember the first time she had slept with Justus, and the second, and the third . . .

'Olivia?'

'Hmm?'

'Shall we get a taxi back to my place? If you still don't want to eat, that is. I can at least offer you a drink.'

As the taxi rolled down Kensington Church Street, Olivia leaned forward and asked the driver to stop.

'I'm staying just around the comer. We might as well go to my place.'

Jerry stepped into the drawing room of the flat and studied the décor with a professional eye.

'Nice place.'

'Liar.'

'All right, it's not my taste. I wouldn't have thought it was yours either.'

'It's not my flat.' Olivia waited for Jerry to ask to whom the flat belonged.

'It doesn't feel very lived-in.'

'The owner's hardly ever here.'

'Didn't you offer me a drink?'

'Look in the bar. I don't know what there is; if there is anything at all.' All at once she regretted bringing him back. It wasn't fair to Justus.

Jerry opened up the large and ostentatious mahogany bar as the telephone rang. Just after the answer-machine clicked to receive the call, Olivia leaned across the table and snatched the phone but the machine did not immediately cut off. Justus said, 'Olivia? Shoot. I wanted to hear –'

'Hello. I'm here.' She held the phone close to her lips, her eyes fixed on Jerry's back as he squatted before the bar. 'I'm fine. Yes, it's absolutely fine . . . No, not yet, just very briefly. Uh-huh. I can't – I can't really talk now. No. Let me get a pen – hold on.' Jerry drew a pen from his inside pocket and offered it to her. 'Thanks . . . Go ahead . . . Is that a mobile? OK. Later tonight. Oh, I don't know . . . An hour or so? Fine . . . You too . . . Yes. I miss you too. 'Bye.'

'We're spoilt for choice. Armagnac, Calvados, Cognac, three or four different malts, wine, champagne . . . Your host – or hostess – has expensive taste. What's your poison, these days, Olivia?'

'Whatever you're having.'

There is something pleasantly distracting about busying oneself with the practicalities of setting out drinks, finding ice, looking for an ashtray as a prelude to a conversation that neither party wants to have, and both Jerry and Olivia drew it out as long as they could.

'Is that all right? Do you want water?'

'It's fine. Thanks.'

'Soda? I'll go and look in the kitchen.'

'No, it's fine.'

'Jerry . . .'

'Yes, Olivia?'

'Look, this isn't really working. I'm sorry. I shouldn't have, you know . . .'

'How did you intend it to work?'

'Oh, damn. I thought if I just saw you, looked at you, I'd feel better about everything. Be able to put it all in place . . .'

'And tidy it away, and settle it?'

'Yes.'

'Do you feel better?'

'No. Worse.'

'Do you know how I feel?'

'No.'

'Did you think what effect seeing you might have on me?'

'No. I didn't intend you to see me at all.'

'Are you sure about that?'

'No. I'm not sure.'

'Are you playing some sort of a game here?'

'Absolutely not.'

'I wish you hadn't come back.'

'So do I.'

'Shall I tell you what I think is going on? What you're doing here?'

'If you must.'

'I think that when we were together, you always knew that I wasn't enough for you.' Olivia opened her mouth, and Jerry held up one hand. 'Listen. I wrote this to you so many times, you probably know it by heart. I certainly do. I'm not saying you didn't love me, as I think you did, but you did not love me enough. You stayed with me because you knew that I loved you utterly, and that was a comfort, but in the end, you quite sensibly decided that wasn't enough. Now you come back. You tell me that you are getting married, and you want to settle unfinished business. I am unclear if that unfinished business is really with me at all, or if it is in fact with your intended husband. I suspect that I am to be used as a catalyst, and there's nothing intrinsically wrong with that. It's happened before; I have done it myself. I simply wish you would get on with it. By all means use me, but let's be straight about it, and not waste resources unnecessarily.'

'Jerry, are you involved with somebody?'

'I would describe my present relationship as semi-detached.'

'Do you believe that we each have only one perfect soul-mate that we are destined to be with?'

'At one time I thought so, then I didn't, now I don't know. It is a theory with considerable charm, but it seems improbable.'

'Tell me about the women you have loved.'

'*Loved*? That's very easy. There have been only two.' Jerry watched her closely.

'Oh.'

'You hoped I would say there had only ever been one? No, I fell in love with you, and then, some time later, I fell in love with Pip.'

'Pip? I see.' Somewhere in the back of her mind, Olivia had

known this; she had certainly suspected it from the moment Pip had laid her hand so protectively on Jerry's shoulder in the pub. The confirmation of it made her feel irrationally bleak. She struggled to keep her voice level. 'I guessed as much.'

'You asked if we had stayed in touch. We lived together for several years – until about a year ago.'

'What happened?'

'Who knows? Something didn't happen.'

'Was it mutual – breaking up, I mean?'

'Pip and I didn't break up any more than you and I did. I love her very much, she is my dearest friend. She is one of very few people that I know whom I regard with the highest esteem.'

'That doesn't sound very passionate.'

'It wasn't intended to. You see, Olivia, after you left – or, rather, after I gave up hope of finding you – I didn't have a romantic involvement for several years. It was my second attempt to live according to the Vaishnav principles, and I failed as miserably as the first. I then forced myself to have girlfriends, felt relieved every time I got one, and delighted every time we broke up. All the while, I saw Pip. We had dinner at least once a week; she helped me to believe in the idea of the gallery. Initially, I clung to her because she was the only person I could talk to about you, the only one who didn't laugh at me when I said that I was still in love with someone I hadn't seen or heard from in five years. It took me several years to recognise that, as time went by, we were no longer talking about you, only about each other, and eventually things fell into place.'

'And you were happy together?'

'As happy as I've been.'

Olivia did not know if he meant 'as happy as I've been since', or 'as happy as I've ever been'. He did not enlighten her, and she hated herself for wanting so badly to know.

'And why aren't you still together?'

'We are still together. Pip has never had any doubts, not ones she expresses . . .'

'But you're unsure, and you've told her so,' Olivia concluded. 'I'm glad I know. I'm seeing Pip tomorrow, and I might have put my foot in it.'

'How? Said, "At least you're not with that loser Jerry"? It would have amused her.'

'You hate me, don't you?'

'I only wish that I did. What would you like me to feel towards you?'

'I wish you'd asked me that ten years ago.'

'Oh, but I did. That was my big mistake. I think it's time for me to go home.'

Olivia didn't move as he put on his coat and walked to the front door. 'Will I see you again? Perhaps when your fiancé returns we could all go out to celebrate your engagement. That reminds me. If you've really taken a fancy to the El Fharmi miniature, I would like to give it to you as a wedding present. Let me know.'

Although he had known ever since seeing her in O'Neill's that he loved her still, Jerry felt a sudden and irresistible impulse to say something that would startle, something that would even – was it conceivable? – hurt her. 'In the meantime, give Justus my regards, would you?'

'How did you know it was Justus?'

'I would recognise that voice if I hadn't heard it in forty years. Goodnight.'

# The Rules of the Game 3

**Oxford, February 1986**

The word *avgolemono* rings with a certain magic; it is the sort of word you can intone out loud, rolling it sensually around on the tongue – *avgolemono, avgolemono* . . . It is redolent with Mediterranean olive groves, spicy evening air, the scent of citrus blossom; it sounds like a Greek fishing village, or an Italian aphrodisiac . . . It means, sadly prosaically, egg-and-lemon, a soup that lends itself well to student entertaining, being very easy to make, extremely cheap, and appealingly exotic. It was a staple on 12 Kingston Road dinner-party menus, particularly on those nights when George was cooking.

'Should I use two stock cubes or one?'

'Live dangerously – splash out on two.'

Pip was racing through the last two pages of an essay on Balzac due for a crack of dawn (i.e. nine a.m.) tutorial. Olivia was chatting to George while supposedly helping him make dinner and painting her nails a brilliant orange.

'OK, the stock's boiling. Now what?'

'Where's the chicken?'

'I forgot it. Surely there's enough chicken in the stock cubes?'

'There's meant to be real chicken in it, you turkey. Our cook on Chios used to use two whole ones. You poach them, shred them, and use the carcasses for the stock.'

'Great, Liv. If you just want to give her a quick bell, perhaps she'd like to pop over and cook it for us?'

'I'm just telling you what it's meant to be like.'

George stabbed at a ratty paperback titled *Effortless Entertaining*. 'It says here, "Boil stock; season; add rice; when not quite cooked beat egg with lemon juice and chuck in". It does *not* say, "Locate typical ethnic family retainer and transport to kitchen; let ancient crone get on with it while you paint your nails".'

'What are you doing for the main course?' George held up a tin of curry powder. 'Oh, God. If we're having your curry I might just make myself a bacon sandwich now.'

'Don't forget you're doing the pudding.'

'It's done. Three tubs of ice-cream and mushy raspberries. I don't know why Pip isn't helping. I bet she'll end up bunking off tomorrow.'

'I don't approve of skipping tutorials,' George said pompously.

'Oh, yeah, like you've never bunked off work?'

'I work very hard. I positively sweat.'

'You need to. Some of us get by on innate brilliance.'

'And others are lazy shits. You can divide Oxford undergrads into five essential categories: scientists in anoraks; working arts students; non-working arts students; incredibly diligent lady linguists; and people who read geography. And then there's us.'

This was one of several rules – Upton's Rules of Oxford Life, George called them – that he liked to declaim to anyone who would listen. His personal favourite was that Oxford was the best university in the world provided you managed to avoid either of two colleges – Keble and St Cats. Olivia and Pip had become deaf to this nonsense, but occasionally a newcomer to the house would take him seriously and all hell would break loose.

'Talking of diligent lady linguists, is Sarah coming tonight?'

'Dunno. I was going to call, but I don't want her to get the wrong idea and think I'm getting serious or committed or anything.'

'Heaven forbid. Personally, I think she's great.'

'You do? Not too dull? Not too conventional?'

'Not for you, no.' She dodged the wooden spoon George chucked at her head.

'The problem is, if she's free, I don't know that I want her to come, and if she says she's busy it will really piss me off.'

'Just call her, you dimwit.'

'You watch the soup. It's beginning to look incredibly like scrambled egg.'


'Ten people, right? OK. My ideal dinner party would be Marilyn Monroe on my right, Samantha Fox on my left, David Gower, Machiavelli, Bob Dylan, Cher . . .' George paused in his reverie while the rest of them grinned . . . 'JFK, Oliver Cromwell, me and – and. . . a Marilyn Monroe clone.'

'JFK would keep both the Marilyns busy,' Olivia pointed out, 'and you've got zero culture.'

'You don't call Dylan culture? He is the *sine qua non* of culture.'

'It's not a good mix. None of them would get on with each other. I'd have a round table, heaped with chocolate puddings and tons of really good wine, and I'd ask Simone de Beauvoir, Indira Gandhi, Dorothy Parker, Jane Austen, me, of course,' Pip reached the fingers of her second hand, 'somebody to ruffle a few feathers – let me think – Mary Magdalene –'

'What is this, some kind of lesbian love-in?' Michael mopped up the remains of Pip's curry with the last of the naan bread.

'Livvy, I'll have you too, so we can analyse it afterwards. Maybe Balzac so he could help me with my essay, and I need two perfect blokes, absolutely perfect – don't volunteer, George, you wouldn't get a look in.'

'Lancelot and Heathcliffe,' Olivia supplied.

'No fictional figures allowed,' George ruled. 'Otherwise I would have had O, as in *Story of*.'

'Pervert. Well, I'm still entitled to Lancelot. You don't think he had some disgusting sixth-century skin condition, do you? Boils or something? My final guest will be Sidney Poitier when he filmed *Guess Who's Coming To Dinner*.' Pip shrugged at George and Michael's knowingly raised eyebrows. 'It is meant to be about fantasies, after all. Jerry, who would you choose?'

'I think I'd have my mother at the head of the table,' Jerry ignored the catcalls, 'with Carl Jung to keep her on her toes. Down the middle I'd put the Marxes, Karl and Groucho, then Wittgenstein and Thomas More because I'd like to hear what they had to say to each other. At my end I'd have my best girls – Livvy and Pip, because I can't imagine being without them – and I'll chuck in Henry James to keep Livvy sweet.'

'You – are a real darling.' Olivia kissed him lingeringly.

'You – are a real creep,' George amended, putting his finger down his throat. 'And a liar, and an obsequious, oily, smarmy ladies' man. If you had a shred of honesty you'd admit you'd much rather have an intimate *tête-à-tête* with a page-three stunner with simply enormous boobs –'

'I've already bagged them,' Michael interjected. 'All of them. Me, eight pairs of thirty-eight DD breasts, plus whichever old bastard is going to mark my finals papers, so I can slip him a wad of used fivers under the table once he's well and truly plastered.'

'How disgusting.' Sarah shook her head.

'Go on, then, Sarah, who'd you have?'

'I'd have a really good cook, Raymond Blanc or someone, to do the dinner.'

'Eminently practical.'

'And I'd like to have Rilke and Rimbaud' . . . Sarah started off strong but ran out of steam. She would have liked to include George, but seeing that he hadn't mentioned her, and had gone on about breasts and Marilyn Monroe, she abruptly decided not to. 'I'd like to have somebody really funny – Peter Cook. Maybe a great musician to play afterwards – Mozart –'

'Not that little shit!'

'OK, Bach, then. And somebody nice and easy just to talk to – maybe somebody like Jerry,' she ventured nervously, uncertain how far she could goad George at this tentative stage in their relationship. 'And Shakespeare, I suppose.'

'Where's the sex?' Pip pointed out. 'You haven't got any lookers, Sarah.'

Jerry grunted. 'Thanks *very* much.'

'I'm just saying it's not a dinner party I'd cut my arm off to attend.'

'Seeing as she's not inviting you, Pip, that's all right.' Pip stuck out her tongue at Jerry.

'How many have I got left – two? OK, Gandhi –'

'Call him a looker?' Pip scoffed. 'He may be very worthy, but he doesn't ring my bells.'

'Leave her alone, Pip,' Olivia said quietly

'And Elvis Presley before he got fat,' Sarah finished breathlessly.

'I'd like to be there.' Olivia lit a cigarette and began to clear the table.

'Come on, Livvy, tell us who you'd have.'

She stood in the doorway with plates lined along her forearms and the cigarette gripped between her teeth as she replied, 'I'll think about it while I get the pudding.'

When Olivia returned she stood until they all looked at her expectantly, then held up her hands for complete silence.

'OK. I've got it, but the conditions are, first, that it's a buffet, right? I don't want anyone sitting down and getting stuck all night with someone they don't like. And, second, I'd have to have already met Thomas More at Jerry's, because otherwise I'd have him too. Here goes – Henry James again, providing he was good value the first time,' she nodded at Jerry, 'and Jerry, William Faulkner, Cleopatra, Joan of Arc, John Keats, Abelard, Virginia Woolf and Napoleon. If Henry James doesn't give good conversation, I'll drop him and have Justus O'Keefe in reserve.'

'Why on earth Justus O'Keefe?' Michael asked.

'Because she fancies him.' Pip placed her elbows square, peevishly annoyed that Livvy had excluded her, and still smarting at being rebuked for teasing Sarah.

'No, mainly because Jerry hates him, and a little bit of tension's good – most dinner parties are disastrously dull because the guests like each other too much. And I'd ask Justus, like Napoleon, because I think he's interesting but probably ninety-eight per cent a shit, and I'm interested in shits. And I'd like to see how he'd handle Cleopatra and Joan of Arc.' She gazed around the table. 'Hey – it's *my* fantasy, isn't it? Who wants ice-cream?'

only shooting a crapola costume drama . . .

Justus hung around in his hotel room trying to read a new script for well over an hour, then took his mobile down to the hotel bar to join assorted members of the crew. He had a good reputation as a mixer and had made firm friends with some of the more lowly members of the cast and production team, who rarely got as much as a nod from the star. He had a good reputation for pretty much everything, with pretty much everyone, except the script-writers and editors. Eleven years after leaving Oxford, with a highly successful TV series to his name plus a box-office-breaking feature film, producers regarded Justus as a runner with potentially endless legs, several directors regarded him as a barely tapped well of talent, and the audience, by and large (and large they were) regarded him as a heart-throb. The English script-writer and American script-editor of his current film, *Roderick Hudson*, regarded their eponymous star as a pain in the arse, because he insisted on interfering in their work.

They were in the process of shooting the very end of the film in the late middle of the shooting schedule and the whole charabanc had therefore moved from Rome, where they had shot the bulk of it, to France, which was masquerading as Switzerland, before they would return briefly to the States to shoot the opening scenes. So far it had been a good shoot, as shoots go. Justus had knowingly exaggerated the shortcomings of his female co-star, Ophélie Arcier, for Olivia's benefit. He did not, in truth, find her attractive, but she'd done a perfectly good job to date, and that mattered more to Justus than her appearance. His male co-star, who played his mentor and patron, Rowland Malet, was an American actor Justus had known from way back, when Justus had been struggling to get cast in off-Broadway musicals, and Martin Benucci had already been a household name. Now, their fortunes had changed: Justus was to take top billing; Martin was making his comeback.

'Hey, guys. What're you drinking?'

Martin shrugged. 'I didn't see the label, but we charged it to your room, so I hope you like it. Here, have a bottle. We ordered plenty.'

Justus ordered a mineral water in French, raising wolf-whistles and a round of slow applause from his companions.

'Yeah, yeah – don't tell me – multi-faceted,' Justus said, self-mockingly. 'I even learned it in Italian, too, you know that?'

They were chatting half-heartedly about the day's shoot when Justus's mobile bleeped. He stepped away from the bar.

'Hi,' he said softly. 'I've been waiting for you to call back.'

'That right? Well, I've been waiting for three fuckin' days for *you* to call back, chum!' his agent's voice bellowed, as if it had to carry unaided all the way from LA.

'OK, OK,' Justus soothed. 'What's so urgent?'

'What's so urgent with you you couldn't return my call? Too important to check your own voice-mail? Too busy to remember that I dragged you out of the gutter and put you where you are now? I'll bet you're not too goddamn busy to return a call from fuckin' ICM, huh? What the fuck are you so goddamn busy doing, anyway? You're only shooting a crapola costume drama, for fuck's sake, *against my best advice*, and don't forget I put that on paper – what's so busy with wearing a frilly shirt and pretending to be a sculptor, huh?'

'I died today. I was kind of tied up.'

'Great. I can take your name off my list, then – clear my automatic dialler for some guy with real talent, not some one-reel dead-beat schmuck. So you died, huh? Hope it was painful.'

Justus grinned.

An actor who had found success early might be excused the occasional error of judgement in accepting a script, but one with Justus's experience could not afford to take such risks; he had, after all, so much more invested, and so much more to lose. In many ways Justus was a rarity in the make-or-break film industry. He had determined on an acting career back in England when he was twenty-four, and had leapt at an offer from the older brother of a school friend of a role in an off-off-Broadway production. He'd immediately packed his bag for New York, but it had taken him ten years to clamber to a position even close to power. Six years of barely seen and unreviewed stage roles, accompanied by second-rate made-for-TV movies and unsuccessful pilots, only to hit the jackpot via a protégé of Steven Bochco and *The 87th Precinct*. The serialisation of Ed McBain's novels, and his own portrayal of Detective Steve Carella, had made Justus O'Keefe a household name, but ten years of hard grind had given him two things that many of the 'talent' did not have: first, a finely developed instinct for critical self-appraisal and, second, cynicism. He was quite immune to the flattery of agents and producers, as well as would-be agents and would-be producers. He was fully conscious that a good performance could not rescue a weak script, nor good directing salvage a feeble concept. The release of his first feature film, in which he had portrayed a dedicated but ultimately corrupt mayor of New York, had brought him a large Internet fan club, a house in the Hollywood Hills, and the offer of a three-movie studio deal. 'This is it, boy,' his agent had said, bringing him the deal – the same agent who was now bawling him out in France, and the same agent who had always represented him. 'This is it. We're here, we've arrived.'

'The question is, are we going to stay "here", or slide slowly into celluloid Siberia?'

'Celluloid suburbia? What the fuck's that?'

'HBO.'

'Nah. Don't be such a pessimist, Justus. When you should have been, you weren't. Now you're talking like an old lady. They love you. They love your profile. They love your promotability. Son of WASP Wall Street lawyers, Ivy League, Oxford University, England, Broadway – they die for all that shit.'

'Do they also love my acting?'

'Sure, sure, sure they do, take it as read.'

But Justus hadn't. He had ignored his agent's best arguments, tantrums and tears, and refused to sign. Being in a position of power, particularly such a fragile one as offered by Hollywood, meant nothing unless it meant the power to be selective. He was so driven to achieve success that success, now it had come, was something he could neither enjoy nor rely on. He had insisted on taking the role of Roderick Hudson, whom his agent insisted on calling Rock. The decision to escape typecasting was strategic; the initial script adaptation was intelligent; the director up-and-coming; the appeal of a classic literary work not to be underestimated and the idea of a long shooting schedule back in Europe had been appealing, not least because he was planning to extricate himself from the last in a series of half-hearted relationships he should not have entered into. Even Ophélie Arcier had been a draw, for at least the first week. During the

third week in Rome he had been waiting around the set at Santa
Maria della Pace, waiting, as he spent so much of his time, in full
costume, and had strolled down a side-street and almost into the
arms of Olivia Fletcher-Smith. That was the moment when he'd
known he had been destined to play the role of Roderick
Hudson. His agent was still flinching at the deal he had turned
down.

'OK, Laura. You've had your fun. What's up?'

Her voice changed at once. 'I'm just checking up you're OK.
How's your lady?'

'Far away. In London. I called her tonight and she kind of cut
me off.'

'You thought I was her?'

'I *hoped*. . .'

'Listen, babe, don't go all lovesick on me. It was bad enough
when you called to say you were getting married to some girl you
hadn't seen for ten years. If she throws you over now, I'm not
going to be around to clear up the mess, know what I mean?'

'I don't want to think about it.'

'She's a jerk if she lets you slip the noose, my lamb. Tell you
what, if she dumps you at the altar, I'll take her place. I'll even cut
my commission to ten per cent. Deal?'

'Deal.'

'I can tell you want me off the phone, so I'll be brief. What d'you
think of the rewrite of *The Spider House*?'

'I haven't looked at it.'

'OK. No problem. Just think sweet thoughts of Morocco – you
could make it a honeymoon trip, no? Yes. Call me. 'Bye, cute-
cakes.'

Laura gazed out of her office window and prayed Justus would be
OK. She hadn't decided if she wanted him to get married or not –

Justus was as far from impulsive as any man she knew, let alone any actor. In her experience, very few indeed approached their careers and their work with the single-minded rigour Justus possessed. Whichever way he went, she wanted the best for him. She punched a series of numbers into her dial pad.

'Matt? Yeah, OK . . . He's hard to get hold of, know what I mean? But I pinned him down somewhere in the mountains. . . *The Spider House*? He *loves* it. He loves it so much it's chokin' him. We're just waiting for the word on the new Bond . . . Bond – as in James, you jerk-off. You mean you haven't heard?. . . Well, *sure* he's the hot tip. You didn't know? Where've you been? Outer Mongolia?'

Justus spent a sober hour in the bar and then went to bed. After a shower he took a long hard look at himself in the mirror, then sat on the bed holding a photograph of Olivia. He only had two; his favourite was back at home, buried somewhere in a desk drawer. He'd come across it from time to time and never been able to throw it away. It had been taken at the Merton Commem. Ball, just after the first time he'd really kissed her. They hadn't gone to the ball together: she'd gone with Jerry and he'd gone with some girl whose name he couldn't even remember, but they'd found each other in a comparatively secluded corner of Mob Quad when he'd been trying to lose the girl, and she'd been running. . . Escaping Jerry, he knew, however much she'd later claimed to be looking for a loo. She'd been wearing an exotically draped dress that left half her bosom exposed, and all her back, and he had caught her in his arms mid-flight, pushed her bare back against the glossy leaves of a magnolia trained against the stone wall and drained the breath out of her. Best of all, they hadn't exchanged a word – not one, not even when, walking sedately and a foot apart back to the main marquee, a photographer had stopped them and Justus had handed over ten quid for a photograph of them as a couple. He wished he had that picture here with him now, with her head thrown back and her hair coming down and her throat exposed like she wanted him to bite it.

The photograph of Olivia he now held had been taken unawares by one of the stills photographers. Justus had managed to persuade her to visit the set in Rome just once, in the Borghese Gardens. Olivia had skittishly refused to be introduced to the director and cast. When he tried to catch her arm, she had dodged behind a tree, and the photographer had caught her, arms wrapped around the trunk, chin and half her mouth hidden, and those saucer-wide eyes flashing in playful defiance.

He dialled his London number again and was rewarded with a sleepy 'Hello?'

'Darling . . . You didn't call.'

'Oh, Justus, it's *so* good to hear you. I'm sorry. I was upset, and I didn't want to worry you, so I didn't call, and then I fell asleep . . . I'm so glad you've called.'

'What upset you?'

'I don't know. Everything. Being back here. Feeling so alone. Seeing Pip . . .'

'You said you just saw her briefly.'

'Jerry, too. It was horrible. I wish I'd stayed in Rome and waited for you.'

'So come over now. I'll get you a ticket right away, Olivia, I'll come and fetch you myself.'

'Darling . . . I'm OK now. I'm seeing Pip again tomorrow. I *have* to talk to her properly. I love you. I miss you. I'm longing to be married.'

'I like that. Say it again.'

'I'm longing to marry you, more than ever now.'

Juliette Mead

They talked until they were both nearly asleep and Olivia had to beg him to hang up. At three a.m. he woke up with a dry mouth and wondered why she had added the 'now' to 'more than ever'.

116

nothing left to say to each other . . .

Waiting for Pip on Saturday morning, Olivia whiled away the time by revising her notes on *Midsummer Night's Dream* even though she was still undecided if she was going to resume teaching after the wedding. She constructed a chart on the ebb and flow of the various relationships between the *dramatis personae*, concentrating on the friendship of the two girls. She jotted down some *aides mémoire*:

1. Lysander says he met Helena one May morning in the woods where he plans to meet Hermia. (What was he doing in the woods alone with Helena? Was something going on between Lys and Hel?)

2. Helena says she's generally considered as good a looker as Hermia; then says she is ugly as a bear. (Classic female schizophrenic vanity / insecurity.)

3. In the woods, Helena decides all three are taking the piss out of her; she's angrier with Hermia than Demetrius – lists all the things they shared, the secrets, sisters' vows, childhood, schooldays, sewed the same sampler, sat on the same cushion, sang the same song in the same note, two cherries on one stem. Bangs on about their 'ancient love'. Says Hermia's mockery is a

strike against the female sex, and at least as a woman, she deserves Hermia's pity, not her scorn. (NB – the Sisterhood more important than 'lurve'? ref to latent schoolgirl lesbianism? Lizzie will like that.)

4. Hermia turns on Helena – canker-blossom.

5. Helena gets on her high horse, calls Hermia a puppet.

6. Hermia rages against Helena; calls herself dwarfish, and Helena a maypole.

7. Helena begs the boys to protect her; Hermia goes mental. Helena says she always loved Hermia, never did her harm, begs to be allowed to go back to Athens. Says she's simple and fond; Hermia tells her to piss off then.

8. Helena implies Hermia was a bitch at school; Hermia goes for her. (ref. bullying? ref. Pip?)

9. Boys also insult Hermia's vertical challenge – 'you minimus of hindering knot-grass made' and go off fighting.

10. Puck does the business –

Jack shall have Jill:

Nought shall go ill:

The man shall have his mare again, and all shall be well.

11. Theseus & co wake the lovers. Theseus overrules Egeus, says they'll all go have a bloody good dinner, then get married.

12. The four lovers act completely stoned. Lysander wishes Theseus a happy sex life, cheeky sod.

13. During the mechanicals' play, Lysander and Demetrius crawl up Theseus' arse trying to out-quip each other; the girls, of course, are silent.

Olivia paused; she didn't like leaving it on 13, but had exhausted the girls' relationship, which was clearly not one that had inspired the Bard. Nor did she like the similarities that were being thrown up between her and Pip. It would have struck those who knew

Olivia well – at least those who had known her in her teens and early twenties – as disingenuous to claim that the parallel between Shakespeare's thinly sketched females in the *Dream*, and Pip and herself had never occurred to her before. This would have been an injustice to Olivia, if only in that she had never recognised Pip as a rival until the previous night. As Olivia could not blame Puck's incompetence for Jerry's attraction to Pip, she was tempted to examine the friendship a little more closely, perhaps, than Shakespeare had.

Jerry had volunteered the first and most attractive explanation. Pip had been the other person closest to Olivia, and if, over time, intimacy had formed between the two, it could have been a brother-sister thing. An appealing explanation, but not a wholly plausible one because there was one piece in the jigsaw that didn't fit at all, that belonged to some altogether different puzzle – why should *Pip* have entered into a sexual relationship with Jerry? Unless, *unless* Pip had always nursed some secret crush on Jerry. In which case, Olivia's confidences through all those long Oxford afternoons when they should have been studying, when the two of them had effectively embroidered the same sampler and sat on the same sofa – if not cushion – had given Pip all the ammunition and inside information she needed to have Jerry for herself. In which case, Pip's behaviour had been a treachery of the worst kind, a betrayal of sisterly devotion, a disloyalty and cunning of such . . .

Olivia shook her head, dismissing the notion. If only she was still prepping *Lear*, her head wouldn't be full of such nonsense. She was talking about two people she had walked out on and hadn't seen for ten years; what they did was their business, and didn't in any way concern her. Except – she jumped as the door buzzer sounded and pushed her papers aside before opening the door.

'Darling!'

'*George*?'

'Surprise! I know you're expecting Pip, but there's been a change of plan. You're coming to Suffolk with me. I happened to give Pip a call this morning, heard the happy news of the prodigal's return, and insisted on driving down right away to swoop you off.'

'George, I can't believe . . . Let me look at you.'

'Not until I've had an armful.' He lifted her off her feet in the exuberance of his embrace. 'You look *glorious* – a sight for sore eyes. Now off you go and get a nightie or whatever.'

'Georgie, really, I can't –'

'Nonsense. It's all arranged, you just have to go with the flow. Pip's meeting us down there, bringing Jerry, and we'll have a wonderful reunion. I'll have you all to myself for at least two hours providing the traffic's bad enough.'

'I'm sorry, I can't just go like that. I have, well, I have things I have –'

'Miss O. Fletcher-Dunn, Miss O. Fletcher-Dunn, Furnish'd and burnished by Aldershot sun, What strenuous singles we played after tea, We in the tournament – you against me!'

Olivia's eyes watered at the nostalgia of the Betjeman lines. 'Oh, Georgie, it's *wonderful* to see you again! The best of all!'

'Go get that bag – I'm double-parked. We're expected back for lunch, and it's high time you met my sprogs. Bring something decent you can play tennis in – or indecent. If you haven't got anything, you can always borrow something of Sarah's.'

As George's Mercedes purred down the M11 towards Cambridge, Olivia sank deep in her seat and listened to George with a smile on her face. Ten years, marriage, fatherhood, the City, her own absence hadn't changed him at all; he was the same old George, still her George.

'You were an absolute little fool, Liv, if you don't mind my saying. I ought to paddle your backside for disappearing like that, and I would, too, don't for a moment think I wouldn't, if it wasn't so nice to have you home, and if the idea wasn't slightly perverted. You always had a smackable rear end, still do, from the brief glimpse I got. Good God, I can just about understand why you didn't want to phone Jerry, but did I deserve to be cut off, poor loyal George? Talk about a bum rap . . . But I'm not a moaner by nature, so we'll put that behind us. Now, you know Sarah and I tied the knot? And you know about my boys?'

'Pip said you had two.'

'Arthur's an amazing chap – bright and eager, and has the makings of a fine batsman. Little Will is still tied to his mother's apron strings, but he'll come into his own in good time.'

'How's Sarah?'

'Oh, fine, fine. You know Sarah, solid as a rock.'

'I don't know Sarah actually, George. Hardly at all. Are you happy together?'

'Happy? Of course we are.' George fiddled with the mirror, so that he could see Olivia's face better. 'Not lovey-dovey newlyweds, you understand. Having children around soon sorts out that malarkey, but yes, we're very happy.'

'I'm so glad. I'm longing to see them all.'

'Now, are you going to tell me what's going on? Where on earth you've been, for starters.'

In the mirror, Olivia might have been asleep. Her face was relaxed, her eyes shut; a few strands of hair fluttered loose, caught in the light breeze of the air-conditioning.

'George, when I left I didn't have any idea of what I wanted to do except get the hell out of London. I went home. To see if I could salvage anything with my parents.'

'Could you?'

'No. They thought I was a mess, and packed me off to Chios for a couple of months. Dad was quite sweet, now I think about it, but my mother regressed to her usual pattern and arranged a series of visits for me with members of the family – as far-flung as she could find them. I spent six months in Hong Kong working as an assistant to one of my uncles, then New York, where I tried to work for my cousin while he tried to get my knickers off, and eventually to Washington, because they managed to track down a second cousin in the Greek embassy. I stayed there until my grandfather died. After the funeral, I went back to Rome, and somehow never left. I've been living there for about six years.'

'And doing?'

'What do you mean?'

'To earn your living.'

Olivia laughed. 'I don't know that I do earn it . . . I teach literature, or at least I try to teach it, to the top class of the New School. Most of the time I just live in Rome, which is a perfectly acceptable thing for a Roman.'

'And you're happy?'

'Yes, I suppose I am. I'm getting married.'

'Why, that's wonderful! Congratulations.'

'Thanks.'

'Decent bloke?'

'Um-hmm.'

'My little Livvy getting hitched . . . What a shame.' It was an echo of Luca's 'Che peccato!', said with exactly the same inference.

'I didn't have much choice. All the best men have long gone.' She poked a finger in George's ribs, and he squirmed.

'Just say the word, Livvy, just say the word. It's never too late.'

'It's way too late, Georgie, not like you don't know that, and I know you didn't mean it. But thanks for the flattery. I need it.'

'Why? Who is this man you're marrying?'

'It's nothing to do with him. It's being here. I don't know if I can face Pip. I saw Jerry yesterday. It was grim.'

'Because he's still got the hots for you?'

'Because he hasn't.'

'Oh, Olivia! I'm ashamed of you! Can't you let even one little fish get away? You know, don't you, that Pip and Jerry are an item?'

'Jerry was pretty vague about it. I gather they used to live together.'

'It's been an on-again, off-again kind of thing – I can't keep up with it.'

Olivia twisted in her seat to face him. 'George, have I made a mistake coming back? Tell me the truth. You're the only person who ever has.'

'It depends why you've come back, Liv.' George spoke slowly, his eyes flicking between her and the road ahead. 'If you've come back in order to prove to yourself that Jerry still loves you, I'd think that was a mistake. Not necessarily for you, but for him. If you've come back to have a wild pre-marital fling with me, I'd call that a sensible decision.'

She leaned her head against his shoulder, comfortable for the first time since her return to England.

Sarah Upton, *née* Matthews, was in the garden with the two boys as the car pulled into the drive. Olivia looked at her carefully – although she had not admitted it to George, she had not been able to recall what Sarah even looked like. The only thing she could remember about her was that she'd been a nervous bunny, perfectly nice, but a bit of a bore. Now she was met by a slim, sleek-headed woman wearing a guarded smile and possessing all the clean elegance of the brunette in the Peugeot commercial.

Sarah embraced her, laying a cool cheek against Olivia's. 'Olivia! I'm so glad you were able to come! We're going to have a lovely weekend. Boys, come and meet Daddy's friend.'

The taller of the two children stepped from behind his mother's skirt and held out his hand. 'How do you do?' The little one bounded forward and then back, and asked, in a stage whisper, 'Has she brought me a present?' for which his elder brother punched him.

'They're lovely, Sarah. And they take after you. How lucky you are!'

'You wouldn't have said that if you'd seen them at six this morning,' Sarah sighed, 'but yes, they are rather nice, if I say so myself. George, did you remember the parsnips for dinner?'

George slapped his forehead. 'Went clean out of my head. Sorry, darling, you know you shouldn't ever give me any domestic responsibility. Have Pip and Jerry arrived?'

'Oh, yes, they've just gone for a walk. Come in, Olivia, do, and talk to me while I finish off lunch. Are you here on business, or a holiday?'

'Let's say a bit of both . . .'


When Pip and Jerry walked into the farmhouse kitchen, wellies caked in Suffolk mud, which is stickier than any other, they saw George and Olivia sitting at the kitchen table with the two boys. Olivia was peeling carrots, George was between his two sons, constructing a K-Nex Ferris wheel.

'It doesn't go there, Daddy, that's the wrong bit.'

'No, it isn't, Arthur, just you wait and see. Trust me.'

'George, could you take that bit of plastic out of Will's mouth?' Sarah didn't need to turn from the stove to sense that her younger son might have put himself in peril.

'Wow! We could all be back in Kingston Road!' Pip kissed

Olivia. 'I hope you didn't mind the change of plans. You know what George is like when he gets something into his head.'

Yes, Olivia thought, and there's safety in numbers. 'It was a wonderful idea. It lets me see Sarah and the children.'

'Maybe you'd like to drive back with us tomorrow, so we can have a proper chat? I told George we'd bring you down, but oh, no, he had to come and get you himself.'

'Bloody hell, Pip, stop talking about leaving when you've only just arrived! Jerry, get a bottle out of the fridge, would you, there's some Chablis there we can start on. Unless you'd rather take over here? I can't seem to get this piece to fit.'

'I told you, Dad, it's the wrong one.'

'Let this be a lesson to you women – never have children unless you're willing to abandon your self-esteem.' Both Olivia and Pip looked distinctly uncomfortable. 'Tell you what, Arthur, we'll finish this after lunch. Let's clear the table now, there's a good chap.'

Olivia sat between George and Jerry and wished she hadn't come. Pip talked busily to Sarah about nursery-school education, and promised to send her the transcript of a series they had recently released on the pros and cons of formal schooling for the under-fives. Olivia smiled, and tried to ask suitable questions of everyone, George about his work, Jerry about his work, Pip about her work, and Sarah about her children. After the main course, she excused herself along with the boys and went into the garden for a cigarette. Or two.

'Well? Does anybody know why she's here?' Pip turned from face to face. 'Did she tell you, Jerry? George?'

'For God's sake let it go, Pip. Can't you just accept she's an old friend, we haven't seen her for a decade, and now she's here so let's just enjoy it? She's getting married. Maybe she's shopping for her trousseau.'

'She didn't tell me she was getting married. I asked her if she was married, and she said no. She didn't say not yet, or nearly or anything. Did she tell you, Jerry?'

'She mentioned a fiancé, I believe.'

'And none of us knows who this mystery man is? Well, for God's sake.'

'Why on earth are you so worked up, Philippa? Give her a bit of time to find her feet.'

'Like ten years isn't enough time?'

'I, for one, am extremely glad she's come back at all,' George asserted. 'What's the possible danger in seeing an old friend? She seems just the same to me.'

'No, she's more beautiful now than she was at Oxford,' Sarah corrected her husband, adding thoughtfully, 'much more. Would anyone like cheese?' Nobody replied to the question.

'Anyone for tennis?' George pushed his chair back. 'No? Then I'll have to persuade Livvy. I hope she hasn't kept her game up, or I'll be slaughtered.'

'Darling, weren't you going to finish the boys' model?'

'They've forgotten all about it, Sarah. No point reminding them!'

'Well, do you think you could pop into the village and get those parsnips?' but her husband had already gone into the garden.

Pip insisted that she and Jerry did the washing-up while Sarah put her feet up. Sarah didn't want to put her feet up, but knew when she wasn't wanted, and joined the boys watching the tennis match. She'd offered Olivia a skirt, but her guest had opted for a belt and a pair of George's shorts, their bagginess emphasising her slim legs. Sarah's trainers were too small for Olivia, so she was playing barefoot. As she watched her husband and Olivia play,

126

Sarah decided that she really ought to get round to having tennis coaching. Either that, or abandon her attempts at the game entirely. Her attention was caught by a pair of birds courting on the lawn: the male was treating her to his full repertoire, strutting, preening, puffing out his chest and making all the right noises, while the female, drab, brown little scrap that she was, stood stock still and watched him sceptically. When he got to within three inches of her she took off vertically, straight up in the air, and landed on the window-ledge of the guest bathroom. Sarah saw the male cock his head slowly, like a clockwork bird, first to one side, then the other, almost shrugging his shoulders, human in his bewilderment. When Pip and Jerry joined her, Pip was scowling. Things did not augur well for the rest of the weekend, although the axis of tension that Sarah felt did not seem to lie between Jerry and Olivia, as Sarah had predicted, but rather between Pip and everyone else. Sarah decided to remove herself and used the children as an excuse, a trick all mothers are entitled to use when the need arises.

'If you two don't mind, I simply must take the boys fishing. It's a terrible bore, but we promised them, and George looks settled in for the rest of the afternoon.'

'Would you like some company? It's a long time since I've been fishing.'

'Thank you, Jerry, but it wouldn't be much fun for you.'

'Oh, go on, take him with you. He's only going to sit around like a lump all day if you don't.' Olivia would have recognised Pip's expression from the under-thirteen hockey finals, if Olivia had been looking at Pip, which she wasn't. 'Tell you what, Sarah, I'll do my godmother bit at bedtime and read the boys stories. Right now, I can hardly tear myself away from the game.'

'Stop it, Pip. All right? You're behaving like a child.'

Sarah blushed at Jerry's rebuke. Her role this weekend, apart

127

from hostess, cook and nanny, would be to keep Pip from going for Jerry and anyone else who crossed her path; it seemed expedient to let George have Olivia, and enrol Jerry as her own assistant. She asked him to get the rods and wellies from the garage, and laid a cool hand on Pip's arm. 'Will you make yourself at home, Pip? We won't be too long.'

'Is it all right if I have a bath?'

'Of course. There are towels in your room.' Sarah coloured again, and took the other woman aside. 'Pip? I'm sorry about this . . . I've put you and Jerry in the same room. George wasn't sure how things, I mean, whether you and Jerry . . . The point is, I can easily put Jerry in the attic if you'd rather. I thought you two should decide, Lord, how silly. . .'

'Why don't you just ask him? I couldn't care either way.' Pip glared at Jerry as he approached with the rods. 'Oh, blast. I'm sorry – I don't know what's got into me. It doesn't matter about the room, honestly, Sarah. Leave it as it is.'

Although the river passed through the bottom of the Uptons' garden, the boys were eager to walk a mile down the lane, where it flowed faster and deeper under a little bridge. Jerry rolled up his trousers and sat between Arthur and Will, fumbling with worms and hooks and nets and occasionally looking over his shoulder to where Sarah sat on the bank. 'I did warn you I hadn't been fishing for a long time.'

'Don't worry – nor have they. They just like messing about in the water.' The boys proceeded to prove her right, soon abandoning their rods, taking off most of their clothes and plunging into the river. Arthur stepped carefully over the rocks, but Will held his head under the water and then shook his whole body like a dog, laughing with delight. Sarah moved closer to the bank to be on guard and dabbled her toes.

'How does it feel to you, Jerry, seeing Olivia again?'

'I've been trying to work that out. I like watching her, I know that, and it's easier when other people are around. Yesterday, we spent some time together, and I found myself quite unable to function. Whether it was embarrassment, whether it was that we had simply been apart for so long that we had nothing left to say to each other, I don't know. I do like looking at her.'

'She's very beautiful, isn't she?'

'It's not that, it's something more than beauty. I find her . . . intriguing.'

'Does she seem happy to you? I never knew her well enough to tell.'

'I don't know that I've ever seen Olivia what you would call happy. It isn't an Olivia state, if you know what I mean.'

'I suppose . . . I don't know if I've ever seen *you* really happy, for that matter.'

Jerry laughed uneasily. 'Maybe it's not my natural state either. Maybe that's why Olivia and I hung about with each other so long; we were reciprocally unhappy together.'

Sarah dissected a strand of river weed with her carefully trimmed nails, her head bent so close to it she appeared to Jerry like a miniaturist or jeweller at work. 'I always thought you were perfectly matched. Did you love her very much?'

'Oh, very, very much, yet I don't know why. Even at the time I couldn't have given you a list of reasons. Perhaps I liked having something other than ideas and religions to study and worship.' Sarah smiled. 'Does that sound funny?'

'Oh, not at all. I was just thinking about me and George.'

'You worship George?'

Sarah laughed, the sound unexpected and charming. 'No, I'm not a worshipping person. I love him. George has always been everything I wanted.'

'Then you're a lucky woman to have found him. And he, you.'

'It *was* lucky, I suppose. I used to look up to you lot so much. You seemed so much older than me – with so much more ahead of you. Now, it doesn't feel so bad. I mean, you can end up anywhere, can't you? When you're twenty-one, and making all those plans about the future, and having all those ambitions, how you're going to conquer the world, it feels like you can choose anything, anything at all, and then you find yourself somewhere, in an office in a city, or a children's nursery, and you think, hang on – how did I end up here? Why here? What am I doing?'

Jerry didn't reply, but looked at her closely.

'You think I'm rather stupid, don't you? All of you always did, especially Olivia – I used to catch her looking at me oddly, as if she could read my thoughts. My only worry, ever, about George, was that all his friends would convince him I was far too stupid to marry.'

'I don't think any of us thought you were stupid. Did you want to conquer the world, Sarah?'

'Me? No, I'm not the conquering kind.'

He took her hand in his. 'Nor me. We'll leave that to the others, shall we? I'd much rather sit on the riverbank.'


Pip had poured the remaining half-bottle of something called Christmas Essence into her bath. She reckoned that seeing it was June and Sarah hadn't used the stuff, and had put it in the guest bathroom, then she must want it used up, and if she ended up smelling like a tart's boudoir, then no one was interested in her anyway. It would probably clash dreadfully with her perfume, a bottle Jerry had given her for Christmas. She had been pleased when he gave it to her – he normally gave her an African mask or a Turkish flask and the perfume had been strangely flattering, until she'd realised that he must have picked it up in some duty-free zone and had probably asked the assistant which her favourite perfume was. Nonetheless, she'd chucked it in her overnight bag that morning when George had phoned and suggested they all spent the weekend in Woodbridge together. She'd had to bully Jerry into coming; he'd been all set to go to the cremation of some nonentity in Mortlake. On reflection, she hadn't had to bully him nearly enough . . .

The water came up to her ears, one advantage of being short. She had to paddle her hands under her buttocks, treading water to keep afloat. The house was very quiet: George and Livvy were presumably still thrashing about on the court, and Jerry would be listening to Sarah witter on about the boys, and then they'd all have a bloody awful dinner, and it would be embarrassing as they all waited to retreat to their bedrooms without it seeming like they were running away, and no one except George would have the nerve to ask Livvy anything. To cap it all, she'd stupidly suggested she drive Livvy back to London, which would mean what? Her driving, Livvy in the front, and Jerry crouching in her small back seat like a huge dark beast sitting on their shoulders. She could fake car trouble, and suggest they all went by train, which would at least mean she could get a drink. Or George could volunteer to drive Livvy when he went into work on Monday, or Livvy could break her ankle playing tennis, and have to be ambulanced back to London – helicoptered back to Rome, in an ideal world – and they'd never have to see her again, married or not. What the hell was she doing here, in this beautiful house, with these people? What the hell was she doing in the bath at five in the afternoon? Asking herself, well, how did I get here? How do I work this? Same as it ever was, same as it ever was, same as it ever was. . . She slid under the water and wondered why she couldn't get David Byrne's paranoid voice out of her head. When she surfaced, Olivia was standing in the doorway.

'Hi. Can I come in? I was hoping to get a shower.' Olivia had deep rings of sweat under her armpits and was standing like a stork examining the black soles of each foot in turn.

'I'll be out in a minute, if you can just wait. Outside.'

'I really want to talk to you.'

'Well, can you just hang on till I'm out of the bath?'

Olivia sat down on the edge of the tub and Pip looked in vain for a flannel. 'I want to say a couple of things, then I'll go. I know you're mad at me. All I wanted to say was that I'm glad you're with Jerry, and thank you for – well, for not saying anything to him when I left. OK? That's it.'

'Hold on. I'm not "with" Jerry – not at the moment, probably not at all.'

'Well. It wouldn't matter to me if you were, other than you two being happy.'

'I should never have agreed to this stupid weekend. I should have just come to see you.'

'We've got time. I'll be around for months. A month, at least. Probably.'

'Still not making any firm commitments, huh? OK. I want to book a day while you're here – a week, whatever. I still – you're still my best friend, damn you.'

'Thanks. I love you too. Don't use up all the hot water, OK?'

'You think George will charge us for it?'

Olivia grinned. 'Is he still such a stingy bastard? See you later. Oh, Pip – tell me about Sarah?'

'She's just the same. She tries too hard, that's the problem. She's so nice she'd probably send you a good-luck card if she heard you were going for a haircut.'

'Ouch! Give me a quick summary.'

Pip rested her elbows on the edge of the bath, chin cupped in her hands. 'How quick?'

'Ten words.'

Pip counted them off on her fingers. 'Nice. Maternal. Dull. Dutiful. Corporate. Eager-to-please (that's one).' She bent the thumb of her right hand back and mused. 'Practical. Long-suffering. Middle-aged. And . . .'

'And?'

'*Enduring*. I'll go for enduring.'

'Has she got any good smellies for the bath?'

'Yup, but I used them all up.'

'Selfish cow.'

'Liv, who's the man?' Pip called out as Olivia left the bathroom.

'Tell you later.'

# so sorry there weren't any parsnips . . .

'Liv? Remember the night when Pip said she was going down to Balliol to "have coffee" with Michael, and you and I waited till two a.m., and then went to his room to deliver her toothbrush?'

George and Olivia rocked with laughter. 'Yeah, you said, smirking your head off, "We thought Philippa might need this." Michael was wearing only a small hand towel, if I remember correctly, and took the toothbrush and sidled off, looking like a dog sneaking away with a stolen pork chop.'

'Very, very funny. You slay me. Bastards. I only went there that night to see if he'd read his essay the following day so I didn't have to write mine.' Pip threw a cushion at each of their heads.

'And, in exchange, you stayed the night? Good trade. Admit it, Pip, it *was* incredibly funny. You did everything you could to pretend you weren't sleeping together, and everyone knew . . .'

'Everyone except Michael. He was so stoned most nights the creep barely knew I was there.'

'So why did you keep going back?'

'A girl has to have some sex life. You and Jerry were at it all the time, George was working his way down Walton Street and up Kingston Road – oh, *shit*, where's Sarah?'

'Probably putting the kids to bed, but it wouldn't matter if she heard. We have no secrets. She knows what a reprobate I was. She rescued me.'

'How sweet. Sweet Sarah.' Olivia drained her wine glass.

'How smug. Smug Georgie.' Pip followed suit.

'Let me top up your glasses, girls.' George had only called girls 'women' until he hit twenty-four; ever since he had been religiously calling women 'girls'. This night, he was as happy as he ever remembered being, with his wife putting his children to bed, and reliving the days when he and these two girls had held the world in their palms.

'I wonder what happened to Michael?'

'I know. I carried on seeing him for the odd bonk – odd being the operative word – and then one day he said he wanted to ask me something important, and I thought, Uh-oh, how am I going to deal with this and let him down gently? Then he asked if I'd read the lesson at his *wedding*. So I said yes, and he married some girl he'd known since he was five years old. It was a hell of a party. Dope wall to wall.'

'You never saw him again?' Olivia asked.

'Oh, I still see him. He lives in Devon, makes furniture, and has four kids.'

'Four?'

'Yep. One of them's my godchild. I saw them a month ago.'

'You're incredible, Pip.'

'No, Livvy, I just make an effort to stay in touch.' The words came out of her mouth before she thought. 'I didn't mean anything by that. It's just my big mouth.'

Sarah popped her head into the small sitting room to see Pip sprawled across the sofa, Olivia in the armchair, and her husband sitting on its arm

'George? Did you remember the parsnips? I'm just going to dash upstairs and change. Would you mind keeping an eye on the roast?'

'I didn't realise we were dressing for dinner – I don't know if I've brought anything.' Olivia stood up, in faded jeans and a man's shirt knotted at her waist, still barefoot.

George pulled her back down. 'You look fine, Liv. Why not have a bath, darling? Take a glass of champagne up.'

'I'm all right, thanks. There isn't time for a bath, and Jerry's in the shower, and I haven't put the boys to bed –'

'That's my job!' Pip slowly raised herself from the deep cushions. 'I promised. Where are the miserable little blighters?'

'George? Couldn't you put the boys to bed?' Sarah's voice was soft but firm.

'And screw up their bonding with Auntie Pip? No way.'

'Lead me to 'em.'

George, from his superior position on the arm of the chair, looked down at Olivia and smiled.

'*Salut.*'

'Bottoms up.'

He bent so swiftly that she couldn't have moved away if she'd wanted to. George kissed her on the edge of her mouth, slightly lingering, but not busting wide the rules of propriety.

'Olivia. My friend.'

'George, you're pissed.'

'Not as pissed as I intend to be. Anyway, I'm allowed to kiss an old friend, aren't I? Are you going to tell me about this mystery man?'

'Later. Tonight, I'd just like to be with you lot, and remember the old days, and pretend we're all young again.'

'You're young, Livvy. You've always had old eyes . . . but, hell, that's got to be better than being old and having young eyes.'

'Is it? I'm not sure.'

'Can we make a pact? This is it. No heaviness, no serious, deep, meaningful conversations, just enjoying being together again.'

'No Notker? No Einhard?'

'No shit. Do you know when I last thought about Charlemagne? I'll tell you. The day I got my degree. The bastard hasn't crossed my mind since. Yet sitting here, looking at you, I can't help thinking –'

'Of the eighth century? Thanks. I know I'm ageing, but not that fast.'

'You don't look any older than you did ten years ago.'

Jerry came in, sweeping his sleek hair, made sleeker by the shower, back off his high forehead. 'May I help myself, George?'

'Why break the habit of a lifetime, Jerry? Except you never used to ask.'

'Pip is upstairs reading your children *The Prophet*.'

'Makes a change from *Thomas the Tank Engine*.'

'Undoubtedly.' Jerry sat opposite them, his eyes steady on Olivia. 'Good tennis?'

'George thrashed me.'

'She let me thrash her.'

'I'd better go see if I can help Sarah.'

As Olivia rose from the chair, George grabbed her hand and brought her fingertips to his lips. 'Thanks for the game.'

As Olivia left, she glanced at Jerry, hoping he would follow her. He did not.

They sat down to dinner at a round table. Olivia, George, Sarah, Pip, Jerry.

'I'm sorry about the odd numbers – I thought of asking one of the local bachelors, but George didn't think it was a good idea.' Sarah looked up round the table and saw Olivia and Pip exchange a quick look. 'It wasn't a good idea. He was right. Do start, everyone.'

George was drunk, and barely touched his food. 'God, this is good, darling,' he said, as he pushed his plate away. 'Bloody fantastic.'

'It is, really,' the others echoed. 'Absolutely delicious.'

'It really ought to be served with parsnip mash, but . . . I'm not much of a cook. I ought to take some lessons, rather than just bashing away with a cookbook I can't understand. Livvy, tell us about life in Rome. Is it wonderful? Is it glamorous? Do you go to endless cultural events?'

'No, not at all. I just teach. I'm teaching *A Midsummer –*'

'Talking of cultural events, isn't Justus O'Keefe's career stagger-ing? Who's seen *Mad City*?' Pip's eyes sparkled. 'I'm telling you, I always thought Justus was a looker, but in that movie, Jees-us – talk about lust! Jerry, remember that bit when he's in his office, and he takes his shirt off, and I grabbed your hand? Why bother with a Rhodes Scholarship when you've got a body like that?'

'I went with a friend from the village who refused to believe I'd actually met him.' Sarah brought the pudding to the table, a golden apple pie. 'George didn't want to go. He said it would be a girls' movie.'

'You dickhead, George. It was a boys' movie, it just happened to star a sex god. He was brilliant in it, too. Did you see it, Livvy?'

Olivia rubbed her neck, avoiding Jerry's watchful eyes. 'Not yet. Most films in Italy are dubbed, and I hate that. Maybe I should try to see it over here.'

'You'll die. He's far sexier than he used to be. *Far.*'

'Nobody give Pip any more juice, OK?' George leaned across his wife to move Pip's glass away. 'She might over-heat.'

'How do you teach *A Midsummer Night's Dream*?' Jerry asked. 'Is there that much to say about it?'

139

'Not much. There are the obvious good lines, but it's a case of trying to whip up some enthusiasm. I've had three years of *King Lear*, which was a joy. Each class is different, and responds differently. It must be like that for you, Jerry – each piece being different, each client looking at it differently.'

'I've never before seen any similarity between selling specialist works of art and teaching Shakespeare, but if you say so . . .'

'More pudding?'

Jerry stood up. 'I don't want to break up the party, but there's something on television in five minutes that I'm sure you'll all be interested in – the women especially.'

George refused to allow a television set in any of the reception rooms, so they gathered around the one in the boys' playroom. Jerry switched it on to BBC1; Olivia stood at the back of the room, leaning against the wall with her arms folded across her chest. After a few minutes, during which Pip tried to make herself comfortable between Jerry and George on a sofa, and Sarah perched on a five-year-old's wicker stool, the logo of *Film 97* came on the screen.

'Why are we watching this crap?'

'I told you the women would like it. Be patient.' Jerry looked over his shoulder at Olivia, who at once walked out of the room.

'I'm going to bed. Goodnight, all.'

Jerry followed her into the hall and grabbed her arm. 'They're featuring an interview with your boyfriend.'

'Stop it, Jerry.'

'Aren't you proud of him? You're not *ashamed* of him, are you? Come on, Livvy, sit down and watch, in the bosom of your family – isn't that what you always said? That we were the family you'd never had? Don't you want us to share your pre-nuptial bliss?'

'Fuck off, Jerry, all right?'

'I'll fuck off, so long as you come back in and watch.'

'What is this? Some kind of penance?'

'Do you feel you ought to do penance?'

'Do I have a choice?'

He held her arm tightly just above the elbow, and led her back to the playroom. Barry Norman was wagging his sweet, melancholic head from side to side, bemoaning another shoddy remake of a classic. Olivia and Jerry stood shoulder to shoulder against the radiator, Jerry's hand still loosely around her arm, behind her back.

*'Well, that's as may be. Now, moving on to brighter subjects – for some time I've been trying to get in touch with one of Hollywood's newest stars, Justus O'Keefe. O'Keefe's meteoric rise since portraying Detective Steve Carella in the world's favourite TV drama, to a record-breaking box-office take in* Mad City *seems to have taken him by surprise, if not we critics. I managed to track him down on location in the Alps, where he's filming* Roderick Hudson, *yet another adaptation of a novel by Henry James . . .'*

The screen switched to Justus running his hand through his hair with a devil-may-care grin.

'Jerry! You're brilliant! How did you know he was going to be on?'

'It said so in the newspaper.'

'Livvy, come and sit here!'

Jerry's grip on her arm tightened.

*'Justus, how are you enjoying fame and fortune, after what can only be termed a meteoric rise?'*

*'Life could be worse, Barry.'*

Justus O'Keefe's soft New England accent filled the Suffolk playroom as Pip turned up the volume.

*'But I have to correct you on one point; I wouldn't call ten years in*

*daytime soaps, television dramas and B films a meteoric rise . . . More phoenix than meteor.'*

'Holy Mother of God. He's stunning.' Pip hugged a cushion to her chest and glanced back at Olivia.

'Shut up and let us listen.'

*'Well, sure, I'm proud of Mad City, Barry, but the credit has to go to Cyrus St Paul. It was a real privilege to work with him. I've admired him for a long time. And I had plenty of time sitting in the bleachers to admire him!'*

Justus laughed, throwing back his head and baring a set of perfect teeth.

'He could have been yours, Livvy,' Pip murmured, 'if you'd made a bit more effort.'

*'Now, Justus, while Hollywood claims you as its own discovery, we in England are entitled to a degree of patriotic pride in your success. I'm right in saying, am I not, that you spent several years at Oxford as a Rhodes Scholar? And became President of the Oxford University Dramatic Society?'*

*'What makes me think you've been talking to the PR team? Yeah, I stood, but I didn't make President, luckily for the society. I did get to act a bit – I was fortunate enough to have that experience, and it was a formative time for my career.'*

'What a charlatan.' Jerry's hand closed harder on Olivia's arm.

*'I started acting at Oxford in a production of The Winter's Tale and then went on to A Man For All Seasons, A Midsummer Night's Dream and The Crucible.'*

'Remember seeing him in *The Crucible*, Liv? Right before finals?'

'Uh-huh.'

'He was amazing. But Oberon was best, remember, he was just about naked – Livvy, can you believe you actually *bonked* him? God, am I showing my age? Does anybody even say bonked any more?'

'All that and an M.Litt. degree too. An illustrious start, by any measure.'

'Well, Barry, you have to remember that I had the benefit of excellent tutors and fellow students and I can't pretend my early performances were memorable. Somebody said to me quite recently that my Oberon was unforgettably . . . awful. If anyone out there had the misfortune to be in the audience in those days, I can only offer my humble apologies.' Justus's blue eyes twinkled at them and at thousands of others across England.

'I don't believe I'm hearing this. Seeing it.'

'What can you tell us about Roderick Hudson?'

'Like many of the best films, it comes from a great book.'

'It's a love story?'

'It's a film you can see on many levels. There's a love story in it, but it's also the story of a male friendship, and a study of creative talent. I play Roderick, a sculptor of supposed genius. Without getting heavy,' Justus laughed again to prove he could get heavy if he wanted to, 'I'd say it's a classic Jamesian story of the careless creator versus the careful consumer of art. And the story of Americans struggling in Europe, which we're still doing! I'm lucky to be working opposite Martin Benucci, a friend, and an actor I have always admired.'

'As well as the truly lovely Ophélie Arcier.' Barry paused for a reaction.

'Yeah, she is kinda cute, isn't she?' Justus flashed another grin.

'And what does the future hold, after Roderick Hudson, which will no doubt be a runaway success?'

'Hey, Barry, like they say, the show's not over till the fat lady sings, right? In the meantime, I'm looking at various options.'

'We've heard rumours stretching from the new Bond, to another literary interpretation – The Spider House, possibly with our own Helena Bonham Carter?'

'It's all in the air, like I said.'

'And – I hope you won't mind my asking you this, or consider it prurient, but as you will understand the private lives of the screen stars are open season – there have been rumours of wedding bells, and you and Ms Arcier have been romantically linked?'

'Holy shit! I want an invitation to that wedding!' Pip breathed out hard. 'Can I have another drink, George?'

'Help yourself.'

'I can't – I can't tear myself away. This is like living in a movie.'

'Barry, may I be perfectly frank? I spent ten years struggling to get parts, and during that time it was hard work persuading the waitresses in my neighbourhood coffee-shop to go on a date with me. In the past two years, I can't think of an actress I haven't been romantically linked with by the press. Does that answer your question?'

'It certainly does. So Ms. Arcier?'

'Is a very talented professional,' Justus concluded.

'Perhaps you're just too busy these days to think about settling down, and making a romantic commitment?'

'I wouldn't say that.'

'So there might just be a lady out there who could persuade you to take your mind off work?'

'I'm going to bed,' Olivia repeated, to no one in particular. Jerry's hand tightened once more.

'I certainly hope so, Barry. In fact, I believe I have found a very special lady, the right lady, and much to my amazement she has agreed to take me on.'

'I don't suppose you're going to give us a name?'

'You don't suppose right.'

'Can we at Film 97 be the first to congratulate you? Thank you very much, Justus O'Keefe, and our best wishes for the success of Roderick Hudson.'

Barry went back to the studio and George switched off the telly.

'I'd say we could all use a drink. I suppose O'Keefe's the biggest celebrity of our generation. Can anyone think of a rival?'

'I think Olivia would like to say something. Wouldn't you, Livvy?' Jerry nudged her forward, as the rest turned expectantly.

'This is incredibly stupid. I was going to tell you, I was just going to tell you tomorrow.'

'What?'

'Well, the thing is . . .'

'Livvy, what?' Pip knelt backwards on the sofa, facing Olivia. '*What*? You're not – Oh, God, you *are*.'

'Our friend Olivia is a very special lady, the *right* lady.'

'Noooo – you're kidding.' Pip stared in complete amazement. 'Livvy, you're marrying Justus O'Keefe? Nooo!'

'But, yees!' Jerry corrected. 'Now isn't that what you call a fairy-tale ending?'

Olivia's shoulders sagged. 'Yes. I'm getting married to Justus. Next month, or August, if I can ever get to the registry office. I guess you're all invited to the wedding. That's why I came back, Pip. To get married, and to ask you to be our witness.'

Nobody spoke for several long seconds. Then Pip scowled.

'I wanted to go to his wedding if he was marrying Ophélie Arcier somewhere glam. I don't know if I can be bothered, seeing he's just marrying some old slag I've known since I was ten.' She climbed over the back of the sofa. 'Oh, Livvy, I'm so happy for you. Congratulations!' Jerry released Olivia's arm and left the room. 'What on earth am I going to wear?'

Sarah came over too. 'Congratulations, Olivia. I can't imagine marrying someone like that.'

'Like what?'

'Oh, you know, so famous, so good-looking. . .'

'Thanks, darling.'

'You know what I mean, George. I'd spend my whole time

worrying about which new gorgeous actress he was, well, you know – pretending to be in love with.'

'I don't think it works like that.'

'Of course it doesn't. I don't know anything about actors.'

'Girls! I've an idea. Why don't we crack open some more champagne, to toast Olivia and Justus, and then play a game – for old time's sake?'

'What? Guess who's coming to dinner?'

George waggled an empty bottle. 'Livvy? Why not? We know your little secret now.'

'Sure. I'll play. On one condition.' She tipped up her chin and folded her arms tightly across her chest. 'I'll only play if Jerry plays.'

'Where the hell is Jerry? He didn't even congratulate you.'

'Oh, yes, he did. In his own way.' Olivia, wearing a determined expression, slipped her arm round George's waist.

Pip found Jerry in the garden and persuaded him to come back to the little sitting room. Pip, it has to be said, was excited: she did everything but paw the carpet. In time they settled down, Sarah pressed close to George for security, Pip and Olivia side by side for solidarity and Jerry out on a limb by choice.

'Like old times,' George whispered.

'Same as it ever was . . .' Pip sang tunelessly. 'Who's going to start? I know. Our hostess.'

'I haven't done this since we were at Oxford.' Sarah spun the bottle, and it picked Jerry. 'That's a relief! Umm, Lord! OK, here goes – I suppose we're all old enough friends. Ah, how many people in this room have you slept with?'

George looked at her as if she had farted audibly and unashamedly. 'Are you drunk, Sarah? For Christ's sake.'

'Leave her alone, George,' Jerry commanded. 'Just remember

who taught her the rules of the game. Let me answer. Two. I'll be absolutely precise about that. I am not including myself, as a cute little trick, nor am I counting the night when I had to share a bed with George. I have slept with Philippa – on the left, and Olivia, on the right.'

The bottle pointed to Pip. 'Why are you so nervous about Olivia being here?'

'Is that your question, Jerry? I'm not,' Pip said, turning red to her roots. 'I'm *not*, not any more. You're the one who's nervous.' She could barely grip the bottle, let alone spin it, so it was not surprising that it ended up two inches to her left, pointing at Olivia.

'If you could wish for one thing, what would it be?'

'That Justus was here right now.'

'You coward.' Jerry leaned forward and stroked her cheek with a finger. Olivia flinched. 'I never knew you were such a coward.'

Olivia watched the bottle's slow revolution. 'George, what would you change, between nineteen eighty-six and nineteen ninety-seven? What one thing?'

'I wish I'd won the Deutsche Telecom deal. Or maybe that England had won the World Cup.' No, I don't, I wish I'd slept with you, Livvy, just once, George thought.

'There speaks a fulfilled man. God bless you, Upton!' Pip gave him a wet kiss on the cheek.

The bottle returned to Olivia.

'Look, could we actually have a full one as well as an empty one?' Pip staggered to her feet.

'In the kitchen. Dearest Livvy, why *did* you leave London so suddenly?'

Olivia looked steadily at George and at George only. Pip paused apprehensively in the doorway. Sarah picked bits of fluff off her sweater and Jerry watched Olivia, who spoke very calmly, and rather softly. 'Because I was so suddenly pregnant, Georgie. So suddenly pregnant that I suddenly had a sudden abortion and suddenly decided to leave.'

George cleared his throat; the sound was amplified in the stillness of the room. 'I see. Did you find that bottle, Pip?' He waved her into the kitchen. 'You know, this is beginning to remind me of another game – remember Consequences? Bugger Bailey met Margaret Thatcher in the A house bike-sheds, and he said to her, "That's a rather smart frock you're wearing," and she said to him, "What's it to you, big boy?" and the consequence was they invaded China . . . Do you remember those, Livvy?'

Olivia kept her eyes lowered to the floor.

'They weren't really worth remembering. Well, I guess that just about wraps up games for tonight. What shall we do tomorrow, for sport? D'you fancy going after a few duck, Jerry?'

Pip placed the bottle in the middle of the table. It had taken considerable will-power to return to the room at all. 'I think I'll go to bed now.'

'I'll come up with you, Pip,' Sarah moved quickly, 'just in case the boys hear you on the stairs and wake up. Goodnight, Olivia, Jerry. George, aren't you coming up? I think it would be best, perhaps. I'm sorry the lamb was so overcooked. It was disgusting, really, wasn't it? I'm so sorry there weren't any parsnips.'

George poured himself a large whisky. 'We're down to three little Indians. Now, the obvious question, Livvy, is the one I won't ask. I can at least remove myself from the list of suspects. The real question is, were you all right?' There was something about George, a hide-like skin that made him infuriating, but oddly comforting. He could always be counted on to state the obvious.

'I was fine,' she said flatly. 'I am not telling you this because it was some dark, dreadful secret, or because I'm overcome with remorse. It was not traumatic – not nearly as traumatic as I expected it to be, or not in the way I thought it might be.' Olivia looked swiftly at Jerry: his brows were pulled together with an intensely sad and preoccupied expression. She decided to ignore George as he didn't have the sense to leave them alone. 'I don't know if you were the father. You might have been. There was never any point in trying to work out who the father was, you do understand that? It wasn't the pregnancy – it was everything else I had to get away from.' Jerry didn't blink. Olivia sighed. 'The pregnancy was my problem, my responsibility. Pip was the only person I told, the only person I've ever told until tonight.'

'Including Justus?' Jerry asked.

'Including Justus.'

'What did Pip say? At the time?' Jerry spoke as if he were interrogating a witness in a murder investigation.

'Not a lot. That she'd help me whatever I decided to do, and finally she agreed with me that I didn't really have a decision to make.'

'Does this have any bearing on your decision to marry Justus now?'

'I don't think so, except that later there were certain . . . oh, coincidences that made me feel maybe he had been the father, that it was fate we should meet again, by chance, as we did.'

'And when we met again, that wasn't fate?'

'I wish it had been, but I engineered it. I don't think you're allowed to help fate along.'

'Why are you so bothered about what you're allowed to do and not allowed to do?'

'There are rules, Jerry. There are rules whether you recognise them or not.' Olivia lit a cigarette and took a sip from George's glass. 'Moral, social, I don't know, I just know there are rules.

'Would you two rather I buggered off?' Embarrassment had finally tracked George down.

Jerry and Olivia spoke simultaneously: 'Yes' and 'I don't mind either way.'

'I'll bugger off then. Liv, if you want me, just shout. I'm a light sleeper, you know that. I'll lock up, shall I? Don't worry about the lights, we always leave the hall light on anyway, so no one falls down the stairs.'

'Goodnight, Georgie.'

'Do you want to run these rules past me one more time?'

'It's just that there are things that happen, things that we do, that are right or wrong, good or bad, and if they are bad, they need to be corrected – I'm not saying they need to be paid for, exactly, but they have to be put right, as best as one can.'

'I'm lost. What was the bad thing you actually did? Sleep with both me and Justus?'

'No,' Olivia said impatiently, with an edge of irritation. 'Well, yes, in a way, but they're different. I intended to sleep with both of you – I *chose* to. Getting pregnant was completely careless, that was what made it so bad. Can't you see that?'

'I'm not sure that I can at all. Wasn't *that* just fate?'

'You're doing this deliberately to annoy me. You can only attribute those things to fate that have no human involvement, like bumping into someone on the street. Or getting killed by a drunk driver. Fate has nothing to do with having or not having sex, getting pregnant, or deliberately arranging to 'accidentally' bump into somebody.'

'Let me get this right. You carry about some sort of a moral code book, and when anything crops up, you flip to the back index, look it up, and say: "Ah, *yes*, now that was clearly a bad thing, and I must reverse it; that was a good thing, so we'll just let it be, or that was just pure, unadulterated fate, so I'll go along with it." Is that how life works for you, Olivia?'

'If that's the way you want to describe it. It clearly amuses you –'

'*Amuses me*? Good Christ! It's hardly amusing that you have no control over your life whatsoever. Far from taking responsibility, this is just a means of avoiding it. You're fundamentally dishonest.'

'Don't you dare call me dishonest! I have never lied to you, I've never hidden anything from you,' Jerry's eyebrows arched dramatically, 'that you had any right to know.'

'If you decide who has the right to know and who doesn't, you'll always win. You'll always have your feet planted firmly and unshakeably either side of what you mistake for the moral good. I had every right to know everything. What you felt about Justus, when and why you were sleeping with him, why you carried on with me. That was my right.'

'So if I'd told you I was pregnant, and that I'd slept with Justus too, and didn't know which of you was the father?'

'It wouldn't have mattered a damn to me.'

'How easy it is to say that now.'

'I'm speaking the truth. It would have hurt my pride, but that wouldn't matter a damn. I loved you. I would have married you, whatever –'

'But I didn't want to be married "whatever"! I didn't want to be married at all! Do you know what it would have meant? That at twenty-one, I was married to you, or to Justus, it wouldn't have mattered which, and having a baby I didn't want to have. What would have happened to my life?'

'What happened to it anyway?' Jerry snapped grimly. 'Giving the teenage children of the privileged a superficial introduction to Shakespeare is not what I would call a purposeful life.'

'As compared to buying and selling overpriced works of questionable art to the privileged?' Olivia jumped to her feet.

'You're as certain of your moral rules as you claim I am. There's no difference between us.'

'Perhaps we should have stuck together. Tell me, Livvy, did you ever love me?'

'I don't know any more. It doesn't matter either way.'

'It matters to me. How many times did you sleep with Justus?'

'Back then, you mean?'

'I have no interest in hearing the specifics of your current sex life.'

'I slept with him three times.'

'And how many times did you and I sleep together?'

'Is this a trick question?'

'No. How many times?'

'Oh, God, Jerry, I don't know . . . Two thousand? A million? How can I remember? What are you asking me to count – penetration, or every time we went to bed?'

'Either; any of them. I'll tell you. It was three hundred and twelve.'

'You're mad. What did you do – write it down every time?'

'I had a lot of time to work it out. I might be out by five or ten per cent either way, but three hundred and twelve is a pretty good estimate. It seems such an insignificant number. Three hundred and twelve quite different women.'

'What the hell are you getting at? Are you trying to say you loved me a hundred times more than Justus did, or are you still calling me dishonest?'

'What I'm trying to say is that no man sleeps with the same woman twice, if the woman is worth anything at all. Each time it's a fresh encounter. Embracing the same woman night after night is no more thrilling than climbing under a familiar duvet. Comforting, perhaps, but only that. But, by the way, I probably still love you a hundred times more than he does.'

'You're wrong.'

'He cannot understand you. He will not.'

'You're wrong,' she repeated.

'I'm very right, and you know it too. Good night, Olivia. Don't finish the bottle. And don't run away again. You have no reason to now.'

Olivia's tennis practice had not improved her aim in other target sports: the bottle she hurled at Jerry's head missed him by at least a foot and smashed. He watched the pale yellow liquid trickle down the white wall.

'On second thoughts, do run away. I'd rather mourn your memory than mourn what you've become. Goodnight.'

# The Rules of the Game 4

**Oxford, March 1986**

Olivia was in such a state about her revision of the metaphysical poets that Jerry literally had to carry her away from her desk to the door. Jerry was alone in not being at all fazed by finals. His own academic performance was brilliant but spasmodic; his philosophy tutors despaired of him one week, and marked him for an early fellowship the next. His politics tutors were certain that he was destined for an academic future. His economics tutors, while he had them, were baffled as to how he had secured entrance to the university in the first place. They all knew Jerry was not a contender for an upper second or a gentleman's third. Most were of the opinion that so long as he could be persuaded to sit all his papers, he could be awarded a first, perhaps a congratulatory one, but a couple doubted he would achieve a degree at all. That afternoon was a case in point – he was determined to attend a lecture by a visiting American psychologist on a subject that had nothing to do with any of his papers: the relationship between physical disease and psychological traits, the complex and inextricably linked relationship of body and mind. He was equally determined that Olivia should accompany him.

'All work and no play makes Jill a boring pain in the arse, and she lands up with a third.'

'Right now, I'd get on my knees and thank God if I could be sure of a third. If you'd just let me do some bloody work –'

'You're overworking, darling –'

'Ten weeks spread over three years? You call that overworking?'

'Sure. It's like a fat guy who's done no exercise in his life suddenly running the marathon. You'll keel over dead. Moderation, that's the golden rule.'

As they walked home to Kingston Road that evening, Olivia was brimming over with enthusiasm for the lecture.

'C'mon, Jerry, just admit it, you're a prime candidate for cancer. That's what he said – it's all about the repression of feeling, and compulsive worrying and all that stuff. He was talking about *you*, don't deny it.'

'Rich coming from the drama queen of Schools, or have you forgotten all that whining about how you were going to get a third?'

They came in the front door to find Justus sitting on the sofa next to Pip, and George in the act of unscrewing a bottle of Teacher's.

'Hey, Justus! I didn't know you were coming over!' Olivia kissed him on the cheek. 'I thought we'd banned booze till finals were over.'

'Pip and I were too stressed – anyway, blame Justus. He brought it.'

'Then pour me one.'

Jerry leaned against the door frame. 'And what about Donne?'

'Olivia, if you're working on Donne, I'd be happy to help.'

'Thanks! See, Jerry? We'll call it a revision tutorial. That's my story. . . Anyway, what about your banging on about Jill being boring?' Eyes alight, she turned back to her housemates to tell

156

them about the lecture. 'What he said was that every type of physical illness, cancer, diabetes, heart disease whatever, can be at least triggered – maybe *caused* – by a particular type of psychosis. It was gripping. Come on, tell me what your physical problems are, and I'll tell you what kind of nutter you are – let's see if it works. Go on, Jerry; you heard it, so don't cheat.'

'I have only one recurrent physical ailment,' Jerry began. 'Dodgy ankles – I'm always falling over and spraining them.'

'Perfect. Proves the point. Essentially, some inner part of you doesn't want to move on. You're frightened of moving forward – you want everything to stay the same forever and ever, so you unconsciously incapacitate yourself from forward action.'

'Or backward action,' Jerry amended good-naturedly.

'You're scared – scared of moving away into the unknown. George?'

'I don't suffer from any health problems. I'm as strong as an ox.'

'Georgie, if you don't tell, I will . . .' Pip winked at him.

'I don't know what you're talking about.'

'What did I have to pick up for you at the chemist just last week? What is the bathroom normally *full* of?' Olivia and Pip began to giggle.

'Just because I occasionally, very occasionally, suffer from what our American friends would call "regularity" problems . . . Thank you, ladies. Thank you for sharing that.'

'Repression. Compulsive Retentive Disorder. Emotional blockage,' Olivia recited. 'You don't want to let anything go. You store it all up inside. It's all down to your mother sending you away to prep school when you were seven. You'll probably need enemas all your life – colonic irrigation, even. You're a textbook case of British male repression at the anal development stage – blocked emotionally and physically.'

'You've brought new meaning to my morning routine, Liv,'

George said huffily. 'Let's hope understanding it makes my passage in life easier.'

'Pip?'

Pip thought for a while. 'Sore throats? Ever since I was a child. Constant sore throats, strep, tonsillitis – you name it, I got it.'

'You talk too much. Exactly the opposite of George in fact. You have no self-control at all – it all gushes out. Verbal diarrhoea. Justus? What about you? Now don't be shy.'

'Well,' he drawled, 'why don't you just hazard a guess, Olivia? I reckon you'd get it right first time if you thought real hard.'

'Genital herpes?' Jerry volunteered innocently. 'Gonorrhoea? Syphilis? Brewer's droop? Something in that line?'

'Sounds like you're a real authority on sexual malfunction, Jerry. I don't know much about it, myself. To be frank, I guess it would be to do with the lungs – shortness of breath, something like that.'

'That doesn't count,' George complained. 'That's just because you smoke Camel unfiltered day and night.'

'Maybe it *does* count,' Olivia laid a hand on Justus' thick brown hair. 'Maybe he's trying to kill himself. Subconsciously. He's denying himself the very air he needs to breathe. It's a type of slow suicide.'

'Now why ever would I want to do that?'

Olivia studied him. 'I don't know. It could be a different kind of repression. It could be a kind of dramatic urge – you could just like the idea of breaking all the natural rules, doing something different, electing to do something you know is wrong for you . . . pushing the limits to see if you're beyond the rules of ordinary mortals. It could be a kind of arrogance. Wanting to be Superman to see if there's anything greater than you. Maybe you hate yourself.'

Justus took out a cigarette and a book of matches. 'It's just a cigarette, Olivia, see?'

'Funny that.' Jerry grunted. 'Trying to be different and beyond it all by doing something that seventy-five per cent of the Oxford population do. Smoking seems pretty run-of-the-mill to me. So, Ms Freud, what about you? Can the physician diagnose her own disease?'

'Of course. I'm painfully short-sighted. I can barely see beyond my own nose,' Olivia replied, and stretched languorously.

'Egocentricity, if you ask me.'

Justus smiled at Olivia. 'Sounds like you and me should be picking out china patterns, darling. We're obviously made for each other.'

'Can you help me with Donne before we go shopping? Are you sure you can spare the time?'

'All the time in the world.'

'Jerry, are you coming back later?'

'No, thanks. I'm going to do some work myself.'

'Suit yourself.'

Olivia and Justus went upstairs to her room. Jerry hung around pretending to listen to Pip while straining his ears to hear Olivia, then walked slowly back to New College.

never, ever try to live dangerously . . .

On a Sunday evening in mid-June, George Upton sat in his garden wondering if he had been insane to embark on the New York venture. Two minutes after finding out he had to go to head office, he'd been on the dog to Olivia asking if she'd wanted to come along for the ride, and two minutes after that it had all been settled, split-splat. Now that it was a *fait accompli* – he was to meet Livvy the following morning at Heathrow – he was astounded he'd had the balls to suggest it. He sat at the fretwork table near the river, supposedly enjoying a quiet drink in the bosom of his family, while Arthur and Will played in the sandpit. Arthur was carefully excavating the fortifications for a castle; Will was just as carefully trashing them. Sarah sat opposite him, her sewing basket on the grass next to her, and her head bent over a pair of small grey school shorts. Although she was not a good seamstress, she enjoyed the small repairs and stitching of nametapes, the endless maternal chores that her boys required.

'When are you due back?' she asked. Her voice was level, and she kept her eyes on her needle.

'It depends how my meetings go,' George replied, swallowing his whisky and water. He'd had to buy a new litre bottle after Livvy had somehow kicked over the last one that weekend. 'Thursday, perhaps, if I'm lucky. Certainly within a week.'

'Where will you be staying? Just in case I need to contact you?'

'Uh . . .' He normally stayed at the bank's apartment, as Sarah knew perfectly well, but he'd had his secretary book the Mark, which had the advantage of discretion. 'It's been a little tricky. The flat's been offered to some client or other. I'll have to sort it out when I get there, and call you.'

Sarah permitted herself a fractionally raised eyebrow. 'I thought you stayed at the Waldorf when the flat wasn't available. Hasn't Sue booked it yet?'

'There's some international hi-tech conference on. Sue's had a devil of a job trying to find a room anywhere. Nothing confirmed yet.' He prayed that she'd drop the subject, and for a moment or two, it seemed as if she had. She folded the grey shorts neatly, and took a white pair out of her basket. 'I see. Well, don't bother to call, I know you'll be busy. I'll check with Sue myself.' She sewed in silence for a moment or two, while George looked across the river morosely. 'I know how you hate hotels. Won't you be lonely?'

'Ha!' her husband barked. 'Chance would be a fine thing. It's a work jaunt. Jack will be a very dull boy when he comes home. Tedious stuff, arse-kissing the Yanks, morale bullshit, living the corporate values . . .Why d'you ask? You don't fancy coming along, do you? You could if you want.' He had no option except to go for the full double bluff to head her off at the pass.

'Perhaps. I hadn't really thought about it until now. It might be a pleasant break.'

'What about the boys? We're cutting it a bit close to sort out a baby-sitter.'

'Damn.' Sarah sucked her finger where she had pricked it; a drop of blood marked the white tennis shorts.

'You all right, darling? Need a plaster? It's not that I don't want you to come, Sarah – I do, naturally. It's just that you might find New York a bit of a let-down, especially in midsummer. If it was San Francisco, I wouldn't have a second thought, but New York's a cesspit, this time of year. If you're really keen, come along by all means – nothing could make me happier. Just don't say I didn't warn you.' He rattled the ice cubes in his glass. 'It's no place for a holiday: nothing but a vast office block, and there isn't even any decent shopping.' He winced as he listened to himself – surely Sarah would never fall for that? 'Since the dollar surge it's more expensive shopping on Madison Avenue than on Faubourg St Honoré.'

'Still. It would give us some time together.'

George was sweating, and felt chilled by the light summer breeze. He finished his drink and put it down firmly on the table. 'It *would*, if only I had a moment to spare. You don't want to be cooped up in some nasty hotel day and night, do you? If you feel like a break, darling, why don't we pop over to Normandy for a weekend – perhaps next month – longer if you like? We could take the boys. July's a lovely time of year. I've just got such a tight schedule in New York, meetings day and night, dinners, the lot. It's not that I don't want you to come, love, I just dread you being bored. I'd feel responsible. Fancy another swift one before dinner, darling?'

'No, thanks. Won't Olivia be bored, cooped up in a nasty hotel all day and night?' Sarah looked at him calmly. 'Won't she, George? She *is* going with you, isn't she?'

He stared back at her and panicked. 'I don't know what leads you to that conclusion,' he said huffily. Standing on your dignity was the last resort of a desperate man. Never go back, never apologise, never explain, as his father had told him, and characteristically his father hadn't seen the need to explain how to brazen your way out of a situation like this one. Knowing his

163

father, he would have succumbed to the first swift cuff on the metaphorical ear from his mother.

'Probably the fact that you've booked two tickets, and booked a room at the Mark, and haven't asked me to go. I know you don't fancy Sue – anyway, she was the one who told me about the hotel. She said something about how sweet it was of you to take your cousin. It must be Olivia.'

Oh, fuck, fuck fuck! he thought. 'Oh, Sarah, Sarah, Sarah,' he groaned, 'if you could only hear yourself . . .' It flashed through his mind to say that it had all been a surprise, a surprise for *her*, but now she'd ruined it by trusting him so little. It might just work. It would be tricky, with the flight tomorrow morning, and the ticket in Olivia's name sitting in his briefcase, but he could perhaps wangle it. He could blame Sue, Sarah might yet fall for it, and he could give Sue a well-deserved bollocking for opening her big mouth at the same time. It would mean calling Olivia surreptitiously and coming up with some sort of story, and the risks involved, and the sheer nervous sweat of pulling it off, and giving up his last ever chance to be alone with Livvy before she got married . . . And so it all came out. Some of it, anyway.

'All right, goddamn it. Yes. I *did* suggest to Livvy that it might do her good to get away. I've felt responsible, you know, ever since that bloody weekend here, and Jerry being such a shit. I thought she needed a shoulder she could lean on and a change of scenery, time to think things through. There's nothing else in it, I promise you. We're very old friends, after all, as you know. Perfectly natural. I didn't tell you, because. . . because . . .'

'Because?' Sarah prompted patiently.

'Because I knew you'd get the wrong end of the stick, just like you are doing. I didn't want to upset you, Sarah. And there. I *have* upset you, haven't I? It was all I was trying to avoid. I knew you'd misunderstand.'

'I've never done that, George.' She held the shorts loosely on her lap, her warm brown eyes steady on his face. 'I know perfectly well that you're in love with her – you always have been. I knew it when I met you and I knew it when I married you. I've known it for the past twelve years. I knew it most of all when she came back. You might have given me a little more credit.' The mildest of all possible rebukes. 'You fell in love with her when you were barely more than children. You fell in love with her that afternoon, playing tennis. You've told me so yourself, more than once. And you've been in love with her ever since. I may not be as compelling as Olivia, but I am not a complete fool.'

'I never thought you were,' he said, and meant it.

'No.' Despite her gravity, she smiled at him. 'You've always thought I was nice, decent Sarah. Not a complete fool, but certainly a little foolish, hmm? I always knew you weren't in love with me, George, but I didn't mind. I still don't, not really. I've always known you couldn't help yourself. I love you, and I know that you are a decent man, and that you'll always do the best you can for me. I've never minded much about Olivia, honestly.'

'This is all absolute nonsense, Sarah. Of course I'm not in love with Livvy. What a preposterous idea, and rather offensive, too. Just because I had a little crush on her at school . . .' George leaned forward, gripping his empty glass in his hands. 'And if it were true, which I assure you it is not, how could you not mind? Why wouldn't you mind, Sarah?'

Resuming her sewing, his wife replied coolly, 'What good would it do if I did? If I had ever said I minded, could it have stopped you loving her?' Of course it couldn't, George thought, and then he wondered if it might have . . . Might just have changed the way he felt, have swung the balance. 'Of course not,' she continued. 'I'm not cut out for that sort of drama, anyway. I don't like scenes, and I certainly don't like causing them. People don't fall in love with me, they never have and they never will, and I am perfectly accustomed to it. I wanted a nice quiet life as your nice quiet wife. That didn't seem out of the realms of possibility. That's what I had, up until now. Olivia left a long time ago. She gave you to me, really. She knows it and so do I. My only question now is, does she want to take you back?'

'You sound as if you find this all monumentally tiresome. You sound as if you're choosing an insurance policy.'

'That's an unfortunate simile, darling. I never had any insurance – the risk was always there. I imagined it to be minor because it never crossed my mind that she'd return. Who would have predicted that? Maybe it was always on the cards, and I was too stupid to see it. Now that she has, all I can do is be practical about it, assume that she's going to go ahead and marry Justus, and then we'll go back to normal.'

She had always been a sensible woman. George faced her, running his hands through his hair in helpless frustration. He watched her bend low over Arthur's small shorts, biting the thread free of the waistband with her even white teeth, and imagined those same teeth sinking into his neck and slicing cleanly through his carotid artery. Nice, quiet little Sarah. 'You must hate me. Or despise me. Or both.'

She laid a cool hand on his knee and patted it. Using the low, patient voice with which she reprimanded her boys, she soothed, 'Nonsense, darling. I love you. Even if I didn't, I couldn't ever hate you. I wouldn't know where to begin. Let's be rational: even though you don't love me, it doesn't mean that you hate or despise me, does it?'

'I love you. I – I care greatly for you.'

'Thank you. That's sweet.' She flipped her little wrist and looked at the gold watch he had given her as a wedding present – pretty, but practical, valuable, but unostentatious, above all, long-lasting.

It was time to prepare the potatoes, and while they boiled she could put the boys in the bath; while they washed, she could lay out George's clothes for his trip, then drain the potatoes and pop them in the warmer while she read the boys a story. The skate would only take a minute to grill. 'Arthur! Will! Five more minutes and into the bath, all right, darlings?' George caught her hand as she passed him. 'You're a very decent woman, Sarah.'

'I know I am. That is my great misfortune.'

When she had gone inside, George rolled up his trousers and stepped into the shallow stream where his sons were paddling. It was all far too complicated for him. He didn't want to be put on the spot, he simply wanted to be somewhere else, like his father, no questions asked. 'Well, lads, found any tadpoles yet?'

An hour later, Sarah Upton had packed her husband's bag, put her children to bed, placed their repaired and neatly folded clothes in their drawers, put on the laundry, prepared dinner and set the kitchen table, put out a note for the milkman and wormed the cat she had never wanted to own. George stood disconsolately in the kitchen while she watched the skate, flipping through his papers and waiting for her to speak, dreading what she would say.

'Would you mind very much if I didn't eat with you, George?' she said at last, putting the fish on the table next to the new potatoes and the salad. 'I'm tired, just longing for a bath.' She walked slowly up the stairs to their room without waiting for a reply.

In the bath, she slipped down so that the water came up to her neck, letting her soft brown hair float around her. She reached for the soap and experienced a familiar clash of sadness and resentment that the week-old bar, so delicately carved when newly unwrapped from its expensive paper, already looked cracked and dirty. In what was, for her, a virtual fit of pique and shocking disregard for money, she climbed out of the bath, threw out the offending bar and reached into the cupboard for a new box of Crabtree & Evelyn geranium-scented soap. Returning, she submerged herself completely in the comforting water and decided George should sleep in the downstairs guest bedroom that night, if only so that he wouldn't wake the children when he left for the airport. She moved his bag down and laid his dressing gown out on the bed. In the middle of the night she woke to Will's cries, padded barefoot to his room, lifted him silently and took him back to the master bed. Cradling him in her arms, feeling his pouting still babyish lips against her throat, and his soft, steady breath, she lay awake in the dark remembering how she had adored his first infant weeks, and how she had wallowed in that bed with the scent of vanilla rising from her hot breasts, the same slightly sour scent thrown back at her on the baby's breath. She inched away from him to fetch some aspirin, knowing that it wasn't the pills that would cure her headache, so much as the water she drank with them, and the sleep they allowed her; just as it wouldn't be betrayal that killed her marriage, so much as the side effects that went with it: his guilt, her inability to trust, their mutual ungenerous reluctance to forgive or forget.

Olivia had arrived at the terminal before George. He spotted her wearing a sleeveless black dress and huge dark glasses, looking like an elongated Jackie Kennedy all the way from her elegantly shod feet to the Mona Lisa smile on her lips. The taxi had collected him from Woodbridge that morning, and he had paused beside the master bed, looking down at his sleeping wife and younger son, but had not disturbed them. On the long drive to Heathrow he had tried to study his notes, but found himself gazing through the window, wondering if Olivia might not turn up, and whether it would be better, after all, if she didn't. His pulse quickened when he saw her standing at the British Airways business-class check-in, leaning over the counter and chatting to the clerk. Something overly familiar in the clerk's manner irritated him.

'Ah, Olivia, you beat me to it.'

'Good morning, sir. Your lady friend was just speculating that she might have to make the trip on her own. That would have been a shame, wouldn't it?'

His lady friend? George blustered, annoyed that the clerk hadn't assumed Olivia was his wife, flattered that he was seen as a man with a lady friend, nervous that he might meet someone he knew who might jump to the same conclusion, apprehensive that Olivia wouldn't let the comment pass.

Olivia was discretion itself as she kissed him on the cheek. 'Morning, darling. He's having you on. I only just arrived.'

They didn't talk much until they were well on their way, when Olivia said, 'I am grateful for this, Georgie, really I am.'

He patted her hand. 'How are you, Livvy?'

'I'm all right. How's Sarah?'

'Hmmm . . . Would you like a drink?'

'At ten a.m.?'

'Live dangerously? Time change and all that.'

'Maybe the best plan is to drink heavily and then sleep till we land.'

George summoned the stewardess, made a great fuss over the brands of champagne and vodka, and settled on a Bloody Mary and a half bottle of fizz. Olivia had reclined her seat as far back as it would go and had her eyes closed. Perhaps she was asleep already?

'Didn't Sarah mind at all?'

'No. Not a jot. Why should she?'

'I would have, in her place. It's not a completely normal situation, is it, us going to New York together? You married, me engaged. Justus thought it was weird, till I told him we had a long history of sharing rooms and beds without having sex. Presumably you told Sarah we'd be in separate rooms?'

George fiddled with his peanuts.

'George? We *are* in separate rooms, aren't we?' She opened her eyes, and looked at him from an angle well below and well to his right – rather, George thought, the angle he'd see if they were in bed together. A slow smile spread across her face. 'You only booked one room, didn't you? I don't mind what you've booked so long as you aren't counting on us having sex and so long as you told Sarah we had two rooms. George? George!'

'I didn't tell her anything.' He had no desire to tell Olivia what Sarah had said, even less what Sarah had surmised. None at all. If he did, she might turn tail in New York and get the next flight home before they'd even had a chance to talk.

'You are a moron. It would have been so simple to tell the truth, and instead you've just made things more complicated. I shouldn't even be sitting next to you. You should have ignored me at Heathrow, put me in a different row, and then we could have accidentally bumped into each other at JFK . . . God, you're an innocent, Georgie. You really are. Never, ever, try to live dangerously. You're not cut out for it.'

She touched his cheek lightly, then turned her face to the window and went to sleep. She wasn't angry with him, that was the important thing. He sat beside her, watching her breast rise and fall, and thought again about making love to her. George had had a couple of women before he went up to Oxford, half a dozen or so before he'd met Sarah, and – not that anyone, *anyone* knew about it – he had even had a couple more in the years since he had married, but none of them had really compared to Olivia with whom he had never had a sexual relationship. None of them had left the sexual imprint that she had without even trying. He didn't know why, and he was not inclined to speculate; he simply knew that he had never stopped wondering what it would be like since that first tennis match, and whether it could ever happen. It was probably – almost certainly – out of the question, but there was no harm in imagining it.

On arrival at the Mark, George feigned surprise when the clerk said they were holding a suite. Olivia merely shrugged. When the porter took them to the room, with its huge bathroom, and a double bed that was almost the size of the private terrace, Olivia shrugged again.

'I could ask for a twin-bedded room . . . Or I could use the sofa in the sitting room . . .'

'Yes, you could,' she agreed, 'but why go to that hassle? It's lovely. It's the nicest room I've ever stayed in. I might spend the whole time in bed.'

She didn't, as far as George could see. Olivia spent most of the week by the pool, in a series of cinemas, or on the phone to Justus. When he awoke, she would often be already at the pool, having breakfast, a book open on the table. When he returned from his meetings, that's where he found her, on the same lounger, by the same table, always alone, and on the same page of her book. They ate out in the evenings, wandered the streets for a little, and returned to the hotel bar for a nightcap. They undressed separately in the privacy of the marble bathroom, and then Olivia would begin to read, and George felt too uneasy to interrupt. On the fourth night he took her to dinner with an Australian colleague and her husband, and introduced Olivia as an old schoolfriend he had had the good fortune to bump into at the airport. The foursome spent a pleasant evening, dutifully swapping tips on restaurants and shops in Rome, London and Sydney. Olivia promised to visit the Frick, with no more intention of keeping it than the Australians had of visiting Santa Maria della Pace on their next stop in Rome. All the time, every minute, George watched Olivia and pretended to himself that she was his wife, his mistress, anything that belonged to him. All the time, he thought about how badly, how madly he desired her, twelve inches apart from him in the bar, six inches away from him on the banquette during dinner . . . Olivia played along, although George saw her spine stiffen at the end of the evening when he made a laboured point of telling the Australians that he was staying at a quite *different* hotel, on the other side of town, but would see Olivia home first. She was silent in the taxi, and stayed poker-faced in the bar.

'Livvy?'

'I'm fine.'

'But you're angry with me?'

'Yes, I'm angry with you.'

'Why? What have I done? Tell me.'

'You're enjoying all this – you're enjoying the deceit. You think it's a terrific lark to pretend that I'm some long-lost schoolfriend and let people speculate that I'm your mistress. You're wallowing in the fact that Sarah doesn't know I'm here. You're praying those two tonight are going to assume we're having an affair, and be too discreet ever to say or do anything more than give you a sly smile – I *saw* him do it when we left.'

'Good God, Livvy, you were the one who suggested it – you were the one who said we should have travelled independently, and "just happened" to bump into each other.'

'I didn't think you'd get such a kick out of it. That was between us. Now you're using me, and you're using Sarah. You haven't even called her since we got here.'

'You don't know that. You wouldn't know if I'd called her twenty times a day.'

'Have you?'

'That's not the point.'

'And what is the point? That I should at least be screwing you, if I've agreed to come on this trip?'

'For God's sake, Livvy, no, of course not. The truth . . .'

'I'm waiting?' Her eyes flashed at him, her mouth set tight.

'The truth, as if you didn't know it, is that I love you. Oh, bugger. I don't mean in any disgusting way, I mean, I love you, I care about you, I wanted to make you happy. I'm not at all sure you're doing the right thing with Justus. I have the feeling you're letting go of your life, somehow, in some way I can't put my finger on. You're letting everyone else make decisions for you. Perhaps I've been stupid, and all right, fuck it, *yes*, I like it if people think you care for me, or that there's something between us. You're a very desirable woman – I'd be a eunuch if it never crossed my mind, after what we – had. Is that such an evil thought? Does it do anyone any harm? Have I laid a finger on you, ogled you, made you uncomfortable, once? I can't understand why you won't talk to me. You're a million miles away, and I'm your best friend – aren't I? Still? Why can't you just talk to me?'

'What about?'

'Anything, everything. Whatever you like. The book you're pretending to read. The old days. Your sodding parents. Look, I'll cancel my meetings tomorrow. It's a charade anyway – these bastards don't give a shit about what we think in London. I've seen everyone I need to – I'll plead urgent business and cancel. Let's spend tomorrow together, even go to that sodding art gallery, if you like. And we can talk about everything. Justus. Most of all, Justus.'

Olivia was white. 'I came because I trusted you, because you're my oldest friend. I came back to England, and I came to New York, for my own "time to pause" – you remember *Midsummer Night's Dream?*'

'I remember you dragging me to see it at Worcester when Justus was in it.'

'I thought this would be a pause – time for me to think.'

'Quite right too. You ought to think very carefully about it – it's a big step, marriage. Most people leap into it with their eyes closed, and then a few years later find themselves wondering what if I'd married X instead.'

'I'm going upstairs.'

'Can I come with you?'

'No. Not now. Not for a bit.'

Within minutes of Olivia reaching the bedroom, the phone rang. She knew it would be either George calling from the bar to apologise, when he owed her no apology, or Justus.

'Hello?'

'Olivia?' Olivia shivered. 'Olivia, it's Sarah. Sarah Upton. I'm so sorry to call so late. I hope I haven't woken you up?'

'No . . . Hello, Sarah.'

'You sound a million miles away. Silly me, I suppose you are! Actually, not quite a million, is it? Something like three or four thousand, if I remember from the air-miles accounts. How are you? Are you having a good time? How's the weather?' Sarah had a gift for meaningless pleasantries: she'd had to keep many an office wine-and-cheese do on a gentle simmer for hours.

'It's all fine,' Olivia replied.

'Oh, good. I expect you'll come back with a glorious tan, and we'll be green with jealousy. I was hoping to speak to George. Is he with you, by any chance?'

'No. As far as I know he had a meeting tonight. I haven't seen him. He may be in his room.'

'That's naturally what I asked for – perhaps they put me through to the wrong extension? Hotel staff must be selected for incompetence in every country. Never mind. Could you give him a message for me? I'm sure you're more reliable than reception. Could you tell him that his father's not very well? My mother-in-law just called – it's very early here, but I suppose she was anxious to let us know. He's had a fall, but I'm going over to see him now and he's absolutely all right, nothing to worry about and George absolutely mustn't rush home. I'm worried his mother will call and be hysterical and make George fly back unnecessarily. He's not to. I'll let him know if there's any cause for concern, but it sounds like nothing that a day or two in bed won't cure. The boys and I will go over to help out. All right? We'll probably stay the weekend. Don't let it disturb George's plans. Oh, and by the way, Olivia . . .'

'Yes, Sarah?'

'It might be best if you don't answer the phone in case Cecily – my mother-in-law – calls. She wouldn't understand. She's rather old and, oh, dreadfully old-fashioned. No point in upsetting her as well. And I do so hope you enjoy the rest of your break, Olivia. Goodbye.'

'Sarah? Sarah. Hold on a minute. I don't want you to think there's anything – you know, there's nothing . . .' Olivia sighed heavily. 'I'm not sleeping with him. That's all I want you to know. That I'm not.'

'You're not? Poor George! He will be disappointed! 'Bye now.'

Olivia sat on the bed for ten minutes before summoning George back to the room and repeating Sarah's call.

'Why on earth didn't you tell me? I was stunned you hadn't told her. Now I'm stunned that you did. What are you playing at, George?'

'I thought it would be best to say as little as I had to.'

Olivia was too tired to feel angry. 'Aren't you going to phone your parents?' As George obeyed, Olivia went into the bathroom to undress but left the door open unselfconsciously. She unbuttoned her silk shirt and dropped it on the floor, undid her bra and chucked it on top, then reached for the waistband of her linen shorts. George watched her reflection in the long mirror. It could be, it could yet be . . . Olivia stripped to her pants, draped the thick white robe around her and belted it tightly as George hung up. She looked at him expectantly as she stepped back into the room. 'He's fine,' George confirmed. 'A bit bruised, but fine.'

'Good. Let's sit on the terrace for a bit.' She stood at the sliding doors, one arm extended in invitation, the robe, which was both too long for her and too wide, gaping open to show her breastbone.

'You're looking bloody thin.'

'Thanks a bunch. Stop criticising me and come outside. Then you'll have to sort out your flight home.'

'I told you, Dad's fine. He quite often falls, it's nothing to worry about.'

'I wasn't worrying about your father.'

'You mean Sarah? She's fine too. She must have relished an excuse to call and speak to you. She knows it all, you see.'

'She certainly knows a lot more than I do.'

'No. Both of you know everything, and I'm the mug. It's just as Sarah said, after all.'

'Which was?'

'That it's all up to you. That she knows, and you know, that if you want me, I'm yours. Always have been, Livvy,' George said, with a resigned sigh. 'You must know that? Ever since you thrashed me at tennis. Ever since you told me you had a place at Worcester, and ever since I discovered you snogging that shit from B2, the prefect, whatever his name was.'

'James.'

George closed one eye and looked at her balefully.

'Whatever. I love you, Miss O. Fletcher-Dunn. I can't help myself. God knows I've tried, and it's been all right by and large – it was all fine so long as you were gone, and now I look up and see you opposite me, and it's not fine any longer. Perhaps I'm too old.'

'Perhaps we're not old enough.' Olivia had heard similar romantic guff from George before, and had never taken it seriously. She was well aware that he desired her, but desire was controllable most of the time, and she was convinced he would never jeopardise his marriage. In the past she had teased him and hustled him into laughter; tonight she felt too old and too weary.

'You think this is growing pains? Jesus. I'd leave Sarah, if you'd have me, Livvy. I'll probably leave Sarah if you won't. I could cry, Livvy, when I think of it all, I really could. Who knows . . .'

But it was Olivia who began to cry, and George couldn't stand that. He picked her up, and he carried her to the bed. He stroked her hair until she slept, and for the first time sincerely examined his heart as to whether he could, in fact, leave his wife.

moving gently around the body

of another . . .

On their last day in New York, Olivia wouldn't let George
cancel his meetings; she wanted to be alone. She didn't like
New York much but she was determined to find something that
she could take home with her – a memento, a pleasant image, a
memory. She walked until her feet were sore, zigzagging from
Fifth Avenue, across to Bloomie's, back across and down into the
lower West Side, where she found a little gilded wooden tableau
that had been stripped from a lacquered chest and, once
decently mounted, might suit Pip's living room. As she walked,
she occupied herself by trying to list all the names of the States
in alphabetical order. Alabama, Alaska, Arizona . . . She met
George, as arranged, on East 4th Street, where Manhattan's
Indian restaurants were concentrated. They had spent so many
long hours over bhajis and dopiazas from the Curry Inn at
Marlborough to the Dildunia, or 'Dildo' as their local Oxford
Indian had been known, it seemed appropriate to go for a curry
in Manhattan. They wandered the blocks before selecting the
Star of India.

Olivia dropped her head to study the menu. George had made

up his mind. Olivia was still looking for the wardrobe that led to
Narnia, and if anyone could provide it, it was George.

'Are you glad you came, Livvy?'

'Yes, I am. Last night I regretted it, but tonight – tonight I feel
fine. I'm glad you're here too. I don't think anybody else would put
up with me the way I've been.'

'What rot.'

Idaho, Illinois, Indiana, Olivia heard in the back of her mind.

Some of the food was very, very good and some of it was horrid,
but that was typical of Indian restaurants and made the occasion
all the more nostalgic. And the wine was decent, and the evening
air balmy, and they were both able, for a short while, to forget all
about England. As they were finishing dinner, a woman came into
the small dining room. She was Indian, but in Western dress,
barring a gauzy scarf draped over her head and round her neck,
and the bhindi on her forehead. She was of uncertain age, possibly
in her forties, perhaps younger. She greeted the waiter warmly,
then spoke quietly to an elderly couple at a table near the entrance;
Olivia strained to hear what she was selling, but could not make it
out. The couple were clearly discomfited, smiling with
embarrassment and shaking their heads. The woman floated over
to their table. 'Good evening, sir and madam. Do you choose to
know what the future holds?'

'Not half!' George grinned at Olivia.

'I have the gift.'

'Oh, no, George, honestly. . . I'd rather have a long-stemmed
rose.'

'You get that in Little Italy, not here. Go on, Liv, don't be such
a coward.' Olivia glanced quickly at the woman and smiled, and
George pulled out his wallet with an indulgent grimace.

'I assume this is going to call for a lot of crossing palms with
silver . . . You know it's a fearful tourist trap, Livvy, they shouldn't

really be encouraged, but if it amuses you . . .' He extended a twenty-dollar bill towards the fortune-teller. 'Only the lady, thanks very much.'

The fortune-teller tilted her head on one side and looked at him for a moment. 'Thank you, but I do not want to be paid now. When I have finished the lady can pay me what she considers suitable. It is not good to be paid in advance. People who pay in advance think they buy a perfect future.'

'So you're not offering any guarantees, hmm?' George winked at Olivia. 'She's no fool. If the punter sets the price beforehand and gets a great future, that's it – no upside for her. But if you leave the payment open-ended the sky's the limit. Sound commercial practice, in her business.'

The waiter pulled up a chair, and the fortune-teller perched on the edge of it, close to Olivia, who stretched out her hand across the table, palm up.

'No, thank you, madam, my gift is not in reading hands. May I?'

The woman rose to her feet and stepped behind Olivia. She placed her hands on either side of Olivia's neck, and held it firmly between cool fingers. Then she touched her temples briefly, before pressing down on her cheekbones. Olivia half wanted to laugh. They had attracted the attention of the few remaining diners who watched, chewing silently. The woman moved to Olivia's side, took one hand and then the other, and seemed to be checking her pulse. With the lightest of pressure, she touched her arms inside the crook of the elbow, and then pressed both hands, one over the other, against the hollow at the base of Olivia's throat. George did not speak as he watched them; he found the sight of one woman moving gently around the body of another disturbingly erotic. The fortune-teller then knelt at Olivia's feet, and, again asking permission, unbuckled her strappy sandals and held each foot in her hand. Olivia was visibly unsettled by this apparent servility.

The woman replaced her shoes, crossed to the far side of the table and sat down again.

'You are a fortunate woman. The signs are good for you. You have money, enough I think, and you will continue to have money. You do not want it or need it as much as you think you do, but money will not interfere with your life.'

'Oh, good – that's good, isn't it, Georgie?' Olivia was disappointed. She had expected something less mundane.

'You have friends who are important to you. I don't think you have family, I am not sure. I cannot see children in you.'

'Not ever? Won't I ever have children?'

'I do not know.'

'I thought that was the whole point of the exercise – lots of money, a happy marriage, and three beautiful kids.'

'You will be married –'

'Of course she will be, she's wearing an enormous engagement ring, for God's sake –'

'But you are not presently. You may not marry for some time yet.' The dark, intelligent eyes of the Indian woman gazed across at George with reproach. 'You are looking for someone, or something, someone you have lost. That's why you are here . . . You loved a man once, and you hope to find him again. It will not be as easy as you think.'

'What if I've found him already? Haven't I?' Olivia had turned pale beneath her light tan. George felt a quickening of interest, that conviction of being on the brink of something uncertain but of certain significance. He paid more attention to Olivia's questions than to the fortune-teller's statements.

'You have not found him, although he is before you. He is not free. You could not see him if he was. There is a blindfold over your eyes that stops you recognising the person fully.'

'I don't know what you are talking about.' Olivia put her hands in her lap. George knew; he was certain now.

'You have not been happy. There are many shadows, but I see light – I see a man who loved you. It was a long time ago. He loved you very much, and you have forgotten. I see you with him beside a river, somewhere far away. There are others there, but only one you loved. When you left his embrace, you were lost. Sometimes when you leave a lover's arms, it is to journey to a greater love. Sometimes that is where love ends.'

'Thy love is one thou'st not yet known,' Olivia murmured, before pulling herself up. 'I don't want to know about the past,' she corrected the seer. 'I *know* what happened in the past. You're supposed to be telling me about my future, whether I'll have a long life, whether I'll travel, settle down, go into business –'

'You live yet in the country of the blind. It is hard to see a way forward.' The stranger stood up, and pulled her headscarf more tightly around her.

'Don't go! You must be able to tell me more.'

'Have you consulted the Tarot?'

'I want *you* to tell me. Please.'

'I will try. Give me your hands.'

The Indian woman took Olivia's hands in hers and closed her eyes. 'For you it is all about love. There is nothing else of any importance. People die if they are not loved enough. Someone died. . . You must learn how to read your past, and you must search your memory. A person who reads his past is able to read the future without my help.'

'*Help* me.'

'Livvy, this is stupid. It's nothing to do with you. It's not about you, it's to do with tourism –'

'Shut up.'

'I feel the presence of a man. He is . . . I don't know. A spiritual man, a man of family . . .'

'That's Justus out on two counts.'

Although the woman held her hands very loosely, Olivia felt physically drawn towards her. 'He is not alone. I see others . . . A friend, and a guide. These people are marked by you, but do not be mistaken: you, too, bear marks. These people who love you, they are too near. I can't see . . .'

'Livvy, this is one hundred per cent unadulterated bullshit. Any woman your age is bound to have had a fling or two. It doesn't mean anything. It's nonsense –'

'I'm marked by them? Where?' Olivia searched her hands as if for visible scars.

'I cannot see it, I feel it. Don't you?'

'No.'

'You will.'

'Will I ever be happy?'

The Indian woman opened her eyes. 'Happiness means different things to different people. You are not happy now, you will be happier, but that is not important. You need to look carefully before you cross the river.'

'What should I do?'

'Open your eyes. Stand still. Search your heart.'

'And don't forget to use the crystals!' George chipped in, but neither woman heeded him. The fortune-teller pressed Olivia's hands and released them. 'I wish you good luck. And joy.' She left without another word.

George paid the bill and put away his wallet. 'At least she's got some conscience then. Unless she gets a cut from the waiter.' Olivia scored the tablecloth with a toothpick, but did not reply. 'Liv? You don't believe in all this stuff, do you?' She shook her head. 'She would have said exactly the same stuff to anyone. Every thirty-year-old woman's got a past. The secret is being so obscure that the punter can apply it to whatever she wants. It's all crap, you do know that?' Another nod. 'It's like fortune cookies. All the fortunes are good.'

'Except mine wasn't.'

'If you've got doubts about marrying Justus, discuss it with people you trust, not crackpots. Talk to me, for God's sake. You're far too intelligent to be superstitious. I've always had you down as a healthy sceptic.'

Olivia smiled wistfully. 'My mother was obsessed with the Tarot. She used to do it all the time, said it had told her about Dad, long before she met him, about me, everything. Maybe it runs in the blood. Maybe that's the only thing I inherited from the old cow. Superstition.'

On the plane home to London the next day, George held Olivia's hand in his and bounced it slowly up and down on his knee as he talked. 'If you ask me my honest opinion, straight up, and putting aside any ulterior motives, I don't think you should marry Justus.'

'I didn't ask, actually.' Olivia felt she was going a little mad. She attempted the States in reverse order as George babbled, naming them in time with the rhythm of her hand bouncing on his knee. Wyoming, Wisconsin, West Virginia, Washington . . . She took pride in remembering West Virginia.

'You've got nothing in common – even less now than you did at Oxford. What is he, at bottom? A man who earns his daily crust pretending to be something else. If that doesn't make you suspicious, what can? I admit he's good at it, not that I'm any judge of thespian talent, but so the rest of the world seems to think, and he may well be a stud, but what *is* he, at bottom? You don't share any background, for God's sake. Even if you're attracted to all that celebrity, the fame thing, it won't make you happy. You won't like living in his shadow. Let's face it, Liv, you've always needed to be adored. A man like Justus hogs the limelight. Sarah was right –

where will it leave you? You'll always be wondering who he's with, about some co-star, about his sex scenes. It'll drive you mad.'

New Hampshire, Nevada, Nebraska, Olivia thought. Shit. Had she forgotten Oregon? Didn't everybody forget Oregon? She looked sad. George – decent, reliable, honest Georgie – could not stand to see her looking sad, because when she did, he felt that they really were just old friends. He wanted her to be feisty, to bark at him; he wanted her to throw care to the winds and get on with life, and seize experience in both hands while she still could, and he still could. He wanted her to roll her head to one side, look at him with that confrontational yet tired-of-the-world expression she had perfected at sixteen, and say, 'Oh fuck it, Georgie, let's go and have *fun*.' Then he'd be back on safe ground at last, not panting after a ghost. He brought her clasped hand to his lips and she looked straight at him, her eyes full of fervour.

'I love you, Olivia.'

'I love you, too.'

She was deliberately refusing to hear what he was really saying. He drew in his breath. 'No, I mean more than that, much more than that. I mean I *love* you and – you need me.'

'Yes, you're right, I do. But do you need *me*, George? I don't think so. Justus does, in a funny way. Justus and I have more in common than you know. I understand him, and I know I can give him what he wants. You don't need me.'

'Oh, yes, oh, yes, I do – you're the only woman who's ever really known me, Liv, all of me, the only person I could ever say everything to, the only one who's been strong enough – you're the only woman I've ever wanted that I haven't –'

'You haven't had? Oh, *George*. How boring. If that's all it is, if it's all just about sexual fantasy, then for God's sake let's do it and put you out of your misery. Honestly. I don't believe you've been thinking about me all these years – you've made a very nice life for yourself, just like I always knew you would. Don't get hung up on some crappy notion about pining for me now. It doesn't wash.'

George was still picking over her first sentence. Could she genuinely mean what she had so casually suggested? He closed his eyes for a moment and saw himself on a beach on the Calabrian coast, watching Olivia and Pip. The two girls stood knee deep in the Aegean, washing tomatoes for lunch, their faded cheesecloth skirts, one pale yellow, one salmon pink, tucked into their M&S knickers. During that impromptu picnic his heart had swollen with love and tenderness for them both, for their youth and modesty, their girlish high spirits. Yet after lunch they had stripped down to those white knickers and lain stretched out on the pebbles to catch every ray of sun, with Jerry, in shorts and a T-shirt, perfectly at ease between them. The sight of them, their breasts flattened against their ribcages, the sight of their nipples, the way Pip had propped herself on a elbow and leaned two inches from Jerry's face to whisper a confidence that had made Olivia shake with laughter – a confidence about him, he'd assumed, a joke, until he'd realised that all three were wholly unaware of his presence, and he had stormed down the beach, smoking furiously until he could bring himself under control.

'I've always loved you, always desired you. If you knew how many bloody long nights I spent aching in some cold metal bed . . .'

'That was a schoolboy crush.'

'No, after school. Do you remember that holiday in Italy, with Pip, the summer of our second year?'

'And Jerry. Don't forget Jerry was there.' Olivia remembered the holiday vividly, when the four of them had driven down the coast and caught the ferry to Sicily, then meandered slowly back to Rome. It was long before Justus had arrived on the scene; it was the time that she had been quite blissfully happy with Jerry, and convinced she could keep that contentment forever. He had made her laugh so; she thought of the day they'd stopped for lunch at the beach at Maratea. Jerry had made them laugh so hard telling them about Gandhi battling temptation by forcing himself to sleep between gorgeous naked women, begging them to let him re-enact the scene to test his own resolve, imploring Pip to lean still closer, to make the test yet harder, that Olivia had had tears pouring down her face.

George saw Olivia's slow smile as she recalled the trip. 'Since then, before then, but very often since then, I've always wanted you.'

'Oh, Georgie! You got over it easily enough.' She patted his hand.

'Till you came back.'

'You're such a big baby, such a big, sweet baby. OK, here's the deal. When we land, if you really want to go through with this, then we'll go back to Justus's flat, take our clothes off, get into bed, if that's where you'd like to do it, and have sex. OK? It's cool by me.'

George didn't think he wanted that at all, not quite that. He wanted to have that twenty-year-old, all or nothing, heart over head, stomach-churning experience before he turned forty. He wanted to find Olivia so overwhelming that the thing was bigger than both of them, that they were swooped off their feet and into another world that lay beyond Sarah and the children and the bank and Justus and the past, that they could say, 'This was bigger than both of us' – and he wanted her to feel it as acutely as he did, and did he ever want to feel it acutely. Try as he might, he was not disabled by desire for her, but he was as close to disability as he'd ever been, limping badly, if you like, and part of him suspected this was as close as he would ever get. Not passionate enough to discard her pragmatic offer, but too passionate to refuse it, he kissed her fingers again, and kept a watchful eye on her through landing, customs and the taxi rank, half expecting a sudden reversal, mockery, even tears. In the event, Olivia didn't have to do anything at all, and George was not to discover, not that night at least, if she intended to go through with her bargain or not. When she opened the door to Justus's flat, the first sight that met their eyes was a large bouquet of white lilies thrown on the hall console; the second was Justus himself, talking on the telephone.

'Well, hey!' he said to his unknown listener. 'The wanderers have returned. Yeah, I can see at least ten Saks Fifth Avenue bags . . . does ten bags a trousseau make? D'you want to say hello? Hold on.' He kissed Olivia as he passed the phone to her. 'It's Pip. And if it isn't George – this is a surprise! It's been a long time. What were you doing sweeping my fiancée off to New York, without asking my permission, huh? I ought to knock you down.' Instead he shook his hand.

If George found the transition from arriving in the flat with the sole intention of bedding Olivia to making light conversation with her intended mate difficult, he showed no sign of it. He sat down without an invitation and shifted his attention to Justus.

'So what's it really like? Hollywood, the lights, the action – all those women?'

'It's just a job, years of hard grind, rewarded by a short spells of success – probably very short in my case.' Modesty, like most things, came easily to Justus O'Keefe. 'What are you up to these days, George? Livvy tells me you're in the City.'

'For my pains. I'm with an American outfit – Bartle Greenberg?'

'Sure. My dad was on the board. He may still be, now I think of it. What's your area?'

'Capital markets, new issues – that was the idea. What you end up doing is always rather different; sixty per cent trouble-shooting, thirty per cent sitting on planes, ten per cent sacking people. I hear you met Livvy on location – is that what you people call it?'

Justus looked at Olivia with loving eyes. 'That's right. She fell into my lap, so to speak. Out of the blue. I didn't even know she was living in Rome.'

'Nor,' George smiled archly, 'did anyone else.'

'A lady of mystery.' Olivia grimaced at Justus in the middle of talking to Pip.

'So you're all set for the wedding? Congratulations, by the way.'

'She wasn't easy to persuade, but after I'd beat her up a couple of times, pulled out the old photos and threatened to sell the negs to the *National Enquirer*, she finally gave in. Can I offer you a drink, George?'

Olivia put down the phone. 'George has to get back home. He was being gentlemanly escorting me to the door but he has to drive all the way back to Suffolk.'

'Oh, I don't think I'll go down tonight.'

'You must, really. Sarah will be waiting.'

'Give her my best, will you, George? I hope we'll be seeing you at the wedding – if Livvy ever gets round to booking a day.'

'Wild horses wouldn't keep me away.' George stood his ground looking at Olivia, who was trying to lead him towards the door. 'I'll give you a call tomorrow, Livvy . . . Don't worry about that woman in the restaurant, will you?'

When they were alone Justus put his arms around her. 'Woman in the restaurant?'

'No one. A fortune-teller.'

'Oh, yeah? What did she say?'

'Wouldn't you like to know?' Olivia ruffled his hair. 'She said I was getting married, and I hadn't been happy, but I would be, and that it was all about love, and there was someone I'd known a long, long time ago . . .'

'And I'll bet George thought that meant him?' One expressive eyebrow lifted.

'Oh, I don't know about that. He's just being protective.'

'He thinks you need protecting from me?'

'No, he thinks I need protecting from *me*.'

'Olivia, when we're an old married couple, will you still talk in riddles?'

'Will you still want me to?'

'No. More than anything, I want to know you, all about you. I want to know what you're like when you've got a headache, and what you'll look like when you're sixty, and whether you'll get ingrown toenails.'

'God – how romantic! Aren't those things better left covered by a discreet veil?'

'No. I want to know everything that affects you.'

'Then you shall, I promise. The first thing is I'm a martyr to jet-lag.'

'You're tired? You want to go to bed?'

'I want to go to bed, but I'm not tired. How about you?'

'I don't remember feeling more awake.'

Olivia was no longer nervous in bed with Justus; she had been, electrically so, during their first few weeks of renewed courtship in Rome. She had been apprehensive that her memory may have cheated her – could it be as good as it used to be, could it possibly be as good as she had remembered? Torn between the horror that she would disappoint, and the dread of her own disillusionment, she had decided to do it and be damned. It had all been far more straightforward than she had expected. Justus was at ease and in control: he acted as if a week had passed rather than a decade, and the languorous release she found with him was an acceptable replacement for erotic obsession.

'Justus? What would have happened to us if we hadn't suddenly met in Rome?'

'No point asking. We did.'

'But if we *hadn't*?'

'I guess I'd have been described in the trade as a "confirmed bachelor", with all sorts of speculation about my sexual orientation. In time I'd have been forced into a marriage of convenience, probably to my agent.'

'Laura? You're crazy about her.'

'I am, but not so's I want to spend the rest of my natural life with her.'

'I bet you'd have made a star-studded match with some actress. I'd've read about it in the papers, and thought, If only.'

'No, you wouldn't. You'd have thought, Stupid schmuck. So what would have happened to you if we hadn't met?'

'If you hadn't picked me off the shelf? I'd have stayed on it.'

'Crap. You've never been on a shelf, you've just been on a pedestal.'

'Same difference.' She rolled on to her tummy to look him in the eye. 'I had a terrible time with Jerry.'

'You saw him again?'

'We all went down to George's for a reunion weekend. The highlight was watching you on Barry Norman.'

'So that's it . . . I thought you'd shut down on me. You're pissed because I talked about you.'

'God, no, I was glad. It made it seem definite for the first time.'

'It better be definite. That thing on your finger didn't come out of a box of Crackerjack.'

'It made it *public* was what I meant. Up until now, it's just been you and me.'

'That's the point of getting married, isn't it, the public commitment, having witnesses? So you told them all the news?'

'Um-hmm. Pip was thrilled, but she'd rather you married Ophélie.'

'And Jerry?'

'He didn't really comment. He wanted to talk about the old days, and I didn't.'

'You never do.'

Olivia looked at him gravely, her eyes nearly black in the dim light of the bedroom. 'You're quite wrong. I'm perfectly willing to talk about it to you, so long as you don't overreact.'

'Me? Overreact? That's a capital offence in my line of work.'

'Justus, when you left England, in eighty-six, do you remember what you said to me?'

'Yeah, I said I was catching the next flight to New York for an audition. I called you from the airport. And I said I'd come right back.'

'I don't mean to be a pedant, but actually you said you'd be in touch.'

'And I was. I called a couple of weeks later. You'd already gone away.'

'It wasn't a couple of weeks. It was over a month later.'

'Maybe three, maybe four weeks. I called when I'd got everything sorted out. George or Jerry or one of them told me you'd gone away and they didn't have an address. The trail ended there.'

And you didn't once try to look for me, Olivia thought, knowing she couldn't blame him for that. 'Before you left, do you remember what we said, what we agreed?'

'Sure I do. We've already been through this. We agreed that whatever had happened between us, we weren't going to talk about it, and we weren't going to pursue it, because you felt so bad about Jerry. It was your idea to call a halt, Livvy, not mine.'

'You didn't take a lot of persuading.'

'Jesus, what was I meant to say? No way? Challenge Jerry to a duel? You have a pretty selective memory, if you don't mind me saying. You told me straight up that you had zero interest in commitment. You said there was a lot to do in life, and you didn't want to be tied down to anyone. You said it wasn't meant to be.'

'I know, I just didn't expect you to accept it.'

'We're not all patsies. Jeez, Olivia, I watched you that last year running rings round Jerry, blowing hot and cold. You think I wanted to put myself in his shoes?'

'So what changed?'

'You did, you fool. You stopped being a bitch. When I met you in Rome you were a completely different woman – just as attractive, but a hell of a lot nicer.'

Olivia climbed out of bed and slipped on his discarded shirt, slowly doing up the buttons while she thought how to voice what she needed to tell him. 'Justus. I know you didn't call for a month, because a week after you left I found out I was pregnant.' She shook her head at the startled expression on his face. 'No, I'm not about to present you with a ready-made ten-year-old child. I'm not sure I'm doing the right thing to raise it even now, but you said you wanted to know about my toenails, so I guess you ought to know about this. I was pregnant, but I didn't know if it was you or Jerry. I didn't do anything at all for ten days. I couldn't tell Jerry about us, I just couldn't, and I couldn't tell Jerry I was pregnant and not tell him about you. You didn't phone, but that wasn't the point – I don't even know that I'd have told you if you had. I spent almost a whole week in the loo, praying I was wrong, and that it was a mistake. In the end I told Pip, and she helped me arrange an abortion.'

'I left you my parents' number. You could have called me.'

'How could I? I'd said goodbye, I'd decided it was over. How could I have called you and said, I've changed my mind, and by the way . . . ? Look, Justus, I wasn't even thinking of you. I hate to say this, I do, but if I'm honest then I was only thinking about me, and thinking that my life was over unless suddenly it hadn't happened at all. I was completely selfish. I was for years. Do you know the funny thing?'

Justus wore a puzzled, veiled expression as he considered how he should react. Olivia lifted herself up so that she was sitting on the dressing table, swinging her legs. 'The funny thing is I don't feel guilty, or ashamed. I don't feel scarred. I don't remember it very well at all. Sometimes I'm not even sure it happened – it felt like an episode from somebody else's life that I'd picked up at a cocktail party.'

'Then why did you run away?'

'It didn't feel like running away. I just didn't know who I was. I didn't want to have to discuss it with everybody, pick over it all, you know, have people telling me exactly what I should feel, until I'd gathered myself together. It just took a lot longer than I thought it would, and by that time there didn't seem to be any point in coming back. I don't think I would have brought it up, ever, but that weekend, the weekend we were all in Suffolk, it came up.'

'You told everyone?'

'Not the way I just told you, but sort of. We were playing Spin the Bottle.'

Justus got out of bed and walked to the window. Olivia stared at his silhouette against the street-lamps' peachy glow and took a packet of cigarettes out of her bag. He turned around as she lit one.

'Boy, you're full of surprises tonight. Is there anything else I should know?'

'No. That's everything, really.'

'Good. Let's get some sleep, OK? I've got to get back to the set in the morning.'

'I assumed you'd finished the shoot.'

'Nope. I just dashed back to see you. A romantic gesture. I guess it's a good thing I did.'

'Oh, Justus, I'm sorry . . . I've been wanting to get everything straight, clear up all the loose ends . . . How's it all going?'

'Olivia, I'm real tired. Let's leave it for tonight. And put that thing out – it'll kill you, and you'll smell like an ashtray.'

Fifteen minutes later Justus reached across the wide bed and pulled Olivia close against him. A man who believed in facing adversity with courage and the future with confidence, he was not prepared to let the past, however surprising, interfere with his plans.

'Livvy,' he murmured into her hair, knowing she was still awake, 'just book the day, OK? Book the day, and I promise you everything will be all right. I'm glad you told me. I love you. You can even smoke, for all I care. Just not in the bedroom.'

# The Rules of the Game 5

**Oxford, April 1986**

'Come. Please.'
  'I'd rather have lunch at the Trout.'
'We can do that first.'
'I can't understand how you have the nerve to turn up at the funeral of someone you don't even know. It's morbid. It's preposterous.'
'Don't be so narrow-minded.'
They were sitting in a carrel of the English Faculty Library; Jerry had a copy of the *Guardian* unfolded on to the gazette entries of births, marriages and deaths, and had circled one of the deaths with a red pen:

**Swithun, Arthur Geoffrey (Lord Swithun of Felpisham)** died on Friday 3 April in the John Radcliffe Hospital Oxford. Funeral on Friday 10 April at 2 p.m. in the Oxford Crematorium. No flowers by request, but if desired, contributions to Student Hardship Fund, c/o Vice Chancellor, Sheffield University, would be very welcome.

'It's disgusting,' Olivia hissed. She had four or five books strewn on the desk in front of her, but hadn't looked at them since Jerry's unannounced arrival. 'If you feel so moved, why not just make a donation? Going in person is so . . . weird.'

'Don't knock it till you've tried it.'

'What if they ask who we are? What if they work out that we didn't know him?'

'It's a mark of respect. Why should it piss off the family?'

'There's something very odd about you – very odd indeed. Occasional bursts of eccentricity are all very well, but this is something else . . . I don't know whether to blame your mother, or blame Pusey House, or Hinduism or what, but whichever it is there is some part of your poor brain that's just not properly connected. Maybe there was too much algae in your gene pool.'

It had taken Olivia a week from their auspicious meeting at the start of their second year to piece together Jerry's brief biography. He was the second son and third of five children sprung from the loins of a psychotherapist mother and an academic father who lived outside Cambridge; he had flourished at a highly successful grammar school, and won a scholarship to New College to read PPE, but had rapidly dropped economics; politics bored him and he abhorred most sports – certainly all sports that required 'team spirit'. She had seen immediately that he had a natural rapport with women and animals, but there were several things about Jerry that Olivia discovered more slowly. It had taken him three months to tell her, for example, that he had spent much of his first year at Oxford dallying with the Jesuits of Pusey House while flirting with Hindu mysticism, finally deciding at the end of his first summer term to quit Oxford and become a Vaishnav monk. For ten weeks of that summer vac he accepted the full austerities of the discipline – no meat, no fish, no hot water, what food he ate taken cold, meditation six hours a day, six days a week, until his therapist mother drove him back to Oxford, took him to dinner at the Elizabeth and told him he would have plenty of time to subdue the flesh and channel his emotions after he had completed his degree. Some three weeks later, Olivia had run him down in Radcliffe Square. Only three weeks after that, he told her that he adored her, and always would. Only when she had pressed him about his frequent disappearances had he confided that his primary interest outside the mystics was attending the funerals of complete strangers.

'You're quite wrong. It is far more normal and healthy to embrace death as part of life than to be terrified of it.'

'OK, Jerry, I'll come with you just this once, but if we get caught I'll say you drugged me, kidnapped me and brainwashed me. What shall I wear?'

'I don't think Swithun, Arthur Geoffrey, will mind much.'

When they left the Trout at one thirty the following day, Jerry opened the boot of Olivia's car, took out a carrier bag and stripped off his upper clothes in the car park. Olivia leaned against the car watching him in disbelief.

'I've met blokes who keep their football kit in the boot of the car, but having funeral kit is ridiculous.'

When he'd exchanged his T-shirt for a white shirt, plain tie and dark jacket worn over faded jeans, he jerked his head towards the small suitcase in the boot.

'Don't call me ridiculous, Liv, not given your double-0 seven escape bag. In the realm of human eccentricities, that would bring to mind the old pot-and-kettle dispute.'

'The fact that I keep an emergency overnight bag in the back of my car cannot compare to your obsession with funerals. Mine is perfectly sensible – if I ever have to go somewhere suddenly, I've got a toothbrush and a clean pair of knickers in the car. Are you going to give me directions? I haven't got a clue where this place is.'

'The Crematorium? I know it like the back of my hand.' Olivia gagged at the wheel. 'I promise you, you'll feel perfectly at home – he's bound to have been an academic, definitely an Oxford man, what could be more natural than students turning up to pay their last respects?'

When they arrived the room was full, but they were able to slip into a back row, nodding at the elderly couple who squeezed up to make room for them. Throughout the service Olivia kept her eyes on the floor or on the order of service that had been handed to them at the door. Jerry sprawled back in his seat, gazing around the room and nodding at fellow mourners like long-lost friends. During the address he leaned forward and his face mirrored the changing sentiments of the speaker. Olivia was terrified he would burst into applause if not tears, but the service was over mercifully quickly and without disgrace. She leaped to her feet as the final chords of the hymn died out, and grabbed Jerry's hand.

'Come on – let's get out of here before the family spots us.'

Instead, Jerry held her hand tightly to his side and pulled her towards the front of the room where an elderly lady in a pale blue suit and hat stood surrounded by members of the congregation patiently waiting their turn to speak to the widow. She turned from person to person, pressing hands, smiling, offering her powdered cheek to friends, as a middle-aged man and woman stood supportively behind her. As Jerry and Olivia took their place in the impromptu queue Olivia's eyes again returned to the floor, and she found herself praying. She did not see the widow's eyes rest on Jerry, turn quickly to her son behind her, and then back, with a slightly embarrassed query.

'Lady Swithun? I'm Jerry Milton. That was a very powerful service – a great tribute.'

'It was, wasn't it? I'm so glad you thought so too. I've been dreading it, yet I found it rather uplifting. Arthur would have been very touched so many came, I'm sure of that.'

'He certainly would, not that I knew him very well. I regret that I didn't have the chance to know him better.'

'So many of his young people have said that to me . . . Arthur was so very fond of his students. You knew him from Balliol?'

'Indirectly, yes.'

'I hope you'll come back to the college with us for a drink. Arthur was most insistent when we discussed the arrangements that everyone should be offered a decent drink after the funeral – you'll remember what a stickler he was for social etiquette, dear man . . .' As she sniffed, her son put one hand lightly on her back and one on Jerry's, urging them gently but persuasively down the aisle. Outside the crematorium, Lady Swithun pressed Jerry's hand again. 'You will come back to the SCR, won't you – Jerry, is it, and . . .?'

'Olivia – Olivia Fletcher-Smith,' Jerry volunteered. 'Yes, of course we will. We would be delighted.'

'There's some sort of transport, a bus, if you don't have a car . . . You must meet the rest of the family,' she ended brightly. 'Everyone's managed to come back – Helen even flew in on Tuesday from California, bless her.'

As Jerry dropped behind the straggling line of mourners making their way towards their cars Olivia's grip on his hand tightened. 'We *can't* go to Balliol,' she whispered urgently.

'Don't be ridiculous. These people don't care about how or why you knew him, or whether you knew him at all. They deserve the assurance that he was loved and will be remembered.'

'And exactly how are you going to do that?'

'I do remember him vaguely, I went to a lecture of his in my first term, but that's not important. What matters is recognising him as an individual, acknowledging he lived, the people he loved and influenced. I'll remember his cremation and the faces of his family, and so remember him.'

An hour later, Olivia leaned against the panelled wall of the Balliol SCR smoking a cigarette. Jerry was sitting with Lord Swithun's daughter-in-law, his head bent close to hers, listening intently. Olivia saw him smile and make a comment that she couldn't hear, but the woman laughed loudly enough to show the fillings in her upper teeth, and the sound made the widow turn and smile in relief. Two old men approached Olivia and refilled her glass.

'Were you a pupil of Arthur's, my dear?' one asked.

'No, I'm sorry but I never met him. My boyfriend,' Olivia pointed to Jerry, 'was very keen to come.'

'Arthur would have been tickled pink to see all these young things show up for his final bash. I won't get half this turn-out when my own time comes to meet my Maker.'

'You won't get a tenth of it, old boy,' his companion corrected. 'Not sure I'll bother to tip up myself!'

'What was Lord Swithun like?'

'Putting aside his obsession with disproving the Albigensian myth – and that messy business with Harold Wilson – he was the ideal sort of chap to have around college, a man of great loyalty, and considerable vision. And, of course, a great family man, something academic life rarely encourages . . .'

The two old men began a discussion in which Olivia was no more than an attractive and outwardly attentive centrepiece. While she pretended to listen to them, she watched Jerry moving around the room, solicitous, thoughtful and entirely at ease, like the documentaries she had seen of elephants tenderly and respectfully nosing around a dead member of the herd.

As the guests began to leave, Jerry rejoined her. 'Are you itching to go?' he asked.

'Only if you're ready.'

When they said goodbye to Lady Swithun she kissed Jerry's cheek, then patted it with her gloved hand. 'You have such a look of him, when we first met. It's quite uncanny. He was very much like you. Now, you will remember to come next month, won't you? I'd like to know you had something of Arthur's to remember him by. Just phone Mallam's for the date, and join us for dinner afterwards? Your young lady's most welcome to come.'

Before she started the ignition, Olivia gripped the steering wheel and peered ahead through the windscreen.

'Just tell me why you like going to funerals. Just explain.'

'I don't like the idea of a death, a life, being unrecorded – any life. There's a great deal to learn from observing that final passing, seeing who and what mattered to an individual, what they leave behind. I almost always feel like a member of the family. I can't really explain it, but I do. It moves me intensely.'

'But, Jerry, you're going to the funerals of relatively famous people – people whose death notices go in *The Times*, not some nameless, penniless, lonely stranger.'

'I've been to all sorts of funerals. I admit I haven't often been to the funeral of a homeless person, or a beggar, but that's not because I don't want to. I've quite often stopped and followed a hearse.'

'You'd better be at my funeral.'

'I wouldn't miss it for the world.'

'In the meantime, would you kiss me?'

'It would be an enormous pleasure.'

## three swords plunged through a heart . . .

From the outside, the house looked like a perfectly ordinary Hammersmith house. There were no crystal balls hanging, no inner eye painted on the white front door. The door was opened by a boy Olivia guessed to be about fifteen; he stepped aside to let her in and shouted up the stairs, 'Mum! Your lady's here for you.' Perhaps divination had been passed on genetically, or perhaps Olivia looked like all the other mixed-up hopefuls who came to Rosie Ferguson for Tarot readings and directions of a spiritual sort. Inside, the house was disorderly, littered with sports equipment, school satchels, books thrown everywhere and the hall made near impassable by assorted pots of paint. A woman came down the stairs wiping her hands on a rag. She was wearing jeans and a man's shirt, and had her long dark hair pulled into a pony-tail that gave her a chaotic and youthful appearance. She looked rather as Olivia herself might in ten years' time.

'You must be Olivia. I'm Rosie. No trouble finding the house, I hope? Come upstairs, but watch where you walk – we're redecorating. At least, my son and my husband are meant to be redecorating, but they keep getting called to higher things, like football, so I'm doing most of it. And, as I'm sure I don't have to tell you, I'm not very good at it.' She opened a door into a small, neat room with a sofa on one side and a couple of armchairs drawn up around a low wooden table. Above the fireplace were family photographs, a lurid abstract painting and a small flowerpot overflowing with trailing geraniums. Olivia made a vague gesture around the room.

'It's not what you expected? You thought there'd be hocus-pocus? Charts of the zodiac, curtains showing the celestial symbols? A black cat kneading the sofa? I bet you thought I'd have grey hair, and wear a long robe of some indescribably rich foreign fabric.' Olivia smiled ruefully. She'd been given Rosie's phone number by an eccentric Italian friend who had once lived in London and swore by her, and Olivia had indeed expected something on the far side of wacky. 'Don't worry about it. I don't go in for that sort of stuff. Have you had a Tarot reading before?'

'No. My mother used to do it, just for her own benefit, and that sort of put me off.'

'I can identify with that. My mother used to cook – for her own benefit too – and that *really* put me off. I can't boil an egg – well, of course I can, but I certainly can't scramble one. However, I've been studying the Tarot for nearly twenty years, and I'm relatively competent, as much as one can be. Sit down wherever you like and get comfortable – you don't have to take your shoes off, unless you want to, and I won't ask you to close your eyes or imagine you're lying in a field of daffodils or meditate on a small bowl of water. Would you like something to drink? Tea, water . . . I can normally persuade Sam to waiter for a small cash incentive – Sam!' she shouted, before Olivia had a chance to reply. 'Put the kettle on, would you?' She sat opposite Olivia in one of the armchairs. 'Now. Do you have any questions before we begin?'

'Do you do this for a living? Is it your job?'

'I *wish*. No, I'm a GP. I've always been interested in the Tarot as a route to the subconscious, and as a meditational aid. I did it purely for myself for many years, and then I started doing readings for friends, and it grew from there. Are you asking if I'm a registered professional?'

'No, not at all – I'm quite happy with whatever you are.'

'There isn't really an official body of approved Tarot readers. There's some sort of society of psychics and clairvoyants, of which I'm not a member. Whatever the outcome of your reading I will not tell that you're about to go on a long journey to a hot country, that you'll have three children, or that you're likely to receive unexpected news in the form of a letter or telegram. OK? I *certainly* won't tell you you're about to win the lottery. There may be people who can do that, but it ain't me.'

'So the Tarot can't predict the future?'

Rosie Ferguson thought for a moment, then sighed. 'Let's say prediction isn't its primary or most beneficial function, even if it can be bent to that. It isn't magic. I like to say it's a way of reading certain unconscious patterns. The cards represent universal symbols, they have meanings that are ascribed by tradition, and although I can guide you as to their meaning, only you will know what they really mean within a specific context. It isn't my role to predict the future – that would imply you have no free will, and can never live freely, and it would be unfair to make heavily suggestive statements. People who do that are exploiting vulnerability.' She screwed her face up. 'Does any of this make sense to you, or am I bullshitting? Do say.'

'No, it makes sense. I'm not really so suspicious.'

'Suspicion is healthy. Now, the only thing I have to ask you is what you want to know from the readings: do you have a question about a specific situation, or a decision you need to take, or are you looking for a more general summary of your overall position?'

'I want it all. General, specific. Most of all I want to know if I should marry the man I'm engaged to.'

Rosie glanced at Olivia's left hand. 'I'm tempted to say stuff the cards and grab him – that's one hell of a rock you've got there. Sorry. Flippancy is my worst trait. Good boy!' Sam appeared with a tea-tray and left it on the side with an adolescent grunt-and-shrug combination. 'Olivia – let's see what comes up. Think about the specific question, and we may get a general direction as well. While we're preparing, I ask you to be quiet, and breathe deeply – we're not looking for a trance here, just a small spell of peace.'

She instructed Olivia to shuffle the pack of cards and cut them three times, then to pass them back to her. She dealt them face up, placing each card in a specific position. One central card, the second laid horizontally over it; four surrounding the cross, and four going up the right-hand side. Olivia suppressed a desire to laugh.

'We call this the Celtic Cross spread. It's the most traditional of the Tarot spreads.'

'It's funny – until now I could never have described it, but I watched my mother do this almost every day. It's odd that I had completely forgotten it.'

'I don't know that it's odd. There are memories that can be unlocked, and picked over in recall, others tend just to wash in and out.' Rosie bent low over the table, looking at the cards. Olivia leaned back. It looked rather dull; she'd hoped for a dramatic array of portentous cards – Death, the Hanged Man, the Moon, but instead she'd been dealt a motley run of numbers. She felt inclined to ask for a second bash, just as she used to restart Patience when the outcome did not look promising. Rosie covered her mouth with the fingers of both hands, her chin resting on her thumbs, and studied the cards in silence.

'Well, this certainly addresses your central question. I should also say that these cards point to a considerable amount of struggle in your past.' Her index finger trailed over the three cards on either side and below the cross. 'It's the preponderance of Swords. As a suit, they indicate suffering.' As she talked, her gentle eyes kept flicking to Olivia's downcast face. 'Let's go through them in the order you placed them. This first card tells how you feel about this question, and it is very fitting that it is The Lovers. It puts your relationship as the central issue. It represents all that is human in the ways of love, the mysteries of the male and female relationship. Look at the image, Olivia. What does it mean to you?'

'Well, they're naked. Am I being too obvious? There's a tree behind each of them, and a snake on the one behind the woman, so I guess it's the Garden of Eden or something. Adam and Eve. Jack and Jill.'

'The traditional reading would be that you need to look closely at this relationship, to decide if it's what you really want.'

'Is it significant that the man's looking at the woman and she's not looking at him?'

'It could be. Is that significant to you? It could be that there's a need for more spiritual values; it could be that attraction can only be resolved by commitment and decision. It's very striking that The Lovers are crossed by the Three of Swords.' Rosie's fingernail tapped the card that she had placed second. 'That would imply to me that something's not right with this relationship and, seeing the two cards together, it's quite clear that there is a very important issue here, about this man. The Three of Swords on its own carries with it feelings of separation and loneliness, perhaps deep distress, and possible problems due to disloyalty.'

'Yes, OK.' Olivia licked her lips and pushed her hair back.

'Olivia,' Rose continued softly, 'I see a lot of sadness in these cards. This one below The Lovers, the Nine of Swords; the position of the card represents the root of your situation. This is a card of mental pain, a difficult and confusing past – perhaps something to run away from? The fact that this card has appeared signals we need to analyse the spread very carefully. It indicates desolation. Do you want to look at it?'

'Not very much,' Olivia said, nonetheless leaning closer. The card showed a woman sitting up in bed with her hands covering her face; nine swords hung on the wall above her. 'I can't say it means much to me, but it's not very uplifting, is it? It's clearly not a good omen.'

'You mustn't try to see it – any of the cards – as an omen exactly. It is what colours and imbues your current situation, the wash, if you like. It is not an entirely negative card. It also has the interpretation of someone who is able to free themselves from sorrow by turning it into wisdom.'

'If I could do that, I wouldn't be here, would I?'

'Perhaps that's why you *are* here . . . To the left of the cross you have the Eight of Swords.'

The card depicted a bound and blindfolded woman in a barren landscape, surrounded by eight swords plunged into the ground.

'She doesn't look like happy families, either.'

'This represents what you are in the process of leaving. The image of the blind is key – the interpretation is very much of feeling trapped, confusion, isolation. It carries a great deal of anxiety, and the sense that you feel unable to make decisions. Olivia?' Rosie covered one of Olivia's hands with her own. 'Are you all right? Does this make any sense? Would you like to ask anything?'

'No.' Olivia leaned back away from Rosie. The cards made perfect sense in the way that an abstract painting does; perfect sense, that is, until an expert begins to explain it, when it suddenly ceases to mean anything at all. She knew that the three swords plunged through a heart represented Justus, Jerry and George; whose heart they pierced she did not choose to know. 'They all look awful and ominous. Don't even tell me what *that* one means.'

She stabbed a card to the right of the central cross with her finger, the Six of Swords.

Rosie continued in sequence. 'The crowning card, this one at the top, is the Ace of Cups, which represents the principle of Love. It is this quality that informs the whole reading, this quality that you want to bring into being. It is the seed of love and joy.'

'I bet you say that to everyone.'

'To anyone who is dealt exactly these cards in this position, yes. I can't say I've ever seen a spread like this before. The card you fear isn't a bad one.'

'I thought you said all the Sword cards were bad?'

'Not at all. They represent adversity, not defeat. The Six of Swords, in this position, is not negative. It is what we term the passageway card, what lies ahead and must be travelled through, what must be faced. What does the image say to you?'

'The river Styx. The boatman. "Guide me o'er, thou Great Redeemer". Death. A shrouded woman. It looks like there's somebody next to her in the boat – a child? I don't know. Look at them all – arms behind their backs, hands over their faces, blindfold, bound. I don't seem to have one woman who's showing her eyes, or looking directly. Aren't there any in the deck?'

'Oh, yes, there are some ahead. Olivia, the cards are designed as eternal and absolute symbols. They are intended to be strong images, but not to be taken literally. If you see images of blinding and binding, you need to explore which aspects of yourself these may reflect on. The cards do not concern physical reality – they are symbols only, if powerful ones. The Six of Swords tells me that there is a spiritual journey that you need to make, and indicates mourning, an old sorrow, but a sorrow that you may have felt for so long that you no longer feel pain, it has become a part of life.'

'Look, if you're talking about the fact that I had an abortion ten years ago, I have to tell you that's not something I've been suffering over. I don't have any deep, long-buried angst about it at all.'

'I must repeat the cards cannot be that specific. I would not have interpreted this card around the mourning of a baby, although the second card, the Three of Swords, can refer to miscarriage or termination. I would not have mentioned it myself. As I said, I do not believe the cards deal with actuality so much as states of consciousness. What I say may not mean anything to you, or it may mean a great deal. The Six of Swords can represent a journey by water. It certainly speaks to me of spiritual evolution and the way ahead. It is the bridge card into the rest of the spread.'

'Which says?'

'At the base we have the Two of Cups, again a male/female image, one of love and friendship, and representing what you wish to achieve. It indicates deep understanding, the binding of two hearts in a common purpose, a nurturing and inspired love. What does it mean to you?'

'Jack and Jill with clothes on. So that's me and my fiancé?'

'No. The position of the card relates to you yourself, and your own needs and feelings. It also, in repeating the suit of Cups, reaffirms that the overall principle to you, the matter of import, is love. The card above it is The Wheel of Fortune, followed by The Empress and The Tower, which gives a very strong final reading – there are four of the Major Arcana cards here.'

'I don't understand all the mumbo-jumbo . . .'

'The appearance of the Major Arcana, what you might think of as the medieval symbol cards – The Moon, The Sun, The High Priestess, et cetera – informs the reader that there is a strong and general message in the Tarot. It is, if you like, an indication of significance.'

'Well, great. I need all the help I can get.'

'The Wheel of Fortune describes the surrounding situation. It indicates the broad picture, the general state of play. It is a karmic symbol.'

'The Samsara, right?'

'Yes, that's part of it.'

'I had a boyfriend once who was really into all that stuff – Hinduism, laws of karma, harmony, wheel of life, rebirth, the works. I can't say I had much time for it all.'

'Perhaps you do now. Its appearance here implies that things are not quite as they seem. You may need to re-evaluate – as the wheel has turned, your needs may have changed. It is a symbol of transformation and rebirth. The fact that The Empress lies above it is very positive – The Empress is a strong card, symbolic of the female principle. This card,' Rosie's finger stroked the image, 'conveys sensuality and sexuality, in a grounded woman. The Empress is the bestower of life and love. She also takes them away. It is the card that denotes individuation, being in control of your own sexuality and sensuality.'

'That sounds good at last. So I'll achieve that when I marry Justus?'

Rosie did not reply directly; her face was veiled. 'The tenth card portrays the outcome of the decision under review.' She sighed. 'The Tower is such a powerful card, particularly in this final position, that I would have to advise you to take stock of what you are doing – take a long, cool look at what you are about to do.'

Olivia twisted her head to study the card. There was a lot of black in the picture, and the top of the tower had been struck by lightning and erupted into flames, sending a crown toppling. Two figures were in free-fall – a bareheaded man and a crowned woman. 'It looks to me like Jack and Jill falling down the hill, Jack broke his crown, Jill put it on and came tumbling after.'

'Nursery rhymes also work through eternal symbols, Olivia. I once had a patient who told me she habitually recited nursery rhymes during intercourse. I probably shouldn't repeat that, but it's always struck me as fascinating. Now, where was I? The Tower. Well, the Tower represents a shattering of dreams, also perhaps a shattering of personality. Change is inevitable. I feel obliged to say that, according to the wisdom of the Tarot, the outcome of this relationship is not positive. It is an image of collapse and disintegration – perhaps occurring most where you seek to protect yourself, in a metaphorical tower? Do you feel secure with this man? Is that his attraction?'

Olivia shook her head, but more in disbelief than total disagreement.

'The Tower is not a bad image, even if it does not bode well for your current relationship. It does imply a break from the past, a release from the old life. Sitting as it does above The Empress, I feel that your own instincts are against this relationship. The overall reading is that we are talking about a real relationship, not the fantasy of or desire for one, and although all the cards are significant, the one and two cards – The Lovers and the Three of Swords – balanced by the two final cards, The Empress and The Tower – would lead me to say that you are on the right path to fulfilment and release from a path of pain, but this relationship is not the way. You may risk everything.'

Neither of them spoke. Every sound in the house became distinct to Olivia in the hush of that room: she could hear a clock ticking slowly, and Rosie's son whistling reedily somewhere downstairs. She could hear the sound of her own breath.

'Well. That's quite an eye-opener.'

'Is it? I had the feeling nothing surprised you very much.'

'I'm surprised that it meant anything at all. I'm rather a sceptic when it comes to fortune-telling.'

'You know, Christianity and most other religions take a very dim view of fortune-telling. They are almost universally opposed to it. I suppose if you accept predestination, and thus the possibility of predicting the future, you deny the notion of free will and responsibility. It's very important to remember that you have choices – many. The goal is to make those choices from an informed and responsible position. You make your own history, don't you agree?'

'What happens to fate? To things that just happen, with no input from anybody else?'

Rosie looked puzzled. 'Give me an example.'

'I knew my fiancé a long time ago. We weren't engaged then, or anything. We lost touch. A few months ago I bumped into him completely by chance. Neither of us had any intention of meeting. I didn't even know he was in the same country.'

'And?'

'Well, isn't that significant?'

'Let me tell you a story – not one that reflects well on me, but never mind that. When I was a little girl, a bird built its nest on the balcony that faced our back garden. My parents wouldn't let me have any pets, so I adopted this bird and cared for it as if it belonged to me. I thought it had been specifically sent to me. I fed it scraps of bacon rind, and crusts of bread, and one day I was delighted to see four little eggs in the nest. A couple of days later, I was coming in from the garden when I felt something on my head and put my hand up to find my hair covered in bird-shit. I looked up, and there was my own little bird, its bottom waggling over the edge of the nest, just over my head. I got a broom from the kitchen, marched straight upstairs, flung open the window and swept the nest off. The eggs smashed, the mother bird flew away, and I never told anyone.' Olivia smiled: the image of the outraged little girl was vivid, and the crime not so very great. 'I know it sounds funny, but the thing is I connected each action together: my need to love, the bird's nourishment, its betrayal. I made a

215

connection that wasn't there. The bird had no idea where the bacon rind came from, nor did it know who stood below when it crapped. There was, if you like, no *significance* in the crap.'

Olivia laughed out loud and Rosie joined her. 'It's a good thing I'm not earning my living telling parables – I wouldn't get very far. What I'm trying to say is that just because you and this man happened to be in the same place at the same time doesn't mean you need to marry him.'

'I love him; he loves me.'

'That's a completely different issue then. Forget my bird, OK? You can forget all about the reading, too, if you like. What you might want to remember is why you came in the first place. Were you looking for an excuse to call this off, or were you looking for some outside force to confirm that it was the right way to go? You should trust yourself a little more.'

'Do you mind if I write down the cards that came up? Can I borrow a bit of paper?'

'I'll even let you have one, I'm that generous.' Olivia quickly sketched out the Celtic Cross as Rosie watched her. 'Ask your mother how she'd interpret the reading – it never hurts to have a second opinion.'

'I'd never do that. I haven't asked her opinion about anything since I was five years old.'

'Hello, Dad. It's Olivia.'

'Sweetheart! How's old London town?'

'The same as ever. How are you?'

'As well as can be expected. Not as young as I was, of course, but there's life in the old dog yet. Have you set a date for the wedding? We need to make plans if you and Justus are still set on this summer. We're due to attend an opening in Paris, and I thought I'd take the opportunity of seeing my tailor while we're with you. We'll also need a room at Claridge's – they get so busy in the summer with all those travelling Americans. Could you possibly pop in and book us a room as soon as you've picked your day?'

'Yes, Dad, I will. Is Mother there?'

'Your mother? Would you like to speak to her?'

'Don't sound so surprised.' Olivia could hear him calling through the apartment, 'Darling? Darling! Olivia wants a word . . .'

'Mother? I wanted to ask you something . . .'

'I'm honoured. I thought I was too démodé to be of any use to you. What is it? Is it your dress, or have you finally decided to have a reception?'

'Mother, I want to ask you about the Tarot.'

She could hear her mother dragging on a cigarette, and imagined her lips releasing a thin trail of smoke. She could visualise her mother's cheekbones in sharp relief as she sucked in the smoke, her well-cared-for skin nonetheless crazed with fine lines like a porcelain heirloom.

'Go on.'

'I had a Tarot reading today.' Olivia looked down at the sketch she had placed on the table before her. 'About marrying Justus. What does The Tower mean to you?'

'Oh, Olivia, so many things. Where did it come? What surrounds it? You are far too inclined to look at these things simplistically. It is a very complicated art; it takes time to know the wisdom. I would need to see all the cards.'

'Have you still got your pack?'

'Of course.'

'Would you go and get it?'

She knew her mother would be torn between curiosity and reluctance to do as she was asked without seizing the opportunity to complain about it. Domenica permitted herself one small, world-weary sigh, then, 'All right.' Olivia described the position of the cards one by one so her mother could lay them out in Rome. 'Well? What do you think?'

'What were you told?'

'That I shouldn't marry Justus. That was the gist of it.' Olivia waited, amazed at herself. If anyone had ever told her she'd find herself connected to her mother via a telephonic Tarot reading while they both smoked she would have laughed herself sick. 'Well?'

'There is no single message. Whoever you saw can't have any feeling for the cards. I would say the reading says you *should* marry Justus.'

'And what about The Tower?'

'The Tower signifies a break from things past. Justus will lead you to a new life. Darling, even you must admit that anything would be better than rotting away teaching ungrateful children for the rest of your life. If old ties are to be broken, that must be a good sign, no?'

'Talking of old ties, Mother, why didn't you tell me that Jerry came to Rome?'

'Tsk. I'm sure we did. You were a very determined woman at twenty-one. You made it clear – very – that whatever had happened in Oxford had not resolved any of your problems or your restlessness. I knew Oxford was always a mistake for you, and it was only your contrariness, your stubborn refusal to take my advice, that made you insist on going there. That's probably where all this nonsense about teaching came from. You must remember telling us you did not want to go back to England and that you wished to close the door. If your father and I chose to obey your instructions, you should not reprimand us for that. We had your best interests at heart, as we always have – not that you have ever given us credit for it.'

'But you did see Jerry? You talked to him?'

'Some boy turned up on our doorstep once or twice, perhaps three times. We were never formally introduced. I don't even remember where you were – perhaps on Chios? You'd flown off somewhere in a temper. As always we obeyed your instructions and said we did not own you and did not know your movements. I sent you all those ridiculous letters.'

'All of them?'

'Good Lord, Olivia, I have a great deal to do, I am not a postal service! Perhaps some were lost. If some misguided boy writes inappropriate letters every day, I can hardly be held at fault. Surely this is all irrelevant?'

'It probably is, Mother. You're right. I'm just feeling a little confused.'

Domenica's voice dropped to a low and urgent note. 'Olivia, my dear. You have been fortunate enough to find a charming and successful man who loves you and wants to look after you. You should thank God for that and put away all these childish notions. It would be foolish to ruin what you have now. Don't . . .'

'Look a gift horse in the mouth?'

'I don't understand you.'

Nor I you, Olivia thought. Why couldn't her mother understand that she did not want to be looked after? 'I know you don't. I'll book you a room at Claridges – unless you'd rather stay with us?'

'Make sure it's a large room, darling, if not a suite. Some of their rooms are dreadfully poky. You can also book me an appointment at a hair salon – there's one in the hotel that's not very good, but it will have to do.'

219

# The Rules of the Game 6

**Oxford, June 1986**

Three days after the Merton Commem. Ball, Olivia sat on her bed with approximately one hundred bits of paper spread out around her in haphazard piles – her own essays, other people's essays, summary revision notes, reams of quotes she had copied and copied until she knew them by heart. She was undecided whether she should throw them out or keep them for posterity. Finals were over; student life was over; everything was over, and she had no enthusiasm for what the future offered, not being certain that it offered anything at all. She picked up an essay at random and read the title 'Variations of style in Joyce's *Ulysses*: are they an integral part of the novel?', before flipping through to her tutor's assessment: 'An essay of this length is far from ideal, but within these terms you have done well. I fear examiners would find your discourse on Fra Angelico unprofitably pretentious. β+++.' Little did her tutor know that she had fallen back on the Fra Angelico stuff (dimly remembered from Doc Peters' history of art lessons) because she had not, in fact, managed to read *Ulysses* at all, and had spotted an opportunity for filling at least one side of paper with other stuff she might just get away with. On grounds of sheer ingenuity alone, the essay deserved more than β+++. That's what it boiled down to, three years of studying the master and some of the minor pieces of English literature, only to be chastised for pretentiousness.

To cheer herself up, Olivia turned to a borrowed essay submitted by her tutorial partner, on the bottom of which Dr Graves had scrawled, 'This is absolutely hopeless. You have cited two poems and quoted four lines from one of them. It's almost inconceivable to me that one could write on a poet in this way. It's a totally wrong and misguided approach. *Nothing* is worth saying about poetry or literature (*pace* certain stupid Marxist critics and other imbeciles) that is not demonstrable and demonstrated every inch of the way by the texts, *BY THE TEXTS!* What you say may be right, but that doesn't make it of any use to me. I will not grade this essay.' Olivia kicked the papers off the bed, letting them fall in random drifts, and lay back with her hands behind her head. She could hear Jerry downstairs talking to Pip, and waited for him to come up.

Jerry grinned when he saw her in the middle of the piles. 'Spring cleaning?'

'Should I keep the essays or chuck 'em?'

'Keep them for posterity. For your biographer.'

'I'm not sure I'd like posterity to see them, even if posterity wished to do so. Which it won't. No one's ever going to write a biography of me, for God's sake. My outside chance would be a tiny entry in somebody else's. That might be more fun, actually.'

'Oh, you'll probably appear in the index of the biography of some great man: Fletcher-Smith, Olivia. First meeting with X, 8. Influence on X's life, 94 – 112. Influence on X's work, 231 – 275. Influence on X's divorces, 300 – 318. Responsibility for X's subsequent seventeen suicide attempts; 318 – 437.'

'You're fantasising about some poor sod wanting to write a

biography of *you*. I've got a title for it – "The Martyred Monk".'

'Wouldn't sell. If you're going to carve out a career in publishing, you'll have to brush up on your titles. What about something simpler, closer to the bone? "Sex God", perhaps?'

'What about "Delusions of Grandeur"?'

'What about "An Uxorious Monk"?'

'What about "The Fallacious Philosopher"?'

'I still think "Sex God" makes the punchiest title.' He lay down beside her and took her in his arms.

Pip knocked loudly on the door after she'd opened it. "Scuse me, you two, but it *is* noon. George and I are going to Brown's – want to come?'

'Sure. You go ahead and get a table.'

Jerry picked up the essay on *Ulysses* and watched Olivia over it as she took off her dressing gown and collected possible items of clothing from the floor, the open chest of drawers, random hooks and discarded hangers.

'You are a complete slob. You *ought* to do some spring cleaning.'

'I don't like the word "ought". Anyway, it's high summer, and we're leaving. It's too late to start putting my house in order.'

She stood in front of the mirror in underpants, either artlessly unaware of his observation, or too accustomed to his presence to care whether he observed her or not. He assessed her as he had before: neck and limbs – Modigliani; the elongated hips and belly by Cranach; the high and rounded breasts by Botticelli. What a composite, what variations of style – the whole, an Aphrodite. She took a huge, wide-brimmed black hat with stiff gauze wings coming off it at all angles, plonked it on her head and wore it throughout her search for a clean T-shirt.

'D'we really have to have lunch with Pip and George?'

'We've got to talk about finding somewhere in London to rent. George can't buy somewhere unless Old Man Upton coughs up the down-payment, which he won't do until he sells this place, and he won't sell this place because the market's dead, or something like that. We'll have to rent. George wants to be in Notting Hill – Shepherd's Bush at least – and Pip wants to be in North London. She wants to find somewhere right away, so we'll have it over the summer, before real life starts. Ugh.'

'Sounds like we should leave them to sort it out.' Jerry sighed and shifted restlessly on the bed as she dressed. He had pretty much committed to doing his doctorate at King's, but knew he was only leaving Oxford because Olivia was. He was not going to have funds to contribute to renting the sort of London flat that the other three were likely to want. Nor had he and Olivia actually discussed whether they would be using one room or two. Between her risible salary as an editorial assistant – assuming she eventually managed to find a job in publishing – and his grant, they might just be able to fund one. She was brushing her hair so roughly he felt sorry for it.

'Has Pip heard from the BBC trainee scheme?'

'Only that she's on the shortlist. She's not talking about it.'

'And George?'

'All set for pinstripe glory. They're paying him the most enormous whack – about ten times what I'd be getting.' Olivia stroked Vaseline on her lips and preened in the mirror. 'There.' She turned back to face him and held out a hand to pull him off the bed. He pulled her on to it instead.

'Do you want to get married, Livvy?'

'As a general concept? Ever? Or now – to you?'

'I know you'll say no to me now.'

'You don't know that. Try me. You might just catch me at the right moment.'

'So, how about it? Do you want to marry me?'

'Why not? Yes. It'll be fun. Come on, let's go.'

'Are you serious?'

'Perfectly.' She pinched his cheek. 'Almost definitely'.

During lunch, George spelt out his remuneration package, ticking off the items on his fingers. 'Salary, annual profit-related bonus, company car after the probation period, mortgage subsidy, health insurance . . . I must have forgotten something. I know, share options after the third year's employment.'

'Piss off, would you?' Olivia complained. 'My only perk would be choosing books from the remaindered pile. That's all you lot will get for Christmas and birthdays for the next fifteen years.'

'Jerry, make me and Livvy feel better by telling George he's selling his immortal soul. Tell him about Mammon and what happened to Faust.'

There was such naïveté about them in those days, about all of them, never more obvious than in the easy assumption that life was simple, and that people and professions could be neatly divided into categories: Art, good; Commerce, bad. Given how quickly students learn far more complex lessons like how to drive a car and how to blackmail their parents, it is mystifying how most of them fail to see through such clichéd categorisations. It would take Pip several years to understand that at a dinner party of publishers, novelists and television producers, the conversation is most likely to centre on money, advances and who has the most aggressive agent. It is the stockbrokers who will be avidly debating the relative merits of the early and late novels of George Eliot. It is precisely those who spend their university years writing essays on Eliot's moral and ethical framework who find themselves peculiarly preoccupied with pension plans.

Jerry poked his pasta morosely. 'Why do I feel you are all about to board the great Train of Life, leaving me stranded on the platform like a part-time porter?'

'Oh, sweetie, we'll always make room for you! I'll share my ticket, for what it's worth.' Pip cradled his head against her breast. 'Look – there's Justus!' She waved him over from the bar to join them.

'Hey, it's the Four Musketeers. You know, people are talking . . . There's a nasty rumour doing the rounds that none of you actually exists unless you're all together. How're you going to cope, alone in the big bad world?'

'Just because you haven't got any real friends, Justus, you shouldn't knock it,' Pip scolded. 'After all, friendship is meant to be the great Oxford legacy.'

'And all this time I thought it was education. What a horse's ass!' Justus pulled up a chair and straddled it. 'Hi, Livvy.' Olivia's head was angled sharply away from all of them, apparently absorbed in the study of a large potted palm while she trembled at the memory of their illicit kiss at the Merton Ball. 'So what's the news on the job front? Finals front? Any front?'

'I'm waiting to hear from the BBC,' Pip rattled away, 'George is pretending to wrestle with his conscience before sailing into the murky waters of corporate finance, Livvy's got an interview with Secker's, and Jerry's going to be an eternal student.'

'I'm going back to school too,' Justus offered. 'Well, drama school, at least. I've got a place on the Webber-Douglas post-grad course.'

'So you'll be staying in England?' Pip asked. 'Maybe one day I'll get to cast you in a radio play.'

'That'd be great. I could do the sound effects.'

'I've got some news,' Olivia announced. 'Jerry and I have decided to get married.'

They all looked first at Olivia and then at Jerry. He shrugged with don't-look-at-me resignation. Justus held out his hand to him. 'No shit. Now that's what I call real grown-up, long-pants stuff . . . Congratulations, Jerry. I'm sure you'll both be very happy. I'd better be getting back to the guys, but if any of you are at a loose end, Rich is having a farewell party tonight in the BNC beer cellars. You're all welcome, any time after nine. Maybe I'll get to see you later.'

Pip put her elbows on the table. 'Is this a joke?' she said suspiciously. 'Liv? *Jerry*?'

if only Catherine of Aragon had been better in bed . . .

On his return to Suffolk from New York, George Upton had assured his wife that his relationship with Olivia was platonic, if profound; he did not entirely manage to convince Sarah, but she seemed willing to give him the benefit of the doubt. Once back in London, he phoned Olivia two or three times daily. He was no longer capable of crossing the road without the thought simultaneously crossing his mind that if he were knocked down by a bus he would go to his grave without having made love to her. He was convinced that the infection could be purged by one single act; he did not dwell in a Cloud Cuckoo Land of thinking that he and Olivia would be transported into some blissful union that would sweep them up and beyond the rest of his life. Since New York, he had given up calculating the logistics of divorcing Sarah, paying alimony, arranging visits with the children, and structuring his life around Olivia. Charming as the image of a shared future with her seemed, he did not seek anything beyond the moment of consummation, beyond avoiding the absolute horror of dying without it. He was lovesick as he had never been, and the symptoms were misinterpreted by his colleagues as stress-related.

Having failed to persuade Olivia to meet him for lunch, George was unable to stay at his desk and went for a walk. He found himself standing outside an antiquarian print dealer, and went inside to buy her a present. The prints were all too impersonal to act as a gift of love; he searched in vain for one that might represent 'our place' – a mood at least, but it was not to be found among the assorted etchings of the 'Bridge of Sighs' and 'Cornmarket Street *circa* 1836'. He continued past jewellers, knowing how negatively Olivia would react to a ring, past florists, past bookshops, past traditional *parfumiers* – nothing seemed to represent the pure essence of his desire.

He rang Olivia's number on his mobile and left yet another message, then phoned Pip at work to ask where Olivia was. She was not very helpful. 'I haven't got the foggiest. Sorry, George, gotta dash, or I'll get demoted to reading the shipping forecast.' He made one final and very uncharacteristic call back to his secretary to say he suddenly felt ill and was going home to Suffolk, and might not make it back to town the following day. It was the first time he'd bunked off work in ten years. It was seven o'clock by the time he got home, and he could hear Sarah upstairs in the bathroom with the children. He loitered on the stairs listening to them before entering just at the point when Sarah lost her temper. She was kneeling by the bath shouting at Will, and when she saw George in the doorway she gave a little scream that frightened the children more than her shouting.

'What are you doing here?'

'I just decided to come home early. Hello, boys!'

Sarah sat back on her haunches, wet from the splashing, without makeup and without having washed her hair. She was in the habit of washing it on Friday and Sunday mornings, and didn't bother during the week. She watched George step towards the bath as his boys cried 'Daddy!' and 'Dada!', then step back sharpish as the water sloshed over the edge and over her.

'Right. That's it. Out, both of you. Right now. Not another word.' As she stood up, her eyes went quickly to the mirror. She looked dreadful, pinched and tired, with a heavy crease over her brow. She put up a hand to smooth it. 'So, are you sick or what? Or are you flying off again tomorrow?'

'Neither, I just felt like coming home.' George took Will on his lap and wrapped him in a towel, leaving his toes out. 'This little piggy . . .'

'Went to market!' Will shrieked.

'Dad?' Arthur stood at the loo having a pee. 'Do you know what I learned today? I went to Harry's house, and before I had a pee, the water was blue, but after I had a pee, the water was green. Harry's mum said it was about magic colours, and blue plus yellow makes green. Did you know that?'

'There's nothing to eat. I was going to have bread and cheese and an early night.'

'Fine. I didn't, actually, Arthur – I haven't thought about that for a long time. This little piggy had roast beef . . .'

'Arthur, stop dawdling. There's no need to show off just because Daddy's home.'

'Leave them be, Sarah. I'll put them to bed. Go make yourself a drink and relax.'

She turned in the doorway. 'You must be sick.'

George closed his eyes for a moment.

When he came downstairs Sarah had changed into a dress and pulled her hair back. There was a bottle of red wine uncorked on the kitchen table, a pot simmering on the hob and she was chopping carrots.

'Bread and cheese would have been fine.'

'I know, but I had some chicken thighs in the fridge. I would only have had to cook them tomorrow and freeze them. It's no effort. It would only have gone to waste. I'm trying a recipe from that book you gave me at Christmas, remember? The one about healthy cooking. It's quite interesting, very little fat, a lot of steaming, and vegetables.'

George handed her a glass of wine and sat down heavily. 'God, I'm tired. Maybe I *am* coming down with something.'

'Maybe it's just delayed jet-lag. You do far too much travelling. I thought you said this year it would ease up.'

'That's always the theory.'

'You work far too hard.'

'You think it makes me dull?'

'No, but it worries me.' As she tested the casserole, the juices boiled over and spilt on her dress.

'Oh, fuck!'

'Good thing the children are in bed.'

'You think I'm a bad influence?' She swung round angrily. 'Honestly. I'm with them day in, day out, and the one night I happen to feel down, the one night I've run out of patience, you decide to come home and criticise me. Well, you can fuck off, that's what I think.'

'Dearest, it's all right. I wasn't criticising you. I don't care how much you swear. To be honest, it's rather a relief.'

'I'm not such a goody-goody, George. You're making a big mistake if you think that.'

'Come here.' Sarah clung to the oven. 'Come here now and sit down. No – next to me.' When he had topped up her glass, George kissed her cheek. 'Now, can we start again? Hello, darling! I've come home early for a change!'

Sarah looked at him sadly. 'You really do think I'm a fool, don't you, George? You have no respect for me at all.'

'Sarah, please, not tonight. I'm tired, I want a bit of peace.'

'Why didn't you go and see Olivia, then?'

'Because I wanted to come home, damn it! You're incapable of thinking about anything except Olivia. I told you last weekend. She's a very old friend, she's in a mess, we went to New York as *friends*. How many times do I have to say it?'

'Until you mean it.'

'Just call her. Call her yourself and ask. Go ahead – be my guest. Christ, I wish to God I *was* having an affair. At least I'd be getting something in return for all this flak!'

'Just tell me honestly. Are you and Olivia sleeping – having sex together?'

'No. As far as I recall, for the past few weeks I haven't been having sex with anyone at all, including my own wife!'

'But you do want to sleep with her?'

'Sarah, you've got some notion in your head. It's an obsession of your own making, nothing to do with me, and I wish you'd snap out of it. Why on earth are you so suspicious? Sometimes I think you're the one with a guilty conscience, you're the one who's having an affair, and this is all some reverse psychology thing – what do they call it? Projection.'

'Even if I wanted to, who d'you think there is for me to have an affair with? The milkman? Mr Evans? The man at the garage?'

'You see? You're actually contemplating it.' He wagged his finger at her, hoping to make her laugh.

'It's not funny. Look at me, George. Who could possibly desire me? I'm thirty-one years old, and I look forty-five. *Look at me!*'

'You're a beautiful woman, Sarah.' He really did look at her, trying to assess how other men might see her. She had a 'homey' prettiness that did not immediately lend itself to sexual suggestion but then, there were men who found that the most intriguing of all. He'd always found her beautiful, the softness of her hair, the delicacy of her small chin, her heart-shaped face and melting eyes. That her appearance was rather undramatic did not mean that she

233

wasn't desirable; there was an immensely comfortable feel about her, and she'd kept her figure, so far. 'You are a beautiful woman,' he repeated.

She went back to the stove. 'You know, sometimes when I'm alone, particularly these past few weeks, since Olivia came to stay, I keep wondering if anyone's ever going to really desire me again – I mean, really, really want me. You know what I decided?'

'I'm all agog.'

'I decided that the closest I'm ever going to get to that would be with some future school chum of Arthur's. You know, maybe when Arthur's sixteen – I don't know, maybe it happens younger, these days, fourteen, say. He'll have some friend for the weekend, and while I'm cooking their tea, or taking them lemonade,' she stabbed at the chicken with a wooden spoon, 'maybe I'll suddenly see a look of admiration, even desire, in his eyes. That'd be something.'

'It would indeed.' It was one of those times when George stared at her with narrowed eyes, when his clear blue gaze was so intense that she had the feeling he was looking at her through burning smoke. Several years ago she had concluded that when his gaze was fiercest, his thoughts were least with her. She knew he was thinking then of the probability of an interest-rate hike, or whether the central banks would continue to support the ailing lira. 'I never knew you fantasised about toy-boys.'

'Do you know how many women in their thirties, after five or ten years of marriage – maybe even less – begin to wonder if they made the right choice, if they wouldn't have been happier with someone else? Do you think that I'm the only woman on earth who hasn't had that fantasy? In my case, I try not to think about it, because of the boys and because I'm too old, and it's too frightening to try to start again, and I've never been the sort of woman men fall in love with. So I am stuck with the choice I made,

234

providing you stay with me, and I am trying to make the very best of it, but I can't help envying Olivia. I can't help envying her for having a second chance, getting to look at it all again and make her mind up.'

George thought it wasn't only women who fantasised about having a chance to start all over again, but it was typical of the female sex to claim it as their own exclusive right. 'I'm astounded, Sarah. I had no idea . . .'

'There's plenty you don't know, George. If you spent only half the time thinking about our marriage that you spend thinking about work, maybe things would make more sense to you.'

'Sarah, dear, if you want me to be some sort of new man and bang on about my emotional needs and your emotional needs and all that wank, then think again.'

'Why don't we discuss it as if it was work? Let's pretend it's some sort of currency.'

'What is?'

'Love. Let's assume it can get devalued, or revalued or whatever you call it, and it's subject to all sorts of pressures – deflation, stagnation,' she continued to pulverise the chicken, 'you see what I'm saying?'

'I haven't the foggiest.'

'Soaring inflation. When you first fall in love, a pat or a kiss mean nothing, they happen all the time – they're given away. Over time, the value inches up a bit more. To get a caress, you have to have sex, or cook a really good dinner, or have the office round for a party. Then suddenly, bang. Prices go through the roof, and you can't get it for love or money. All of a sudden, those little endearments that you take for granted cost ten, twenty, thirty times the price, and even then the trade isn't willing.'

George was genuinely confused. He wasn't sure if Sarah was trying to imply that he was 'dealing' in some other currency, or whether she was simply bemoaning a lack of demonstrated affection.

'You're quite the budding economist, sweetheart.'

The spoon pointed at him. 'You can fuck off with your patronising crap, all right? I've had enough of it.'

'Darling, please,' he moved to embrace her and she went rigid in his arms, 'shush . . . I do understand. Really I do. I'm sorry, I've been far too neglectful. I do not, absolutely not, patronise you. You're beautiful, and intelligent, and informed. You're an outstanding wife and mother . . . Sarah? Sarah, darling, don't cry, this isn't like you . . .' Every woman he went near spontaneously gushed like a fountain. Sarah had very rarely wept, and George had always found tears the most powerful weapon in the female arsenal.

While George was window-shopping, Olivia went to Jerry's gallery. Although they had not spoken since the weekend in Suffolk he showed no surprise at her appearance.

'Am I disturbing you?'

'There's no one else here. Tuesday morning is rarely rush-hour.' She picked up the Persian miniature she had admired on her first visit. 'Ah, I see. You've come back for it. I did promise it to you. I should have taken it off the display. Have you set a date?'

'No, not yet. I'm going to sort it out this week. I was in New York last week.'

'So I heard.' He took the El Fharmi battle-scene from her and placed it on his desk. 'I'll wrap it for you.'

'There's no hurry. I don't want you to give it to me, anyway. I thought I might buy it as a gift for Justus.'

'As you like.'

'You will come to the wedding, won't you, Jerry?'

He sat down at his desk and opened his diary. 'I'm travelling a fair bit this summer. If I'm in town I'll certainly come, but without knowing the date . . .' He shrugged. He began to rub the miniature lightly with a soft cloth, then picked up an eyepiece to examine it more closely. 'It is a nice piece – you have a good eye. I must point out that there's a hairline scratch, here, at the bottom corner, just above the signature. Ivory is a softer material than you might imagine. It doesn't affect the value significantly, but I mention it in case you'd prefer something in perfect condition.'

'What's Samsara?'

'It's the name of my gallery.' Jerry continued polishing until he heard Olivia stamp her foot. He looked up in initial bewilderment that changed to amusement. 'It's a perfume, Olivia. I couldn't positively identify the maker, Guerlain, I believe, but it's certainly a perfume. I gave Pip a bottle of it quite recently.'

'Don't make fun of me.'

'All right. Samsara is the wheel of life; birth, death, rebirth. It is the universal cycle. May I ask why you want to know?'

'No.'

'It is the cycle of pain and suffering through which we all travel endlessly.' He looked at her steadily.

'There's no getting off the ride?'

'To escape Samsara one must accumulate positive karma, generally over the course of many lifetimes. When one achieves the complete realisation of one's true nature, or Atman, one achieves Moksha, or complete enlightenment, and thus escapes Samsara.'

'And karma? What does that mean exactly?'

'Exactly? Not a word that translates well in Vedanta philosophy.'

'I remember: "Those who know do not say; those who say, do not know."'

'That's Tao, actually, but let me try, at the risk of proving I no longer know. Karma is both each individual committed act, and the accumulation of good and bad acts through the course of an individual life. Unlike Samsara, karma is up to the individual. You are able to affect it through your actions. The Hindu texts are full of metaphors and images for the meaning of these concepts, most of which I have forgotten, but the inability to escape your karma is likened to a calf being able to find its mother in a herd of hundreds of cattle. Likewise a good or bad deed will always return to its perpetrator. I'm a little rusty on all this. If you want a crash course in Indian philosophy, you should ask somebody else – or consult a book.' He turned the pages of his diary. 'I'm out of the country almost the whole of August. Unless you marry in haste, I will have to decline. Sad, but there it is.'

'Please talk to me, Jerry. I can't stand this.'

'I don't find it very enjoyable myself.'

'Then talk to me.'

'How did you enjoy your jaunt with George?'

'Why are you doing this? Why are you being so horrible?'

'That was not my intention.' He rubbed his eyes. 'All right, Olivia. One last try. What is it exactly that you want to know? What do you want from me now?'

'Everything. I need to know everything that happened. Why it didn't work for us, where it went wrong . . .'

Jerry drew in his breath through his teeth and pinched the bridge of his nose. 'Forgive me for stating the obvious, but are you really asking *me*? Am I the right person to answer those questions?'

'Fine, if you want me to say it I will. Tell me where *I* went wrong, what *I* did wrong. I'm willing to take the blame.'

'No, Livvy. You have never been willing to take the blame. You've never been willing to take any responsibility at all, as far as I can see.' Jerry realised that unwittingly he had been pushed into exactly the position he most wished to avoid – checkmated in three moves. 'Christ. I can't have this conversation here.'

'Can we go back to that pub?'

'I don't want to have this conversation anywhere. It's over, Olivia, dead and buried. Just get on with your life and leave me to deal with mine.'

'I'm sorry, but I can't do that, not until I understand everything.'

'Then you are stupider than I ever dreamed possible.'

'Jerry, how can I – any of us – deal with the present without finally understanding the past? Can you say absolutely that if Neville Chamberlain hadn't had two whiskies too many one night and woken up with a hangover then war would have been averted? Can you say if Cleopatra's nose had been misshapen, or a little longer, or a little shorter, or even more perfect, that the Roman Empire might have been spared from collapse? That if only Catherine of Aragon had been better in bed, England would still be a Catholic country? Even if it doesn't change anything, don't you want to *know*?'

That if Justus had been a year older, or a year younger, he might never have crossed Olivia's path; that if he, Jerry, hadn't gone to the King's Arms but had waited at that appalling BNC party for her, that if he'd been tougher, fiercer, more demanding, bit her on the ear until she lay still, that if she'd only been able to ride a bicycle with competence . . . As she moved across the room towards him Jerry saw himself as an animal lured into a trap, but the image didn't quite fit. He knew that he should run and didn't: the charge of entrapment wouldn't stand up in court if the defence could prove he had been compliant. Standing still made him a collaborator, like a fox holding up a red flag to bring on the dogs. She still represented something that he wanted; she suggested the sumptuous, the exclusive, the reserved. He stood up just as she reached him and walked around the outside of his desk like a nervous virgin avoiding a predatory suitor. 'Let's go and have some lunch. I just need to make a phone call.'

George had returned to his office for the weekly syndicate meeting but was distracted, his thoughts ricocheting between Olivia and his wife. He sat at the conference table making paper planes and chucking them at his team, who pretended to be amused at their boss's playfulness and privately labelled him a victim of an early mid-life crisis, or worse, if any of them were able to think of something worse than accelerated middle-age.

'Who's going to represent the Energen bid? George, who do you think should handle it?'

'Hmm? Oh, doesn't matter much. Mark can have it.'

'I can't, George. If you remember I've got the final signing for LHM that week. I can't do both.'

'Frankly I don't see why not. Rather a defeatist attitude, young Mark,' George chucked another dart, 'but if you don't feel up to it, fine. I'll go myself. I can't seem to get off bloody aeroplanes these days. Might as well live on one. Anything else, chaps? Ladies? Then back to work and earn some more money.'

One of his colleagues loitered over his files until the others had left the room. 'George, I wanted a word about the Man-Comm negotiations.'

'Umm,' George grunted. He'd just had an inspired idea; he'd decided to pay a call on Jerry Milton and see if he had anything that might tickle Olivia's fancy. So greatly did the idea please him that he failed to notice his colleague's obvious discomfort. 'What about them? I thought it was all going fine.'

'You know what these tin-pot privatisations are like. They want a proportion of the fees passed back under the table.'

'That's pretty standard, Bill, particularly in Indian deals. What's the problem?'

'It was suggested to me by the Deputy Minister that we might,' Bill cleared his throat, 'consider a further off-the-record donation to a charity of his choice, in consideration for our getting the mandate.'

'The charity of his choice being?'

'Certain trusts not a million miles away from the Minister.'

'I see.'

'And in consideration for *our* consideration, he would like to offer a token of his personal respect.'

'A token. I see.' A token of his personal respect was exactly what he wanted to find Olivia. 'There's nothing wrong with tokens, if the beneficiary's happy.'

'It could go to a charity of our choice . . . Yours, mine . . .'

'Well, Bill, I'm quite confident you can handle any matters that arise, but you'll understand this isn't an entirely appropriate conversation. I'll give it some thought and get back to you if I have any doubts. It's not the first time we've come up against this, after all. You can make arrangements as you see fit on your next visit to the Minister. I wouldn't want to show up and upset the apple-cart at this stage.'

'What would you have done if I'd told you I was pregnant?'

'That's impossible for me to answer. I cannot really know how I would have acted then. In all honesty, I believe I would have been glad.'

'That I'd slept with Justus?'

'Why do you insist on saying such stupid things?'

'Because I want to be sure. I don't want to get anything wrong again.'

'Fine. I would not have been "glad" that you'd slept with Justus, but at that time your fidelity was not the linchpin of my feelings for you – far from it. Had you told me the truth, and trusted me, that might have counted for more than the fact that you had slept with another man.'

'I asked my mother yesterday why she hadn't told me that you'd come looking for me.'

'And?'

'She said,' Olivia put on a heavy, sultry drawl. 'Darling, how can I be expected to remember? I lead a very busy life. Maybe some boy came, maybe he didn't . . .'

'I came, all right. I haunted them. Your father threatened to call the police if I darkened their door again.'

'If you had, maybe . . .'

'Oh, no, don't even suggest it. That's quite outrageous.'

'I'm sorry. You're right. That was an awful thing to say.'

'There were times when I thought if I had only tried harder, waited longer, but I stopped beating myself up like that years ago. I did everything I was capable of at that age to be with you. You had only to raise your little finger . . .'

'I know, I know.' Olivia spoke softly. 'I told you, I know I was to blame. If I could reverse it –'

'You wouldn't. Everything's worked out for the best. You're going to marry Wonderboy – or is it Superman? And you'll live happily ever after.'

'I just wish you'd be there to dance at my wedding . . .' The look in her eyes was so beguiling that Jerry found himself smiling back. 'Jerry, are you in love with Pip?'

'I think she is absolutely wonderful. I depend a great deal on her.'

'I can't help wondering why she never told you about me and Justus, or about my being pregnant. In her shoes, I couldn't have kept my mouth shut.'

'Unlike you, she's a person of great integrity and loyalty. You had asked her not to. If she had told me, I would only have increased my efforts to find you.'

'She *is* very loyal.' Olivia studied a beer mat with intensity. 'She was furious with me about seeing Justus, so protective of you. You know, it doesn't surprise me at all that you and Pip got together. I often thought at Oxford that she had a bit of a crush on you.'

'Did you?'

'Yes. I never imagined she'd do anything about it.'

'I was the one who made the first move.'

'Well, I'm sure she was happy when you did. You still haven't told me if you're in love with her.'

'I don't believe that I have been in love with her, as you put it, but I love her dearly.'

'And what's the difference?'

'That I'm happy.'

'Maybe you never have been in love. Maybe you don't know what it feels like.'

'Oh, I was in love with you . . .'

'So you say.'

'No one's really been in love unless they've been in love with you. No man can possibly know what a bloody miserable thing it is to be in love unless he's had the misfortune to love you.'

'Thanks for sharing that thought, but I don't agree with your reasoning. The loved object is irrelevant, neither here nor there. It's the action of being in love, the state of it, the experience that matters. That's what we're all trying to recapture, now, in our advanced years. That delirious feeling. Can any of us bear the idea that we might not ever feel it again? Everyone experiences the same sensation.'

'What on earth would you know about it?'

'You think because I haven't experienced it I can't imagine it? Shakespeare didn't have any problem imagining how Lady Macbeth felt.'

'Because he had some affinity with guilt and remorse; some knowledge of betrayal.'

'You don't even like me any more, do you?'

'Not very much, no.'

'So shall I go? I will if you say so, Jerry. You have to admit, the one thing I've always been good at is going.'

Jerry avoided her eyes. He had already said so much more than he had intended to, and the conversation had been so familiarly circuitous that he felt years younger, unhappy, but years younger and on familiarly unhappy territory. He knew all these paths and their unexpected twists and dead ends: he could walk them with his eyes shut. He knew that however powerful dreams and fantasies were, they were not respecters of possibility; it was better to leave them well alone, and not ask them to live up to the gymnastics of the subconscious. The knowledge that he could not lose the same limb twice gave him a feeling of security, sufficient that he returned to her as she stood poised to leave.

'I do love Pip, and I don't like you much any more, but that doesn't mean I want you to go.'

The confirmation that he loved her still was as refreshing – and as deliciously private – as the physical sensation she used to get from standing naked in front of the bright, icy chill of the fridge on a humid Roman night. She was young enough still to cling to the belief that opportunity is endless, and that there is nothing you cannot eventually have, even if you're not sure what it is that you want.

# The Rules of the Game 7

There were so many official and unofficial parties, post-Schools parties, farewell parties, end-of-an-era, drink-the-Buttery-dry, is-there-life-after-Oxford? parties, that the final weeks merged into an unreal netherworld of drunken promises, hangovers and sober-in-the-cold-light-of-day arrangements to regather the following evening. Students ran the gamut in their handling of the dreadful realisation that the Oxford idyll was over; a few seemed relieved, but the Kingston Road circle, both intimate and extended, knew that *the* party was over, even if there were a few remaining events to distract them during its death throes. Pip and George adopted the strategy of attending every party to which they were invited, and several to which they were not. Olivia found it increasingly difficult to accept that her life was changing at all; so long as Jerry was at her side, what changes there would be insignificant. But because Justus had asked, albeit so casually, she agreed to go along to the BNC bash after seeing her tutor at Worcester for a farewell sherry.

Dr Graves delayed her longer than she'd anticipated, for three large sherries rather than his customary two small ones.

'Well, Olivia, so you're off into the exciting world of publishing?'

'I hope. I've got an interview at least.'

'Perhaps one day I may find myself submitting essays to you for correction.'

'Oooh, I don't think so, Dr Graves! I don't think I'd ever be capable of that.'

'Please feel free to call me Humphrey, my dear. A peculiar practice, I acknowledge, that intimacy between tutor and undergraduate is invited only as we are on the brink of parting, but then many of Oxford's customs may be termed peculiar. Perhaps we do not prepare you adequately for the rigours of the life outside this,' he waved his elegant hand loosely, 'sanctuary. That has often occurred to me, never more vividly than at this time of year, when it comes time to bid adieu.'

'I'm sure I'll be back.'

His eyes twinkled at her through his glasses. 'I don't believe you will, although I hope time proves me wrong. Nathaniel and I,' he referred to his fellow fellow, 'have a little wager this time every year on which of our undergraduates will come back to call, and which will not. I have you marked down as a non-recidivist. I'm certain you'll find far too many things to occupy your time to come back here looking for your lost youth.'

Olivia smiled uneasily: she was impatient to be off, much as she liked the man, and much as she owed him. 'I'll at least have to come back to collect my degree – providing they give me one.'

'That need not disturb you, although I warned you many times that you should not be banking on a first. Your indulgence in extra-curricular activities, attractive though they doubtless were, precluded serious scholarship. I hope you do not come to regret that choice. Make sure you let me know when you're in town. Perhaps you would join me for dinner at High Table?'

'Umm, that would be lovely.' Olivia hadn't eaten in college since the end of her first year.

'And in the meantime, Olivia, may I be so bold as to give you a few final words of advice?' He did not wait for permission to continue. 'Try not to spread yourself too thinly. In the resultant dilemma of quite how to distinguish between what is truly significant in life and what is fundamentally inessential, adhere to the Jamesian principle.'

'Which one? He had a few.'

'Do all that you can to be classified among the blessed body of people "on whom nothing is lost". Exercise the receptive facet of your nature, and I am confident it will never disappoint you.'

Outside in the quad, she looked up and saw him standing at his second-storey window, hand raised in salute, creamy nasturtiums trailing below him against the pale yellow stone of the college. He surveyed his empire like a benevolent but puppet monarch, quite content with his impotence.

By the time she arrived at BNC the party had spilled out of the beer cellar and into the rear quad. She picked out Pip quickly: Pip was always easily found – or easily avoided; she might as well have worn a flagpole on her head if she wished to be in-conspicuous.

'Have you seen Jerry?' Olivia shouted over the thumping music.

'He went to the King's Arms for a drink with someone, can't remember who. Said he'd come back and find you later.' She threaded her arm through that of a blond man Olivia had not met before. 'This is Peter. Say hello, Liv.'

'Hello, Peter.'

Peter swayed unsteadily in spite of Pip's support and grinned amiably, roughly in Olivia's direction.

'Guess what? Peter's got a flat in London.'

'How nice for Peter.'

'A flat in London that he doesn't use, you berk. In Covent Garden. He's looking for *tenants*.'

'You're doing such a good self-promotion job, I'll leave you to it. Where's George?'

Pip gestured into the throng. 'Somewhere in there, dancing with Sarah – if you can call what George does dancing.'

Olivia did not go to find them; she wandered back to the front quad intending to join Jerry in the pub. She wanted to ask him if she was someone on whom nothing is lost. At the porter's lodge she saw Justus on the phone, his back to the wall so that he would miss nothing that passed. She smiled and tried to walk by, but he put out a hand to stop her without interrupting his conversation. Olivia waited for ten seconds, and then tried to shake herself free.

'Hey, wait – gotta run, Mark. I'll call you tomorrow, OK? There's someone I've got to catch before she disappears out of my life for ever.' He held the phone between his head and his shoulder, grasped her with one hand, and made a circular motion with the other as if to speed up whoever he was talking to. 'Yeah, it's a girl. Yeah, yeah, she's gorgeous . . . OK, OK, I'll ask.' He covered the phone. 'He says, do you want to come round to his place for a drink later?'

'Who is he?'

'A creep.'

'Good friend of yours then?'

'No, Mark, she says you're a creep and she's too busy. OK. See ya.' He replaced the receiver without taking his eyes off her. 'So where are you running away to? I've been waiting for you all night.'

'I'm meeting Jerry at the King's Arms.'

He slapped his forehead. 'How could I have forgotten about Jerry? The fiancé, no less. Well, seeing you're going to spend the rest of your life with him, can't you spare an hour for me?'

'I'm late.'

'It's early.'

'I'm not in the mood. For anything. It's just hit me that I am not and never will be a Jamesian heroine.'

'Shall we go somewhere quiet and talk about it?' Draping an arm over her shoulders, he bent his head low to her ear and kissed it softly. 'What did Henry James know about anything, anyway?'

Jerry came back to BNC, but found only Pip.

'She was here a minute ago – well, an hour ago. Looking for you. I thought she'd gone with George and Sarah.'

'Gone where?'

'I don't know. You know Olivia, she's your girlfriend. She doesn't exactly put stuff in her diary. Maybe she went home.'

'I better go and look for her. Have you seen O'Keefe?'

'Not for hours. He left when you did. Come on, Jerry, lighten up! She'll get here sooner or later. Olivia's turning you into an old woman, and you're not even married yet. Come *on*, come and dance with me or I'll get stuck with Michael again.'

'OK, let me just phone the house and make sure we haven't got our wires crossed.' Jerry went back to the porter's lodge, got no reply from Kingston Road, and returned to where he had left Pip. She wasn't there. Just as he decided to go back to his room, in case Olivia was waiting for him, he heard a whistle and looked up to see Pip's red head leaning out of a window above him.

'Up here, Jerry, it's all moving up here!'

'Is Livvy there?'

Pip's head ducked in and out. 'No – hang on – yeah, I think so.' The window slammed, slicing off music and laughter like a blade. Jerry took the stairs two at a time.

Justus and Olivia walked aimlessly. It was dark, and Olivia, never confident when she could not see clearly, leaned close to his side, listening intently.

'I guess we're talking about a gift of complete perception, like drawing back the curtains and seeing absolutely everything under the stars perfectly clearly, if only for a moment. That's one reason why I like acting. There's that great moment when you know, absolutely know for sure, that the audience has forgotten they're watching a play, forgotten who you are, who they are, forgotten about everything beyond the stage. I'm not saying I have those moments, but I'm certain they're out there, waiting.'

'I don't know about that. I think James meant being receptive, being wholly sympathetic to whatever went on around you, and how other people felt. Caring. Sometimes I've been able to tell what someone feels – like Sarah Matthews, how uncomfortable she is when we play games – but I haven't bothered to do anything about it.'

'You always have to make a choice, Olivia, when it comes to caring about other people. At least you've got all it takes to have that choice. Many people don't. You're bright, you're beautiful. Best of all, you know you are. What more do you want? You have to make a choice between whether you want to play the game, in which case you are never going to see the whole picture, or whether you want to sit on the sidelines and be able to watch it all play out.'

'Which is more fun?'

'I don't think spectating is ever as absorbing as playing. Speaking personally. At least when you're playing, you can ignore the rules and go ahead and foul, forget about them from time to time. Like you do. Like you're doing with me.'

'What do you mean?'

When he kissed her, standing square with his thighs pressed against hers, Olivia turned liquid. Since the Merton Ball, she had imagined the feel and touch of him so often that she could not distinguish the reality of kiss after fierce kiss from her fantasy of them. When he stopped, holding her by the shoulders and staring into her eyes, she was overwhelmed by the force of the moment, so that she was quite literally powerless – unable to speak, walk, talk, barely able to stand unsupported.

'What do you want, Olivia?' he asked softly. 'Tell me what you really want. Forget about what you ought to want.'

'I don't know what I want. I feel like I'm walking through a minefield. I don't know where to put my feet.'

He picked her up in his arms and held her. 'Fine. I'll decide where we go, then. Is that OK with you?' She nodded, rubbing her cheek rhythmically against his sleeve. 'Only we better pick somewhere close by. I'll make an ass of myself trying to carry you all the way back to Magdalen. I knew the day would come when I'd wish I was at Worcester.'

George and Sarah walked back to Kingston Road with Jerry and Pip. On the doorstep, George exchanged a whisper with Sarah and tossed Pip the keys. 'I'm going back to Sarah's for a bit, Pip. Don't lock me out, OK?' The final admonition was solely for the sake of good manners – and Sarah's blushes.

Jerry went straight to Olivia's room. On finding it dark, something made him turn on the lights. There was no sign that Olivia had been home since early evening. He walked out of the house and looked up and down the street for her car, but could not see it.

'Her car's gone.'

Pip was eating a chocolate bar and scanning the notepad where they left their messages. 'So I noticed.'

'She hasn't been home.'

'She doesn't need to, does she? She's got everything in the boot.

She could go anywhere. Maybe at last she's found a reason to have that bag packed, ready and waiting for emergencies.' She sucked the chocolate off the Crunchie thoughtfully. 'Would it make you feel any better if I told you her car's in the garage? It died when George borrowed it yesterday.'

'You might have told me right away.'

'Why? It was much more fun seeing you sweat.' She instantly regretted speaking to him like that, even if it *was* for his own good, and offered him the denuded Crunchie. 'Sorry – d'you want a bite? Listen, Jerry, it's time you and I had a man-to-man talk. You're silly about Olivia, really silly, I mean all this crap about getting married. You're not serious, are you?'

'Of course we're serious.' Jerry stood at the window holding back the curtain and gazing out into the night with his back to Pip.

'"We're".' Pip repeated quietly. 'Are you sure you mean "we", and not me?'

'What do you mean by that?' Jerry swung round to look at her.

'I mean you're not going to get anywhere moping like some Christmas puppy abandoned on the M1. You should either give her a free rein or a kick in the teeth. You should point blank refuse to marry her – tell her you want to play the field a bit. Play the game, Jerry – you know how Olivia *hates* feeling tied down.'

The savagery of her comment made Jerry wince; he turned back to the street. He could not imagine anything worse than playing the field. A few nights ago, an hour earlier, he would have welcomed the chance to talk to Pip about his relationship with Olivia, and he would have respected her insight. Now he felt too damaged to confide in her at all. He could not tell Pip that he felt frightened when Olivia was out of his sight, a twilight-zone fear, as if he'd woken up in the middle of the night to find his pillow was not there, not anywhere, when it had been beneath his head as he fell asleep. Not being able to feel one of his limbs. A presentiment of disaster.

'Tell me more,' he said quietly.

'Let me try to explain. Olivia plays games for a purpose, most of all with you. I think she's setting you a test. If she treats you like shit and you put up with it, then you're crap and worthless to be so devoted to someone as nasty as her. If she treats you like shit and you walk out, then you're noble and she loves you to death, but it also proves you never really loved her in the first place. That's the way I see it, anyway. It's the classic female game, and you're damned either way.'

'All the more reason not to play. I don't think Olivia does treat me like shit.'

'Don't get me wrong. Olivia loves you, I know that. She's never felt that way about anybody else.' She threw herself on the sofa. 'Oh, shit, I don't know what I'm talking about, just ignore me. Liv probably bumped into someone when she was looking for you and she's gone off for a drink. Talking of which, why don't we have one? She'll be back in a minute, but if not, no big deal. What are you going to be like when you're actually married?'

'We won't get married.'

'Of course you will.'

'No, we won't. She'd have forgotten the whole subject if Justus hadn't appeared at Browns.'

'Justus? Justus is nothing but a pair of walking biceps. That type's never appealed to Livvy. She uses him to nark you. Trust me, I've seen her do it before. She once invited some braindead Marlburian cricketer to Chios simply to piss off George. And everyone always takes her dead seriously. Whereas me, well, however hard I try, people can't take me seriously at all.'

'I do.'

'My arse you do!' She wagged her finger at him. 'You spend time with me because I'm Livvy's best friend, and you're smart enough to know I might hold some keys to doors you can't open.' Jerry was beginning to feel uncertain about why he spent time with any of them, yet longed for Olivia's return.

'And why do you spend time with me?'

'Because I like you. I like you a lot. You're the best of them all, Jerry. I'm not just saying it 'cause I'm pissed, though I am pissed, royally. I mean it. You're the best of the bunch.' She curled up on the sofa, and her eyes suddenly filled with tears. Rubbing them away streaked the mascara across her white cheeks and Jerry found her smudged face far more touching than her made-up one.

'Oh, Pip!'

Her hand shot up to ward him off. 'Don't – *please* don't be nice to me, Jerry. I haven't got the strength to be comforted. I'm tired of people feeling sorry for me.'

'I don't know anyone who feels sorry for you, Pip, certainly not me. There's no reason to.'

He was baffled by her sudden collapse.

'Then I'm tired of feeling sorry for myself because I haven't got a proper boyfriend. Haven't got one?' she scoffed. 'Never had one, more like.'

'What about Michael?'

'Michael isn't so much a boyfriend as a convenience. He's like . . . like one of those handy slots in smart American fridges, where you shove your glass under the spout for ice or iced water. You walk past it twenty times a day without even seeing it, unless you're thirsty. I'm just the same to him, too.' The tears flowed again, making her nose sniffle. 'It's not funny – don't you dare laugh at me!'

'Pip, you're five foot high, you have the physique of a seven-year-old boy – and a not very robust boy at that – and red hair. I've never seen anything less like a fridge in my life.'

'So now you're insulting my appearance?' Pip smiled. It was the prettiest thing about her, normally seen at its finest when accompanied by a barbed comment.

'You're very attractive. Very.' Jerry sat down next to her and looked at her severely before punching her gently in the shoulder, as he might a large dog. 'I don't want to hear you spewing this rubbish again, and I will not share a flat with you if I'm going to be subjected to it.'

They had stopped talking about literature long before they reached Justus's rooms, and were not to resume the conversation. It seemed later to Olivia that they had been seized by a profound and mutual sense of relief. They surrendered to each other, each more willing than the other, desperate to be the first to give themselves up. For a time, Olivia believed that she was indeed a person on whom nothing is lost. That moment would stand with her throughout life, isolated, whole and not to be repeated. If she knew that what she did in going to bed with Justus was wrong, she knew also that not going to bed with Justus would have been more hazardous, in that the rest of her life would be scarred by curiosity. More than anything, she feared the unquenchable power of denied love. Olivia was not a woman to be haunted by the sentimental, namby-pamby notion of 'if only'. The rough impatience of their lovemaking set it apart from any other intimate encounter, and the subsequent intimacy was gentler and more poignant than the comfortable post-coital cuddles and whispers she shared with Jerry. Olivia lay on her back in his bed, with the sheets tangled around her legs and her arms flung behind her head in complete abandon.

Justus kissed her like a skinny cat poaching cream; the salty, sweaty surface on the ridge below her breasts made his tongue fizz. When she began to speak he propped himself up on one elbow, transfixed by her closed eyelids. They reminded him of the fragile, whispery, mauve-pink tissue on some luxurious, exotic delicacy – Turkish delight, Amaretti biscuits. Then with his lips against her ear, he whispered, 'Tell me stories . . .'

'Like Scheherazade?'

'She'll do . . .'

'At school, when other girls were crossing off the days on their home-going charts, I'd start to panic, knowing my mother would be on the phone arranging for me to go to Chios. She once told me my face was so morose that she got a headache just looking at me. She considered Rome unsuitable – "an unsuitable venue for a twelve-year-old's vacation", she said; she often referred to "venues"; still does. "Is it a 'desirable' venue?" That's what she said when I told her I'd got a place at Worcester. Justus, d'you mind if I smoke?'

He reached to the floor by the bed, shook out two cigarettes and lit them, passing her one.

'*Very* Humphrey Bogart.'

'Keep talking.'

'Anyway, one summer, when I was fourteen, summers on Chios changed. That summer I became a whipping boy, an object of ridicule.' She inhaled deeply and let the thin vapour of smoke curl out before she opened her eyes again. 'My cousins pretended they couldn't understand me when I spoke Greek. They laughed at how clumsy I was swimming and diving – I was a klutz, terrified of diving off the rocks, but I thought I had to do it to keep up with them. The only one who was nice to me was my cousin Matthias. He was sixteen.'

'And don't tell me, your first true love.'

Olivia ground out her cigarette on a saucer. 'No. He stayed behind with me one day and took me to a cave off the beach. When he started groping me I scratched his face so badly he had to pretend he'd been attacked by the compound cat. One of the gardeners wrung its neck.'

Olivia climbed out of bed and threw him a glance over her shoulder as she picked up her scattered clothes. 'I'd like to talk, but I have to go.' He waited until she was dressed before he felt the need to stop her. He believed she would stop of her own accord; perhaps he was uncertain if he wanted her to stay.

'You know you don't have to go.'

'Oh, yes, I do.'

'Don't go back to Jerry. Not tonight, at least. I can't stand to think of you with him. You deserve something – different. Stay with me.'

'You sound like a jealous lover. It's not a good role for you – you're more convincing playing it cool.'

'Maybe I feel like a jealous lover. Maybe I've fallen in love with you.'

Olivia leaned against the door. 'Maybe pigs can fly. Don't mess it up, Justus. Tonight was special. We're friends. Let's leave it at that.'

'Hey. I was only teasing.' He yawned. 'Give me a call sometime, OK? At least invite me to the wedding.'

Sex with Pip was different from what he had grown accustomed to, and not just because it was the first time. Even the first time he went to bed with Olivia, she'd had a way of withdrawing herself, looking over his shoulder as if she were half expecting somebody else to arrive. It was not boredom, simulated or genuine, he knew that: it was a curious blankness that had nothing to do with her physical responses, and not much to do with him. Sometimes Jerry indulged himself in the belief that he had been able to transport her into a semi-conscious erotic trance. Sometimes he could not settle himself, and would have to resist the impulse to crane his neck to see what she was looking at. The difference with Pip was that he felt so very closely observed, so very much present; her eyes never left his face, never shut, never shifted, not even inches away from his. She was consummately alert, and the nervous intensity of her attention prohibited him from being able to stop long after he knew he should, and long after he wanted to. He barely knew how they'd ended up in her bedroom at all; working out an exit route was a far more pressing concern.

'Look, Pip . . .' Shame-faced: that's how he knew he looked. Shame-faced.

'You don't have to say anything, Jerry. It never happened, OK? Except that it's good that it did, because now I get to say it never happened in a different way from saying it never happened if it actually *hadn't* happened. As far as Olivia's concerned, it never happened. God – don't look so tragic! I know you're not interested in me, and I can live with that, OK? It's fine.'

'It's not fine at all. It's a mess.'

'Rubbish. Remember the great Train of Life? Think of tonight as a pre-boarding preliminary check on the buffet. So, you didn't buy anything. So what? Nothing ventured, nothing gained. Honestly, Jerry, it just happened. Or, rather, *didn't* – not for you, at least. I still think you're great. I still think you're the best of the bunch. Now either get the hell out of the house, or get up to Olivia's room before she walks in the door. *Go*. Scram.' She fumbled, trying to unbutton her pyjama top so she could get her head through.

'I'll have to tell Olivia.'

Pip shook her hair free of the collar. 'Do whatever you want, but you'd be making a big mistake . . . If you tell her, she has to react. If you don't, then believe me, it will never cross her mind that anything ever happened between us – and let's be frank, nothing did, did it? Go on, go.'

'Pip. I've always believed one thing, even when I was certain I was destined to be a brahmachaarin.'

'A whaty?'

'Celibate bachelor.'

Pip giggled. 'Oh yeah, *that*. I hear it's a common stage boys go through post-puberty.'

'I've always known that an affair should begin, at least *begin* in the belief that it will last for ever. You have to believe that it will never end before it starts. It's criminal to start with the foresight of it ending.'

'So what were we doing just now?'

'I don't know.'

'Jerry, I don't have all that wacko hare krishna stuff under my belt like you,' he winced, 'but what I do know is this. We're young, learning is all about trial and error, and between people like us, there's a kind of equality in the game. Maybe, when we've all grown up, we'll have to think about responsibility for others, and salvation of our souls and all that shit – but right now, we've got time on our side, and the inclination, and the appetite, and the opportunity. I think it's "criminal" not to take it. Don't be a bore now. We can forget all about it, OK? Now *get out*.' As Jerry hesitated in the doorway she added, 'I love you, you screwed-up nutter.'

Jerry went upstairs. He did not agree with Pip that youth entitled individuals to play fast and loose. He believed that people of every age bore responsibility for the health of their own hearts as well as those of others. When Olivia came back sometime later, much later, he pretended to be asleep. Olivia was glad he was there; it did not occur to her to question his right to sleep in her bed without an official invitation. She was relieved he wasn't waiting up for her. Jerry was equally relieved she'd come back, but he still did not find sleep easy. He watched over her as she slept, and prayed for the chance to stay watching over her for ever.

In the morning, Olivia stayed in bed and said she felt ill. She certainly looked it, disproving the theory that falling in love gives women a special radiance. Most women, when they fall in love, or begin – even contemplate beginning – an affair, look far from radiant, just as pregnancy very rarely brings a glow until it is irrevocably established and public knowledge. Olivia looked tired and jaded. The thought of Justus brought on waves of nausea, a liquid stomach, leaden legs and aching thighs. She felt unable to concentrate, drugged, drunk; she didn't want to discuss the ailment with anyone. Jerry and Pip decided she had summer flu; even George appeared at her bedside with a thermometer and a couple of trashy paperbacks. Their solicitousness only aggravated her symptoms, and despite her resolution to be someone on whom nothing is lost, she failed to notice Pip's red eyes.

## not a note; not a word . . .

'OK. Cut and *print*.' The assistant director pulled his hat low over his eyes and slumped back in his chair. They had been shooting a tiny yet crucial scene, a scene in which Rowland and Roderick lay on their backs in an Apennine valley while Roderick threw a wobbly about leaving Italy and heading for the Swiss Alps. Although the journey had taken several days for Rod and Row, the 'Italian' valley was but a stone's throw from the 'Swiss' destination for the film crew, and both were solidly within French borders. Christina Light, a.k.a. Ophélie Arcier, had a few days' rest and had gone to Paris to discuss her next venture. An American ingénue, Lily Danziger, had rejoined the set in France for the next scene, in which she played Roderick's fiancée Mary Garland. When they broke for lunch, she reclined on the grass next to Justus.

'I hear on the grapevine you're gettin' married.'

'That's right.'

'That's grand,' she drawled. 'It's grand to hear of people like you doing normal stuff like getting married. God surely knows how you find time to meet any normal people.'

'We go way back.'

'So she's not part of all this shit?'

'No, she's a teacher. She teaches in Rome.'

'Real normal, then. How delicious. Sometimes I wish I was a teacher in Rome. Oh, it's OK for guys like you, you're made already, but nobody ever told me what hard work all this was.'

'It's a job. All jobs are hard work.'

'Endless toil, or you don't deserve the reward,' she replied with a smile. 'Tell me about it.'

The request was rhetorical, and Justus didn't have the energy to chat about the profession with yet another young hopeful. When he thought about it, which he didn't often, Lily was a good actress, he appreciated her cynicism, had some affinity with her non-theatrical background, and liked her unpretty face, but he was tired of talking shop. He picked up the script and pretended to concentrate on it.

'So this is the bit where you risk your life on the rocks to get me a flower, an' I realise, all serious wide eyes and stuff, that you don't love littl'ol' me, after all?'

'Un-huh.'

'And then I walk around for a bit with Rowland, while he tells me that he does really love me?'

'Un-huh.'

'And then I read aloud to you, and find you're not listening to a word I'm saying?'

'Un-huh.'

'Just like you're not listenin' to me now?'

Justus grinned at her. 'I'm sorry, Lily. You must think I'm rude. I just have other things on my mind.'

'Forget it. I was just trying to get in character. It's clear as glass you're already in it.'

Justus had been thinking about Olivia, and wondering whether she would accompany him on location in the future. He refused to acknowledge that he expected her to do so, only that he hoped it would be true. He was not marrying her because he needed a consort, nor did he want to be cherished and mothered, but he badly needed somebody other than himself to look after. Bottom line, Justus O'Keefe was bored by his own issues and pursuing his own goals; he bored himself. He had found the filming of *Roderick Hudson* far more arduous than he would have been prepared to admit to Barry Norman or any of the host of film critics who interviewed him about his work. Unlike *The 87th Precinct* and *Mad City*, *Roderick Hudson* had made him think of earlier times, at Oxford, when he and other friends had weighed the merits of Henry James and William Faulkner. He had perfect recall of an evening alone with Olivia, not long after they'd first met, when he had teased her about seeking a deep interior life. Now, if not then, she gave the impression of having one, and his concern was that he had been so busy with his exterior life that the interior had slipped out the back door while he wasn't looking. Marriage to Olivia would ground him, he was confident of that. As his enchantment with success faded, so he looked for another goal to pursue, and he would be as tireless in his pursuit of the real thing as he had been in pursuit of an altogether more artificial one. His initial reaction to Olivia's admission of a past pregnancy was a tribute to his acting skills; he had been far less affected than he had shown.

Justus was not perturbed by the notion of what might have been, so long as he had a good grip on what could be. He wanted to have children and to be a good father, but the notion that eleven years earlier there had been a biological possibility of paternity did not move him. Nor did it come as any surprise that Olivia had been sleeping with Jerry Milton over the same period that she had been making love with him; he had always been aware of that. His dominant feeling had been an uneasy uncertainty about how he would have reacted if she *had* phoned him in New York and told him she was pregnant; it would remain unresolved. He hoped he would have done the decent thing, but was relieved that it had not been put to the test. Personal morality, he thought, was a little bit like a fire extinguisher, one of those things you only used in an emergency, and couldn't just test to see if it worked before your life was dependent on it. He had required more selfishness then than he did now, and was glad he had not been left holding the baby, as it were, although he hoped he would have found some way of living with it if he had. Justus was now concerned only by what he termed Olivia's hesitancy: as they got closer to a wedding date, he was increasingly aware of some vague waywardness on her part. Without a trace of vanity, he did not put this down to doubt that she loved him; Justus knew what was lovable and what was not in himself, and he believed they were well matched. The timing of their needs had fallen into place with the neatness and simplicity of the cracking of an egg. His issue now was to co-ordinate the wedding and the final shoot in Massachusetts, and to get Olivia the hell out of the grip of the Oxford cronies he still regarded as children.

'Justus, there's a phone call for you. I've had it put through to the trailer, OK?'

Justus walked slowly across to where the trailer was parked precariously on the edge of a steep mountain path. Laura had been harassing him for a decision on *The Spider House*, which he wanted to discuss with Olivia before committing her to a working honeymoon.

'Go away, Laura. Leave me alone. I still haven't decided.'

'That's going to be a big problem because I've just booked us a date with the Chelsea Town Hall registrar.'

Justus laughed. 'Hello, my darling. You did it?'

'Bright and early this morning, but only by dropping a hell of a lot of names – rather, dropping your name a hell of a lot of times. We're pencilled in for August the nineteenth, which is a Tuesday.

No chance of a Friday or Saturday, and you still have to go in and show your passport, and get some kind of release or deposition from the embassy – I don't know, you may have to get a letter from the U.S. ambassador. There's a ton of red tape, but at least we're sort of in the book.'

'Thank God for that. I dreamed last night you told me you were getting married to George Upton.'

'You did?'

'Yeah – a real sweaty nightmare.' He hadn't dreamed anything of the sort.

'Maybe you subconsciously *want* me to marry George Upton.'

'Maybe I consciously want you here right now . . .' he growled in return.

'I'd come like a shot, believe me, if there wasn't so much paperwork to do.'

'I can fly back this weekend if it helps.'

'It probably would, darling. If you were there, in the flesh, maybe they'd take me more seriously. They probably have ten women a week turning up and claiming they're marrying Brad Pitt.'

'Say the word and I'm there. *Shit.*'

'What?'

'We're all meant to be in the States from Saturday.'

'So tell them you can't go – say your wife won't let you.'

'Oh, honey, if only . . . Hey, that reminds me. How d'you like the sound of a ten-week honeymoon in North Africa?'

'Explain.'

'D'you know a book called *The Spider House*?'

'Paul Bowles? Of course I do.'

'D'you like it?'

'I love it.'

'I've got a script – I think it's good.'

'I get it. A working honeymoon, right? You working, me moon-ing around.'

'I hope to hell you mean moping around.'

'Sorry. I haven't got the hang of Americanisms. I will.'

'You better.'

'Justus, whatever you want to do is fine by me. I mean that. I love Morocco. I love Paul Bowles.'

'I'm waiting . . .'

'I love you.'

'And I love you, darling, more than you'll ever know. Liv, they're calling me, can I call you later?'

'Of course. I'm on my way out to have lunch with Pip, but I'll be home tonight.'

'Is she going to be our witness?'

'Yes. We'll talk later, OK?'

'Don't hang up – just tell me you love me again.'

'I love you again.'

'I love you more.'

'Justus, go for God's sake – you've got to be reliable. I'm only marrying you if you can hold down a steady job, remember?'

'And remind me why I'm marrying you, sweetheart?'

'You are marrying me because you don't know anything about culture, or books, or scripts, or art, and you need me to choose your films for you. Send me this script, OK? And find out where we'll be staying. *The Spider House* is Fez, right? Then it's got to be a suite at the Jamai Palace or I'm not coming.'

'I'll get it in the contract.'

When Justus reached the set, and after Makeup and Wardrobe had finished with him, they started the cameras rolling.

'Cut.' The director wiped his forehead. 'Uhh, *Justus*. One pointer. Roderick is in the Slough of Despond, yeah? He's abandoned everything. The guy hates himself. I don't know, I don't want to get into all that heavy metaphysical shit, but you could say he hates life itself, his art, the whole shitheap. D'you think you could lose the puppy-dog grin?'

Pip had to sweep the passenger seat free of rubbish before Olivia could get into the car; she threw plastic sandwich wrappers and paper coffee cups on to the back seat, leaving the floor space still littered with magazines and other debris. Olivia picked up a copy of *Cosmopolitan* as Pip turned into Kensington Church Street.

'Remember when we used to pore over these? Why the hell did we buy them?'

'For the sex and makeup tips. Remember when we tried smearing that white highlighter stuff down our noses to make them look thinner? That was some schmuck's brilliant tip.'

'Why do you buy them now?' Pip threw her a quick sideways glance and grinned as they said in unison, 'For the sex and makeup tips . . .'

'Actually, the only stuff I ever read are the problem pages – they always make me feel better.'

'I still like the multiple-choice quizzes.'

'Here's one for you: You are about to be married to a famous film star. Spending the weekend in the country, you bump into a former lover. Do you (a) Treat him as an old friend and invite him to the wedding (b) Pretend you've never laid eyes on him before (c) Disappear for a final night of wild passion or (d) Tell him he impregnated you ten years earlier?'

'That's not funny, Pip.'

'I'm sorry – I have an uncontrollable impulse to make tasteless comments. It's an addiction.'

'Anyway, you forgot (e), None of the above. I always ended up choosing none of the above.'

'Where shall we have lunch? We could always nip down the M40 to Oxford.'

'Why not?'

As Pip crawled along the Westway she began to recount her various attempts at finding love. 'I did them all, Liv – I ran the gamut of deeply unsuitable relationships. Honestly, I couldn't have covered the ground better if someone had laid a trail. First off at the Beeb I fell in love with my boss, who was not only married but much worse, my *mentor*. Big no-no. It was OK because he made it painfully clear it was unrequited anyway. So then I thought I'd hock my broken heart further afield and went out for a year with a colleague of George's who kept telling me that education ruined women and I was the living proof of it. So that pushed me back into Michael's arms, which was fine – at least it meant I had a boyfriend. Remember you once told me to get a boyfriend and stop messing about in other people's relationships?'

'Please tell me I didn't ever say that.'

'Oh, but you did, and you were right. It was hunky-dory till Michael announced he was marrying someone else. Then all our friends started dropping like flies: George and Sarah had already done it; I don't think there was a single girl from St Mary's who wasn't engaged by the age of twenty-five – at least, everyone who got engaged took pains to phone me and tell me about it. I could have papered the walls of my flat three times over with wedding invitations. Count yourself lucky you missed all that. Then I met a landscape gardener – got him over to look at my window-boxes when I decided that I would be a deeply fulfilled and green-fingered spinster, and the next thing I knew we were in bed and I was spending my weekends trundling wheelbarrows and spreading horseshit. Then I went full circle and fell in love with a guy in the next-door office I was meant to be training, but that was doomed too. I told you I was a slow learner. And now . . .'

'Where does Jerry fit in?'

'Jerry never fitted in, not even when he moved in. I know he told you about us, him and me. I would have told you myself, if we hadn't all ended up in that ridiculous situation in Suffolk. I was terribly in love with him, almost as soon as he came back to England. Eventually, he moved in with me, and a couple of years later he moved back out, just as easily.'

'He didn't tell me what went wrong.'

'You know, Livvy, I don't think anything *did* go wrong. Sometimes I still think we'll get back together. Less so now, but maybe it could happen. I'd marry him tomorrow if he asked. Not that I've ever loved him as much as my first great passion.'

'Who – Sting?'

'Before Sting. Chocolate.' Pip crashed the gears as she accelerated.

'Why don't you ask him? Ask Jerry to marry you?'

'The truth? I'm scared he'd say yes, and then regret it.'

'D'you mind if I smoke?'

'Consider the floor your personal ashtray.'

Olivia looked out of the window for a while: the countryside, if it deserved to be called that, and even the road were unfamiliar, although it was a journey she had covered a hundred times.

'D'you believe in the Tarot, Pip?'

'I'd believe in anything that said good stuff about me. You had some sort of psychic thing in New York, didn't you? George told me about it.'

'Everything gets around, doesn't it? I met a woman who was a sort of clairvoyant. She told me I was looking for a man I'd loved once, but lost.'

'Justus? Or Jerry?'

Olivia replied indirectly. 'George thought it was all crap.'

'He would, wouldn't he? When have you ever seen George

believe anything that isn't printed in black and white and under his nose?'

'This woman said that I was going to get married, but not for some time. I've just booked Chelsea registry office for August the nineteenth.'

'Well, you could say that's not for some time, couldn't you?'

'Are you still going to be our witness?'

'Of course. Don't you want to do the white-dress bit?'

'I can't think of anything worse. I'd like you to help me choose something to wear, though.'

'Fantastic. We'll start looking in Oxford.' Pip resettled her grip on the steering wheel. 'About Jerry –'

'Why didn't you ever tell him about my abortion?'

'I knew you'd ask that, sooner or later. There was only one moment when I could have told him. When you first left. I had no idea what was going on, Liv. For all I knew you might have come back three weeks later pretending everything was fine. How would it have been if I'd told Jerry you'd been bonking the man he hated most on earth, got pregnant and had an abortion? My job was holding the fort till you came back. I didn't like it – I didn't like lying, but I honestly thought I was doing the best thing, and that my first loyalty was to you. Then Jerry said he was going to Rome, and I thought, fine; let him find out whatever he can, or whatever you want to tell him, the ball's in your court – and I was really mad at you by then, for not getting in touch. I didn't see Jerry again for two years. By the time he came back, what was I meant to say? Hey, Jerry, I could have saved you the trip?'

'But for years after – for seven years, you didn't say anything. I always assumed you'd told him. I couldn't understand why he never wrote about it.'

'It was too late by the time he came back. How was it going to help anyone my trying to analyse what had gone on in your head?

I didn't understand it myself. You'd told me often enough it wasn't my business. I wasn't even certain it had happened, to be quite honest. Jesus, Liv, I made the appointment for the abortion, I picked you up, remember? You seemed fine, quiet but fine. Ten days later you're gone – pouf! Bags out, everything. Not a note, not a word.'

'I just got a train to Rome, I didn't know I wasn't coming back, honestly, I just wanted to go away and forget all about it.'

'What an absolute mess.' Pip sighed as they approached the Banbury Road. 'Shall we go to Browns?'

'Where else?'

'You realise we'll be a hundred years older than anyone else in the place?'

'Sod 'em. We're richer, too.'

During lunch there was a great deal of do you remember, do you remember, some happy, some sad, but the two women colluded in selecting mainly the funny memories. The restaurant felt smaller and shabbier than during their time, but the menu had barely changed.

'So where are you going to have the reception?'

'I don't think we're going to have one, maybe just lunch. It's only going to be you, us, my parents and his parents, whom I haven't even met. I don't want to have a big thing. I don't know anyone here any longer. It seems silly to ask them to my wedding.'

'What about friends in Rome?'

'I thought about it. I'd love one or two to come, and I might still ask them, but you know what it's like – it's very hard to pick twenty and not end up asking fifty. I don't want that sort of wedding.'

'It just feels a bit hole-in-the-corner, Liv. I mean, when you're marrying such a celeb, why not really celebrate, ha ha? Otherwise, what's the point?'

'That is *not* why I'm marrying him.'

'Ah-ha! So we finally get to the $64,000 question. Exactly why are you marrying him, may I ask?'

'I love him. I know what he wants and I know I can give it to him. We always had something in common.'

'You had sex in common –'

'We *fit*. We're alike.'

'Hey, don't go overboard on starry-eyed romance!'

'I'm serious, Pip. When I saw him in Rome, I knew it was meant to be.'

'Fate.' Pip groaned.

'Why not? What's wrong with fate?'

'Nothing. You always used to say it was fate that brought you and Jerry together.'

'Fate my arse. It was the fact that I couldn't ride a bicycle.'

'Funny you didn't end up with any of the other people you ran over.' Pip twirled her spaghetti on her fork with a flourish that sent clam sauce splattering over her white shirt. 'Jesus. How come I always look like a pig and you look like you've stepped out of a *Vogue* centrefold?'

'I think you should marry Jerry. I think you should go ahead and ask him. I know he loves you.'

'He loves me, all right, but there's no getting away from the fact you're still his . . .You should have seen his face when I told him you were going to New York with George.'

'He thinks I'm here on some vanity kick, trying to prove everyone still loves me. It isn't true. If I'd been getting married to anybody other than Justus, I wouldn't have come back at all. It was only because it was Justus that I had to.'

'I can see that. I'm sure Jerry can too.'

'No, he can't. He thinks I'm a manipulative bitch.'

'So what do you care if he does? Let him go hang. You've done the decent thing at last, you've come back, said you're sorry – why beat yourself up over it? You love Justus. He loves you. Stuff Jerry. Go ahead and marry him – Justus, I mean. Where are you guys going to live?'

'We've barely talked about it. I guess between New York and LA.'

'*Between*. Spoilt for choice, huh? You're going to have to tell me which before I book my tickets. Which I'd like to do next week.'

'*God*, it's good to see you, I never knew how badly I missed you till I saw you again.'

'I have that effect on people. Out of sight –'

'Tell me about work.'

'Work's fine, really good, in fact. I'm a commissioning editor. I produce some stuff, but it's mainly deciding what we should commission, and when to schedule it. God, I complain about it all the time, but down deep, I love it. The professional side of my life is just dandy – it's the personal side that sucks. I've got a new man in my life. I did, at least . . .'

'Well?'

'Oh, he's a bugger, really. I kind of called it off before it started – I know his type so well. Ever since Jerry moved out I keep attracting men who specialise in the shoe-cleaning approach to romance.'

'You've lost me.'

'Don't you remember from St Mary's? Spit and polish, spit and polish. First they spit on you, then they rub you to make it better. Then when you're all happy and shiny, they spit on you again.'

'So why put up with it? You never would have – not when I knew you.'

'I don't. It would just be so nice to find someone to settle down with. I'd like to have children, or I'd like just to know it was *going* to happen, one day, so I didn't have to keep worrying about it. I'd like to be able to go to a party without it even crossing my mind which of the men there are married and which not. Just not to care.'

'Marry Jerry.'

'Maybe I will – ask him, I mean. It's not like I've got anything to lose. It's not like he can't say no, or I'm worried about what he'll think when he sees me naked. At least I've got over all that. What was it like with Justus second time around?'

Olivia shook her head: it took considerable effort to concentrate on what she'd felt about Justus rather than imagining Pip and Jerry in bed together. 'Oooh, I can't really describe it. In one way, it was scary. Then, in an odd way it was like nothing had changed at all, as if it was only a few days since we'd been in bed together – all very straightforward, and very,' she shrugged, 'nice.'

Pip laughed the throaty, gurgling laugh that their house mistress used to describe as the sound of water rushing out of the tub. 'I can just see the interview headline: "'Sex with Justus is Nice' says O'Keefe's Schoolmarm Bride." That'll do a lot for his ratings.'

'OK, more than nice . . .'

'Don't say any more – really. I get embarrassed enough reading sex scenes in trash novels. They either make me feel ill or so jealous I can't stand it. I don't think I can face hearing a real one.'

'I wasn't surprised by it being good sex – I was surprised by it being so *nice*.'

'You've always had the luck of the devil.'

'Don't say that – not even as a joke.' Pip held up her index fingers in a cross. 'I mean it, Pip, don't say it. It spooks me.'

Outside the restaurant they stood in indecision, looking up and down the street.

'We could try the shops on the High – or Little Clarendon

Street?' Olivia suggested. 'I've got no idea what's there any more.'

'No, I know where we'll go. Follow me.'

'Lead on, Macduff!'

The girl who opened the door looked sulky and hung over. When she saw two middle-aged women on the doorstep she scowled. 'I'm not the owner. If it's about the council tax, you'll have to talk to him.'

Pip did all the talking. 'We're terribly sorry to disturb you, and I hope you won't think this odd. My name's Philippa Renfrew – I'm from the BBC.' She offered the card she used to pass the security guards at Broadcasting House; the girl glanced at it but remained singularly unimpressed. 'My colleague and I are researching a programme on Oxford, working title, *Oxford Now and Then*.' Her pale eyebrows worked furiously up and down as she thought. She leaned back to peer at the number on the dark blue door. 'This *is* number twelve, isn't it? You see, one hundred years ago, this house was occupied by one of the Worcester porters – a Mr Frank Buttle, wasn't it, Olivia?' Olivia nodded gravely. 'And Mr Buttle let a set of rooms to an undergraduate called Finnian McCorquindale who kept a diary, rather a detailed diary for the times, never published, but the original is still in the Bodleian.' The girl looked at her with complete indifference. 'Now the curious fact about *this* house, number twelve, is that there exists a record of every occupier who has ever lived here since it was built in eighteen eighty-seven barring a brief period in the mid-nineteen-eighties when we cannot trace who owned the house, and it seems to have fallen into rather dubious hands – a lowlife pimp called Upton who masqueraded as an undergraduate.' Pip hiccuped, and Olivia turned away to stare intently down the street. 'We have been looking for the perfect house to act as the focus, the *mise-en-scène*, if you will, for the series, and this would seem to be it. You follow me? *Oxford Now and Then* – how the students live, housing conditions, parties, moral codes, academic rigour . . .'

'It's already been done – that show on telly, with the students, where they had the cameras on all the time?' The girl showed signs, albeit faint ones, of life. 'Not bloody likely.'

'No, no no – this is *radio*. Only interviews, nothing intrusive, no candid camera. We'd probably only need you and the other current residents for, ooh, say a couple of hours or so? At a time of your convenience . . . You are, ah, all students here, aren't you?' She turned officiously to Olivia. 'Olivia? Your research did confirm the house was still a student residence?' then swung back to the girl.

'Like I said, I just live here. If you want to do anything, you'll have to talk to the guy who owns it.'

'And would that be possible?' Pip was smiling so hard her jaw hurt.

'It would.'

'Lovely!'

'If he was in. Which he isn't.' Now it was the girl's turn to smile, well satisfied with her handling of the situation.

'I don't suppose we could wait here for him?'

'You could . . . but he's in Paris till mid-September.'

'Then that would be rather tedious, wouldn't it?' Pip snapped. Olivia tugged at her arm, but Pip's blood was up. All the concentrated determination of a one-goal-down hockey team in the closing moments of a match rushed through her veins. 'Now, listen here, sweetheart, I don't think it would really destroy your life to let us have a little peek at the house, and tell us who lives here, would it? If you and your house-mates don't want to proceed after that, fine. I'm sure we can find somebody a tad more accommodating, diary or no diary.'

The girl opened the door. 'Suit yourself. You can look around.

Don't take any pictures, and for God's sake don't touch the hi-fi stuff or Barg will kill me.'

'Barg?' Pip squeaked, in a stage whisper to Olivia. '*Barg?*'

'I'm going back up to my room, OK? I've got to work.'

'Bit late in the academic year for work, isn't it? We thought we'd find the house all locked up – assumed you'd all be sunning yourself on Greek islands.'

'Oh, yeah? That just proves how little you people know about students, doesn't it? Most of my mates are doing summer jobs, but I just failed Mods, so I'm spending the summer working. If I don't pass the resits, I won't even sodding be here when you come back to do the interviews.'

They waited until they heard an upstairs door slam shut.

'Miserable bitch – pig-ugly, too. I'm sure we wouldn't have behaved like that.' Pip stared up the stairs, while Olivia went into the sitting room. She heard Olivia's low gasp, and followed her.

'Pip! Oh, *Pip!*' Olivia grabbed Pip with one hand, and with the other pointed with a trembling finger across the room. 'It's the same sofa – it's George's sofa – and there's Billy's penis!'

The shabby, sprigged sofa had not even been re-covered since their own tenancy. Pip remembered George having such trouble trying to get it out of the front door that he had finally abandoned it. Above it, in sepia swirls, Billy's nude stood rampant, faded but still proud. They stared at it in awe, as rapt as two cultural pilgrims gazing on the ceiling of the Sistine Chapel.

# The Rules of the Game 8

All that month, the 12 Kingston Road household was slowly dismantling. Having failed with the flat-owning Peter, Pip had taken on the burden of finding an alternative in London, leaving George to interview prospective tenants for the following year. Olivia was trying to be kind to Jerry. She had started to scan the death entries in the paper before handing it to him, testing if she could pick out the one that would most appeal to him. One morning she brought him coffee in bed, with the paper folded to the right section, and nudged him awake. 'D'you fancy driving down to London tomorrow? There's a gig on that might amuse you. Not many details, I'm afraid – no stuff about "as courageous in death as he was in life" or "this almost unbelievably extraordinary character leaves a great void in the lives of . . ."' Her index finger tapped on the entry:

> **Bashell, William**, Putney Vale Chapel, 3.30 p.m. Donations to Pro Dog or Airedale Terrier Rescue.

'I bet he left a great void in the lives of his Airedales,' Jerry observed. 'Do you think they'll be at the service, howling away?'

'Probably. They'll almost certainly be his beneficiaries.'

'Shall we go – just to see?'

'Can't say I'm in the mood to support the canine mourners, no.'
She passed him the coffee. 'What have I done to deserve this?'

'Oh, I don't know.'

'Livvy, we have to talk.'

'I was hoping you wouldn't say that.'

'I know, but we do. Something's wrong.'

'No, it isn't. I've just been sick, and feeling sad about going
down, that's all. Really. And bloody tired.' The fact that they hadn't
really talked for several days, and had slept in the same bed but not
made love weighed on them equally; she certainly wasn't tired
from a surfeit of sex.

Jerry pulled the pillow over his head. 'I don't think I want to go
to this party tonight. I'm sick of parties.'

'You don't have to come. We could go somewhere else,
together. We could see a movie.'

'Liv, it's *your* party, your farewell thrash. You don't think it
would look odd if you didn't turn up?'

'George and Pip won't mind, and I don't care about anyone else.
I'll tell them we're too sick. No – I'll tell them we're too *well* to
attend.' She risked cracking a joke but when Jerry barely smiled
she changed tactics. 'Come on, get up. I can't stand you when
you're morose. You can help me pack. I'm going to burn all my
essays tonight on the sacrificial bonfire. Everyone's been told to
bring something to burn. What will you consign to the ashes of
Oxford?'

'How about your suitcase?'

'What?'

'The suitcase you keep in your car. Will you let me chuck that
on?'

'If you hate it so much. You don't even know what's in it.'

'Then it will be even more satisfying burning it. The mystery of it all.'

'You can have a look if you like. Pip took the car to London, but when she comes back . . .'

'No, thanks. When *is* Pip coming back?'

'Sometime this afternoon, she said.'

'I'm not convinced this idea of living together is a good idea.'

'You and me?' She had a queasy feeling of sudden emptiness.

'No, the four of us. It's a mistake. We need a clean break.'

'I can't tell them that – they'll die. They're my best friends. Is this what's been bugging you?'

'Part of it. It just doesn't feel right, Liv. It isn't giving any of us a chance to grow and, boy, do we need to grow. And I'm fed up with playing our relationship out in front of an audience.'

'If anyone should object to that, it's Pip and George. Listen. George is going to end up spending at least half the weekends back in Oxford, anyway, probably here, in his own bedroom, if he lets the house to Sarah, which he almost certainly will. You can't feel uncomfortable in front of Pip.'

'I wasn't only thinking about us, I was imagining how she might feel, that she might feel excluded.'

'Oh, Pip will find a boyfriend in London – she's bound to. Don't be so sensitive. She'd be devastated if we pulled out. Besides, we can't afford anywhere alone.'

Jerry pulled the sheet over his head. The only way out of this was searing honesty, if he could only summon the courage to tell her.

Pip burst into the house and shouted up the stairs, 'Guys – Liv? Everyone? I've got a house! I signed the contract. And you all have to give me a shitload of money or my deposit cheque will bounce. Time to pack our bags and move on – the Train awaits!'

The dress code on the invitations – George's choice – had read 'Prepared for the Future'. George wore one of two pinstriped suits he'd commissioned from a gentlemen's tailor in the High. Pip wore her school gym slip and house sash and carried a teddy bear as a statement that she resolutely refused to give up her grip on youth; besides, it flattered her. Over a hundred undergraduates – in their last few weeks before graduation – turned up during the evening, some in costume and others not. Olivia refused to let Jerry dress as a monk on the grounds that he looked more camp than the fields around Agincourt, so he settled on jeans to signify his continuing student existence. Olivia wore black to signify mourning. Michael Marsden brought three cases of beer he'd bought on tick from the buttery and a packet of Anadin, so no change there. Billy appeared in a fur coat, but once inside the front door stripped off to reveal all – the flesh-coloured bikini underneath left little to the imagination.

'Billy, what on earth are you meant to be?'

'I am prepared for the future.'

'As what, or is it rude to ask?'

'I have decided to be an artist's model rather than an artist. I wish to be a muse. I will make my body my creation.'

Michael drew her into the garden. 'That's an amazing coincidence. Just this minute I decided to be an artist, and I'm on the look-out for a decent muse . . .'

When Justus arrived at midnight, half of the guests were dancing in the garden; those who weren't were sprawled in the sitting room, or chatting in clusters up the stairs. The entire house was littered with bottles and fag ends but George was beyond caring; he had resigned responsibility. He leaned over the top banisters dangling the house keys tantalisingly above Sarah's head. Sarah – in cap and gown, prepared for her own finals – gazed up at him adoringly and worried how their romance would survive

George's departure for London. Justus absorbed everything, the mild debauchery that sought to be so much more extreme than it was, the broken glass, the carelessness of the revellers, their reluctance to bid farewell to the protection that Oxford had temporarily offered them. He helped himself to a drink and wandered into the crowded back garden. Billy entwined herself around him. 'Justus, will you have me for your muse?'

'Sure, Billy, just call me when you want me.'

'Justus, you're not even dressed up!'

'I am, Pip, I just left my props in the hall. A spear, and I brought a couple of friends with me – hope you don't mind.'

'I don't get it. What are you?'

'Third spear carrier. Is Livvy around?'

'Somewhere.'

He pressed his way through the crowds of people, greeting friends and repeating the phrase, 'Yeah, I'm sticking around in London, you won't be rid of me that quick,' whenever he was questioned. All the time he looked for Olivia. After an hour, convinced she was avoiding him, he grew too bored to linger; Justus could not participate in the rituals of leaving something he had never really felt part of. He clambered over the bodies that crowded the stairs and knocked lightly on Olivia's door.

'Don't come in – hang on!' a man's voice shouted as Justus entered.

'Hey – excuse me.' Justus grinned at the unknown couple lying semi-clad on Olivia's bed. 'I just wanted to leave a note for Olivia. Pretend I'm not even here.'

They resumed as he looked for pen and paper amid the clutter on Olivia's desk.

'Hello, sweetcakes,' he scribbled. 'Missed you at the party. Missed you all over. Don't leave town without coming to say goodbye. I'm here till Thursday, then to London to seek fame and fortune – seeking something, anyway.' As he went to the door Olivia walked in, flushed and her hair ruffled.

'Hello, stranger. I just wrote you a note.'

Olivia glanced at the couple on her bed. 'Matt, d'you mind doing that somewhere else? If it isn't too much to ask. You can use George's room if you haven't finished.' She leaned against the door and ushered out the unabashed couple. 'I thought you'd gone. I wasn't sure you'd come.'

'I *was* going . . .' He smoothed a lock of hair off her face. 'I only came to say goodbye to you.'

Olivia stiffened. 'I just came up to get my keys – I've run out of cigarettes, I'm going to the garage to get some.'

'You've been drinking. You shouldn't drive.'

'Who are you, my mother?'

'She never took care of you, you told me yourself. You shouldn't smoke either.'

'Oh, like you don't.'

'I quit as soon as you walked out on me. It was easy. You should do it.'

'There are lots of things I should and shouldn't do.'

'Such as?'

'Oh, nothing.' She squeezed past him and grabbed her car keys.

'I don't suppose you could drop me back at Magdalen on your way? There's a garage just past the bridge. I'll even drive.'

Olivia hesitated for a second. Jerry had gone to dance with Pip; she'd told him she'd be back in twenty minutes. She probably wouldn't see Justus again, almost certainly not. She picked up the car keys from her desk and read his note. 'I don't see why not. But I'll drive. I don't trust you.'

The streets were quiet barring the odd clusters of students spilling out of brightly lit houses or loitering around college gates. The city belonged to them, at least to those who were staying. Olivia pulled up outside Magdalen. A figure loomed out of the darkness and peered in the passenger window. Justus rolled it down.

'O'Keefe, where've you been? Sissy's been looking for you. We're all going to Henry's place – you've gotta be there, man.'

'Sure, sure, I'll be along.' Justus turned to Olivia. 'Thanks for the lift. Isn't this the scene where I ask you in for a night-cap? My folks aren't home . . .'

Olivia knotted her hair into a loose coil. 'Thanks, but I'm dying for a cigarette. And I ought to get back.'

'And I thought you were adventurous . . . Intrepid.'

'You were wrong. I am quintessentially trepid.'

'What's the matter, Olivia? Scared of the consequences? Or scared of me? I'm harmless. Come in for ten minutes, OK? Just have a coffee before you drive again. Besides, I want to give you something.'

'I can't leave the car here.'

'Sure you can. You can't spend your life worrying about parking tickets and being late back. Tell you what, if you get a ticket, I'll pay. We'll only be five minutes.'

'I want to get some fags.'

He leaned across her and pushed open her door, brushing her cheek with his lips. 'You don't need to. I promise. I'll take care of everything.'

Justus had a quick word with the porter and Olivia let herself be led through the large quad and up the familiar staircase to Justus's room. At the top of the stairs he banged on his neighbour's door. A face peered out sleepily.

'Jack, got any smokes you could spare for a lady in distress?' Justus caught the pack of Marlboro thrown through the open crack and handed them to Olivia as he unlocked his door.

'You see, solutions to all life's problems are always just around the corner. Don't sweat over them. It's a full pack, too. Not that I want to encourage you to smoke. Filthy habit.' He peeled off his sweater. 'You haven't been to see me since . . .'

'You haven't exactly been banging down my door either.'

'I wanted to, but your house is always full. I don't like to disturb you. Besides, I thought I should wait for an invitation. You're the one who's getting married, not me.'

'Don't be ridiculous. Of course I'm not getting married – not immediately, at least.'

Justus offered her whisky but she declined. 'I'm not trying to get you drunk so I can have my evil way. I wanted you to sober up, remember?'

'I know that.'

'Not that I don't want to . . . You know that too, I guess.' He held his hands palms up, in a gesture of innocent enquiry. 'So?'

'Stop looking at me like that. What did you want to give me?'

'Oh yeah, it went straight out of my head. Funny – I must have been distracted.' He held out a book.

'Emerson. Complete works. How nice.'

'I promised it to you, remember? I think you'll like the essay on self-reliance. He makes a great case for nonconformity. You should read "English Traits", too, there's a lot of you in it.'

'That's strange, seeing as I'm not really English.'

'You're very English, Olivia. The fact that you don't want to be only proves that you are.'

Olivia opened the book. On the inside Justus had written, 'To the girl on whom nothing is lost'. 'Thanks.'

'You're welcome. I hope that night we had together wasn't lost on you, Livvy.'

'Not entirely.'

'I hope you didn't regret it.'

'Not yet. I ought to get back.'

'Since when did you develop this strong sense of obligation?'

'Maybe you inspire it in me.'

'Thank God I inspire something. I was beginning to think I left you stone cold. C'mon, Olivia. Sit down and at least have a cigarette, just so I know I didn't go to all that trouble for nothing. The party's going to run for hours. You're not scared about Jerry, are you? If you like, I'll even come back with you and say I kept you out. I'll take the blame like a man.'

'That's a lot easier than taking it like a woman.'

'I'll say I kidnapped you – hey, I could ask for a ransom. What would Jerry pay? What *wouldn't* Jerry pay?'

'Stop talking about Jerry.'

'So we say we spent an hour talking about Emerson. Perfectly innocent.'

'You know, Justus, you're a real snake. You're not interested in me, not really. You just want to prove how powerful you are so you can walk away knowing I couldn't resist you.'

'It's true I want to make love to you again, but you've got me all wrong. I don't get my kicks from making girls want me. Shit, I haven't had a real girlfriend since I've been in Oxford –'

'No, that would cramp your style.'

Justus shrugged. 'OK, don't believe me. The fact is, I hadn't met a girl, till you, that I had anything in common with. Sure I've slept with some – no more than any other guy – but I've never wanted to talk to any of them.'

'How charming. They must have been delighted.'

'And you – you don't even want to spend half an hour talking to me, let alone sleep with me.'

'Have you forgotten we did that, already? Wasn't once enough?'

He shook his head slowly. 'Not nearly enough. "Other women cloy the appetites they feed, she makes hungry"—'

'Just stop it, will you?' Olivia stood in the middle of the room, poised for flight.

'So go. I'm not stopping you. But don't tell me that a tiny little part of you doesn't regret it – a tiny little part of you wants to know what it would be like not to be such a good girl, not to play by the rules.'

'You're the only person who thinks I do.'

'You can pretend to be whatever you want, Olivia, with all those kids, but I've always recognised you for what you are, and I've always admired it. Remember that first night I came to dinner, when you played that schmuck game and said you'd slept with two people in the room? I knew you hadn't. I knew you were saying it for the heck of it, just to see what would happen. I knew you were playing with them. Did Jerry? Did your buddy George? Did Pip? Could one of them have said, hand on heart, that they knew you at all? And don't you love the fact that they don't?'

'It was a game. That's all. If you're so sodding sure of yourself, tell me why I'm not in bed with you right now.'

'The difference between you and your crowd, Olivia, is that none of them really know what they want. The trouble for you is that you know exactly what you want. It just isn't what you think you should want, so you make life difficult for yourself. I want to be around to see you when you finally grow up – you'll be something to see, something rare, I'm sure of that.'

'You're not advocating maturity – you're advising me to act like a little kid, to say I want all the sweets in the sweetshop even when I know they'll make me ill.'

'How do you know what they'll make you do, if you don't try them?' She glared at him with such pure anger that Justus was taken aback.

'OK. Cards on the table. I want to make love to you real bad, but if you don't, fine. We can be friends. I might carry on trying, I won't make any promises, but I'm not going to force myself on you, ever. I think it's a pity, that's all. I don't like seeing people trying to persuade themselves to do what's good for them. Now if you're going, take the cigarettes, OK? At least I'll have given you something.'

'I'll have a whisky – just a tiny one, and then I'll have to go.'

'Won't you give me a goodbye kiss?'

'You wouldn't want me to. Cigarette breath, remember? A filthy habit.'

'A guy who hasn't tasted whisky and cigarettes on a woman's mouth hasn't lived. Come over here.'

Olivia walked slowly towards Justus, and knew she would not be back to bid her guests goodbye. She'd known that when she agreed to give Justus a lift.

He was awake when she opened her eyes very early the following morning.

'*Christ* – I've got to go.'

'I wish you'd quit saying that. Come here, let me kiss you at least.'

She moaned in his arms. 'I don't want to go. I want to stay here and hide for ever.'

'Why don't we do just that? I don't have to vacate the room till the end of the week. Then we'll sneak away, find someplace else to hide.'

'You have no idea how tempting that sounds, what bliss it would be.'

He stroked her hair. 'You're wrong. I know just how it would be.'

Olivia had the strength to resist the temptation of staying, but gave up refusing to let Justus come with her. He argued, lawyer's son that he was, that the best demonstration of innocence was to behave completely suspiciously, and although Olivia did not agree with him, she didn't want to say goodbye. They settled that he would come only as far as her front door.

They had escaped without so much as a parking ticket, which gave Olivia the faint hope that she might escape everything without penalty. It was only as she drove down George Street that her hope dissolved. A mayfly dashed itself against her windscreen and became trapped in the wiper. It took the pretty thing less than fifteen seconds, while she watched helplessly, to decide that freedom was worth pulling its own wing off. Pinned to the front door of Number 12 was a message from George reading, 'Gone to St Septic's. Bring more bottles asap.' The house was a disaster area; only three of the many responsible remained, fast asleep on the sitting-room floor.

'Is that some hospital, or do you guys normally go to church after parties?'

'It isn't a church – it's St Sepulchre's cemetery. It was consecrated when the city churchyards were overflowing due to a cholera epidemic. Jowett, the Master of Balliol, was buried there – you know? "First come I, my name is Jowett; if it's knowledge, then I know it."' Justus looked at her as if she was mad. 'Never mind. We often go there. I'm going to make some coffee and take it down to them.'

'You guys are definitely weird. Are you sure you want to find them? There's still time to run.'

'Look, Justus, I feel like death already. At least now I won't feel any pain.'

'I'm coming with you.'

'I don't think that's a good idea . . . though you could help me over the gate – I won't manage it with bottles. Oh, what the hell. I'm doomed anyway. At least if you're there you can call an ambulance when Jerry kills me. See if there's any booze left, will you? Brandy. Anything.'

It was a cool summer morning, and Olivia took a Thermos full of coffee and two spare overcoats of unknown ownership that she found draped over the staircase. She and Justus did not speak as they walked the short block to the cemetery, but he held her hand deep in his pocket. The gates to St Sepulchre's were locked, as Olivia had foreseen, and Justus gave her a leg up, before passing the bottles and flask through and clambering over himself. The graveyard was bordered on three sides by Lucy's Eagle Ironworks, a disintegrating red-brick factory that had prospered in the mid-Victorian period but was now a sorry sight. Gothic headstones lurched and tilted oddly beneath the towering yews, giving the place more than a touch of the Peter Cushings. Not far from the gates were four flat, raised tombs under a huge rambling rose. George was prostrate on top of one with his hands folded across his chest, still in his city suit, but with his red polka-dot tie now knotted around his head in the style of a Vietnam veteran. Michael was lying on the next-door tomb, singing. Pip was perched on top of the low wall near them hugging her knees to her chest. Further down the cemetery, where there was something of a clearing in the densely packed graves, and the long grass was dotted with flowers, Jerry was dancing with Billy, her fur coat opened and half wrapped around him. Michael spotted them first.

'Aha! The cavalry!' He pulled a bottle from one of Justus's coat pockets and picked up a glass from the grass. 'Pip, where did you put that corkscrew? Livvy's brought more plonk . . .'

Pip jumped down and shuddered at the sight of Michael pouring himself a large glass of red wine. Olivia handed her the Thermos. 'Coffee. Thank God. I was just about to puke.'

'How long have you been out here?'

'An hour? God knows. Billy wanted to be outside to see the

dawn, Jerry was desperate to go to a funeral, George volunteered to be the corpse. I have a horrible feeling we had some sort of a service, but Billy did it in German, so God knows what she said. Michael keeps moaning, "Take me to the river", and we don't know if he's trying to sound like David Byrne or he genuinely wants to go and drown himself. If he doesn't shut up soon, bags I help him out. Cover George up, will you, Liv? I don't think I can walk that far.'

Justus looked at the wrecked revellers and then significantly at Olivia. 'Looks like we missed one hell of a party . . .'

'When did you two disappear anyway?'

'We were there until three in the morning, Pip, not that you would have noticed. Justus came with me when I went to get some fags. I had to go all the way to that shit motel on the roundabout. We decided to stay there for breakfast.'

'Did somebody say fags?' George reared up from under the coat Olivia had tucked around him. 'I'll give my first annual bonus to the angel who can put a cigarette between my teeth and light it.'

'Don't strike a match anywhere near his mouth, for God's sake . . .'

Olivia took the Thermos down to where Jerry and Billy still moved in slow circles, his head resting on her shoulder, his eyes shut. 'Jerry, wake up. Here.'

'Who's that?' Jerry mumbled. 'I was having a dream, such a beautiful dream. I met Sri Ashish, on the mountainside . . .'

'I dreamed of a beautiful man too. We made mad love.' Billy tightened her grip on Jerry as he tried to ease himself away. Olivia was torn between laughter and irritation. Michael was challenging his indomitable liver to a final bout while George choked on the cigarette. Justus watched them from a distance like a benevolent but mildly disapproving parent.

Pip was the first to come to her senses. She took Olivia by the elbow and pulled her away from the others. 'Where the hell were you, Liv?' she hissed. 'You weren't there at three – I wasn't that pissed, and I know you weren't.'

'I told you. I went for a drive with Justus. I wanted to talk to him.'

'Like fuck you did. How can you be such a bitch? How could you bring him back here with you? Jerry's not an idiot.'

Olivia shook off Pip's hand. 'I wanted to talk to Justus and that's just what we did. Talk. About Emerson. Is that allowed? Not something I expect you to understand, but then you're not involved, are you?'

'If you're screwing Justus then you're a fool, but at least you can tell Jerry the truth and stop jerking him around.' Pip was as stunned as Olivia that she'd voiced what was in her mind; she felt afraid of Olivia's cold detachment, and ashamed of herself for feeling afraid.

'I am not jerking Jerry around, and I'm not screwing Justus. And if I were, it would be my business. I wish to hell you'd find yourself a real boyfriend and stop poking your nose into other people's business.'

They'd barely exchanged so much as a heated word since the fifth form. 'What an unbelievably bitchy thing to say.' Pip's bare legs trembled beneath the gymslip. 'How you've got the gall . . .'

'You asked for it. You have no idea. None at all.' As Olivia strode away on her infinitely long legs she remembered that Justus was watching them.

'Justus, would you take Billy home? She's going to get pneumonia. Take my car. And you might as well take Michael at the same time.'

Justus came up close behind her. 'I'd rather take you.'

'Please. Just do it.'

'Come round and see me later? Soon later? I'm holding your keys hostage.'

'I'll try.'

The four of them sat in the graveyard.

'You missed the bonfire, Livvy.' George stripped ivy off one of the headstones to read the inscription; he pulled out his Swiss Army knife and sliced through a stubborn root.

'Shame, all the children must have loved it. George, that ivy's been there for a hundred years. Leave it be.'

'You haven't missed the fireworks, though, not yet.' Olivia shot Pip a glance laden with threat.

'I couldn't burn your suitcase because you'd taken the car.' Jerry slumped against Olivia. 'I went out to look for it.'

'I'm sorry. I only went to buy fags. I had a horrible breakfast at the Trusthouse Forte.'

Pip opened her mouth but shut it at another look.

George was brightening up. 'Talking of which, I could just about face another one. The first never feels right, sticks in the throat somehow, but the second slips down pretty easily. Might just wash it down with a large slug of brandy, smooth the passage . . . Let's drink a toast – come on, you slackers, charge your glasses. Here's to the future! Wha-hey!'

As they had only one glass between them George passed it around and held on to the bottle.

Pip winced as she took a tiny sip. 'The future, and all who sail in her.'

'The future,' Olivia echoed quietly and handed the glass to Jerry.

'And to the past, lest we forget. . . .'

Jerry and Olivia were finally left alone in St Sepulchre's. 'This is where Jude the Obscure's children were buried.' Olivia said pensively.

'Hardy's a miserable old sod, isn't he?'

'My teacher at school used to say that the difference between Hardy and Henry James was that at least James gave his characters *one* chance to get it right, but Hardy's were doomed from the start.' Olivia kicked at a hillock of grass at the edge of a grave, decided not to tell Jerry anything unless he asked her point blank, and shivered. 'Can we go now? I want to go to bed for a week, but I guess we'll have to clear up the house.' She began to walk towards the gates.

Jerry caught her from behind and held her by both arms. 'Let me look at you.' Olivia stood still, barely breathing as his eyes searched her face. Brows knitted, eyes grave, he seemed to be on the point of an announcement. 'I love you, Olivia. I love everything about you.'

'Except the bits you hate.'

'Those are the best bits of all.'

As they continued towards the gates with their arms loosely around each other's waists, Jerry's eye was caught by a glittering in the grass. He stooped to pick up George's knife.

'Wait – wait there for one minute!' He ran back to the middle of the cemetery and stood beneath the canopy of three large trees, looking about him. He selected the central tree and ran his hand down the bark. Squatting down, he began to carve something into the trunk. Olivia approached.

'No, you don't – get back! I don't want you to see it. Go back home, I'll be with you in ten minutes . . .'

'Jerry, you can't do this, someone will see you, you'll get caught.' As she said it, she thought, And won't I? Won't I get caught? What's worse, the thing you do, or being caught doing it? 'You can't vandalise a cemetery. It's against the law, and probably bad karma.'

'I am quite at home in graveyards, thank you. They never bring bad karma.'

'At least let me see what you're writing – or isn't it about me? Are you writing an ode to Billy?'

'Of course it's about you.'

'Then let me see!'

Jerry leaned against the tree and snapped the knife shut. 'Over my dead body. Go home and let me finish in peace. You can come back and read it when you bring our children here. Or our grandchildren. This is for posterity.'

Olivia shivered. While Jerry stood his ground silently her eyes fell to the tombstone in front of the tree. 'In sweet remembrance of our dear little Jack,' she read out loud, and then swung her head up to confront Jerry. 'I bet it's Hardy. I bet you're writing a Hardy quote.'

'I'm not, but I won't write anything if you don't back off.'

'Then it's some weird Hindu thing – "I am what I was, I am that I am," or whatever that crap thing is. Jerry, let's go and have breakfast.'

'I thought you'd had it?'

'Not enough,' Olivia answered smoothly. 'I'm still ravenous. I need eggs. I need bed. I need sleep.'

'That "crap" Hindu thing you are referring to is *Tat tvam asi* – that you are. You've reminded me of another "crap" Hindu thing: a woman's lust to eat is twice as great as a man's, her cunning four times as great and her sexual desire eight times as great.' Olivia turned her back on him suddenly, her fists clenching and unclenching. 'Go home and eat, Liv. I'll see you there.'

'You're so bloody pig stubborn, Jerry. *Please* let me watch. Stop fooling around.'

'No.'

'You're drunk.'

'I may have been, but I am now stone cold sober. Also stone cold, so if you could just let me get on with it . . .'

'Don't write anything horrible,' she said plaintively, almost to herself, but Jerry caught it.

'Now would I do that? Go on, woman! Trust me.'

Olivia trusted him, if not herself. She climbed back over the gates and went home. Pip and George had already gone to bed. She did not go near Magdalen that day, but left a message for George asking him to pick up her car and keys from Justus. Justus sent no message back with them. She did not say goodbye to him before going down for the last time. In the flurry of packing up that occupied their final few days, she forgot all about St Sepulchre's, and didn't remember Jerry's mysterious carving until she was in London, house-sitting, with George and Pip, for a friend of the Uptons while they waited to move into their new place. Jerry was with his family in Cambridge, and in his absence Olivia thought about nipping down to Oxford just to look at the tree, but it seemed, taken out of context, rather childish. As she toyed with the idea, Justus phoned. She met him for lunch in Covent Garden instead of going to St Sepulchre's, resolved to call off what had barely begun. After lunch she went to bed with him for the third and final time and told him it was over.

less than five per cent of an iceberg is
visible . . .

When they left 12 Kingston Road, Pip and Olivia shared a sense of anti-climax. Neither was willing to drive back to London, kiss goodbye, make a date for dinner the following week, and get on with the practicalities of their quite separate lives.

'I ought to phone Justus.'

'I ought to phone Jerry and tell him about the painting.'

'We could still go shopping.'

'We could go to the Water Meadows.'

'I could visit Dr Graves . . .'

'I could visit my old bank manager. If he's dead by now, which I fervently hope he is, I could go and spit on his grave.'

'We could go to Blackwell's.'

'We could try to pick up some foreign students.'

'God, Pip, didn't we do anything while we were here? What can we revisit? What did we actually *do*?'

'We sat around talking and drinking and smoking and playing games, and frantically wrote essays at the very last minute. That's all we did.'

They looked at each other. 'So we should . . .' Olivia began.

'Go somewhere we can talk and drink and smoke. We can always stay the night here and head back to London in the morning. What d'you say?'

'I haven't got any clothes, remember? I haven't got my magic suitcase any longer.'

'Sooo, we go to M and S, buy some knickers and a toothbrush, and hey presto! Or we could live dangerously and wear the same clothes. I never understood your Boy Scout thing about that suitcase but I may even have a toothbrush in my handbag.'

'Not me. I've got a platinum Amex card and some makeup.'

'Doesn't that just say it all? The difference between you and me. You've got lipstick and the flash credit card, and I've got what? A scabby toothbrush, nineteen receipts from Tesco's, maybe some dried-up mascara, a Filofax, three unpaid parking tickets, and half a bar of chocolate. Let's head for the Trout.'

Half-way up the Banbury Road Olivia suddenly made Pip stop the car.

'Let's go there.' She pointed behind them to a dingy-looking pub called the Empress, crowded between an Indian corner shop and a bicycle-repair outfit.

'Why? Is that where we sold your bike?'

'No. I want to go to that pub.'

'If you insist.'

The pub was quite horrible, stained with nicotine and furnished with red-velour bar stools and little else. Pip poked at the single ice cube dissolving in her gin and tonic as if it was a noxious alien body. 'Have you got a drink problem? Were you that desperate for alcohol, you couldn't wait till we got to Wolvercote?'

'It's the name, Pip. The Empress. It came up in my Tarot reading.'

'It's nothing to do with Tarot, you twit. It might just as well have been called the Queen Vic. Who d'you think that old bag is?' Pip indicated a black-and-white daguerrotype hanging over the bar. 'The Queen of Sheba?'

'It hasn't got anything to do with the *pub* name,' Olivia explained patiently, 'it's what it means to me. It's my inter-pretation, the recognition of a universal symbol.'

'I wish the Trout had come up in your Tarot reading – even the Perch. Aren't there any fish cards in the deck? I always liked the White Hart too.'

'Drink your gin and shut up. I happen to believe in co-incidence.'

'There's no such thing. People are always banging on about amazing coincidences when they bump into someone they haven't seen for a while on a crowded street. It's normally a shorthand for "Shit, I haven't phoned you in a year because I never wanted to see you again." It's all bullshit. Like your idea about meeting Justus in Rome. I mean, if you'd been living in some tiny village in Burkina Faso, and Justus had tipped up with a film crew, *that* might have been a coincidence – but in Rome? It was almost bound to happen, sooner or later.'

'Precisely.'

'The only thing that would be really amazing is if coincidences never happened. Do you want another one?'

An hour later they abandoned the idea of driving anywhere else and settled in.

'Did George make any moves on you in New York?'

'No,' Olivia denied stoutly.

'Bet he did. Seven-year itch and all that.'

'He didn't make even a faintly improper suggestion. Other than saying he thought I was making a mistake marrying Justus.'

'It's odd that both Jerry and George are so worked up about it, isn't it? Any normal person would be delighted to be connected to a movie star, however indirectly. I'll be able to say I slept with the man who slept with the woman who sleeps with James Bond . . . That's pretty cool.'

'I don't think he's going to do James Bond.'

'Piss. Hey, Livvy, if I agree to be your witness can I twist Justus's arm and make him do some Radio Four afternoon play for me?'

'Why not? Make it a condition.'

'Are you going to have a prenuptial agreement? Isn't that the big American thing for successful people?'

'We haven't talked about it. My parents would die at the thought.'

'When I get married – if I get married – I'm going to have one.'

'To protect your assets?'

'What assets? No, I just like the idea of having a contract which says what each person can and can't do, what your joint intentions and obligations are. If kids, how many. Clauses that spell out the absolute no-nos. You could have Infidelity, procedure for disciplinary action: first, oral warning; second, written warning; third, dismissal. Spell it all out, that's what I say, then there's no confusion, none of that crap about "I didn't know it would bother you . . ."'

'Would it bother you?'

'My husband being unfaithful? You're darn tooting it would.'

'It would end up a very long document, Pip. What would happen if your husband, let's call him Jerry, snogged some girl, just snogged her. Is that breach of contract?'

'It depends on the circumstances.'

'Umm. And what about if he happened to *touch* some girl's arm in a way that wasn't completely above board, that was somehow suggestive of wanting to touch a whole lot more?'

'Am I there while he does this suggestive touching? Is it in front of me?'

'Does it matter?'

'Yup. If he was trying to humiliate me, doing it right under my nose, of course it would be breach of contract.'

'So the clause doesn't have to say anything about infidelity, it just has to say that he undertakes to protect your feelings and your public image at all times? To always save your face? He doesn't have to worry about what he actually does, but only how you might or might not interpret it?'

'Look, I know what you're getting at. All I'm saying is there's a case for talking it all through before you say, "I will." There might be really simple stuff – if you leave the loo seat up ten times in a row, then no deal.'

'When I told Jerry that I'd slept with Justus, while I was with him, he said he wouldn't have cared. Do you believe that?'

'No. He's just known about it for so long it's lost its impact. Of course he would have cared. Maybe he was so in love with you he would have put up with it, but he would have *cared*. Wouldn't you care if Justus cheated on you, say in ten years' time?'

'Of course. But I wouldn't care if he left the loo seat up.'

'How would you have felt at Oxford if Jerry had cheated on you?'

Olivia chewed her lip. She knew she would have felt battered, vandalised. Most of all, profoundly shocked that she knew him so little. 'To be quite honest, I think I would have felt relieved. It would have been so much easier to admit what I'd done, if it was mutual.'

'I guess.' Pip buried herself in her handbag. 'Do you think it matters, talking hypothetically, who your partner is unfaithful with? Imagine Justus had an affair with some actress – would it make any difference if you liked her or not? Say Michelle Pfeiffer becomes your best buddy, and Justus rogers her in some drunken mad moment? Would it matter who the woman was? Would it be easier if you liked her, or if you hated her?'

'It would be easier if I didn't know her. Why?'

'Nothing.'

'You're talking about Justus, aren't you? That it was much harder for Jerry to deal with, because he always loathed him.'

'I suppose that crossed my mind.'

'Then you have to ask if Jerry hated Justus *because* he knew I fancied him, or if he had a better reason to hate him.'

'And you have to ask if you fancied Justus *because* Jerry hated him.'

'It was never that. I may have been attracted to Justus because he seemed to be everything Jerry wasn't, and because he was a challenge, and Jerry was a –'

'Sitting duck?'

'Bird in the hand. Listen, pal, it doesn't make any difference now, does it? I love Justus, you and Jerry love each other; I think we should make it a double wedding.'

'Do you really, really mean that? I can't understand it. If I were you, some part of me would always believe that Jerry belonged to me, that I'd got him first.'

'No. It doesn't work like that. It can't.'

'That's how Jerry feels about you.'

'No, he doesn't.'

'Yes, he does. I know him.'

Olivia wanted to lean across the table and tell her friend that she could never know Jerry the way she, Olivia, knew him. She leaned across the table anyway. 'I would be very happy for both of you if you got married. Jerry deserves somebody as good as you.'

'He thinks I'm not deep enough for him.'

'What crap.'

'It's what he thinks. Now you, he thinks you're way, *way* deep. That's why he can't believe you're going to do something as shallow as marry Justus.'

'Even though I was shallow enough to sleep with him?'

'Well, Jerry never officially knew that, did he?'

'He knew. He certainly does now. I felt ridiculous confessing it eleven years after the event, when he'd known all the time. I don't know why I felt I had to, but I feel a lot better having done it.'

'That's a result, then. It's a pity Jerry couldn't have reciprocated, got stuff off his chest too, and then you'd both have felt relieved.'

'Jerry never did anything wrong. He was the victim, remember? I was the one who had to make reparations.'

'If you say so. Olivia, do you ever want to have children?'

'Only,' she smiled and winked slowly, 'when there aren't any men around.'

'What a great line.'

'Not original. It's from a movie. Justus told it to me.'

'How honest of you not to take the credit.'

'I'm in the mood for being honest these days. It's high time, hmm?'

'I'm going for a pee, then I'll get another round.'

Pip stared at the graffiti on the grimy walls of the pub loo. 'Trevor has a big dick.' 'Sez who?' 'Sez Trevor Ha Ha Ha.' 'Love means never having to say you're sorry.' 'Fool – Love means sleeping in the wet patch.' 'All men are two-faced lying cunt bastards.' The largest was inscribed within a heart and read simply 'Johnny + Jess 4 ever.' OK, she thought, OK. She collected the drinks from the bar and said very quickly, before she had time to regret it, 'Jerry and I slept together at Oxford. After finals, but before you went away. I'm sorry.'

Jerry stretched back in his chair with his arms up over his head. 'I never had you pegged as a collector, George. Not that I don't welcome your business.'

'I'm just looking for something that catches the eye, you know, something to spend the old bonus on. To be frank, Jerry, I thought I might find something for Olivia.'

'I see. Perhaps I can make a few suggestions – she's had a look around the gallery already.'

'Been here, has she? I didn't know.'

'She dropped by. Took quite a shine to the Persian miniatures.'

'How d'you find her, then, in herself?' George flung himself down in the chair opposite as Jerry looked at him steadily. 'Look, I'm sorry about that weekend. It turned out to be rather a bad idea.'

'I enjoyed it. I liked having a chance to talk to Sarah. It's years since I'd talked to her properly.'

George look faintly surprised, then pleased. 'She made a point of saying how much she liked you. I'm sorry you and Livvy had such a rough time. She's a funny girl, always been a bit tricky. Heart of gold and all that, but tricky. I heard you had a bit of an accident with a bottle of whisky.'

'I'll replace it.'

'Good God, don't even consider it! Plenty more where that came from. It made me think of the good old days, all that raw emotion. I rather envied you. She does go off the rails, from time to time, doesn't she? I imagine it all comes down to not having any proper roots. She drifts about a bit, know what I mean?' Jerry nodded and took the El Fharmi miniature from his desk drawer. 'There's always so much going on with Livvy beneath the surface. People get her wrong all the time. She seems so cool, but then there are all those hidden depths.'

'Pip uses a similar analogy: she claims Olivia is like an iceberg.'

'That's it! Only ten per cent's visible.'

'I hate to be pedantic, old chum, but generally less than five per cent of an iceberg is visible.'

'It's the same with Livvy. She's really a warm, lovely person –'

'How unfortunate that's the side we can't see.'

'Tsk, tsk, no point crying over spilt milk. It all comes down to her useless parents. Did you ever meet them, Jerry?'

'Briefly.'

'Makes one think about one's own parental responsibilities . . . There were times at school when I could quite happily have put them up against a wall and shot the pair of them.'

'Olivia appears to have recovered from any adolescent trauma and settled down perfectly well in Rome.'

'Oh, she's just very good at covering things up, believe me. You don't really swallow this bilge about Justus O'Keefe, do you? I always thought you loathed the man.'

'I think he's a cipher. I don't have any emotional reaction to him at all. Nor do I – or you, for that matter – have any business opining who Olivia should or shouldn't marry. She's a grown woman.'

'So you weren't surprised about the abortion business?'

'I'd rather not talk about it. None of us acted creditably at the time.' Jerry pushed the miniature across the desk. 'This is the piece she admired. It's by an artist called El Fharmi. I have a certificate of origin and provenance on file, if you'd care to see it.'

George peered at the scene. 'Pretty small.'

'That's undeniable. It's a miniature, after all.'

'You're certain she really liked it?'

'Yes, she admired it several times.'

'What'll it cost me?'

'Two and a half thousand pounds. I could offer you a discount.'

'You could deduct all the bloody utility bills and rent I forked out at Kingston Road.'

'I could.'

'It's nice enough, Jerry, if you like that sort of thing. Don't get me wrong – I just had a whim for something more, more . . .'

'Expansive?'

'Yes.'

'Expensive?'

'Why not? I've had a good year so far.'

'Emblematic?'

'Let's say significant. Something with a story attached. Something she'll never forget – that will make her sit up.'

Jerry calmly observed George's restless energy channelled into one jiggling, well-heeled foot. 'In that case, let me show you something downstairs that might suit you better . . . It is one of six ancestral altar tusks from a Benin shrine, early nineteenth-century, commissioned by the king, Oba Obanosa, to commemorate his mother the Empress or Iye Oba Ose. There's a rather strange but fascinating tale attached concerning magic and witchcraft. Would you like to see it?'

George liked it very much, although he didn't make much sense of the story.

'Price?'

'I hope you've had a very good year . . . A very good year indeed.'

'Hit me.'

'I couldn't let you have it for under a hundred and eighty thousand – and that's allowing for the hot water I used. Telephone too.'

George blanched and fingered his tie. 'Pounds?'

'Dollars.'

'That's a relief. I don't suppose you'd be able to take a Swiss franc bankers' draft?'

Olivia and Pip abandoned the car and took a taxi to the Randolph. The receptionist swiped Olivia's Amex card and did not comment on the fact that neither of the two women had any luggage other than a handbag. Olivia called room service and ordered a plate of cold turkey sandwiches and two toothbrushes. Pip fell asleep

almost immediately, fully dressed, but Olivia took off her clothes
and lay awake beneath the sheet, watching the sky turn nearly
black, and then lighten. Shortly after dawn she dressed, left a note
saying she'd be back for breakfast and slipped out of the hotel. She
walked up Walton Street and took a left turn down the little path
leading to St Sepulchre's cemetery. The grass was dewy and
soaked her neat Italian shoes, which soon became clotted with
mud, but at least she didn't have to climb over the gates: they were
unlocked. She picked her way through to the central of the three
trees and pushed aside the long grass that surrounded the base of
the trunk, running her hand down the bark. About eighteen
inches above the earth she found it, and read quite easily, for it had
been carved deep into the flesh of the tree:

> My true love hath my heart and I have his,
> By just exchange one for the other giv'n;
> I hold his dear, and mine he cannot miss,
> There never was a better bargain driv'n.

Olivia then read the tombstone that stood in front of the large tree.

> In sweet remembrance of our dear little Jack, youngest son of E
> and M Rawlins-Inns. Fell asleep on March 29th 1928 Aged 12
> years 8 months. 'He whom we loved so dearly God loved more'.
>     Also in treasured memory of Ernest Rawlins-Inns, father of
> the above. Fell asleep November 6th 1938 age 69 years. 'At rest'.
>     Also in ever loving memory of Martha Emily Rawlins-Inns
> wife of the above who fell asleep August 24th 1954 Age 86
> years. 'Re-united'.

For some time she sat on the damp grass with her long legs
stretched out in front of her. Unbidden, a line from Thomas Hardy

came into her head: 'I shall traverse old love's domain never again.' And, with a rush, a flood of Hardy's poor doom-laden poetic musings came over her, all reiterating the same thing: 'Twice-over cannot be!' She went slowly back to the tree, armed with the nail clippers from her makeup bag, and more significantly, armed with the conviction that the past could not be revisited, let alone rekindled. She pulled out the tiny nail file and searched for a smooth patch. On the far side, opposite the carving Jerry had made, she found another, clearly by the same hand:

Man is too noble a being to serve simply as the instrument for others

She put away the file and thought about the bundles of Jerry's letters that she kept in a trunk in the store room at Vicolo del Piede. She would have to call her father and ask him to get them and burn them. She knew his curiosity, if it surfaced at all, would be too weak to bother to read them and she could not bring herself to read them again.

# the way you chew your lip . . .

Claridge's was booked for her parents; a table for twelve had been reserved at Bibendum for lunch; Olivia had purchased a suit in the palest pink with Pip's help. She waited only for Justus's return. She spoke to him two or three times a day, but resisted joining him as he begged her to do. 'Absence makes the heart grow fonder.'

'Horse-shit. I want you here, at my side, I'm feeling all fuzzy at the edges.'

'I liked *The Spider House* a lot. I think it's a great role for you.'

'I've Fedexed you the revisions. Do you want a part in it?'

Olivia laughed. 'You never saw my mercifully brief appearance in *The Duchess of Malfi*. I can't act.'

'So you'll blend in . . . Seriously, darling, I want you to be involved. You could have a part, or work with the production team, script-editor maybe.'

'I don't want to work in your business just because I'm bathed in the light of your desirability. I don't want to work in your industry at all. I've been thinking about carrying on with teaching. Can I do that in California?'

'You can certainly teach English – language at least. You might have to go back to school if you want to do something more serious.'

'So long as you don't expect me to lie in the garden in dark glasses ordering the pool attendant around.'

'Now where on earth did you get that idea?'

'From the telly. Isn't that what Hollywood wives do?'

'Second wives, darling, only the second wives . . .'

She tentatively raised the idea that after the honeymoon she might return to Rome while he was filming. 'I'd just like to see my kids through one final term. Finish *A Midsummer Night's Dream*. I don't like leaving them in the lurch without even saying goodbye.'

'So maybe we should go back to the States after the wedding – my folks are ranting they're not going to have a chance to get to know you – then we can go somewhere for a few weeks, wherever you like, and you can be in Rome while I'm in Morocco. I could come over a couple of days a week – I could do a workshop with your kids.'

'Lizzie would die. But she'd probably get an A, too, so it would be worth it. I'd like to see what you made of Luca.'

'Is he the good-looking one? The one you say's better-looking than me?'

'That's the boy.'

'OK, but I get to cast him as Bottom.'

'Who are you going to be?'

'I'll let you choose.'

'Maybe Theseus? I'll work on it.'

And so she did. The obvious angle was to keep stressing the 'time to pause', that her students might see the Athenian wood as the internal life of the protagonists, which they needed to explore before they took life-determining decisions, and where they lost themselves. She could then lead them gently into looking at Lear's time on the heath, Macbeth's encounter with the witches, and the entire period on the island in *The Tempest*. This interpretation would reduce the play's effectiveness as a comedy but then, there wasn't all that much to reduce. If Justus would come along to do a workshop that might kick-start some life into the thing, enough to get the students' minds working without her. Her own mind lacked all inspiration. Olivia was reading Lysander's speech, 'What, should I hurt her, strike her, kill her dead? Although I hate her, I'll not harm her so,' when the doorbell rang. Play in hand, she pressed the intercom.

'Delivery for Miss Fletcher-Smith.'

Justus was nothing if not efficient, but when Olivia opened the door expecting an envelope, she was met by three men carrying a seven-foot-long object.

'Are you sure that's for me?'

'If you're the lady on the label, it's all yours once you've signed for it. Just tell us where you want it, because it weighs as much as a fuckin' elephant, 'scuse my French.'

Olivia knew what it was long before she'd peeled off the brown paper, untied the rope and unwrapped the heavy sacking that surrounded it. The tusk stood in incongruous splendour, dwarfing the small entrance hall. Olivia went straight to the telephone.

'Jerry? What do you think you're doing?'

'My expenses, if you must know.'

'There must be a mighty big hole in them. As soon as you've finished you can come right over here, pick this up and take it back with you, OK?'

'I can't possibly do that. It doesn't belong to me.'

'It doesn't belong to me either.'

'If you read the card, I think you'll find that it does.'

'It's not funny, Jerry. It's tasteless and – and – nasty, and I wouldn't have thought you'd behave like this.'

'Read the card.'

'I've read quite enough, thank you. D'you know what I read a

313

couple of days ago? I read that inscription you carved in St Sepulchre's.' There was no response from Jerry. 'Have you forgotten about it? This strikes me as bloody bad timing. Just get it taken away, all right?'

'Read the card, Olivia.' Jerry hung up.

Heedless of its value, Olivia kicked the wooden mount of the tusk hard several times before she looked for the envelope amid the discarded wrappings.

> Darling Miss O. Fletcher-Dunn, Here's a little keepsake made for one Empress and given to another. Call me when you get it. Love always – Your Georgie.

Olivia prodded redial on the keypad so hard that she broke a nail. 'This is your fault. Whether it's from you or not, I know you're behind it.'

'I'm flattered you think I'm so influential, but I assure you, it was George's choice. I advised him to buy the miniature.'

'You have to come and take it away, Jerry.'

'I simply can't. If you dislike it, I suggest you contact the African Art Department at Sotheby's and ask them to collect it. They have a Tribal sale coming up – let me look at my book – yes, in Paris in early November. I'm sure they'd happily accept it.'

'I want *you* to take it and give George his money back. Now. I thought you said you'd bought it for a client anyway?'

'I did. He was quite happy to take an immediate profit. The Tusk belongs to George. It *did*. It now belongs to you. I'm sure you can find a spot for it in one of your several houses. Perhaps you should present it as an early wedding gift, and wait to see whether your husband likes it before going off the deep end?'

'You are a bastard.'

'Again, you flatter me, if not my mother.'

'Why, Jerry? What's the point of this? What are you trying to say?'

'I'm flabbergasted by your reaction. It's a very important piece that most collectors would give their eye-teeth for. It's not a gift to dismiss lightly. It is a magnificent gesture on George's part. The motifs are powerful images of female protective magic and ritual, and their ability to overcome the dangerous forces lined up against their men –'

'Shut up! How could you let George buy something that would only remind me of you? How could you use him like that?'

'I don't believe I have ever used another human being, Olivia. Certainly not knowingly. Can you say the same?'

'You lied to me.'

'Never.'

'You let me think I was a bitch, and cheating on you, and all the time you were just as bad.'

'I can quite understand how that idea would horrify you, but it isn't true.'

'Well, these days I'm having trouble trying to work out just what's true and what isn't.' Olivia's voice had dropped to a tremulous whisper. 'How could you want to hurt me?'

'I could not. I cannot.'

'Then *why* . . .' she wailed.

'Livvy, Livvy, hush, I'm sorry. I'll come round right now. I'll take it away. I had no idea, no intention – I promise you. If I had any inkling of how this would upset you, I promise you I would not have allowed it. George wanted to make a bold gesture, that was all. I can see now – Livvy?'

'I have to go, Jerry. I really have to go now –'

'I'm coming round. I'm on my way.'

When Jerry's taxi turned left off Kensington Church Street on to

Sheffield Terrace, he saw Olivia bumping a suitcase down the steps of the house. Tossing a ten-pound note at the driver he leaped out of the car and bounded up the steps. 'No, you don't.'

'Jerry, go away or help me get a taxi.'

'No.'

Olivia sat down on the step. 'You don't have anything to say, and you have no right, no right at all to tell me what to do.'

'I agree. But if you want to get rid of the tusk then you need my help. You can't just leave it up there and hope it will disappear – it isn't *that* magic. At the very least, you need to insure it. Stop glaring at me like that. Let's go upstairs and sort this out calmly.'

'Stop talking to me as if you were my father.'

'I have never felt the least bit paternal towards you, least of all now. Come on, get up.' He picked up the suitcase in one hand and offered her the other. Jerry nearly impaled himself on the artefact stepping into the flat. 'I admit, this isn't its ideal setting. It does lend the place some character, though. Now sit down.'

'Stop telling me what to do!'

'So stand. Do you mind if I sit?'

'I don't give a fuck what you do.'

'What a gift for language you have. Your school must value you a great deal.' Jerry sprawled on an armchair. 'Come on, Livvy. Put your dukes up. Let's have this out once and for all.'

'You bonked Pip.'

'Straight for the jugular. Yes, I did.'

'And I spent ten years feeling guilty because I'd betrayed your trust. And all those last few weeks at Oxford, when I was so miserable and hating myself, you never said a word about Pip.'

'That's true, although I didn't notice you hating yourself. And I don't believe for a minute that your past ten years have been spent in a frenzy of tormented guilt.'

'Why did you sleep with her?'

'Because I was angry with you and I suspected you were either screwing Justus or planning to.'

'That was enough?'

'No. I was also twenty-one; I was attracted to her. We had something in common – at the very least we had *you* in common. We both orbited around you, or at times it felt as if we did. It was tempting to do something that excluded you, however childish that may sound. I'm not excusing it, Livvy. I have to admit that as I was driving over here, I even felt rather pleased that you had reacted so strongly. You might not have cared at all.'

Looking at her he could see her struggling with herself, her jaw and lips moving as she tried out phrases on her own ears, her expression in turn determined then confused. To have her vulnerability laid out before him like a body on an operating table was curiously painful. 'Olivia. Can we find a way to bury this? I don't choose to be the cause of pain, any more than I choose to feel it. Would it help if we said our goodbyes – we never did, remember? – and left it at peace? I can't with any honesty say we can be friends. I can't look at you and not know what I used to feel. I can't look at you without feeling a strange disjointment that I spent so much a part of my life expecting to share it all with you. I'm not explaining this very well. I can no longer see you as a separate person, an independent life, because you are so confused with an image I have of myself. I sound egocentric, I know. I have tried to look at you in a detached way, and tried to make sense of your life. I cannot. I cannot wish you joy with Justus, but I cannot wish you harm. I can't understand you outside that time we were together.'

'So for you, I stopped existing in nineteen eighty-six?'

'Not at all.' He ran his hands through his hair. 'You stopped existing, as you put it, in nineteen ninety, maybe even later. That was when I decided you would never come back.'

'But I did.'

'Not to me.'

Olivia paced the room. 'I came back to George . . . He doesn't have any trouble picking up where we left off, and being friends.'

'You didn't leave George. You didn't leave Justus either. You left me.'

'So is it pride, Jerry, that stops us being friends?'

'Of course not.'

'Is it Pip?'

'How like a woman. No, it's not Pip.'

'And if I said I loved you?' Olivia swung round to face him with her arms folded tight across her chest. 'I'm not saying I do, but if I did?'

'It couldn't make any difference, even if you meant it.'

'I don't believe you.'

'That's your problem, then. If you don't want to marry Justus, don't look to me as a way out. You've done that before – you turned to him as a way of running away from me.'

'So you don't love me? Not at all? So all that stuff about undying love was crap? "My true love has my heart and I have his"?'

'There never was a better bargain driven. You see, Livvy, it *is* meant to be a bargain, one you reneged on. I never had your heart.'

'That's not true.'

'I think it is.'

'When did you write the other one?'

Jerry flipped through a magazine and answered idly, 'Oh, the Rousseau? I don't remember. Not long after. Does it matter?'

'To me, yes. Were you talking about me, or about yourself?'

'I was talking about all of us, as far as I can remember.'

'Will you do something about the tusk?'

'May I?' His hand reached towards the phone. At Olivia's nod Jerry called a friend at Sotheby's and quickly arranged for its

318

collection.

'He's delighted. They'll pocket two commissions in one year – I bought it in a Sotheby's sale in New York. Have you spoken to George?' She shook her head. 'I doubt he'll lose on the sale, he might make a profit. I'm sorry, I am presuming you intend to return the money to him?'

'Of course I am.'

'How will you explain your decision?'

'I'll think of something.'

'I'm sure you will.'

'I told Pip I thought she should propose to you.'

'What a kind thought.'

'Would you marry her? I'd hate her to ask if you were going to say no.'

'I really can't say.'

'Justus and I are getting married on the nineteenth of August.'

Jerry stood up. 'Then I have time to think about a gift – and one that won't provoke such a violent reaction.'

'Will you come?'

'I told you, I'm out of the country most of the month.'

'Will you come? If you're here?'

'No.'

'Would you kiss me goodbye, now?'

'No.'

'Would you find me a taxi then?'

'It would be my pleasure. Where are you going?'

'Do you care?'

'Yes, oddly, I do.'

'I'm going to Heathrow.'

'And then?'

'I have absolutely no idea.' She tossed her head.

Jerry groaned. It was her indomitable haughtiness that wore

him down, finally, against all his best intentions. He prepared himself for renewed rejection, and found it very easy. 'That's it. You've won. I love you. I don't want to love you, I've done everything I can *not* to love you, and I stand here and look at you and all I can think of is how much I love you. You've worn me out, Livvy, drained everything out of me, except some impenetrable, primordial sludge that makes me want you still, more than ever. I could never erase that. What it is to desire only one woman . . . There must be something wrong with me. It takes so little to switch it on, you see. A certain look on your face, the way you chew your lip, a tremor in your voice, sticking your chin in the air like you just did, and nothing else matters any more. Please tell me that's all you wanted – please say you just wanted to be sure that I hadn't, and wouldn't, get over you. Don't ask me to come to your wedding.'

On the opposite side of the room Olivia burst into tears. 'Livvy, dearest, don't cry – please don't cry. Come here, don't break my heart, I adore you, Livvy, Livvy . . .' When he held her Olivia's sobs increased. 'Do you still want me to kiss you? Dearest, don't cry . . .' And he did kiss her and she kissed him back, even though her nose was running and her mascara was running and it was not the way she intended things to be, but she knew she loved him, and that the time was right, and there was a way of going back, even if the path wasn't the one she had chosen, and even if it was just the once, just one time when she could hold him and know she loved him, even while the knowledge made the future far more difficult, she didn't want to think about the future and she didn't want to think about the past, and there was nothing, after all, nothing wrong with living for the present . . . And then she pushed him away, and asked him to leave.

When Jerry left, Olivia felt not the victor's triumph but the pervasive ache of utter misery. When she tried to find the exact spot to stick the pin in, she was left with the sense that not only was her life over but it hadn't even been a satisfying one in the first place. There had been no repeat of earlier indiscretions, no sexual betrayal and no forfeit, only a kiss, and kisses were so easily forgotten and forgiven.

# like dogs meeting in neutral territory . . . .

'How did Jerry get stuck into Eastern philosophy? I didn't think the Oxford syllabus bothered with even the Continental philosophers. They kind of stuck to the Anglo-Saxons.' Justus stroked Olivia's back tenderly. 'I hate it when you smoke, I really do.'

'I'm going to stop on our wedding day, I promise I will. I intend to give up all my vices in one fell swoop.'

'That sounds far too dangerous. Tell me about Jerry and the Buddhist bit.'

Olivia lit another cigarette. 'Hindu. In his first term at Oxford, before I knew him, he came across some guy who told him to read some book by some other guy –'

'That makes it very clear.'

'I didn't really pay much attention at the beginning. He was going off it all. He was very keen on an Englishman, a mystic, called Sri Madhava Ashish. That was his monastic name at least, and Jerry went off to his ashram, met him, got very excited about it all and decided to become a Vaishnav monk. By the time I met him, his mother had talked him out of it. Anyway, something stuck, and he was always coming out with weird stuff.'

'He got a first, didn't he?'

'He got a congratulatory first.'

'Then he must know what he's talking about. I always thought it was a tad pretentious, an affectation.'

'If there's one thing you can't ever accuse Jerry of it's affectation. He's all genuine, right or wrong.'

'And he still follows it?'

'In a way, I suppose. I think it's all connected, for Jerry. That's one thing I always envied. He had a way of seeing and accepting a pattern in everything. We once had a very heated argument about trying to understand the "ought" in oughtness. I remember saying that ought *not* was far more interesting, and Jerry got absolutely furious, and said "ought" and "ought not" were exactly the same thing.'

'So you two spent all your time together having heavy philosophical conversations? No wonder you turned to me.'

'Don't knock him, Justus. He was a wonderful man. He was fun, too. We always had fun, even if we argued a lot.'

'I'm not knocking him. I wish I'd known him better. Whenever I saw him, he was like a cat on hot bricks, but then, he never liked me much, did he?'

'No, I don't think he did.'

'Is he coming to the wedding?'

'He's going to an auction or something.'

'D'you buy that?'

'It's his choice. I'd like him to be there, but if he doesn't want to . . .'

'I bet he still hates me, doesn't he?'

'Of course not. He never even knew you.'

'You don't have to know someone to hate them.'

'Oh, you do if you're Jerry . . . Do we have to spend the only night we've got together talking about my ex-boyfriend?'

'I love the way you call him your boyfriend. It's cute.'

'Justus. I kissed him yesterday.'

324

'So?'

'So don't you care?'

'That depends. Did you?'

'I don't know. I don't know why I did it. I felt very angry with him.'

'An original excuse for a snog. Remind me to watch out when you lose your temper.'

'I'm actually trying to be honest here. You're not helping.'

'Well, did kissing him make you feel that you don't want to marry me?'

'No. I just felt it had to happen.'

'Do you want to do it again?'

'No. I wanted to know what it felt like.'

'And what did it feel like?'

'Odd. Not so odd now I've told you about it.'

'I'm a great believer in confession on a need-to-know basis, Olivia, d'you know what I mean? I would have made a lousy Catholic.' She lay close to him, rubbing her cheek against his chest. 'When we're married, if there's something you want to tell me, you just go ahead and tell me. If there's something you don't want to tell me, but you think I ought to know, then you only have to tell me if I really *need* to know. So . . . Is there anything about you and Jerry that I don't know and need to?'

'I think you know everything about me and Jerry.'

'Fine. Then I don't care if you kissed him.'

'Justus. . . what if there was something I *wanted* to tell you, but I thought you ought *not* to know?'

'I like things nice and simple. Need to know, don't need to know.'

Telling the truth was far simpler than Olivia had expected.

In the morning Justus told Olivia that he needed to visit a

producer and would pick her up at one for lunch, before they went to the Town Hall to confirm the booking. He took a taxi to Jerry's gallery. When he walked in, Jerry was with a customer. They both turned as Justus came in, but Justus was growing accustomed to stopping traffic, let alone conversations, and didn't break his stride. 'Jerry, great to see you. It's been an age.' He took Jerry's hand in one of his, holding his upper arm firmly with the other in a technique that was simultaneously intimate and assertive.

'Excuse me – aren't you? You're Carella – the guy in *The 87th Precinct*?' the third man asked. 'Uh, Justus Someone?'

'Yeah – Justus Someone. I like that. Good to meet you. Don't let me interrupt – I'll look around till you're through.'

Even though Justus retreated to the far wall, the gallery was far too small to ignore him; Jerry did his best. 'They're not easy to find, Stephen. Christie's sold one last year, but we're probably talking about a private sale. I'm more than happy to keep an ear open.'

'I'd be very interested if anything came up.' The client dropped his voice. 'I didn't know you had such an illustrious clientele, Jerry. You could exploit that.'

'He's not a client – not yet, at least. Just an old friend.' Jerry surprised himself by the description, and after a few more words on the rarity of late eighteenth century Ottoman marble fountains bade Stephen farewell.

'Is there something I can help you with, Justus, or is this a social call?'

'It's good to see you again, Jerry. You've got a great place here – great stuff.'

'Thank you.'

'You should open a place like this in LA – or New York. You'd do very well.'

'Actually, the Americans are more advanced in their appreciation of these types of artefacts. Even though most of it was our imperial heritage, they caught on to its artistic collector's potential earlier. I would face far more commercial competition in the States than I do in London.'

'Competition makes for a healthy market. Higher prices.'

'True,' Jerry mused, 'but, then, I'm not really in it for the money.' The two men regarded each other like dogs meeting in neutral territory – tails wagging guardedly, toes stiff. 'I hope Olivia passed on my congratulations? I'm very happy for you both.'

'Thank you, that means a lot to us.' Justus studied an inlaid backgammon board. 'I've come to ask you a favour, Jerry.'

'I hope I can oblige, but I'm not prepared to recommend on wedding presents. Only the other day I advised George Upton very unwisely.'

'The tusk? Yeah, I've seen it – well, you can't really miss it, can you? I'm trying to persuade Livvy to keep it. I kind of like it, don't know why she doesn't.'

Justus did not seem in any hurry to name his favour and Jerry played along, saying with deliberate banality, 'I liked your last film. I never saw your TV series, but I did like *Mad City*. I went to see it with Philippa Renfrew – do you remember her?'

'Of course I do. She's going to witness our wedding.'

Jerry swung away. 'I thought that you were busy shooting a film now.'

'We've just wrapped up in France. I still need to do a week or two back in the States.'

'A Henry James novel, isn't it?'

'Yep. *Roderick Hudson*.'

'Ah, yes, that's it. Any good?'

'It's not bad. A good cast. Jamesian tales of repression and wasted opportunity seem to have hit a chord with the public.'

'And how do you find acting as a profession? You certainly stuck at it.'

'I do stick at things, Jerry. That's my way.'

'How exactly can I help you?'

'It's about Olivia; about our marriage.'

Jerry raised his eyebrows. 'And . . .?'

'I want to ask if you'll come to the service.'

'As I explained to Olivia, unfortunately I'll be out of the country.'

'So she said. I want to ask you to change your plans and come.'

'I really can't see why it would make that much difference to you. Normally, of course, I would be delighted, but in the circumstances –'

'It's precisely because of the "circumstances" that I'm asking you to come.'

'I meant that I have to be in New York. It is the nineteenth, isn't it?'

'That's right.'

'Then I can't oblige. I have to attend a sale.'

'I thought you guys did that stuff over the telephone these days.'

'Not in this case, no.'

'Then maybe we can change the date. When d'you get back?'

'Flattered as I am, Justus, I cannot understand why my presence is quite so essential.'

'It matters to Livvy. If you're not there, it will upset her.'

'I assure you, the last time I spoke to her I had the distinct impression that Olivia would be far more comfortable if I'm not there.'

'That's crap and you know it.' Justus sat down in the chair behind Jerry's desk, stretching out his long legs and tapping a pencil distractedly on Jerry's diary. 'Olivia needs to have friends around her, supporting her.'

'I disagree. Olivia needs you, and you only. In any case, Pip

328

will be there – George, I'm sure, and his wife. Livvy's aunt and uncle?'

'None of them matter the way you do, you know that. I'd hate for her to think that you didn't approve.'

'And what makes you think I do approve?'

Justus laughed easily. 'Hell, Jerry, I know you don't! All I'm asking is that you do everything you can to show Livvy that you do.'

'Wouldn't that be dishonest, assuming that you're right?'

'Wouldn't it be kind, assuming that I'm right?'

Jerry covered his eyes with his hands and rubbed his forehead wearily. 'I have always found weighing the relative merits of consideration against integrity very . . . *complex.*'

'I can believe that,' Justus said softly, 'and I have some sympathy with it, though I know that will surprise you. But if you put honesty first, then tell me this: can you say that your refusal to come to our wedding has nothing to do with what happened at Oxford?'

'Of course I can't, but that doesn't make it less valid. None of us can unlive the past; not even actors.'

'But if we're brave, and if we're kind, we don't have to *re*live it, do we?' He bent to retie the laces on one of his trainers, an action so deliberately casual that it infuriated Jerry. 'Tell me why you don't think Olivia should marry me. I'd like to hear why.'

'I have no opinion on the matter.'

'Hey, Jerry, *c'mon*! I'd let you get away with being dishonest, and I'd let you get away with being a pompous asshole, but not both at the same time.'

'All right. I don't believe you have Olivia's interests at heart.'

'So why else would I marry her?'

'I have no idea. Perhaps you consider her an asset – a fitting consort.'

'I do consider her an asset, but not to my career, if that's what you're getting at. Olivia's not a trophy wife.'

'I'm sure she'd be thrilled to hear you say that.'

'There's nothing I wouldn't say to her, nothing I wouldn't tell her. And nothing she wouldn't tell me. But I'm asking *you* for the truth, not Olivia.'

'How do I know the truth? Any of us? Truth's a slippery old bastard, impossible to unravel. I'm not convinced that you know Livvy very well, that you love her.'

'Like you do?'

'As I did.'

Justus grinned. 'Well, if that's all, no problem. For a second there I thought you were going to say she didn't love me, but if that's your reason, I can live with it easy, because I know you're wrong. Tell you what,' he pushed back the chair and stretched languorously, 'see if you can make it on the nineteenth, OK? We'd both be delighted. See ya, buddy.' He slapped Jerry lightly on the back and left the gallery while Jerry watched him through the window.

He had barely gone twenty steps down Boyle Street when two girls stopped him for his autograph. Jerry watched his former rival, gesturing expansively, signing his name with a flourish, then bending his head to kiss each girl on the cheek before going on his way.

Justus was only slightly late to collect Olivia, but as they were pressed for time they decided to eat locally at Kensington Place. As they went through the revolving doors, Justus pressed up so close against Olivia's bottom that she nearly fell into the restaurant and into the arms of the maître d', who stood at his little lectern studying his table plan.

'Hello – can we have a table for two please?'

'Reservation? Name?' he asked briskly, without looking up.

'No, we didn't.'

'In that case we don't have a table until three o'clock.'

Justus moved Olivia out of the way and leaned his elbow on the stand, dwarfing the smaller man.

'That's a real shame. We're only in town for a couple of days, and I'd set my heart on eating here. I've heard such good things about it. Just last week Ophélie Arcier told me it was her favourite place in London.'

The maître d' looked up with his face set in a frown. 'Oh –'

'–phélie. Yeah, she said you beat the pants off most Parisian restaurants.'

'I'll see what I can do. Would you mind waiting at the bar for a moment? I'm sure we can arrange something.'

Justus ordered a bottle of champagne.

'You are shameless.'

'Why? I dropped Ophélie's name, not mine. The least she can do is get us a table.'

'It's still shameless.'

'So what? Here he comes . . .'

'Justus, do you think we should have a marriage contract?'

'Marriage *is* a contract.'

'I mean a pre-nuptial agreement.'

'You want one?'

'No, I thought you might.'

'How can I get it into your stubborn head that all I want is to marry you and hang out for ever and ever?'

'Not till the ring's safely on my finger, buddy.' Olivia leaned close to him. 'I'm glad we got in here.'

'Food's good, isn't it?'

'The food's great, but the best thing is the customers are all far too cool to stare at you. I can actually feel anonymous for once.'

'You *are* anonymous.'

'Bastard. They're probably just used to grander people eating here. If you'd only manage to get a role in a *serious* drama . . . So where did you go this morning? Just had to nip out and get your daily fan fix, I bet?'

'I landed a couple,' he forked up a griddled scallop, 'but I went to see Jerry.'

'Oh, for God's sake! That gallery's becoming Paddington Station. First George, now you. Why didn't you tell me? I wish you wouldn't do this. You didn't punch him, did you?'

'Not so he won't recover . . . No, I said we'd both really like him to be at the wedding. To kiss the bride.'

'But I don't want him to come – I mean it, I really *don't*. Everything's settled, end of story. All I want to do is cast my school production of *Midsummer Night's Dream*.' Olivia took a dog-eared copy of the play out of her handbag and opened it at the list of characters. 'We'll go with you as Theseus, Cobweb too –'

Justus declaimed: 'From Oberon to Cobweb in ten compresséd years, the mirror of so many theatrical careers . . .'

'Thank God you act and don't write. Quiz: What comes after, "And with the juice of this I'll streak her eyes"?'

'"And make her full of fateful fantasies".' Easy. I played Oberon, remember?'

'You certainly bewitched me.'

'That was my intention.'

'Did you know that eighteenth-century doctors thought romantic – or sexual – obsession was a disease? A surgeon wrote a paper on it, saying it was the one affliction above all others people should be inoculated against.'

'Sounds like a fun guy. Hey, what do you call a mushroom?'

'I don't know, what *do* you call a mushroom?'

'A fun guy to be with.'

'Maybe I'll get a job teaching in a kindergarten. I'll be well qualified, married to you.'

After seeing Justus off at Heathrow, Olivia went back to the flat, expecting – hoping for – a message from Jerry but finding two from George. His voice sounded uncharacteristically tense, and she regretted teasing him about having sex. It had been meant as a joke, not a good one, but one that had seemed perfectly safe at the time. When she called him at work she was told that George would be out of the office for several days and she did not phone him in Suffolk. Instead, she opened the Yellow Pages looking for a telephonic Tarot reader. There were several ads under 'Palmists and Clairvoyants', neatly sandwiched between 'Painters and Decorators' and 'Panel Beaters'. Olivia chose the largest, which promised Instant Phone Consultations.

'Hello, Miranda's Mystic Meanings,' a male voice answered. 'How can I help?'

'I was wondering how you do Tarot readings over the phone. Do they work?'

'Oh, yes, it makes no difference at all.'

'What do I need to tell you? How much do you – need to know?'

'Well, we take Amex, Visa, Access, so long as we have your details . . .'

'But I don't have to know people's birthdays? What time they were born? Star signs?'

'No, unless you want to combine with numerology. If you have Miranda herself, you're looking at about a week for bookings. Let me give you some prices: twelve ninety-nine for the first five minutes with Miranda then eight pounds for each subsequent five-minute block. If you call the Instant Prediction line, that'll be twenty-four ninety-nine flat for twenty-five minutes. We can set up a reading within ten minutes, after clearing your credit card.'

'And who would do that?'

'Let me see . . . tonight, myself – I'm Jerry, by the way, or Chrissie and Michele. Obviously, if you want someone in particular, you may not get them immediately. We've got three lines running on instant prediction tonight, so you won't wait long. Tell you what, I'll give you my personal line.'

'And I can ask anything?'

'Whatever you like. If we don't cover it all you can extend. I don't put the credit card through till after the reading.'

'Thanks. I'll call back.'

Let your fingers do the walking and you get idiots, Olivia thought. She'd be just as well advised by a panel-beater as by Jerry. How odd that he was called Jerry . . . Yet she could not dismiss the Tarot itself, and found herself an hour later holding her credit card and calling the number only to hear a business-like American recording, 'Please leave a message for Jerry after the tone.' Jerry must be having a heavy night.

# I'll chuck rice with the rest of them . . .

George slumped at the kitchen table, too shattered to pour himself a drink, too numbed to ask Sarah to do it for him. She stood opposite him wide-eyed.

'I don't understand,' she said quietly, 'I don't believe you.'

'It's true. I can hardly believe it myself, but there's absolutely nothing I can do about it. It's absolutely out of my control.'

'There must be. You can't act so precipitously – you can't just walk out on everything.'

George looked at her bleakly. 'I didn't walk out. I was suspended.'

George had bowled into his office that morning to find an urgent summons from the chief executive. This in itself had not made him prick up his ears: he was a recognised favourite of the CEO, who regularly treated him to chats behind closed doors. That morning his boss looked distinctly on edge and left his door open until they had been joined by the managing director of Capital Markets. George predicted the announcement of major lay-offs, RIPs as they euphemistically called them, or redundancy initiative programmes. While he waited, George prepared his defence why his own department could not afford to lose a single body.

'George, something rather unfortunate has occurred.'

'Hit me with it, Graham.' Perhaps two or three he could spare, but which two or three? He loathed giving people the boot. He prayed it wasn't an across-the-board RIP – it would be far easier to spare one or two of the juniors.

'There's been a hitch in the Man-Comm bid.'

'Oh.' George sat up with surprise and relief. 'Right. I haven't heard of any problems, but I haven't been handling it myself, not since we approved the fee structure.'

'I'm aware of that. I believe you passed the deal on to Bill Fanshawe.'

'Under my overall supervision, yes. Bill's a very competent chap. Have we hit a stumbling block? I haven't had a chance to catch up with Bill since his last trip to Delhi.'

'You could call it a stumbling block. I had a call yesterday from the energy minister, Vikram Desai.'

'Why on earth would he call you?'

'To inform us that they are pulling the deal and intend to publicise their reason for doing so. Would you care to hazard a guess what that might be?'

'I haven't got the foggiest. Unless Bill blew it in some way. I would have thought he'd call me.' George racked his brain trying to remember the final details of the privatisation package.

'Bill blew it in a big way. They are accusing us of corruption, that Bill negotiated a bribe, a personal bribe, in exchange for adjusting the fee structure.'

'That's ridiculous!' George had a faint but chilling memory of a conversation about something, tokens, beneficiaries, gestures, something along those lines, which he had associated entirely with Olivia. His heart began to thump erratically.

'I'm afraid it isn't. I am quite convinced they have proof. Of course, underneath, it's all an attempt to disgrace the American

336

banking community. It's all about their own domestic politics, probably a set-up, but it's quite clear that Fanshawe played straight into their hands.'

'I'll talk to him immediately.'

'He's no longer in the office. I've already spoken to him.'

'Much as I respect your judgement, Graham, I'd still like to hear what he says myself. I'm not prepared to condemn him without hearing his defence.'

'Oh, he defended himself very convincingly.' George relaxed. 'He said that he acted with your full knowledge and authority. I'm afraid we're going to have to suspend you pending an investigation. I don't know quite what I'm going to do to keep this out of the press. If the Indian papers run it, you can bet the scum here will be on it faster than a bugger on a choirboy's back.'

'George, how do you feel?' Sarah touched his cheek hesitantly.

'Know the painting by that Norwegian chappie, Munch? That's exactly how I feel.'

'Oh, darling . . . Let's just be calm and think this through sensibly. There's no evidence you were involved, is there?'

'There's no evidence because I wasn't bloody involved.'

'Then how can they implicate you?'

'Because Bill says that he discussed it with me and I tipped him the wink.'

'He's obviously just trying to save his own skin. I can't believe it – wasn't he the man who came for the weekend in March?'

'Umm.'

'He can't prove it.'

'No, he can't.'

'So it's his word against yours. How dare Graham not believe you?'

'He says he does. They have to have an investigation anyway, to prove they're clean. That we're all clean. There never was a transfer of funds anyway, not even to Bill, as far as I know. But what do I know?'

'Then it's fine. You'll be back at work by Monday.'

'It isn't that simple, Sarah. I handed over all my accounts, bank statements, you know, so they can see there haven't been any mysterious deposits, withdrawals . . . These things take time. Oh, *shit* . . .'

'Darling, there's no point worrying about it. It will be fine, however long it takes. It will be obvious that Bill was lying and he'll be sacked. It's a pity for him, and I know you like him, but if he indicated he would accept a bribe then he deserves to pay the price.'

'It isn't that simple,' George repeated. 'Bill *did* say something to me.'

Sarah looked at him in horror. She knew George very well, and although she would have sworn he was an honest man, Sarah did not put professional ethics in the same ballpark as personal ones. Certain of her husband's fundamental integrity, she had no idea what sort of shenanigans went on in financial negotiations; she'd never wanted to know.

'Well. Whatever happens, we'll manage, all right? I'm sure you didn't do anything hundreds of others haven't done. There are other jobs, other banks.'

As George watched the expression shifting on her face, saw her regroup and read her doubt, he felt angry for the first time since hearing the accusation. He spoke very quietly, his jaw clenched. 'I did not approve a bribe. I am not corrupt. Let me say that again: I did not authorise Bill to negotiate or accept any form of payment, for himself, for me, or for the bank. Not ever. Do you believe me?'

'Of course I do. If you would just tell me what Bill did say, exactly . . .'

George pushed back his chair, scraping it harshly against the slate floor. 'There's something else. I have to phone Olivia.'

'Because she'll believe you, when I don't? Or because you went off your head and took a bribe so you could run away with her?' George stopped as though she had slapped him. Sarah dropped her voice. 'I *do* believe you, I believe everything you tell me. Wanting to know the truth doesn't mean that I don't – I just want to prepare myself for whatever's going to happen. Why can't you tell me whatever you're going to tell Olivia? I've been your wife for eight years – doesn't that mean anything? Doesn't it count for anything?'

George leaned against the kitchen wall and closed his eyes. His feelings for Olivia and Sarah's jealous suspicion paled into something of little consequence. His personal and professional reputation were the only thing that mattered. He laid out the facts succinctly. 'I have to phone Olivia because I bought her a gift, something from Jerry Milton's gallery. A very expensive gift, nearly two hundred thousand dollars. I paid for it from my Swiss account. I gave Graham those account details this morning. It will look suspicious to him. I need to speak to Olivia and Jerry to clear it up.'

Sarah blinked several times. It didn't matter where the money had come from, George certainly had more than enough capital to pay for it without underhand payments, but she could not come to terms with the knowledge that he had spent so much money on Olivia. 'You better phone her then.'

George looked exhausted. 'Oh, what's the point? What is the sodding point of it all? Listen to me, Sarah. I dropped the ball. Bill Fanshawe *told* me he'd been offered a bribe. I was so busy thinking about Olivia, I barely listened to him. It was a two-minute conversation, if that, but he did say something, and if I had been listening at all rather than obsessing about what I could buy Livvy

I would have put him straight in an instant. As it was, I think I told him to manage the deal however he wanted to. It was a misinterpretation, but I know how he reached it. It is my responsibility.'

Sarah hugged herself. 'What *do* you feel about Olivia?' she whispered.

'I wanted to screw her.'

'Oh,' Sarah breathed. She'd never quite thought that, never expected to hear him admit that. While she thought through her options she mechanically prepared two gin and tonics, slicing the lemon into precise half-inch slices and dropping two with a faint plop into the glasses. She even went to the drawing room to fetch a cocktail stirrer. 'George, can you face putting the boys to bed? I can hear them playing upstairs. It's too late.'

George took his drink without a word and walked slowly to his sons' bedroom. Five minutes later Sarah followed and sat down on the top step, her drink next to her, to listen to her husband reading the end of *Penguin Small*: 'There never talked a snowman, Nor penguin ever flew, And there Neverwozanoceros, To make this rhyme for you.' It was infinitely sad, all of it, but she refused to weep, while knowing that tears might be her greatest strength. When Sarah heard Arthur demand a chapter from *The Lion, The Witch and the Wardrobe* she went to get her address book to telephone Jerry Milton.

Jerry picked up the phone.

'Jerry? I need to see you. I really need to see you.'

'Are you still going to marry him?'

'Of course I am.'

He hung up at once. The phone rang again a minute later.

'We've talked enough. There's nothing else to say. I'm fed up with it, the whole thing. Just go away and bloody get married, can't you?'

'Thanks very much! I was calling to ask if you were doing anything for dinner. I hadn't planned on proposing anything more long-term. Who did you think you were talking to?'

'Pip,' Jerry sighed. 'It's you. It doesn't matter.'

'You thought I was Livvy.'

'I'm glad it's you. And yes, I am free for dinner.'

'How about La Famiglia – say half an hour? I'm just clearing up at work.'

'See you there.' As Jerry got his jacket and was on the point of switching on his answer-phone, the thing rang again. He picked it up cautiously.

'Hello? Jerry? This is Sarah Upton. I'm really sorry to bother you, I just wanted a quick word . . .'

Talking to Sarah made Jerry late; Pip had ordered by the time he arrived at the restaurant.

'Oh, there are side-benefits.' She dismissed his apology with an airy wave. 'When you're a single woman and you ask for a table for two and nobody turns up, the waiters think you're such a sad soul they come over all sweet and attentive.'

'Pip . . .'

'It's all right. They probably thought I'd made a date through the Lonely Hearts pages.'

'Pip . . .'

'Hey, Jerry, I'm joking. You're only ten minutes late. I'm starving.' She shoved the menu at him and smiled brightly. 'So how's life?'

'Life's just fine. How's yours?'

'I love talking about me. I edited a programme today you'd have loved. All about people's capacity for goodness. What do you think of *my* capacity for goodness?'

'Simply enormous. Unfathomable. Bottomless. How's your pasta?'

When they left the restaurant, Pip put her arms around Jerry and said simply, 'Come back home with me tonight. I don't feel like being alone.'

'Pip, I don't think that would be a good idea.'

'Even if I promise not to talk about Livvy?'

'Even if you promise.'

'Even if we don't have sex?'

'You're not giving me many incentives.'

Pip sighed in resignation.

About midnight, she was in her dressing gown rereading a proposal from an independent producer when she was startled by cautious knocking on her front door. Olivia waited on the doorstep until Pip ushered her in.

'I'm sorry to turn up so late. I know I should have phoned . . . Have you heard about George?'

'What about George?'

Olivia repeated her phone call with Sarah Upton and concluded, 'Worst of all, she wants to have lunch with me tomorrow.'

'What's the problem? So she's worried about George, and this stupid tusk thing.'

'She's already talked to Jerry. I don't know why she wants to talk to me.'

'It's just Sarah's way. She's very methodical. Don't worry about it.'

'George has been acting so strange –'

'How would you know?' Pip said abruptly. 'Liv, I don't mean to be rude, but you don't know George any longer, do you? Honestly, the best thing for you to do is to forget about all this stuff, see Sarah if it makes her happy, but forget it all and marry Justus. Get on with your own life. You've done without us for so long, there's no point burying yourself in our problems now. God – so George dabbled his fingers in the honey-pot.'

'Of course he didn't! George wouldn't do a thing like that.'

'Livvy, face facts. People do all sorts of things, and most of the time they get away with it. Most people get away with most things most of the time. You know that.'

'I don't believe George would ever do anything corrupt. Have you seen Jerry since we came back from Oxford?'

'A bit. Hmm.' Pip tried not to think about Jerry.

'And everything's OK?'

'Everything's just fine.'

Olivia paced the room. 'Justus came over on a flying visit, I just left him at Heathrow.'

'And it's all set for the nineteenth?'

'All set.' Olivia sat down next to her friend, shifting piles of papers in order to do so. 'Did you propose to Jerry?'

'Of course not. It was a crazy idea.'

'Pip, you know how when you're young you can be incredibly honest, and incredibly irresponsible at the same time?' Pip nodded hesitantly. 'Well, I was irresponsible alright, but I never took advantage of the chance to be honest when I could. Now I feel like I have to be responsible and dishonest, that's what life's become.'

'So maybe when you're sixty you'll get a chance to be irresponsible and honest again.'

'I don't know if I can wait that long.'

'What are you talking about?'

Olivia dipped her head and held it in her hands. 'I think I've fallen in love with Jerry.'

'Jesus, Olivia, what's the matter with you? You're like an incontinent puppy piddling all over the place.'

'I know.' Olivia whispered. 'I know.'

'You can't mean it.'

'You think I would say something like that if I didn't mean it? You're the last person I would have told. I'm not going to say anything to Jerry, I couldn't, and he wouldn't believe me, and he wouldn't want me anyway –'

'Oh, grow up!' Pip shouted, leaping to her feet, and then dropped her voice to a harsh whisper. 'What a nerve you have, after all I've done for you. So you want my permission that it's OK to suddenly decide to fall in love with Jerry after all this time? Or do you want me to act as your go-between? What do you expect me to say to you? You come back, George starts acting like a lovesick teenager, jeopardises his career, his family, everything, all for you. You've got Justus neatly wrapped round your little finger, you make absolutely certain that I love Jerry, encourage me to think everything might still work out for us, and as soon as you know it, you start whimpering that you think you love him too. Jesus, Olivia, I could smack you, I really could. Do you get some sort of a sick kick out of fucking up people's lives?'

'Do you have any idea how hard this is for me, trying to be honest? I'm not going to tell Jerry I love him. I'm not such a fool.'

'So why are you telling me?'

'Pip – I had to tell *someone*!'

'Not me. And actually, you didn't *have* to tell anyone. You could have kept it all bottled up just like you always used to. At least there'd be some virtue in that – you could have gone to your grave knowing that you'd resisted. Like Gandhi – remember Jerry saying he used to sleep with stunning naked women, just so he could prove he could resist them?'

'I'm not talking about sex.'

'Bloody hell, Livvy, I've really had enough of the whole thing.

344

We were all *OK* – happy, even. I wish you'd never come back. Don't see Sarah Upton tomorrow, OK? You might let something "accidentally" slip out, and not be here to face the consequences. Just like you did about being pregnant. For Christ's sake, don't sit there blubbing. It's too late for that.'

'I know. I'm not crying about that.'

'Well what the fuck are you crying for?'

Olivia struggled to pull herself together. 'You're right, Pip, it's much too late. I shouldn't have come back to London, and I shouldn't have come round tonight. It doesn't matter whether I love Jerry or not. I don't. It's a nonsense. I am going to marry Justus.'

Pip dropped her guard a fraction. 'So long as he loves you, you'll be just fine.'

'Do you love Jerry enough to do the same?'

'Fuck off, Olivia. My idea of love isn't yours – it never has been. I've never cheated on anyone in my life, certainly not anyone I love.'

Olivia looked at her gravely; hadn't someone once said that love was a game in which everybody cheated? 'As I said, I'm sorry.'

'I guess you don't want me to be your witness any longer?'

'I want you to be my witness more than ever. With such impeccable moral credentials, who could make a better one?' They faced each other in silence and in that uneasy co-habitation of love and hatred that women tolerate only in their closest female friendships. Olivia stretched out her hand unconsciously. 'I am sorry. Please come to our wedding, Pip. I know Jerry won't.'

'You know Jerry won't what?' Jerry appeared on the stairs, pulling a sweater over his head. 'I don't want to barge in, but you two were making a hell of a din.' Olivia stood up at once, and stepped backwards until she met the wall. 'Evening, Livvy.'

'God. I'm sorry.' Olivia covered her face. 'I'd better go.'

'No rush. I'm awake now. Do either of you girls want a cup of tea?'

'So long as it's not herbal.'

'It's your kitchen, Pip – slim odds on finding herbal tea there. So, Livvy, what was it I won't do?'

Olivia looked around the room for her handbag and made straight for the door. Her throat had closed so tight she didn't trust herself to speak.

'Olivia?' Jerry's voice came from the kitchen. 'You're not running away, are you? Hold on, I'll walk you home.'

'I'm going to get a cab.'

'Then I'll get you a cab.'

Pip took a swallow of tea and picked up her proposal again. She didn't look at them as they left her house.

'I only said I knew you wouldn't come to the wedding.' Olivia searched for a taxi, shuddering with the shock that Jerry and Pip had been in bed together.

'I'll come if *you* want me to – not because Justus tells me it's a good idea.'

'No, you mustn't come – isn't that one free?' She stepped out into the road and Jerry pulled her back and held on to her arm.

'You said "I think I've fallen in love with Jerry."'

'I didn't know you were upstairs, that you'd hear. How could I? I didn't know you and Pip –' she choked in anger, wanting only to be alone, stupefied with jealousy. 'I said it to Pip. For effect.'

'But I did hear.' He put his lips against her cheekbone. 'I heard all of it.'

'Jerry, please.' She tried ineffectively to push him away.

'Did you know Justus came to see me? I told him he didn't love you. That was for "effect", too.'

'Oh, but he does, he does,' Olivia was wringing her hands,

looking up and down the street, at anything except Jerry.

'And did you tell Yankee Doodle that you'd fallen in love with me?'

'Jerry, stop it.' He let go of her so suddenly she staggered.

'Fine. I'll stop it, if you stop playing games. I loved you so much once it very nearly killed me. Don't mess about, OK? For God's sake, don't fuck up your own life. You're right on the edge, Livvy, but you still have choices. It isn't about Oxford any more, not being in love, not secret kisses. It's about real life and, as you so rightly said, it's about being responsible, and telling the truth. You say you've reached a point where you should stop telling lies – that's fine, but it's yourself you have to stop lying to, not other people. Go ahead, marry Justus, but be sure you know exactly what you're doing, and tell the truth. Once you can look me in the eye and tell me that, I'll chuck rice with the rest of them.' He flagged down a taxi. 'Perfect timing – right at the end of my speech. I only wish I'd had time to prepare it better.' He slammed the taxi door.

Olivia met Sarah, as she had agreed the night before, in a café on Kensington High Street.

'Olivia, you look dreadful – are you sure you feel up to lunch?'

'Of course. It's lovely to see you.' Olivia smiled wanly. 'I just had a late night.'

Sarah was precise in her every gesture, from putting on her lipstick to sipping her wine. 'I told you about George's predicament.'

'I don't believe for a moment he had any involvement.'

'George doesn't know I'm here. He knows I'm in London, naturally, but he thinks I'm visiting my mother. I felt it was up to me to sort things out, for my own peace of mind.'

'Yes.'

'George told me that he'd bought you a present, and how he'd paid for it. I spoke to Jerry last night. He told me about the Benin tusk.'

'I asked Jerry to take it back. He's put it in a sale. Of course, the money will go to George.'

'The money doesn't matter at all. You do believe that George didn't accept a bribe?'

'I know he didn't.'

'I'm so glad of that. For a moment, when he first told me, I wasn't sure. You see, Olivia, for the past few weeks, since you came back to be frank, I haven't felt sure that I know what George thinks any longer.'

'Sarah, I told you in New York, George and I aren't having an affair. We never have. We never will.'

'I was rather hoping you would say that you *were*. If you tell me you're not, I believe you, but in many ways it would be easier for me if you *would* have an affair with George. He loves you so . . . And he has such dreams of what it might be like, and dreams can be so very powerful, much stronger than the reality, even when they're misleading. George has slept with other women since we've been married. He hasn't admitted it, but I'm quite certain. It has never interfered with our marriage. I sometimes wonder if the denial of passion isn't more dangerous than the fulfilment of it.'

'I thought exactly that about Justus. Back at Oxford.' Olivia pushed the food around on her plate with no appetite. 'Sarah, are you very politely asking me to sleep with your husband and disillusion him?'

'I wouldn't dream of it. George and I have a good marriage, Olivia, truly. It may not be everything I ever hoped for, but it's most of it. A seventy per-center, as George would say. It doesn't matter to me if George has been professionally dishonest or not, or whether he keeps his job or not. I've never cared much about his career, only so far as he cares about it. I do want to keep him, or what part of him is mine – but I won't fight for him and risk it all, do you understand?'

'What a dreadful thing to say. Marriage at any price.'

'It isn't the marriage, Olivia – it isn't even the children. I'm not saying this from fear, or trying to hold on to security. I suppose it is the marriage, in one sense, but not the being married – it's simply that I love George, for better or worse, for richer or poorer.'

'There's nothing for you to worry about. Certainly not me. Maybe George had a notion that it would be fun to 'realise' our friendship in another way, but it was never more than a fun idea to him, believe me. It's not going to happen, and he'd be awfully disappointed if it did.'

'Oh, no, you're quite an icon to him. Perfect womanhood. And very –' Sarah blushed, 'sexual.'

'Let me tell you a secret. I'm a very bad lay. Always have been. If you don't believe me, you can ask Jerry. I love Georgie far too much to do something as nasty as sleep with him.' Sarah looked at her like a cow that had seen the lethal injection coming. 'Sarah I'm sorry. I don't mean to sound flip. Honestly, I've got enough problems of my own. All I want from George – and you – is your friendship.'

Within moments, Olivia found herself pouring out her heart to the last woman on earth, barring her mother, she had ever expected to confide in.

'I love Justus, I really do. He's a wonderful, talented, sincere, intelligent man. Who could ask for more than that? And he loves me. I was certain that marrying him was the right thing to do. But I'd felt guilty about Jerry for so long – and it all seemed obvious, sign-posted, that I should come back and see Jerry and make amends – because I was marrying Justus, d'you see? In some way, that made everything all right. I thought the worst thing I would feel was embarrassed, no, ashamed – and then I saw him, and I felt so much, so much. And now I think I love him. He positively hates me, and I can't help thinking how ironic it is that Pip loves him and he loves her, and they discovered that through my going away, and then when I come back, I still want him so badly, so very badly, and I don't have any right to . . . I'm sorry, Sarah, I'm sorry I'm being so pathetic.'

Sarah, the only mother among them all, did not become maternal. She became practical. 'Does Jerry know you love him?'

'He overheard me saying so, but I don't know what he thinks. I kissed him, then I told him I was going to marry Justus and he told me to go away . . .'

'And what have you told Justus?'

'That I kissed Jerry.'

'But he still thinks you want to marry him?'

'Oh, yes – and I do! Oh, God, I think I do, I have no idea what I think, I wish . . . I know it's right to marry Justus.'

'Why?'

'Because he loves me, Sarah, he loves me for what I am. He loves me much more than Jerry ever did.'

'I always thought that the way Jerry looked for you to the ends of the earth was the most passionate story I'd ever heard . . . Even if it were true that Justus loves you more, that's no reason to marry him, Olivia. You can't marry somebody because of how much they love you. You can never be certain of that, after all. You marry them because of how much *you* love *them*. I always thought you were smart enough to know that.'

Olivia looked at her wildly. 'God. I think I have to go now.'

you have become what you are, inside
and out . . .

Olivia took to her bed. Justus had left France for Massachusetts. She'd barely spoken to him, only told him she'd
come down with a viral bug, and that every bone in her body
ached. She didn't speak to Pip or Jerry, because neither of them
phoned her. She lay in bed and shivered. George had phoned, and
Sarah too. Sarah had resolved the bribery issue, as she recounted
to Olivia. She had gone to see Graham herself, told him that she
and George had been having marital difficulties and that George
had been understandably distracted as she had only just
announced she was having an affair . . . He may have heard the
words that Bill Fanshawe had spoken, but they could not have any
made sense at the time, because she had created a situation that
made sense of nothing. Dear George had even bought her a
$180,000 present from a gallery. She asked Graham only to
examine George's record along with his financial statements and
come to his own conclusion. With tears in her eyes she had told
Graham that George did not know she was there and would be
profoundly humiliated to discover that she had confided their
private troubles; it was not at all easy for her to admit them herself

. . . Graham, who had had his own share of 'marital difficulties', phoned George that afternoon, slagged off ninety per cent of the world's politicians and demanded his immediate return to the office. George thought his wife a genius and found her cool deception curiously arousing.

He now sat at the bottom of Livvy's bed.

'Can you imagine her doing it, my Sarah?'

'I can, easily. She must have been terrifying.'

'I've just been in to tell Graham he could fuck his job. Well, I told him he could fuck it for two weeks – I'm taking Sarah and the boys on a holiday. We'll be back just in time for your big day.'

'I'm so glad, George.'

'Are you all right, lovey? You're looking very peaky.'

Olivia flapped *A Midsummer Night's Dream* at him. 'I'm fine. I'm just tired, terribly tired.'

'Anything I can get you?'

Olivia closed her eyes. 'Be a love and read to me for a while? Just till I fall asleep. My eyes hurt. I feel like an old woman.'

'I quite often feel like a young one.'

She smiled weakly. 'There – start at the bottom of the page.'

'I can't do voices, you know. I always hated having to read Shakespeare out loud. Makes me feel such a twit.'

'Go on, Georgie.'

'Demetrius, right? Here goes.' He cleared his throat and began to read the text of the play. 'Now it's Oberon: "What hast thou done? Thou hast mistaken quite And laid the love-juice on some true-love's sight:" – Blimey! Sorry, Liv, that was me, not Oberon, ahem: "Of thy misprision, must perforce ensue Some true love turn'd, and not a false turned true." Now it's –'

'Puck.'

'If you know the play backwards it beats me why you want me to read it, unless you want a laugh. Right. So Puck says –'

'George?'

'Um-hmm?' He was flipping through the play.

'Go home now, OK? I think I'm going to sleep.'

'Infinitely preferable to listening to me read this tosh. Shall I call Justus? Let him know you're poorly?'

'He knows. Don't worry about me.'

'Sarah told me about Jerry. About what you felt –'

Olivia rolled on to her side, turning her face away from him. 'I thought she would. Darling, do go. I'm awfully tired.'

'Don't set too much on it, Liv. These things pass – I'm an authority on the subject.'

George bumped into Jerry on the steps of the house; Jerry looked grim, and was perfunctory even when George thanked him for dealing with the disposal of the Benin tusk. 'It was nothing,' he said, brushing off George's hand. 'Is Olivia home?'

'Yes, but she's sick. Reading Shakespeare in bed, which may well make her sicker. Look, Jerry, is everything all right between you two?'

'Why shouldn't it be?'

'Jerry, between us, I've had a word . . . I know there's been some business . . . If I were you I'd tread very softly, she's feeling rather fragile.'

'I don't need advice on how to deal with Olivia. Nor does she need protecting.'

'That's where you're wrong –' George said angrily, but Jerry had bounded up the stairs, leaving him on the doorstep.

Olivia opened the door a bare two inches. 'I'm not receiving callers, thank you. I'm sick. Contagious.'

'So I heard.' Jerry pushed past her and looked around the hall. 'They've already collected it.'

'I was looking for Justus.'

'He's in the States.'

'Olivia, I want to talk to you. Sit down.'

'Don't tell me what to do.'

'Sit down and stop feeling so sorry for yourself. I came to ask you if you wanted to go out – have dinner, go dancing, just go out somewhere.'

'Dancing? You hate dancing.'

'I like it. I just never liked watching you dancing with other people.'

'I'm sick. I'm in my dressing gown, if you hadn't noticed.'

'You're no sicker than you normally are. Go on, get dressed. We'll go and look at paintings, or see a movie. On second thoughts, perhaps not a movie.'

'Why do you want to do this?'

'Why do you always have to have a reason to do everything?'

Olivia smiled at him despite herself. 'Where would we be without motivation?'

'Does good clean fun count as motivation?'

'Why shouldn't it?'

'Do you need drugs?'

'Are you suggesting I'm a candidate for Prozac?'

'Would I ever have the nerve to suggest that?'

'Aren't you scared of catching my bug?'

'Will I get infected?'

'Would that put you off?'

'Is it a fatal disease?'

'No, this strain clears up pretty quickly, or so I'm told by someone who ought to know. I'll get dressed. There's a pot of coffee in the kitchen – help yourself.'

Jerry shouted after her, 'Is it Heaven helps those who help themselves, or Heaven *help* those who help themselves?' but Olivia had turned on the shower and did not hear him.

While he waited, Jerry shuffled through the papers on the desk and came across her tongue-in-cheek notes on *A Midsummer Night's Dream*. Her careless, loopy handwriting touched him acutely and he folded up the top sheet and put it in his pocket. When Olivia came back he was looking out of the window. 'Who's Lizzie?' he asked casually.

Olivia was combing her wet hair, struggling with tangles. 'Lizzie?' She looked confused. 'Oh, *Lizzie*. She's one of my students in Rome.'

'A lesbian?'

'Huh? You read my notes! You know I hate snoopers. No, Lizzie's not a lesbian, not as far as I know. She's closer to the opposite end of the spectrum. She eats up the boys in the class. I was just trying to find a way of provoking a reaction – any reaction. Luckily, Justus has agreed to come to Rome and do a workshop.'

'So you're going back to Rome after the wedding?'

Olivia was sitting on a kitchen chair with her knees apart and her head bent down between them, combing and combing. Jerry focused on the downy V of hair that inched down her long white neck, and shivered.

'For a bit. I'll probably go for a month or so, just till they're up to speed and I can find somebody to replace me.'

'What are they like, your pupils?'

Olivia swung her head up and shook it. 'Not like we were. Much, much older than I was, at least, at the same age. Dreadfully sophisticated.'

'Was Philippa a bully at school?'

'Pip? Oh, God, you really *did* read my notes – that bit about Hermia. "She was a vixen when she went to school, and though she be but little, she is fierce".' Olivia laughed. 'No, Pip was never

355

a bully. She used to take on the bullies – all of them at once. But she was undeniably short, and definitely fierce. Still is.'

'She's protective.'

'Fiercely protective.' Olivia looked at him coolly through her dripping hair.

'How much longer is that going to take you?' Jerry could quite happily have watched her messing about with her hair for the rest of the evening. Longer.

'I'm done. I don't care about drying it.' Her naked face and the damp hair made her look both vulnerable and bold, half schoolgirl, half Celtic warrior queen. 'Where are we going?'

'I'd like to drop in on a private view in Barnes, if that's OK by you. We could walk along the river, and get a bite to eat somewhere.'

'Fine. Am I dressed OK? It isn't a formal do, is it?'

'You look beautiful.'


The exhibition was held in what looked like a private house in a Georgian terrace facing the Thames. Inside, a waitress took their coats and a man in a velvet kaftan greeted them. 'Jerry, I'm so glad you made it – there's a bit of a throng actually. You can't imagine how nervous I've been about this – quite out of character.'

'Can I introduce Olivia Fletcher-Smith? Olivia, this is my good friend Francis Bartholomé. He is hosting the exhibition, and happens to be married to the artist, so watch what you say about the paintings.'

Once out of the hall, the house felt more like an aircraft hangar – two huge rooms, starkly white, comprised the ground floor, and a spiral staircase led to an upstairs gallery. In each room there were only four canvases, each a huge portrait, threateningly dark and simple.

'I wish there weren't so many people here – I can only see the top half of the paintings.'

'That's never the purpose of a private view. Just drink the booze, smile, and tell the artist she's wonderful. Talk of the devil, there she is now.' Jerry nodded up to the tiny balcony that overlooked the lower rooms. A woman was standing at the top of the steps, her profile towards them, and gesticulating extravagantly. Her blonde hair was twisted into a million wild coils by bits of silver wire, and her bony shoulder-blades moved with a life of their own as she talked. 'Recognise her?'

'It isn't – God, it's Billy!'

'A.k.a. Mrs Francis Bartholomé. I've known Francis most of my life, on and off. Three years ago he invited me to dinner to meet his new protégée, and wife, and who should it be but Billy?'

'How fantastic – and this is her work? It's amazing!'

'I think it's very good indeed.'

'Did Pip tell you that her male nude's still on the wall of Kingston Road?'

'Billy would be delighted. It may well turn out to be worth more than the house, not that that's any sign of real merit. Let's go and say hello. We'll have to queue.'

But when Billy spotted them standing at the foot of the staircase she came bounding down. Her deliberate youthful eccentricity had matured into a something far more unusual, a passionate candour that, while still unnerving, lent her a deeper fascination. She looked like a pale silver bird.

'Jerry! You came!'

'How could I stay away? I'm your greatest fan.'

'And my harshest critic. You're wicked to be late, when Francis told you to come early, but as you've brought Olivia with you, I'll forgive you.'

'Hello, Billy. I can't believe you remember me.'

'Of course I do. It was your party that made me decide to

concentrate on portraiture. I should thank you – and I do!' She gave Olivia a fierce embrace, and leaned back to study her. 'You've changed.'

'I've aged.'

'It suits you. I would never have bothered with you when you were at Oxford, not because you weren't beautiful, but you were so obviously beautiful – so boring.'

Jerry laughed. 'As you can see, Billy hasn't changed a jot – as rude as ever.'

'I am not being rude, I am paying her a great compliment. Now that you have become what you are, inside and out, I would like to paint you very much – you will sit for me?'

'I'd love it, but I'm not in England very often.'

'Then I will come to where you are.'

'Olivia's getting married, Billy. She's going to live in America.'

'So, Francis wants to exhibit me there. We'll meet in America, then. Or I could paint you for your new husband?'

'It's a lovely idea, Billy . . .'

'Stay to dinner when these people have gone. We'll talk.'

'I'm afraid Olivia and I have a prior engagement.'

'I will see you again, Olivia.' It was a statement of fact rather than intention, but perhaps that was due to the brusque Germanic tone that lingered in Billy's accent.

They walked by the river. It was dark, but the lights of London sparkled on the water, and they could see each other clearly in the murky light of the street lamps, and the pale moon hung above them in its soft aureola.

'I forgot to tell her about her painting.'

'Don't worry – you *vill* meet again, whether you like it or not.'

'I'd like to see her. I'm not sure that I'd like her to paint me – all her other paintings were nudes.'

'Billy's never liked clothes.'

'No.'

'She'd do a good job of you.'

'I don't know that I *want* anyone to do a good job of me.'

'It would make an interesting wedding present for Justus. Unless you've thought of something else?'

'I haven't been thinking about it at all.'

'High time you did. Nearer and nearer draws . . . Enough of that. I don't know when I'll see you again. Tell me to stop talking. Tell me about your life in Rome. Tell me about teaching. Do you enjoy it?'

'When I'm doing it I don't think so. I've never had the sense that it was my *métier*. I'm not very good at it, to be honest – far too impatient. This past month in London I've rather missed it. Perhaps I just miss Rome.'

'Are you willing to leave it all behind?'

'I've been standing still in Rome for ten years. Although it's the perfect place to do that, there comes a time when you have to move on.'

'I loved Rome. Not that I've been back since.'

'The first time I even liked Rome was when you came out with George. Up till then I'd always hated it. Now it's my only real home.'

'Do you ever go to the Bocca della Verità? I remember you taking us there. I remember how passionately you believed in the legend.'

Olivia didn't answer for a moment. 'I pass it, that's all. I'm not as superstitious as I was. Maybe Billy should exhibit in Rome, in the cloisters of Santa Maria della Pace – it's quite the best venue.' Olivia began to giggle.

'What? What's so funny?'

'Nothing.' Her laughter had the high note of hysteria.

Jerry stopped and shook her lightly. 'What? Tell me. What's so funny?'

'I sounded exactly like my mother. It's not funny at all, it's quite awful,' and as she tried to stop laughing, she found herself laughing all the harder until Jerry began to kiss her hairline, and then her eyes, and her cheeks, and finally her mouth, by which time she had stopped laughing altogether.

'This can't happen.'

'Oh, yes, it can. It has. You can't stop it.'

'I can, Jerry, you taught me that. We make choices, remember? It's a cop-out to say I couldn't help myself. I am responsible. I am in control of this.'

'You should listen to yourself. You're lying. You know you love me.'

'No, I don't "know" – I don't know at all. I don't know whether I'm just trying to make good what I broke. I don't know anything.'

'Olivia, you do love me, even if you won't admit it. You love me now in a way you never used to.'

'But so what if I do, Jerry?' she cried out across the river. 'So what? All right, I do love you, right now, right here, I can say it, I love you.' Her voice dropped to a throaty whisper. 'I was happier with you at Billy's show than I can remember being. But what happens next month, next year? What happens tomorrow night, for God's sake? Will it last? How do I know? How can I tell? Constancy isn't one of my key virtues.'

'You can make it last if you want to. If you want to, you can choose to be with me tomorrow night, you can choose not to leave me tonight. I don't give a fuck about your constancy.'

'I do – I care a great deal! I'm going to marry Justus in three weeks' time. I am going to marry Justus.'

'You don't love him.'

'I do love him, and I'm going to marry him.'

'You don't know the meaning of the word.'

'And you do?'

'Yes, I do. I know that I love you, whatever you do, and I will continue to love you and think about you whether you marry Justus or not. That's all it's about, Livvy. It's about loving someone whether they're with you or not.'

'Then why can't you see that that's exactly what I'm trying to do? You are not the only person concerned, Jerry, however much I love you.'

'Ah, yes, Justus. Let's not forget Justus.'

'Don't be so foul. He's never done anything to you. He's tried to befriend you, for God's sake, and you won't let him get close.'

Jerry's jaw tightened. Though thirty-two, he still wanted to yell, 'Did *nothing*? He ruined my life!' They sat on a bench near the river. Close up, the Thames lost its glittering beauty; the banks were spoiled by litter, the water level was too low, the setting suddenly sordid.

'Can you really marry him?'

'Yes.'

'You can't ask me to come.'

'I know that.'

'So shouldn't we be saying goodbye? We've never managed to say goodbye before.' Jerry saw the tears on Olivia's cheeks glinting in the thin and artificial light. He tried again. 'Livvy, I'm not going to say this ever again, do you understand that? Look at me, damn it. Don't marry Justus. Take your time. You'll be killing yourself if you marry him now.'

Olivia looked at the river and did not know which way to run. Jerry was beside her, but she could not turn to him. Justus was further than the other side of the ocean. She would have liked more time, but asking for time would be the same as telling Justus no, and whatever the future brought, she could not bring herself to say no. She turned to Jerry with a wild smile. 'You always said there's nothing to fear in death. Maybe part of me ought to die.'

'You think that's witty?'

'I'm going to marry Justus.'

'I'm going back to Billy's.' Jerry stood abruptly. 'Are you coming?'

'No.'

'So you're going to sit here all night?'

'I don't know what I'm going to do.'

'I'd do pretty much anything for you, still, you know that – but I won't sit here holding your hand while you steel yourself to marry a man you don't love.'

'You're very certain of everything.' Olivia knew she would say anything, anything, it didn't matter if it made sense or not, just to keep him standing next to her, keep him talking, stop him walking away. There is nothing wrong with prolonging the agony when the agony holds some faint vestige of hope.

'Yes, I am. I'm certain of you, too. Livvy?' She closed her eyes. 'I'm glad you came back. I want to be able to wish you joy – I do wish you joy. I hope I'm wrong about Justus. I admit I don't know him, and I'm a poor judge of character. Say goodbye to me, Liv, say goodbye.'

'I can't.'

Jerry knelt on the concrete in front of her and took her hands in his gently. 'Then think why not.'

'It hurts too much. If it's so good, why should it hurt?'

'Olivia, what you believe lost can be found, but only once you know it is lost.'

'Don't, Jerry, it doesn't help, it never did, all those high ideals, all that spiritual stuff. None of it helps at all.'

'I'm sorry. I hoped – Goodbye, darling.' He squeezed her hands and waited for her to reply. She did not lift her head until she heard his footsteps retreating. She watched Jerry walk away until she could no longer see him in the gloom.

She had not intended to walk home, but she started walking aimlessly and two hours later found herself in Kensington. It had begun to rain lightly, and she had left without a jacket, let alone a coat. When she opened the flat door her T-shirt was damp through to her skin.

'No wonder you wind up with flu if you walk around in the rain at midnight.' Justus was sitting on the sofa with his feet up and a whisky in his hand. Olivia did not have the energy to register surprise; she didn't even feel it. It seemed to her that she was not an agent so much as a powerless part of a chain reaction; she stood still while others made decisions around her. Justus coming back surprised her no more than Jerry turning up had done.

'You're meant to be in Pigsbottom, Mass.'

'There was a technical hitch – meaning the producer got sacked. I made the most of it, faked a tantrum and caught a flight from Boston. Didn't you get my message?'

'I went out without listening to the machine.'

'Come here. Let me get you a towel.'

Olivia put her hand to her head. 'Don't bother, it's fine. How long will you stay?'

'A couple of days. Depends. How long do you want me?' His eyes crinkled up, but the accompanying smile faded fast. He fetched a towel from the bathroom and draped it round her shoulders. 'Sweetheart? What's up? You're not really sick, are you? Are you getting cold feet?'

She sat down on his lap and ruffled his dry and perfect hair. 'No, of course not. Why do you say that?'

'I don't know, I had a strange feeling last time I came through you weren't exactly ecstatic.'

'I just want to get it all over with quickly.'

'Whoa – that's not the classic bridal reply. Don't girls see their wedding day as the happiest day of their lives?'

She punched him softly on the chin. 'Don't boys?'

'I'm not the one who's down in the dumps.'

'It's not marrying you that's making me nervous. It's just the wedding.'

'C'mon, bend over.' He slowly towelled her hair with lulling, circular rubs. 'Don't be scared about the wedding. If that's not the way you want to do it, fuck 'em. We'll run away, elope, go someplace else. Remember the last time we wanted to run away together? Drop your shoulders, you're all seized up. I'll give you a massage.'

Olivia stood up abruptly. 'Not now, thanks. Have you eaten? Can I make you a sandwich?' She moved restlessly around the tiny kitchen while he watched.

'I ate on the plane. What's spooking you about the wedding?'

'My parents, probably. *Your* parents.'

'They'll love you, just like I do. They'll think you're perfect. They've been shitting themselves for years I'd marry some brat-pack kid with a history of drug problems. Have you quit smoking yet? That's the only thing they won't approve of.'

As if he'd reminded her, Olivia immediately reached for a cigarette. 'I saw Jerry again tonight.'

'Oh yeah? Did you kiss him again?' he asked blandly.

'No, I told you, that was just a one-off thing.'

'Don't make a habit of it – you've got what we call an addictive personality. You're pretty addictive yourself.' He nuzzled her neck while she tried shakily to slice a loaf of bread without putting down her cigarette. 'Pretty, and addictive . . . Thank Christ I gave up smoking at Oxford, and didn't have to give you up.'

'I saw him at a private view – Billy's.' Olivia spread peanut butter on the bread so she wouldn't have to move over to the fridge and pretend to look for something she didn't want to eat.

'Billy who? Do I know him?'

'Her. "Anyone who saw the penis of Leigh Bowery would never forget it. It vas Life itself."'

'That Billy! Is she still talking balls?' Justus wrapped his arms around her waist, resting his chin on her shoulder. 'Or were you too busy talking to Jerry?'

'I've told you, I'm not interested in Jerry.' Olivia edged away. 'Darling, I hope you don't mind, but I have to go have a hot bath. I can't stop shivering.'

'Want me to soap your back?'

'No, I just want to soak. I just want a bit of time.' Her hands flew fleetingly to his cheeks in apology. 'I'll be much more relaxed when I've had a bath. I promise.'

Justus stared at the half-made, abandoned sandwich and then went into the sitting room, closing the door behind him. He picked up the phone.

'Laura? Hey, it's Justus . . .' he winced and held the phone away from his ear as a barrage of abuse barrelled across at least seven states before hitting the Atlantic Ocean. 'So I guess you heard, huh? . . . That's what I'm doing, Laura honey, I *am* calling you . . . No, I am not a fuckhead, and I'm not doing drugs . . . I didn't exactly "walk off" the set . . . That's what contract clauses are for, that's what makes you such a damn smart agent . . . I will, if you'd just shut up for a single – Laura, I'm going to hang up, OK? I'm hanging up *now* if you don't let me . . . Right. That's better. In and out, just breathe in and out . . . I told them I had to sort out some personal problems . . . How could I know they'd assume that? I am *not* in rehab, Laura, for Christ's sake . . . I just had to see Olivia . . . If I knew what was going on, I wouldn't have had to fly back, would I? . . . She's up and down,' he laughed, rubbing his head, 'no, not like a pair of presidential trousers, no . . . Yeah, I'm with her now . . . Sure I told them I'd be back in a couple of days, they didn't make a big deal of it . . . Yes, I do absolutely intend to . . . Yes, I know you're fantastic . . . OK, long-suffering . . . Well, your butt could use a bit of working off, between you and me . . . Yeah. You take care of you too.'

When he put down the phone he reached for Olivia's handbag and rifled through it, then turned to the table where her papers were scattered. He found the slim red leather address book, flipped to 'M' then dialled again.

'Jerry, this is Justus O'Keefe . . . Yes, I know, I'm sorry to call so late, and I won't take more than a minute . . . It is kind of another favour, yes . . . I'm sorry about that, I was out of line. I'd be very grateful if you'd meet me for lunch – could you make it tomorrow? I'm only here for a day or so . . . I hate to have to ask you to change your plans, but yes, it is kind of important . . . That's grand. That'll be fine. I'll see you there, one-ish.' He scrawled down an address and shoved it in his jeans pocket. 'Jerry? You're a gentleman.'

# not enough for me, and not enough for you

They met in the Japanese restaurant. Justus had arrived first, and leaped to his feet when Jerry walked in. 'It's very good of you to come. I hope it doesn't mess you up?'

'Meeting you for lunch? No, I don't think it will.'

'I meant your schedule.'

'I know you did, Justus. How can I help you?'

'You won't be surprised if I say I wanted to talk to you about Olivia?'

'I wasn't expecting you to ask me for a few career pointers. Olivia is the only thing we have in common. Shall we order first? The staff here can be touchy.'

'Jerry, we got off to a bad start last time we met.'

'To be blunt, we never got off to a good one.'

'I'd like to start again. I'd like us to be friends. As you said, we share a common interest.'

Jerry smiled tightly. 'I don't know that share is an entirely appropriate word . . .'

'Let me be straight with you, OK? I know you think I'm a shit, and you have some valid reasons for thinking it, and I don't really give a damn if you still think so at the end of this conversation. I came back to London last night because something's not right with

Olivia.' Justus looked carefully at his companion, but Jerry's aquiline face revealed nothing at all. 'When I left Rome, Olivia told me she had no intention of seeing you. I thought she should. I urged her to.'

'Very big of you.'

'It was very sensible of me. I want to make a clean start with her. There's no point having ghosts hanging around if they can be laid to rest.'

'Justus, forgive me for stating the obvious, but Olivia and I hadn't spoken for a very long time. Whatever there was between us was over ten years ago. There are no skeletons in the cupboard that I am aware of.'

'I don't see it quite like that. You were the key person when Olivia was growing up. That's significant.'

'I'm sure Pip or George Upton would claim that distinction. We all have various key people while we are growing up. They tend to disappear. In Olivia's case, quite literally.'

'That's just what bothers me. If the two of you had lived together for three years and drifted apart, then I'd say that was a natural break, but there's something unnatural about the way she worries about what happened that long ago.'

'Then I hope her hankering has been satisfied in rediscovering you.'

'Do you?'

The atmosphere between them was increasingly tense, despite Justus's smiles. Jerry shifted irritably. 'I must say, I'm at a loss trying to understand your purpose here. You appear to be asking my permission to marry Olivia. Even if you required it, it isn't mine to give. You should be having this conversation with Peter Fletcher-Smith.'

'Oh, I have. I'd just like Olivia to feel that you blessed it.'

'Neither of you needs my blessing.'

'Why did you kiss her?'

'Why did *you*?' Jerry tried to catch the attention of a waitress. 'Look, I'm going to have a whisky – do you want something?'

Justus shook his head. 'Are you asking why I pursued her at Oxford? I was very attracted to her, not as much as I am now, but enough for me not to be willing to let her go easily.'

'Would you like me to slap you on the back and say that the best man won?'

'This isn't easy for me, Jerry . . . I think Olivia is a little in love with you.'

'That's something you should ask her, not me.'

'The last time we met, you said you did not believe I loved her. Do you love her?'

Jerry rested his chin on his hands and stared past Justus. 'I can't answer that.'

'Do you think she's in love with you?' Jerry half shook his head. 'Well, do you think she's in love with me?'

'Olivia is more than opaque, she is emotionally indecipherable. She is extremely good at convincing herself of things. That makes her persuasive to others.'

'You think she's trying to love me?'

'How can I answer you? This is the woman you are going to marry. Ask her.'

'And if I told you that I happen to believe that Olivia is in love with you, but won't admit it for fear of hurting me?'

'I'd say that doesn't sound like Olivia.'

'But if it were true, and you were in my shoes, what would you do?'

'I would marry her at once.' Jerry spoke in a clipped voice. 'You forget, Justus, I *have* been in your shoes. I would have married her at any point, regardless of what she felt about you. I always knew she'd fallen in love with you, and chose to ignore it. I suggest you do the same – if your suspicions are correct, which I doubt.'

'You finished? Something wrong?' Their plates were untouched. The waitress looked at them as if they were delinquent schoolchildren. 'You don't like it, you ask for the manager, OK? You want something else?'

'I'll have another whisky.'

'I'll take one too.'

'You just want to drink, go to pub. More expensive here. Two Johnny Walker, OK?'

'Charming place.'

'I hate it. That's why I suggested meeting here.'

Justus nodded slowly. 'I want to make Olivia happy.'

'Don't expect it to be a piece of cake.'

'If I asked Olivia if she was in love with you, she would deny it.'

'Now, there, you're not wrong.'

'But if I told her that I did not love her . . .' Justus said; Jerry looked at him with intense concentration. 'If I said that . . .'

'But you do love her?'

'She's everything to me. More. When I saw her again that morning in Rome, it hit me like a tidal wave. No kidding. She's been like something washing over me, something that's been there all the time, coloured everything I see. She's been the frame against which I look at every other woman. I didn't know it when I left. I had an idea that I needed to achieve stuff first, and then I'd look for a partner. I guess she was there all the time, somewhere in my head, some kind of ideal.'

Jerry stared deeply into his tumbler. He did not feel that Olivia had left a colour wash on his life; he felt that she had personally carved a tattoo on his chest, large, prominent and painful. His attempt to have it removed had taken the best part of ten years, and had not been successful. This was not a thought that he cared to share with Justus. 'If you feel like that, you shouldn't let her go.'

Justus spoke with irony. 'You don't believe me. You think I was just flexing my muscles. Sure, I thought about that. Is she just the last bastion to fall to my irresistible charms? I may have thought that at Oxford – I know I wanted to take her away from you. I wanted her, but I wanted to win her too. Now I just love her. But I wonder if she loves me?'

'Then we're in the same boat,' Jerry admitted finally.

'The question is, if I told Livvy I didn't love her, would she feel free to admit she loves you?'

'Assuming she does.'

'Yeah. Assuming she does.'

Jerry scratched his throat. 'People shouldn't be played with. You cannot trick people falsely into revealing their hand, even as the means to end. If you love Olivia, as I believe that you do, then just marry her and continue to love her. That's all most of us should aspire to, simply to love another person completely.'

'And what will you do, Jerry?'

'Given the circumstances, I shall wear a brave face when I dance at your wedding. But first, I'm going to have another whisky at the pub next door. Don't distract yourself with concern for my feeling. It will be possible for me to say goodbye to Mrs Justus O'Keefe.'

Jerry hoped that Justus would not ask to come with him to the pub: as far as he was concerned, the matter was closed, and in some ways his heart was lighter than when he arrived. Justus insisted on paying the bill, but did not suggest they continued the conversation.

In all the time he'd known her, Justus had so far told Olivia only two lies: they happened to occur within twelve hours of each other, but neither was significant in the big scheme of things. He had told her that the final days of the *Roderick Hudson* shoot had been delayed, rather than explaining he had left the set in order to see her. He had told her the following morning that he needed to meet a director to discuss a project, rather than admitting he was meeting Jerry Milton. He'd bullied Olivia into going to the Moroccan travel-agency to find out how they might spend their honeymoon while he was tied up, and that is where he went after leaving Jerry. Olivia had her arms full of brochures.

'I don't know where to begin . . .'

'You've made a start at least. Here, let me take those.' With the perfect manners of an American, far better than those of any Englishman you're likely to meet, Justus relieved her. 'The only hitch is there's no certainty the film will be shot in Morocco, just because the book's set there. It could be Tunisia. It could be Calabria, or Spain.'

'Calabria would be good – at least you'd be closer to Rome.'

'We'll work it out, OK?'

'Did your meeting go well?'

'Hmm? Oh, that. Waste of time, really, but it pays to be polite. You never know when you're going to need a friend. Darling, I'm going to have to get a flight back tonight, tomorrow morning at the latest. I doubt I'll get back until a couple of days before the wedding.'

'That's OK, I've calmed down. I can handle it. When will your parents get here? Will they stay with us? I could book them a room at Claridge's, although they might end up seeing far more of my parents than I'd like them to.'

'Don't worry about that, I'll call them and sort it out. The thing is, sweetcakes, next time I see you we'll be just about married. I want to go somewhere special today.'

'Like where?'

'I don't know – maybe Oxford?' They were standing in the middle of Shepherd Market, oblivious to the stares of those who passed by.

'I just did a major Memory Lane trip with Pip. Oxford's a lifetime away, and nothing to do with us now. Besides, we haven't got a car. . .'

'Little Miss Practicality. So let's just go back to the flat. Talk.'

'If you'd like to.'

Olivia made every effort to appear happy. She'd bought Justus some cufflinks from the Burlington Arcade and presented them in the taxi on the way home. When he'd admired them and kissed her, she sat beside him pushing her hair up and letting it drop, time after time.

'I've been thinking about having my hair cut off. What d'you think? Do you think I'm too old to go trendy? Would you still love me if it was really short?'

'I'd love you if you were bald.'

'You're not going to go bald, are you? I don't know if I could handle that. . .'

'Prepare yourself for the worst. My dad has about ten hairs left on his head, last count. At least I've checked out your mother.'

'I might not age as well as her. You'll leave me for a younger woman.'

'Not a chance.' He opened the door into his flat, feeling weary and uncertain that he could pull off a performance.

'How many Hollywood stars are still on their first wife?'

'Depends which ones you count . . . Young ones?'

'That's cheating. Do you want some coffee?'

'I've given it up.'

'God, what haven't you given up? What's it going to be like being married to such a saint? Are you still drinking? Would you rather have a drink?'

'I'll have some juice. Get whatever you like. I'm just going to change.'

'Don't change too much, OK?' Her laugh sounded forced even to her own ears.

Justus came back in a T-shirt and jeans, and dropped his overnight bag by the front door.

'So you are going tonight.'

'I see you're on the hard stuff.' Olivia had opened a bottle of wine.

'Why do I have the feeling I've been summoned by the headmaster? I feel like I should be sitting on my hands. I feel like I've been caught smoking in the girls' lats, or jobbing something.' The Marlburian slang for stealing slipped out quite naturally, although she hadn't used it in a decade.

'Maybe you've got a guilty conscience.'

'OK, Justus.' Olivia flung herself down on the sofa. 'I know you're pissed off with me about kissing Jerry, even if you're trying to be cool about it. You're pissed off I even saw him. If you want to tell me off, go ahead. I'd much rather get it over with.'

'I don't want to tell you off about anything, but I do want to talk.'

'Sounds heavy . . . I might just have to smoke through it, OK?'

'Olivia,' Justus began, 'Olivia. You know I love you . . .'

'This sounds bad. This sounds like a script.'

'I wish. I could say it better if it was. You know I love you?'

'Yes, I do.'

'Do you want to marry me, Olivia?'

'Is this some kind of a game? OK, so I went through the pros and cons, but it came out on the pro side. I made my final decision,' she drawled ironically. 'What's got into you?'

'Did it come out by a lot, or just a couple of points?'

'Stop fishing. I'm not going to give you the list. It'll go to your head.'

'Come here.' Olivia slid down next to him. 'Let it go to my head, baby.' Justus held her face between his hands and kissed her deeply. He drew back to search her face, but Olivia had closed her eyes and lay relaxed and limp in his arms. He could not guess what she was thinking and kissed her again, insistently. She offered no resistance, but nor did she respond with the abandon that he sought. 'I think you'll drive me mad.'

'Why?' She sat up abruptly. 'I thought you loved me.'

'Is that what you thought?'

'Justus, don't play games. Don't practise your parts on me.'

'What would suit you best, Olivia? Which role would you like me to play this in? In the manner of Jay Gatsby? Or Romeo? Or would you like something a little more stringent – fuckin' Casaubon?'

'I don't understand. Why are you so angry? What have I done?'

'It's more what you haven't done, Liv.'

'Just tell me what you want. You don't want to get married?'

'Sure I do.'

'But not to me?'

Justus stood up and pulled her to her feet roughly. 'Yeah, I want to get married to you. I'd like that real well.' Holding her by the arm he dragged her through to the entrance hall.

Olivia, half frightened and half laughing, stumbled after him until they stood in front of the large gilt-edged mirror. 'So go ahead – ask me again if you're so unsure!'

'No, I won't.'

'Because you're scared I'll say no?'

'No, because I'm scared you'll say yes. What do you see, Olivia? What do you see in the mirror?'

'You looking like a mad dog . . . Me just looking like a dog.'

'Want to know what I see?' He put his hands on either side of her head and twisted it so she stared straight into the mirror. 'I see someone who's so scared she can hardly breathe. A woman who's trying so hard to please everyone, she's too damn tired to know if she's happy or not. How long have you been saying your lines, Olivia? You're what we call over-rehearsed.'

Olivia's head dropped. She was trembling with shock at his anger. If she had looked up, she would have seen that his face was wet with tears, but she did not, and he saw himself in the mirror and wiped his face with the back of his hand before gently turning her round to face him. She pressed her cheek against his chest, and felt him quiver.

'Olivia. I wouldn't hurt you for anything in the world. Listen to me. I'm not going to marry you. I'd stand there waiting for you to say I will, and I'm too scared that if I heard you say it, I'd just agree, and tell myself that the fact that you don't love me doesn't matter.'

'But I do love you, Justus! I do!'

'No, sweet thing, you don't. Oh, you love me in a way, I'll give you that. But you don't love me enough. Not enough for me, and not enough for you either.'

'I love you more than I've ever loved anyone –'

'You don't. Don't you know it?'

'All I know is that you're the only man I've not been able to forget, the only one I've thought about – even when I left, and afterwards, and when I met you in Rome . . .You're the only one I've come close to loving –'

'Coming close isn't enough. When we were together at Oxford, I fell in love with you easy. Not far enough to stop me doing what I wanted to do, but I did fall in love with you. In Rome it happened again, but this time I fell harder. I would have given up anything you asked. I would have become anything you wanted, so long as I knew that you loved me. Right up until last night, I thought you might just. Given time, and the right circumstances, and a bit of luck, I thought we'd be OK, and that I could make up for what you didn't feel. I could convince you, I could talk you into loving me enough. But then something happened, and I knew I was fooling myself. Worse, you have been.'

'What happened?'

'You reminded me you'd made a decision. I don't want you to decide that you love me, or decide that you'll marry me. That I'll do. You've done nothing but compromise all your life – it's the only thing you know how to do.'

'Justus, I just want to be happy. I just wanted to find the right man, know he loved me and be happy with him. I did. I thought I had. Why can't I just be happy?'

'Darling . . . You will. But not with me. It's the only thing I can really do for you, Olivia, don't you see? Not marry you.'

'But I – but I –' Justus waited, knowing she couldn't finish the sentence. 'You can't go.'

'I have to go,' he said softly. 'You won't kick me out.'

'Justus, don't leave me. I'm so tired of being lonely, please don't leave me.'

'I won't ever leave you. I'll be there whenever you need me, but you won't need me. At worst, I'll be at the end of a telephone, whenever you want to talk. Always. I'll still come to Rome and do your workshop. You keep my number, OK? And you keep that ring. I'd like think of you wearing it sometimes. Now go see Jerry, OK? Talk things through.' He picked up his bag, kissed her once more and left. Olivia wailed as she slumped against the door.

One of the stewardesses on the night flight from London to Boston called ahead to alert a media contact that Justus O'Keefe was on the plane. The photograph of him clearing Immigration at Logan International showed a face so haggard, so wretched, that it stoked the embers smouldering in the trade press which Laura had tried so hard to smother two days earlier. Speculation about a breakdown, drug abuse and the mystery romance he had announced to Barry Norman competed with each other for column inches.

The next morning Olivia cancelled the marriage service and the room at Claridge's and booked a flight to Rome. She telephoned Jerry, Pip and George to tell them that the wedding was off and she was going home. She left a message for both Pip and Jerry, leaving her Rome phone number. George, she learned from his message, was already on holiday with his family. It was only on the plane that she realised she still had Justus's house keys in her bag and his credit card in her wallet. She folded the credit card until it broke into six small pieces, and shoved them into the redundant ashtray; the keys she left where they were. When the stewardess reached her she had only *The Times* left. Olivia flipped to the death entries. There was only one:

**Smith, Olivia Maria (née Schwarz)** of Richmond Surrey on 28 July. Widow of (1) Max von Lienau und Scheinbrun (died Dachau 1943) and (2) Robert Smith. Will be sorely missed by all her family and friends. Funeral at St Sepulchre's, Oxford, at 11.30 a.m. Saturday 6 August. Donations to Age Concern, please, instead of flowers.

She stared at it blankly: there had been a mistake. There hadn't been a burial at St Sepulchre's since 1955. She leaned her head against the tiny window and looked at the clouds.

She refused to think about superstition, about St Sepulchre's, about how lucky she was not to have been married to Max von Lienau und Scheinbrun, or how unlucky not to have been given a second chance with Robert Smith. She would think about nothing at all until she saw Rome beneath her, until she was back safely in Trastevere. She'd make Santa Cecilia her first visit; the saint – at least her effigy – was herself the subject of superstition; much had been read into the position of her corpse, the three fingers extended on one hand, the single finger on the other, the three in one, and all that garbage. Cecilia had died a horrible death – what did she care where her fingers pointed? Maybe Sant' Agnesi in Agone would be a better sister figure: betrothal had brought her to martyrdom. If he or she were a Roman church, which church would they be? Justus might be the classically clean yet complex Pantheon, which had changed its purpose yet maintained its straight façade; George the Aracoeli church, with its one hundred and twenty-five wide marble steps dipped by the knees of generations of lottery hopefuls. And Jerry? Olivia bumped her forehead on the window. Jerry would be Santa Maria in Cosmedin, if he would be anything at all . . . On arrival home she resolved to light a candle in all three.

# to see how it might unravel . . .

**Rome, September 1997**

Olivia Fletcher-Smith, thirty-two-year-old spinster of the parish of Santa Maria in Trastevere, crossed the Piazza del Popolo while opening a letter from George and was nearly hit by a car careering around the centre. The driver screeched to a halt to give her the benefit of his opinion, and Olivia gave him the benefit of her finger before she read the letter. George and Sarah were coming to Rome for a long weekend, and she was eager to know their arrangements.

Darling Liv,

    Writing this from home having quite given up on reading the Sunday papers. I have reached that dubious stage when at least one item in the news is bound to infuriate me – the tell-tale sign of middle age, don't tell me. So glad you'll be free around the weekend of the 15th/16th; we won't stay with you, but are more than happy to leave the choice of hotel to you, so go ahead and book whatever you consider suitable. Sarah pointed out that this will be the first holiday she and I have spent *sine* brats since Will's birth and saying that, I can now tell you our most important news – Sarah is expecting another baby! She didn't want to tell anyone until she'd passed the tricky period, but it is now quite safe. We are counting on you to stand as godmother; at the least it will stop you doing a bunk to Timbuktu.

Arthur's taken the news very well, but Will is struggling to find anything positive in it. Sarah and I are delighted – I confess, I'm surprised quite how proud and happy it made me feel. I have a great sense of a brand new life, although I dread having to go back to reading *Postman Pat*. Talking of godmothers, has Pip told you that she is commissioning a series called *Oxford Now and Then*, and hoping to use 12 Kingston Road as the focus? Sounds a no-hoper of an idea to me – can't imagine why anyone would want to hear how we lived then, but I've agreed to be interviewed, if she wants me. Thinking about the house and all of us back then made me wonder if you and Pip ever settled your final house accounts . . .

It also made me think of more important things. I want to tell you that I'm very sorry about the business with Justus, sorry that things didn't work out as you'd planned, and sorry that I was too selfishly preoccupied with my own insane issues to pay proper attention to yours. Seeing that on paper, I am aware that my current remorse may well be as self-centred as my original sin. I have been a very bad friend (I hope you are disagreeing as you read this) but will compensate for my failure in the future. The last thing you needed was my childish outpourings. I can only say that the expression of devotion at least was genuine. Is this another sign of the onset of the years, that children and friendship become the most important things in life?

Dreadful ramblings – blame the blasted *Telegraph*. This brings my love, and Sarah's love, and we long to see you in the Eternal City. See if you can pull off a papal audience. Doesn't your mother have a relation with influence in the Vatican? *II*

*Papa* aside, the only thing I do not want to do in Rome is be dragged round a series of churches. I daresay we'll have to do it with the children in a couple of years' time, and that's soon enough for me. Take care of yourself and big kisses.

Georgie.

Olivia shoved the letter into her purse and hailed a taxi. 'Cemetario non Cattolico per i Stranieri.'

Access to the walled Protestant cemetery, or the non-Catholic Cemetery for Foreigners as it is correctly known, is from a quiet street in a quiet district of the city. That afternoon, cars lined the street, and as Olivia came in through the door she saw perhaps twenty people gathered in the top right-hand corner, squeezed onto several levels as if clinging for footholds. There are two parts to the cemetery. The 'front room' looks rather like a terraced vineyard in Portugal, but densely packed graves rather than vines cling precariously along the sharply tiered terraces. The 'back room', permanent home to the remains of Keats, Joseph Severn and other notable foreigners who shrugged off their mortal coils in Rome, is quite different, laid out like an English garden, with more sparsely placed graves and paths meandering through them. The whole place is infested with cats: they creep from under benches, behind tombstones, beneath the roots of trees and from the remains of a classical ruin that borders the cemetery wall.

Two old ladies swathed in fur coats huddled on a bench in the sun spot before Keats's grave, gossiping furiously, and eyed Olivia as she walked slowly along the path. She stopped when she reached her favourite grave, a plain, lichen-stained tombstone bearing the inscription:

To the memory of Ruth McEvers of the city of New York, United

States of America. This stone is erected by her affectionate husband James McEvers. While travelling with him for the benefit of her health she was arrested by death on 27th March 1803 and thence removed here and interred on the 29th aged 18 years and six months. She was the delight of a fond mother and family and of an adoring husband.

Jerry slipped his arm around her waist as she stood in contemplation.

'However many times I read that, I always read it with exactly the same reactions. In the first half, I suspect he didn't love her and was glad she died. I imagine him as about twenty years older than her, a well-to-do New Yorker or Bostonian businessman, who snapped up poor little Ruth for her dowry and carted her round Europe trying to make her into the perfect wife, trying to civilise her with some broad brush of sophistication. I hate that word "affectionate". She goes into decline, keeps getting sicker, and paler, and thinner, and finally gives up the ghost in Rome. Then I get to the last line, and every time, I think, No, I'm wrong – he truly did adore her. He probably sacrificed everything travelling with her, desperate to find a cure. He probably nearly died himself because he couldn't save her.'

Jerry kissed the top of her head. 'Do you adjust his age, then, when you get to that point?'

'Always. By the last line, I think he was barely older than she was. I bet she'd always been consumptive, they were childhood sweethearts. Two kids – maybe he was twenty-four or five, but no more than that – lost in Rome, putting all their faith in foreign quacks, going from one to the other, and all the time she's just getting weaker, and his heart's breaking.'

'Meaning that he couldn't have adored her, if he was twenty years older than she was?'

'Only in a paternal or perverted way.'

'You're funny. What can you really tell about them from her epitaph? Nothing much. He might have murdered her. He might have married her for her money, whipped her abroad on honeymoon and poisoned her. He'd certainly still put "adoring husband" on the tombstone, wouldn't he?'

'You don't think that, you're not such a cynic.' She took his hand. 'How was the funeral?'

'Good. I couldn't say much to them, not having my translator with me, but I made all the right noises. I saw you come in.'

'I was trying not to disturb you.'

'I was waiting for you.'

'Are you sure you feel up to dinner with my parents tonight?'

'I've been looking forward to it. Shall we go and have a drink first?'

They spent an hour or so in a bar on the Piazza Rotonda, facing the Pantheon. From their table they could see the rampant irregularity of the rooftops, glimpses of circular red-tiled roofs peeping out from under the swooping pillars and pedestals. The classical ash-white buildings jostled for position with medieval and Renaissance Rome, awash with rose madder, ochre, brick and rust, shutters picked out in dull green, or red the colour of dried blood, some standing out all the more by being unpainted, the bleached wood stark against all that colour. On every terrace, balcony and window-ledge, scarlet geraniums or powder blue plumbago entwined with ivy to trail down along the walls, or seductively embraced erect bushes of laurel and bay. Olivia luxuriated in the late-afternoon sun. A few yards in front of them, a five-year-old boy entertained the outdoor tables by playing the violin along to a compilation tape. Far from resenting the competition, the North African rose touts and local waiters all threw in money and patted him affectionately on the head.

'Now in England, people would be up in arms about that – it would either be seen as exploitative of the child, or of the tourists.'

'He's a regular, part of the scene.' She smiled at the boy as he passed around a plastic bucket, and Jerry chucked in all his change. 'Jerry, I'm not sure I want to go back to London. I don't think I could live there.'

Jerry cocked an eyebrow. 'Are you telling me you'll never come back?'

'It's time I decided what my life was about. Where my roots are.'

'You always said you didn't have roots.'

'I always said a lot of crap. It's not my parents, it's just that I'm happy here.'

'Then you should stay here. It's a great gift to know where you're happy, as well as when you're happy. People underestimate the importance of place.'

'Where are you happy, Jerry?'

Jerry smiled. 'I knew you were going to ask that. You already know the answer. I'm happy with you, dearest. Whenever and wherever. I have always known that.'

Olivia dipped her head. 'Even after all that I've done? I've been so, so – blind. So selfish. So utterly stupid.' She looked up at him with wide and honest eyes, her steady gaze so direct that Jerry felt he could barely breathe. 'I've behaved like a child, chasing after shadows.'

'What on earth have you got against children? If we could have the complete, open happiness that children have, we could put up with a lot of stupidity and selfishness, and all the childish games. We could even enjoy them. There's nothing sadder than an adult who has entirely lost the ability to see and feel as a child.'

When they walked towards the Tiber later that night, Olivia held Jerry's hand and experienced the broad and fearless happiness that had eluded her for most of her childhood as well as her adult life. She did not expect the future to be easy, and she knew that far from tying up loose ends, she had teased the fringes with a mischievous finger-nail, going on to tug at the fraying edge of the fabric without wilful destruction, simply to see how it might unravel. Only when the bare threads lay in her lap had she learned that satisfaction came from the slow labour of creation, not from the finished product. They crossed the river together with light hearts.

# Jack shall have Jill, nought shall go ill . . .

We'll leave them there, shall we, straddling the Tiber, each very far from a Colossus, but both grown considerably in stature since our first meeting, to my mind at least, and both showing at least the potential for continued growth. At least they didn't make the mistake of thinking that the educational process grinds to a halt when you leave university. That is exactly the point at which it begins, and all the time before that is nothing but a warm-up.

Let me review the clues I gave you at the start of this tale: I said that four of them married between the summers of 1986 and 1997, and that was true: as you know, George and Sarah married quite soon after leaving Oxford, and they remain married. I cannot, hand on heart, tell you that George never strayed from his marital bed. He did, and I expect that he will, sporadically, but will always return to it like a dog that forays into the neighbourhood bins and comes home with the shame-faced yet tail-waggingly certain expectation that his own bowl will still be where he left it. Sarah was always there to replenish it, even if at times she was inclined to scold and send him to the doghouse for a week or two. As a woman, rather than a wife, Sarah went from strength to strength: as her family expanded, so grew her capacity for calm and careful management. As George grew older, and grumbled increasingly at the leaders in the newspapers, so his dependence on her increased, and she became a ninety-five per-center, as she came to think of it. Whether her true expectations were raised or decreased in this process, I cannot say. The danger for Sarah was always that she was prepared to settle for the middle ground, to accept most of what life dished up on her plate without complaint. This is a dangerous strategy, to my mind: it may be acceptable to compromise on the colour of your bedroom walls, but not on the person who shares your bed.

You know that Michael Marsden married his childhood sweetheart, and subsequently divided his time between producing children and furniture design. Within the necessary confines of this story, Michael was and is an irrelevance, as I warned you one of them would be. I'm sure he is of primary importance to his family and to his colleagues, and I am certain his death notice will record that he was greatly loved. He was doubtless important within his own tale, but not to this one. Cross him off the list.

And Billy – you know that Billy married. Billy enjoyed a spell of critical acclaim – I believe a couple of her portraits were purchased by one of the Saatchi family, I can never remember which, Doris or Charles, and for a time the fire of her success burned with a brilliant flame. I do not know quite why she ceased to be a darling of the art world, but these things are fragile and mercurial. I know it did not bother her very much. She has a daughter, and she loves her husband, who became one of the most respected gallery owners in London, and Billy did become a muse, to a painter I respect enormously. A painting of her with her baby in her arms hangs in the dining room of the Chelsea Arts Club; she looks down on the members and their guests like a latterday Mona Lisa, holding the secrets of the world in her gaze.

Justus and Olivia nearly married, so very nearly. They should both be congratulated on how hard they worked – and believe me, it was a question of effort on both parts – to preserve their friendship. Justus travelled to Rome from location in Tunisia in October of 1997, his visit coinciding with that of the Uptons, and dutifully spent three afternoons working with Olivia's students on *A Midsummer Night's Dream*. He was surprised to find that he enjoyed it, and it inspired in him a desire to direct. For the next five years, Lizzie encouraged her friends to believe that during those brief three days Justus O'Keefe had fallen passionately in love with her. I did not attend the final performance, but I have been reliably informed that Lizzie's throbbing rendition of 'So will I grow, so live, so die my Lord, Ere I will yield my virgin patent up Unto his lordship . . .' addressed to Justus in the role of Theseus was the least virginal and least innocent Hermia ever likely to be seen on a professional or amateur stage. The following summer, Lizzie was awarded a barely deserved A grade in her English literature A level, although Olivia defended her and said that the ability to fantasise was an essential requirement of literary appreciation. I expect Lizzie will always buy the videos of Justus O'Keefe's films, and her steely eyes will soften when she remembers her teenage glory. Luca made an extraordinarily sulky Lysander, which was an original interpretation, and one lavishly praised by his teacher.

*Roderick Hudson* was not favourably received. In my opinion, it did not deserve the panning the critics gave it, and the blame should have been laid at Ophélie Arcier's door rather than O'Keefe's. Justus works in an industry that takes no prisoners, and one in which it is the matter of a moment to move from darling to *enfant terrible*, even at the age of thirty-six. Most of the critics united, finding, as critics do, security in numbers, in saying that Justus had stretched himself too far in attempting such a classic and literary role, and should have stuck to cops and robbers.

Fortunately for Justus, he was not aware of the critical drubbing he was about to face while he was filming *The Spider House*, and it was the latter, his third feature film, for which he received the Best Actor Oscar. As one body and with one voice, the critics performed a remarkable *volte-face*, and said that he was perhaps the finest actor of his generation. Justus promptly switched to directing.

This leaves Olivia, Pip and myself. I said at the very beginning that one of the characters had been treated badly, but rose above it. I was the person who treated Pip badly, and I carry that on my conscience. I don't wear it too heavily because knowing Pip, as I do, I would never have made her happy and she was ineffably generous when I told her I was going to Rome to follow Olivia for the second time. It is to my great discredit that, nonetheless, our friendship floundered for a short time. That was the only casualty of the summer of 1997, and thankfully not a permanent one. Pip and Olivia talk often, and I am always respectful of the great, private and wholly feminine intimacy of their bond. For a time I believed that I was party to the world of women; now I know I am not, and have ceased wanting to be. Pip and I are gradually rebuilding the close friendship we shared. Even if we do not succeed completely, I will always regard her as a remarkable woman.

I joined Olivia in Rome at the end of August 1997, after I had completed my round of American summer sales. Olivia and I intend to marry one day soon; the date is uncertain, but the venue is agreed – Santa Maria in Cosmedin. It will be a very private service, family members only, which means that the Uptons will be there, George no doubt complaining that we hadn't had the courtesy to do it in October 1997 when they were in Rome anyway. Olivia is keen to have the Upton children participate in the service; I look forward to seeing Sarah gaze on her offspring with that expression of almost unholy pride. We hope that Justus O'Keefe will come as well, and although Peter will doubtless give the bride away, both Olivia and I feel that the generosity of spirit has been entirely Justus's.

Olivia still finds London difficult, and spends as much time as possible in Rome. She still finds her parents difficult, but gradually new bridges are being built, on the foundations of old ones that had fallen into an irreparable state of disuse. I join her in Rome as much as my work allows me, and fortunately that means we are rarely apart for more than a week. Olivia is my guide, my interpreter to Rome, and I am beginning to see the city as a future in-law, perhaps a devoted yet erratic half-sister. It is taking me far longer even to begin to understand Olivia herself, most of all because I had assumed a knowledge of her for so long. Whatever happens, and committed as I feel to my own work, I know that my life will be spent in discovering her and loving her. I do not know if we will reach Moksha, or whether we can reach it together or separately. I do know that if I do not, I will have come as close to bliss as I am entitled to come, and that I came very close to throwing it all away. I remain too anxious, too eager, to achieve spiritual enlightenment; I seek it too aggressively. Olivia will reach it long before me: she views life from a position of peace. I hope she will prepare the way for me. She is inclined, when I fret, to smile at me with her slow, infinitely generous smile, and she whispers to me, inside me, again and again, most often when we are apart, 'Jack shall have Jill, nought shall go ill, The man shall have his mare again, And all shall be well.'

I have never been good at games. I do not like sport; I detest gamesmanship. I do not admire the bargains that people cut every day, in every relationship. Yet I recognise that there is one game we must all play, in which the stakes are higher than we would ever willingly bet, in which the odds are greater than those we could rationally contemplate. I see people all around me struggling to learn the rules of this game, and it strikes me that their primary goal is not to win, but to avoid losing ignominiously. I do not believe there is a way to come second or third and retain anything. I do not believe there is a way of avoiding the game, and being a spectator. I do not think there is any acceptable strategy other than to love and to love completely.